WITCH FINDER

WITCH FINDER

RUTH WARBURTON

*Hodder
Children's
Books*

A division of Hachette Children's Books

For my father Andrew, with love always

Luke lifted his head and sniffed the dusk. The rich smell of roast chestnuts pierced the cold foggy air, above the more familiar Spitalfields stink: horse manure, coal smoke, rubbish. Another day he might have searched his pockets for a farthing, bought a paper cone of hot, burst chestnuts and burnt his fingers as he ate. Not today. Not with his stomach churning like a wash tub and a fluttering sickness in his gut.

Instead he pushed past the scurrying children and sharp-faced errand boys, and stepped into the foetid, muck-strewn road.

At the Cock Tavern the gas-lamps were lit and the working girls called out to him, trying to catch his eye for the evening trade. Their cheap perfume wafted across the muddy street, cutting through the sharpness of the burning chestnut skins. He turned up his collar, readying himself to run the gauntlet.

'Come on now, Luke Lexton!' Miriam called as he drew near. 'A man like you can't be a monk all yer life. I've seen you with those horses, how's about I teach you to ride something a bit more lively?'

'Don't listen to her!' Phoebe twirled her skirts as he passed, flashing her crimson petticoat and stockings. 'I'll give you the first ride for free, Luke. For a birthday present, eh?'

'My birthday's been and gone yesterday,' he muttered into his muffler. 'And I'm late for me uncle.'

'Come back with your uncle and all!' Miriam cried. 'William Lexton's a fine figure of a man too!'

They were still giggling and making eyes over their fans as he rounded the corner.

It was full dark when he entered Fournier Street, the narrow brick houses rising high either side of him. Once these had been the homes of Huguenot silk-weavers, a fine prosperous quarter. Now the silk was woven in far-off India, but on a fine day you could sometimes see bright scraps still fluttering in the windows. Tonight every window was closed and dark, and the yellow-grey fog hung low, trickling between the buildings like a living, breathing thing. The single hissing street lamp barely pierced the gloom, but Luke still pulled his muffler high and his cap low, and he looked up and down the street before he knocked on the door of a shuttered house, three times slow, three fast, three slow.

'Who's there?' The voice behind the wooden door was gruff.

'A man looking for work.' It was the first time Luke had spoken the words, but he'd learnt them by heart long ago. Now, as he said them, his voice low, he felt something tighten round his heart.

'What's your trade?'

'I can wield a hammer.'

'Then enter, friend.'

The door swung wide, a shaft of firelight piercing the fog.

'Come in, young Luke, your uncle's inside.' John Leadingham the butcher stood back against the wall, holding the door as Luke squeezed into the narrow hall.

Inside the small parlour a knot of men were crowded around a smoky fire, their heads low and faces grim. They looked up as Luke entered, and then stood, welcoming him with claps on the back.

'Luke, my boy.'

'Come on, lad, take a seat by the fire. It's a foul night.'

'Are you ready then?' His uncle, a tall broad man with a blacksmith's scarred hands, took a grip on Luke's shoulder, looking at him steadily.

Was he ready? He swallowed and nodded.

'Come on now, cat got yer tongue?'

'Yes, Uncle. I'm ready.'

'Not "uncle" after tonight, lad.' Will Lexton gave him a smile. 'After tonight we're brothers.'

Not if I fail, Luke thought. But he knew what his uncle's answer would be to that: *You won't fail*.

'To the Brotherhood!' Benjamin West raised his tankard high, so that it gleamed in the firelight.

'To the Brotherhood!' William Lexton, John Leadingham and a dozen other voices joined in.

'To the Brotherhood!' Luke said. He had no glass to lift.

'Are we all 'ere?' John Leadingham looked round the circle of faces. There were murmurs as the men looked for missing faces, counted under their breath, then nodded. John gave a final, confirming nod and said, 'Then let the meet begin. Men, put on your masks.'

There was a rustle all around the room as hands dug in pockets and hoods were slipped over heads, and within a few moments all the faces except Luke's were covered with a black hood. Suddenly these were no longer men he'd known since childhood, friends of his uncle's, market traders and bargemen and farriers and smiths, but strangers – strangers with hard eyes that glittered through the slits in their masks. They didn't move, but somehow he had the feeling that they pressed in on him, leaning forward hungrily. He stood his ground, but it took all he had to stop himself from taking a step backwards, out of the circle of glittering eyes, running home through the familiar stinking streets of Spitalfields, back to the forge.

Then one man, gowned as well as masked, spoke. Luke thought it might be John Leadingham, but his voice was hard and harsh, not the hoarse friendly croak that called out the price of meat all day long from the blood-spattered stall in Smithfield market.

'Luke Lexton, you're come here to our meeting house, you've given the secret passwords and entered into our circle. What is your purpose here tonight?'

'I wish to join the Brotherhood,' Luke answered. His voice was very low, but he was relieved that it sounded firm to his ears.

'Before I put to you the trial by knife and the trial by fire and the trial of the hammer, I must tell you this; once you join the Malleus Maleficorum there is no way out except one: death. D'you understand?'

'I do.'

'I give you this last chance; you may go freely now with no hunt at your heels. Do you wish to leave, or join us, now and forever?'

Luke's heart was pounding in his ears and he found his fists were clenched, his bitten nails ground into his palms.

'I wish to join you,' he said harshly. 'Now and for ever.'

'Good,' the man said, and his voice beneath the black mask held a smile. 'Good man.'

He paused for a moment and Luke passed his tongue over dry lips, tasting salt sweat from the heat of the fire and the close-packed bodies in the room. Then the man carried on.

'Three trials you must face, to join the Brotherhood. Three trials, and if you fail 'em you face death. D'you understand, Luke Lexton?'

'I understand.'

'Then let the trials begin,' said the masked man, and there was a hushed murmur around the group, though Luke could not make out any words. He searched for his uncle, but he could not pick him out of the circle. William Lexton was a tall man – Luke was six foot and his uncle topped him by an inch – but in the flickering firelight the silhouettes seemed to wax and wane like shadows, growing taller against the wall and then dwindling back, until Luke could not have said which shape was which.

'First, the trial by knife,' said the man. He drew back his black robe and in his hand was a long knife with a wicked edge and a point that glinted in the firelight.

Luke swallowed. His uncle had told him nothing of what would happen tonight, saying only that it was not worth either of their skins to spill the secrets of the Brotherhood to an outsider. Luke would know the day after his eighteenth birthday and not a moment before. But something in his eyes had told Luke that his uncle feared for him and pitied him, and now he began to understand why. The knife must have been six, eight inches long, and as wicked and sharp as the tongue of a nagging woman.

'Take the knife, Luke Lexton.'

Luke put out his hand. He let it hover over the hilt of the knife for a long moment, trying to summon up the courage to do what he knew he must. It was too late to turn back, too late to run now. As the man had said, there was no way out, except one.

Don't be a bloody coward. The voice in his head was harsh with fear and fury. *Don't disgrace yourself. If you fail now . . .*

His fingers closed over the hilt of the knife. It was warm from the fire and fitted into his palm.

'This test is a test of obedience and purpose, Luke Lexton. By taking this test you show that if you are tasked with something you will do it, without question, without counting the cost to yourself. If you falter, if you lack purpose and resolve, we are all lost. Only by the strength of one can we all succeed. Understand?'

'Yes,' Luke said. His voice sounded strange and grim in his own ears. 'Yes. I understand.'

'Good. Put the knife to your belly.'

He felt sweat prickle across his face and spine and for a moment he didn't believe what he'd heard. This couldn't be right – they couldn't mean him to stab himself, surely?

'What?'

'Put it to your belly,' said the man, and there was a steel in his voice that made Luke realize his role was not to question, but to obey.

He shrugged off his coat and muffler, and then put the tip of the knife to the flesh of his belly, in the soft place beneath his ribs, where there was nothing to stop its slide but skin and muscle. He felt a sickness in his gut as the point bit and a tiny fleck of blood stained the whiteness of his shirt.

'Now, stab yourself, Luke Lexton, and if you value your life and the Brotherhood, hold fast. Do you understand?'

'I understand,' Luke said. A kind of hopelessness rose up in him: the realization that the only choice before him was death or disgrace. He gripped the knife, feeling the hilt slip beneath his sweating palms, and he tightened his grip until his fingers hurt and the tendons on the back of his hand stood out, shadowed in the firelight.

For a minute he thought of dropping the knife, of running – but there was his uncle. And more: at his back there were the shadows of his mother and father and all they'd suffered. If he couldn't do this thing for his own honour, surely he could do it for theirs?

Remember why you want to join, the voice in his head hissed, full of venom. *Remember what it's all for. Do it, you coward.*

He lifted the knife and stabbed it into his gut, gasping as the hilt hit hard against the skin of his belly and he could go no further.

For a minute he felt nothing, but then pain blossomed across his side and the blood began to trickle down his belly, soaking into the worn cloth of his work trousers. He felt sick, sick with pain, sick with the knowledge of what he'd done.

'Take it out,' said the man, his voice hard and clipped. Luke closed his eyes, dreading the slick, grating tug and the mortal gush of blood and guts. Then he pulled.

There was a murmur around the circle, an exhalation of breath and then a few relieved guffaws.

Luke opened his eyes and looked at the knife in his hand.

For a minute he didn't understand. His eyes were blurred with sweat and he had to lift his arm to wipe his brow and clear his vision. Then he saw.

The blade of the knife had slid up inside the hilt, until only a sliver remained – just an inch, barely. It was that which had stabbed his side, making the blood come. But it was not a mortal wound, nothing like it.

'Well done, Luke Lexton,' said the man, his voice warm and strong. He held out his palm and Luke gave back the knife with a hand that shook. 'Well done. You were strong and steadfast, and your courage saved your life. Look,' and he showed Luke the little button in the handle which, if the hilt were gripped hard and firm, released the blade to slide inside the hilt.

'If you'd not held fast, if your grip had wavered, it would've been death to you. D'you see? The switch wouldn't have released the blade, it would've stayed firm and stabbed you to death. Only someone who grips the hilt and drives the knife firmly home can live. It's a test of trust and faith. To show that although what we ask of you may not always make sense, there's always good reason behind it, and only that trust will see us all through.'

Luke closed his eyes, feeling the blood hot on his side and the weakness in his legs, and he nodded, wishing it were all over, wishing he could go home, but knowing it had barely begun.

'You've passed the trial by knife. The second trial is the trial by fire,' said the man. He stepped forward, towards the fire, and Luke saw that there was something resting on the edge of the grate: a long metal handle, with the far end plunged into the heart of the coals.

The man wrapped a cloth around his hand, picked up the handle resting on the hearth and drew the glowing tip out of the fire. It was a brand: he'd seen one often enough to recognize it. Luke's uncle used them on horses and sometimes cattle, if their owners needed them to be marked. He'd even branded a few animals himself, when his uncle was busy, and he'd always winced at their pain and their bellowing cries, but never thought that one day . . .

The end glowed so bright he could not see the design, only the heat that shimmered from it, making the air ripple and waver. Then the man thrust it back into the heart of the fire and spoke.

'Take off your shirt.'

Luke swallowed against the dryness in his throat and he began to fumble with the buttons of his shirt. The men watched, their eyes glinting in the firelight as his reluctant fingers loosened one button, then two, then another, and another, until his shirt hung loose and he could feel the heat of the fire on his naked chest and belly. Blood was already crusting around the cut he'd made, the trail down his side turning black and cracked. He took off the shirt and laid it on the floor at his feet.

'This test is a test of endurance and silence. You must not flinch. You must not cry out. By enduring this test in silence you show that your loyalty to the Brotherhood may be tested, but you will not betray them by any cry or word. Do you understand?'

Luke nodded, not sure that his voice would obey him, but the man shook his head.

'Speak, Luke. Do you understand?'

'I understand,' he said hoarsely.

'Then kneel and hold fast to the chair.'

Luke knelt, holding on to the back of the chair, feeling his breath coming fast and his heart racing beneath his ribs as if he might be sick. One of the other men held on to the seat of the chair so that it wouldn't rock or fall if he flinched or fell himself. Luke heard the whisper of ash as the man took the brand from the fire, and his blood sang in his ears, a strange, fierce, fearful song.

'Hold fast, Luke Lexton,' said the voice.

Then there was a hiss and a heat against his shoulder. For a moment there was no pain and he thought it was all a trick, as the knife had been. But then a roaring, tearing anguish began to engulf his skin and his muscles, until it seemed as if even the bones of his shoulder itself were burning. A great bellow of agony rose up from his guts and he almost cried out, but just in time he remembered his promise of silence and he gripped on to the struts of the chair and bit into his own forearm so that no sound escaped but his tearing, whimpering, ragged breaths.

Beneath his closed lids, constellations of pain exploded and spun and his blood roared in his ears. He wanted nothing more than to beg for it to stop, to scream for water, for pity, for *anything*.

The circle of masks was completely silent, listening to his struggle, listening for any cry. Then, after what seemed an age, the first man spoke.

'Well done, Luke Lexton. You've passed the trial by fire.'

There was a hiss of breaths released around the room and Luke gave a sobbing groan.

'Get something for the burn,' the man said, and one of the masked men came hurrying forward with a pot of grease, like the one Luke's uncle used when he burnt himself at the forge. He felt his shoulder smeared with the ointment and then hands helped him to sit, pulling him to a settle, dressing the burn with a clean cloth.

'You'll have a wound for a few days,' said the man. 'And then a mark, as we all do. As best we know, the meaning of this mark is not known to any outsiders. We show it to none but our wives – and they mustn't know what it signifies. D'you understand?'

This time Luke could not speak, he only nodded, and the man seemed satisfied.

'Good. Good man, Luke Lexton.'

They passed him his shirt and, with their help, he struggled into it, feeling the bandage over his shoulder grate and move as the rough cloth jostled the dressing. There were teeth marks in his arm. He'd not broken the skin, but there would be a welt there for a while.

Someone passed him a half-drunk tankard and he drained it, before he realized that it was not beer, but gin.

It burnt his gullet and then smouldered in his gut, and he half sat, half lay across the settle in front of the fire, feeling the sick cold in his limbs subside a little with the warmth of the fire and the warmth of the gin.

'And now, for the last trial – the trial of the hammer.'

'Wait,' said a voice from beneath a hood, and for the first time Luke recognized his uncle's voice. 'Give him a minute, Brother. He's in no fit state—'

'He's conscious,' said the man in the gown sternly. 'He knows his own mind and can plead his own case. Luke Lexton, are you fit to continue?'

Coward, whispered the voice.

Luke was sick and sweating, but he managed to sit up straighter. He wasn't about to back down now and shame himself and his uncle and the memory of his parents. He nodded.

'I can carry on.' His voice was strange in his own ears. His throat felt tender and raw, as if he had screamed himself hoarse, though he knew full well he'd not made a sound except for shameful pup-like whimpers. He wondered if his uncle had been this weak, or if he'd borne the brand in proud silence, and he gritted his teeth and forced himself fully upright. 'I can carry on.'

'Good man,' said the man in the gown. 'Now, this last trial is different. All we require of you tonight is that you accept the task and undertake to do it to the best of your abilities, or die in the attempt. Tonight the moon is full – when the full moon rises again, either they must be

13

dead, or you. D'you understand?'

'Yes,' said Luke, though he did not.

'Bring out the book,' said the man. There was a rustle at the back of the room and an old masked man limped slowly forward, a huge brass-bound book in his hands. The man in the gown fitted a brass key to the lock and opened the book.

Inside was page after page after page of closely written names, some with a line through, some scratched out so harshly that the paper was rough and hollow.

'This book contains the name of every witch known to this organization – some of them listed thanks to you, Luke – and every one we've sworn to hunt down and kill. The men and women named here have poisoned our brothers and sisters, enslaved them, enchanted them, even killed them. Every one has a heart as black as pitch and it is our sworn duty not to rest until London is wiped clean of their kind. After the trial of the knife and the trial by fire, we ask our Brothers for one more trial to prove their worth – the trial of the hammer: they must pick a name from the book and kill that witch. Do you understand?'

'Yes,' said Luke. And now he did. He stared at the list of names, the faded, scratched handwriting swimming before his eyes. 'What of the ones who're scratched out?' he asked.

'They're the ones your Brothers have killed before you.'

'How do I choose?'

'We let God choose. We bind your eyes, give you a pin.

God will guide you to the name. Are you ready?'

'I'm ready,' Luke said. He sat motionless while they tied a cloth over his eyes and then pushed a pin was pushed between his fingers. Then he felt for the stiff pages of the book beneath his other hand.

He turned the pages slowly, carefully, blindly. There was only one thing in his mind: a figure. A figure he had glimpsed by firelight long ago and the tall shadow it cast on the bedroom wall behind it. It was almost fifteen years since he had seen its shape, but it was still burnt into his mind, and his eye, and all of his nightmares.

This is for my ma, he thought, as his fingers ran down the list, as if touch could guide him to the right name. *This is for my pa*, as he came to a stop, the pin poised in his hand. *Please God, let it be him. Let it be the right one.*

He stabbed with the pin, feeling it pierce the page deep, deep, as he ground it into the book with all the strength of his hatred.

'He's chosen.' The man's voice rang out in the small room. 'Let it be witnessed; he's chosen.'

Luke fumbled with the bandage and opened his eyes, blinking, to the firelight and the circle of faces. Then he bent his head to the book, to see what name lay skewered by his pin.

'Rosamund Greenwood,' he read aloud, with a stab of fury. A woman. He knew nothing about her, except that she was a witch. A witch, but not the one he'd wanted, and for that alone he hated her, as if the rest wasn't reason

15

enough. She'd robbed him of avenging his father and mother and—

'No.' A voice was rising from the back of the room in panic. 'No, no, no. He must choose again.'

'Brother.' The gowned man held up a hand. 'You know the rules . . .'

'No!' The speaker tore off his mask and Luke saw his uncle standing there, his face flushed with the fire. 'You must be mad, John! Her brother's Alexis Greenwood, thick as thieves with the Knyvets, or so they say. To send a green boy up against witches like that—'

'You know the rules.' The gowned man spoke wearily but firmly. 'Put your mask back on, Brother, or you'll be thrown from the meeting.'

'He'll be killed!' William roared.

'She's nowt but a sixteen-year-old girl, William,' another voice tried to put in. 'It coulda bin worse—'

'Worse? Only if she'd picked Knyvet himself, or another of the Ealdwitan! And then I might as well cut his head from his shoulders right here and save us the trouble of fetching his body. Let him choose again, I say!'

'No.' John pulled off his own mask and faced William. His face was both angry and sad. 'The rules are the rules, William. We can't pick and choose for our own, you know that as well as I. God knows, we've had hard choices before – Bates, Jack Almond, young Tom Simmonds. We've lost Brothers and mourned 'em but—'

'Not in a lost cause!' William's voice broke, and he took

16

John by the shoulders. 'We've lost fights, lost men, I know that as well as you. But this is a lamb to the slaughter. Do *not* do this, John. You're a good man – better than this.'

'Hey,' Luke said from where he sat. They took no notice of him. He stood and said louder, 'Uncle! *William!*'

Two faces, red in the firelight, turned to look at him. Luke thought they'd almost forgotten he was there.

'It's my choice,' he said bitterly. 'Mine. And I choose to take the task. A sixteen-year-old girl, you said – and you think I'm a lamb to the slaughter?'

'You don't understand, boy—' William began, but Luke broke in. His fists were clenched so that his nails made half-moons on the skin of his palms.

'I understand. I understand that every other man here's done as I'm being asked to do, and none of them backed down. Don't take away that right from me. I'll not have men say I was too frightened to face a girl fresh out of the schoolroom.'

'Luke . . .' William put out a pleading hand, but Luke turned away from his uncle towards John Leadingham.

'I accept the task. I'll kill the girl. And there's an end.'

2

'Shh, not on the bed, Belle.' Rosa pushed at the little dog and it thudded sulkily to the floor and shuffled over to the window seat, where it circled busily until it settled itself in a neat ring, tail over its nose.

'Watch out if Mama catches you,' Rosa said warningly. Belle let out a little whine of contentment and closed her eyes, and Rosa turned back to her sketch book and the view from the window, over the rooftops of Knightsbridge. The fog was closing in and she could just see, above the yellow shifting sea, dark rooftops and the tips of chimneys, each trickling the coal smoke that made London's pea-soupers so deadly. Not for the first time, Rosa was glad that her bedroom was on the top floor of their tall house. Only the maids slept higher than she, in the attics, beneath the slates.

She swapped pencils for a sharper point and began to fill in the fine detail of the slates and chimneys.

'Down, you god-damn mutt!' The voice came like the crack of a whip.

Rosa jumped as hard as the little dog. Belle leapt to the floor and scurried under the bed, and Rosa's pencil clattered to the floor. She knew who it was, of course, even before she caught sight of him standing in the doorway. He was dressed in riding clothes, his polished boots spattered with mud, and there was a crop in his hand. His face was red with exercise – as red as his hair.

'You might knock, Alexis,' she said bitterly.

'Your door wasn't shut. And why should I knock in my own house?'

Rosa bit her lip. It was true: Papa's death had left Alexis the legal owner of Osborne House and everything in it, but he didn't have to keep reminding her about it.

'The bank's house, don't you mean,' she whispered under her breath.

'What did you say, little sister?' Alexis came into her room, twitching his riding crop dangerously against his thigh. Rosa set her jaw.

'Nothing. Hadn't you better get changed for dinner? It's a quarter after six.'

'That's what I came to tell you. Dinner will be at eight now. And Sebastian is coming, so for God's sake try to look like something more than an insipid schoolgirl.'

'Sebastian Knyvet?' she said before she could stop herself. 'He's back from India?'

'Yes,' Alexis said shortly.

19

Sebastian. How long since she'd seen him? Four years? More? Her stomach curled and she shivered, thinking of those strange, far-seeing blue eyes that seemed to look right through you. He and Alexis had been friends at school and he'd stayed often in the holidays. She remembered the boys swimming in the great lake at Matchenham, their bodies lithe and brown, shining in the sun. And Sebastian, charming a kingfisher out of the tree by the lake, bringing it up to the house with Alexis, the two of them marvelling over the colours of its wings. She'd been charmed too – until she'd realized it was dead.

'You're not wearing that dress, are you?' Alexis broke into her thoughts. Rosa looked down at herself, at the white lawn, and her hand went nervously to the locket hanging at her throat.

'Yes. What's wrong with it?'

'Nothing, if you want to look like a twelve-year-old novice nun. For God's sake, Rose, you're sixteen. It's time you acted like it. Other girls are wedded by your age – and bedded too. You'll be lucky if you get either, looking like that.'

'I'm not changing,' Rosa said furiously. She closed her fingers around the pencil, feeling its point dig into her skin, concentrating on the pain in her hand to distract her from the pain in her heart. Why was Alexis such a beast? Why couldn't he smile and compliment her as other girls' brothers did?

'I'll see you in the drawing room at half past seven.

20

Unless you want bread and dripping for supper, make sure you're smiling. Wear the green dress; at least that's passable. And get Ellen to re-lace your corset. You look like a scrawny boy.'

He turned and stalked to the door. Then he turned back, as if with an afterthought.

'Oh, and take off that bloody locket. It's ugly as hell – and morbid.'

He slammed out, the door crashing shut so hard that the picture on the wall of the stag at bay leapt and clattered against the paper and the gas-light flickered.

'*Lúcan!*' Rosa shouted after him, and the door lock shot across with a sound like a gun, so hard that for a minute she feared she might have damaged the frame.

She sat for a long moment, her heart thumping with fury, waiting for Alexis to come roaring back and shout at her about using magic within earshot of the servants. But he didn't come. There was only silence on the landing outside, the hiss of the gas and the rush of blood in her ears.

Rosa opened her hand, where the pencil lay clenched in her grip, digging into her palm.

She put the point to the paper but, as she pressed, the lead snapped, skittering across the page, leaving an ugly hole in the paper. The sketch was ruined.

She ripped the page from the book and flung it furiously to the floor.

At the sound of the paper fluttering down, Belle's little,

21

pointed, wet nose peeped out from beneath the curtains of the four-poster bed. Rosa scooped her up and buried her face in the dog's warm, shivering back, feeling her breath come quick, catching in her throat like a choke. The locket pressed heavy and warm between them and, at last, when Belle began to whine and wriggle, Rosa set her gently to the floor and drew a deep, shaky breath.

Morbid.

How could it be morbid to want to remember your father?

She held the locket in her palm, looking at the heavy silver scrolling, shiny where it rubbed against her skin and dark in the cracks between. The brass was showing through around the edges, where the plate had worn thin. Papa had given it to her on her tenth birthday and she remembered how sophisticated she had felt – her very own jewellery! Now she saw the cheapness of the thin plate and the old-fashioned moulding. But it didn't matter.

Gently she put her nail to the catch and prised it open. Papa looked out at her, his dark eyes twinkling above his long, dark beard. It was only a pencil sketch. She'd done it one wet afternoon in front of the fire. Alexis had said it made Papa look like Charles Dickens crossed with a potato, but Papa had praised it. *To the very life, Rosa! You'll be an artist some day.*

Rosa shut her eyes, remembering the softness of his beard, the feeling of being hugged against his silk waistcoat, the sound of his laugh.

22

She sighed and clicked the locket shut.

The crumpled paper lay at her feet and she stood and picked it up, smoothing it out with her palm.

'*Gestrice, léaf*,' she whispered. The paper shivered as if a breeze had passed through the room, and where her palm had passed the page was smooth and whole again. Even the hole she'd torn had knitted back together, but as she looked closer she could see it was not quite perfect. There was a faint scar, like a healed wound; a sort of watermark made by her anger. Nothing would get that out. The drawing was spoilt – like everything Alexis touched.

Rosa opened her wardrobe and began to look through her dresses again.

'You look charming, Rosa.' Alexis' smile showed his teeth. 'Quite charming.'

Rosa's stays cut into her waist cruelly, so cruelly she could hardly sit, but, remembering Alexis' threat about bread and dripping, she smiled back, trying to ignore the pain. Ellen had put her hair up and in the mirror above the fire she saw the long white line of her throat, made whiter still by the dark-red curls behind her ears and at the nape of her neck. The neckline of the green dress plunged far lower than she liked and she fought the urge to tug nervously at the bodice.

She had not taken off the locket though – one thing at least Alex couldn't dictate. It lay cold and heavy, just below her collarbone and she shivered; she wasn't used to the chill air on her shoulders and throat. Alexis had moved to look out of the window, and she put out a hand towards the fire, whispering a spell under her breath so that the flames blazed up, licking hungrily at the blackened firedogs.

'Rosa!' Mama's voice rang out like a shot and Rosa jumped guiltily. She turned to see her mother standing in the doorway, her black eyes snapping fire and brimstone. Even the plum-coloured silk of her skirts seemed to crackle.

'What, Mama?'

'Don't say "what", it's horribly vulgar. And you know perfectly well what I mean, Rosamund.'

'But it's so cold in here!'

'Nonsense, it's barely November.' Mama flickered a glance over her shoulder and lowered her voice. 'What if the servants had seen?'

'If we had *proper* servants . . .' Alexis said. Mama thinned her lips.

'If your father hadn't left us knee-deep in debt then perhaps we might. As it is, we're fortunate to have a roof over our head and any servants at all. Now, let me straighten your tie, Alexis darling, and, Rosa, any more foolishness from you and you will be eating in the kitchen with the servants. Do you understand?'

'Yes, Mama,' Rosa muttered.

It was so stupid anyway, she reflected as she pushed past Alexis to the window, to peer into the foggy darkness of the street. She was certain the servants knew what kind of people they worked for – even if they didn't care to put

24

a name to it. Witches. Sorcerers. Demons, some called them. And Mama was hardly one to talk. Ellen would have to be blind not to notice that rents and tears in her best frock disappeared overnight. And did she truly think that anyone would believe dye had transformed her old canary-yellow hat into that ravishing plum-coloured one?

But no. Mama might transform her wardrobe and charm away the lines on her face, and Alexis might seduce Becky the parlour maid with whispered love spells, and heal his lame horse with a poultice of who-knew-what. But she, Rosa, must not even let the fire flare a little higher for fear of watching eyes.

It hadn't always been so. Before Papa's death they'd had servants like them, *proper* servants as Alexis called them. And there had been no need to hide. Rosa had watched enchanted as Papa made her dolls waltz across the nursery carpet and Alexis' toy soldiers marched into battle down the landing runner with their guns puffing smoke. If the bath water turned cold then Rosa's nanny muttered a few words and steam rose up again and she could play with her ducks and boats an hour longer. And when she fell and bumped her knee, a charm was all it took for the pain to lessen and the skin to heal to a silver scar.

But then two years ago Papa had died and the money had vanished, as insubstantial as a dinner magicked from air.

The problem was, magical servants, being what they were, cost money. Money that they did not have, and which the law forbade them to forge. One by one the servants had begun to leave, and two-a-penny outwith replacements had come to take on the work until at last, unwilling to work in a house where even the simplest charm was a danger, they had all left, even Papa's valet, even Rosa's nanny. Now all the servants were outwith. And they were prisoners in their own home.

Rosa stared out into the thick, pressing fog and the darkness, seeing nothing but her own pale face reflected in the glass, white against the gloomy red wallpaper of the room behind. It was only when she heard the *clip-clop* of horse's hooves that she shook herself, and peered into the murk. A hansom cab drew up beneath the feeble gas-light, and a tall, top-hatted figure alighted. It was a man and he was smoking a tiny thin cheroot – she saw the glowing red ember of its tip and the swirl of smoke against the lamp as he took a last draught of smoke and ground it beneath his heel.

He looked up at the window for a moment and then swept off his hat to make a low, oddly ironic bow towards Rosa's silhouette in the frame. Then he straightened, set his hat on his head, and climbed the steps towards the front door. Rosa stood in the window, her cheeks burning. Sebastian. And she knew what he'd thought – the meaning of that ostentatiously elaborate bow. He had seen her watching and thought she was watching for him. Her hand was steady as she pulled the curtain shut. Thank God no one could hear the thudding of her heart.

'Mrs Greenwood.' Sebastian bent low over Mama's soft white hand, and Mama blushed and dimpled.

He'd already greeted Alexis at the door, her brother muttering something under his breath that set Sebastian's mouth twitching and made Alexis himself give a smothered guffaw.

Rosa stood with her back to them both, staring out of the window, feeling her spine grow stiff and straight with tension.

Then she heard a sound behind her and Sebastian's shadow fell across her shoulder on to the window pane.

'Miss Greenwood,' he said, and then, very low, very amused, 'or, if I might – Rosa?'

His voice sent a shiver through her. It was deeper than she remembered, but she would have known it anywhere. Even as a boy it had been low and slightly hoarse, like the voice of an older man coming from a boy's lips. Now it was soft yet rough, like velvet. Rosa swallowed. Then she turned and looked him straight in the eye. 'Mr Knyvet.'

'I hope I find you well?' His gaze was direct, unflinching. There was something uncomfortable in it. It was Rosa who looked away first.

'Quite well, thank you.' She let her gaze drop to her folded hands, playing the demure younger sister. But she watched him from the corner of her eye, taking in his beautifully cut evening dress, the candlelight glinting off his dark-blond hair, still damp with tiny beads of fog. He

27

seemed to have grown taller in the years since they had met, and there was a lithe whip-cord strength about him, as if he might shake off his evening jacket and put up his fists and fight, just as he and Alexis used to do when they were boys. There was a familiar crook in his nose from where Alexis had hit him once, a lucky right-hander that had broken the bone. And Alexis still bore the cluster of scars above his eye where Sebastian had hit him back and carried on punching.

'It seems so long since we last met,' he was saying. 'Where can you have been cloistered?'

Rosa felt her cheeks flush as she remembered Alexis' remark: *like a novice nun.* Had he told Sebastian all that had passed between them earlier? Was that what they'd been laughing about? She felt her cheeks flame.

'I've been in the country with Mama.' Too tedious to be in London in mourning, that had been Mama's verdict. What was the point of London when one couldn't attend balls and parties? Mama had called it 'purgatory'. For Rosa it had felt more like heaven. For a moment she closed her eyes, thinking of Matchenham: the long shadows across the hay meadows where she galloped in the summer evenings when Mama was laid up with the headache; the cool echoing rooms; the vast ballroom which once held balls and levees, where now only mice danced across the scuffed parquet floor.

Then she realized Sebastian was speaking and opened them again.

'I'm sorry?'

'At Matchenham, I was asking. Were you at Matchenham?'

'Yes.'

'Dear old Matchenham.' His pale-blue eyes were the colour of a sun-bleached sky. 'How does it do?'

'Quite well.' Quite well if you ignored the creaking mortgages, and the holes in the stable roofs, and the dry rot in the library. How long could they keep it up, this pretence that they had the same money as when Papa was alive?

'And what brings you up to town?'

Because Matchenham is let! Because there are strangers in my home, their horses stabled in Cherry's stall, their children in my bed.

She kept her face and voice even.

'Mama thought I should see her dressmaker. I'll be coming out in the spring.'

'Next season? Can it really be? Not that I should be surprised, when you're standing before me like this, with your hair twined so seductively above your neck – only it's hard to reconcile you with the little girl I remember, who used to tuck up her skirts to play mud pies with us on the lake shore.'

'I've grown up since then.'

'Yes.' Sebastian's gaze swept her up, and down. 'Yes, I can see you certainly have.'

'Well, gentlemen.' Mama stood with a rustle of silk and looked at her little gold fob-watch and then at Rosa. 'We will leave you to your port. Rosa?'

Rosa stood, thankful to be away from the table, from Alexis' hard stare and Sebastian's disquieting presence on the other side of the candelabra. The candle flames kindled in his cool blue eyes and his gaze followed her as she followed Mama into the drawing room next door. James had laid out coffee and petits fours and Rosa looked wistfully at the tray, wishing, not for the first time, that she could loosen her stays just a little. Eighteen inches was painfully tight, and she'd managed only a few bites at dinner. She would be hungry tonight unless she could persuade Cook to part with a few slices of bread and butter to take to bed.

'What—' she began.

'Shh!' Mama hissed. She closed the door firmly and then put a glass to the wall that divided the room, in the alcove next to the chimney breast. She looked around to check that no servants were likely to come in and whispered a spell. Without warning, Alexis' clear, hard voice suddenly filled the room.

'. . . d'you think of Rosamund then? I'll warrant she's changed since you last saw her?'

'She certainly has.' Sebastian's murmur, followed by the hiss and suck as he pulled on his cigar.

'Quite the beauty, eh? Though she doesn't look as if she knows quite what to do with it, half the time. How do our London ladies compare to the Indian damsels then? From what I heard you had your fair share of caps

30

thrown at your head over there. Is it true what they say about women in a hot climate?'

'What do they say?' There was a laugh in Sebastian's voice.

'Why –' Rosa heard Alexis' chair creak expansively, and knew that he was tilting himself backwards from the table, his arms locked behind his head and the buttons on his waistcoat straining. 'Why, that corset laces are loose and morals looser.'

'I can't speak for their morals, but I probably loosed my fair share of laces,' Sebastian said. Rosa shuddered and felt hot fury flood her cheeks. Her heart was hammering and she looked at Mama, but her mother's face showed no anger, only intense concentration as she strained to keep the spell working.

'If looks could cut, I fear Rosa's stays would have been on the floor,' Alexis drawled. Sebastian said nothing, but Rosa could almost hear his single raised eyebrow and the smile that would be twitching at the corner of his mouth as he sipped his port. 'Though her morals are straight-laced enough to satisfy any maiden aunt.'

'Stop the spell,' Rosa said. Her voice was hard.

'Shh,' Mama hissed.

'Didn't you hear me? I said, stop it!'

'Be quiet, you silly girl. The walls aren't that thick, even without magic.'

'Stop the spell or I'll go in there and tell them that you're spying on them.'

'Rosa!' Mama spun round and flung the glass furiously on to the chaise longue. It bounced up and hit the wooden arm of the chaise, and Rosa flinched as it shattered into splinters that skittered across the Turkey rug. Mama's face was dark with anger and her voice was hard. 'Firstly, if you ever dare speak to me in that tone again you will find that you're not too old for a whipping. And secondly, in case you hadn't noticed, this family is sailing perilously close to the rocks. Matchenham is mortgaged to the hilt and fast falling into disrepair. If our friends find out that it's let, God knows how we'll weather the disgrace. Alexis has just taken a mortgage on *this* house so that we can hold *your* coming-out ball next season. He is clawing his way up the ladder at the Ealdwitan, but without family influence or money to spend, his climb will be slow, if not impossible. We have one remaining asset. You.'

Rosa went cold.

'What do you mean?'

'There are only three things that matter in this life, Rosa: beauty, breeding and power, which is to say, money. God and your family have provided you with the first two. Now it is your responsibility to barter them for the last.'

'You want me to marry for money!' Rosa cried. 'Marry Sebastian Knyvet?'

Images, memories, flickered through her head. Sebastian, his tanned skin glinting in the summer sun as he swam in the lake at Matchenham, his boyish body already halfway to manhood. Sebastian, taking her little kitten and holding it over the nursery fire, and then laughing at Rosa's cries. She remembered his words as he handed the little creature back to her. 'It's so nice to feel them cling to you, don't you think, Rosa? I wouldn't hurt it, you know, not much.' And Sebastian, leaning towards her over the dinner table tonight, his eyes aflame with the candlelight and something more. She thought of his face in the gas-light as he walked towards the house, the way the gas-lamps shadowed his sharp cheekbones, the glimmer of his golden hair as he lifted his top hat . . .

She put her hands to her face, feeling the heat of the fire.

'I don't want to marry – I'm too young, I—'

'You *will* marry for money, Rosa.' Mama's voice was curt. 'And you *will* do it this season. We cannot manage another season for you. This is your one chance: by hook or by crook, we must have a marriage settlement and a protector for this family. Who are you to turn up your nose at Sebastian Kynvet? He's handsome, rich, well connected – what more do you *want*? Dear Lord, his father is a Chair at the Ealdwitan! Think of what a link to his family could do for Alexis, for all of us!'

'I don't . . . I can't . . .' Rosa's face was hot, and suddenly she couldn't breathe, the stays pinching cruelly at her waist until she felt she was about to be cut in two.

There was a noise at the door. The handle began to turn and Mama's gaze flickered towards it and then to the glass on the floor.

'*Gestrice!*' Mama pointed at the fragments and they shuddered, and then a small whirlwind whisked them off the floor and into a swirling mass of glass that spun for a moment above Mama's palm. Then, as the door opened, the glass dropped with a small thud into her outstretched hand and she turned to greet Sebastian and Alexis with a smile.

'I hope you enjoyed your cigar, Mr Knyvet.'

'Oh please, Mrs Greenwood, I beg you to call me Sebastian. It feels strange to be so formal when I scrumped apples from your orchard as a boy.'

'Very well then, Sebastian. Can I offer you coffee? Or brandy, if you prefer?'

'I would love to – but I'm sorry, I must go. Please forgive me. It's disgracefully rude to leave so soon after your charming dinner, but I promised my father I'd call in at the headquarters tonight, and it's getting very late. I hadn't realized how time had flown.'

'Another time,' Mama said with a smile, but Rosa saw the way her rings winked in the candlelight as she tightened her fingers on the glass in her hand.

'With pleasure.' Sebastian raised her free hand to his lips and smiled. 'Thank you, Ma'am, for a delicious supper, and for the charming company.'

Rosa stood, very still and upright, as he turned to her.

'Miss Greenwood . . .' He took her hand and raised it to his lips. For a moment she felt nothing at all – just as if she were carved out of wood or stone. But as his lips touched

34

her satin-gloved knuckles, his fingers found the soft skin beneath her wrist where her glove button gaped. Skin touched skin and she felt something prickle over her – she could not have said what, whether it was excitement, a shiver of longing, or even a kind of fear. She felt Alexis' eyes boring into her back and then she withdrew her hand from Sebastian's.

'Goodnight, Mr Knyvet,' she said. Her voice was low, so low she thought perhaps he would not even hear her. But he did.

'Goodnight . . . Rosa,' he said softly, close to her ear. Then, as he straightened, 'Do you ever ride?'

'I'm – I'm sorry?' she stammered.

'I ride most days in the Row. I wondered if you were ever there?'

'I . . .' Rosa bit her lip. She had barely taken Cherry out since they had come to London. Riding in the Row just wasn't riding – what she wanted was to gallop across the muddy fields and lanes at home, not trot decorously up and down while others cast aspersions at her shabby, old-fashioned habit.

'Yes, often,' Mama said firmly. 'Rosa is quite devoted to riding. Her horse is lame just at the moment, but I have no doubt you will see her in the Row soon enough.' She smiled. It should have been pleasant, but Rosa saw only her teeth and the vein that stood out in her throat. 'Goodnight, Mr Knyvet – *Sebastian*.'

'Goodnight, Mrs Greenwood.' Sebastian turned and

took his top hat from James, who was waiting in the doorway with his coat and cane. He raised his hat to Mama, nodded to Alexis, and left.

Mama watched from the window as he made his way down the dark street, the thick yellow fog swirling in his wake, until it closed around him and it was as if he'd never been there at all. Then she turned to Rosa and her face was hard.

'Tomorrow you will ask Clemency to send for her dressmaker, and we will fit you for a new habit.'

In the middle of the night Rosa woke. It was very late; she wasn't sure how late, but gone midnight. But a light showed faint and flickering beneath her bedroom door, from a corridor that should have been dark. Impossible that the servants would be up so late. And it wasn't Alexis; she could hear his snores coming from the other end of the house.

Gathering her nightgown, she swung her legs out of bed and stood, her heart beating in her throat. It was stupid to be scared. If it was burglars, she had more weapons than they did.

Rosa whispered a spell beneath her breath, a charm to give herself courage. And then she opened her bedroom door.

The corridor was dark, but she could see where the light was coming from: the study door was ajar and the glow of a candle cast a long golden streak across the threadbare hallway runner. Rosa padded closer, her bare feet silent on the soft rug. As she drew near she took a deep breath and held it, tiptoeing the last few feet.

It was the book she saw first, open on the study table. It was bound in thick fading leather with a small brass lock and gold embossed letters that read *The Holy Roman Catholic Bible*. But it was not a Bible. That cover was only for the servants. Inside, beneath the lock, was something very different. Not the family Bible, but the family Grimoire, handed down from mother to daughter, with spells added by every generation, notes on poultices, scribbled additions in the margins: *If rue cannot be found, then the dryed herb will serve very well, only let the mix be steep'd another night . . .*

It was the most precious possession in the whole house – and the most private. And someone was reading it. In secret.

Rosa flung open the door with a furious bang. Then her mouth fell open.

Her mother looked up, her face white, her eyes wide and full of alarm. She was in her nightgown, her hair in a thick plait down her back.

'Wh— Rosa!' She let out a shaking, exasperated breath. 'Good Lord, child. What are you doing sneaking around in the middle of the night?'

'I could ask the same! What are you doing with the Grimoire?'

'It is none of your business!' Mama snapped. She slammed the book shut, flipped the brass lock. But not before Rosa had caught sight of the heading: *A Silver-Tonguéd Charme – to Persuade the Reluctant to yr Course.*

'Mama . . .' They stared at each other in the candlelight. Her mother's handsome face became hard, stubborn. 'Mama, tell me you're not meddling with Sebastian. It would be suicide to do this to an Ealdwitan. If he found out . . .'

'There is nothing to find out.'

'Then why—'

'Hold your tongue!' her mother hissed furiously, and she pointed at Rosa. Magic crackled from her fingertip and Rosa's mouth snapped shut like a trap, so hard she bit her tongue and tasted blood. She breathed through her nose for a long moment, tempted almost beyond endurance to defy Mama, lift the spell, scream back at her.

I am a stronger witch than you, she thought. *And you know it. I could lift this spell and there would be nothing you could do to prevent me.*

But she could not do it. She could not bring herself to defy her mother in cold blood.

She only shook her head, telling her mother with her eyes what she must surely already know – that it would be madness to do this, madness to risk the fury of the Knyvets by ensnaring their son with a charm any hedgewitch could discover and undo. Then she turned and left, feeling the darkness swirling at her heels, as her mother snuffed the study lamp and stalked the opposite way down the corridor to her own bedroom.

* * *

It was only later, in her own room, as Rosa pinched the candle wick and undid the spell in order to rinse her mouth with cold water, swilling away the taste of the blood, that the realization came to her.

It was not Sebastian her mother had been trying to bind.

The spell had been for her.

3

Luke woke, sweating, and with his shout of fear echoing around the bare little room. His shoulder burnt with the pain of the brand, throbbing beneath the dressing, and for a minute he lay, his chest heaving, his skin wet with sweat. Then he turned with a shiver, the bedstead squawking in protest, and drew the rough blankets up to his chin.

But before he could close his eyes he heard the creak of the floorboards in the corridor and the wavering flicker of a candle flame illuminated the doorway.

'Luke?' said a gruff voice.

'It's nothing,' Luke said shortly. 'Only the old dream.'

His uncle nodded.

'Well, you'd have to be made of iron not to have thought of them tonight. I know they were in my thoughts – and it wasn't I . . .' He trailed off. Luke turned his face away from the candlelight, knowing what his uncle had been about to say. It wasn't William who'd hid beneath the settle as his mother and father were butchered before his eyes. It wasn't William who'd stuffed his father's neckerchief into his mouth to stifle his sobs, and watched as the blood ran down the walls and pooled on the rough boards, and the wavering shadow waxed high and black against the wall.

And you never saw his face? they'd questioned him afterwards. Luke had shook his head again and again, wishing there was a different answer, wishing he'd had the courage – not to *save* his parents, for he was wise enough, even as a child, to know that was not in his power and never had been. But the courage just to turn his head, to peep out and see the face of the man who'd sucked his father's life from his mouth and vomited it, red and clotted, against the walls of their little house. But he had not. He had just lain, stifling his whimpers, mesmerized by the rise and shiver of the Black Witch's shadow in the firelight, and the only clue he'd been able to give them was the cane that had rolled across the floor to lie against his leg, the cane with the ebony shaft and the silver head in the shape of a coiled snake. He'd lain there, trembling, as the hand in its black glove had groped closer and closer to his leg, like a monstrous black five-legged spider, creeping across the floor towards him.

And then – like a miracle – it'd found the cane and gripped it. The shadow against the wall straightened from its hunch and stood. Turned on its heel. Left.

The Black Witch had left Luke an orphan. It had left him with the knowledge of his own cowardice, his own powerlessness in the face of evil. And it had left him the dream.

'I'm fine.' He spoke more shortly than he meant to. 'Leave me be.'

'There's nothing to be ashamed of, lad.' His uncle stood in the doorway, the candlelight soft on his face. His voice, usually so loud, came low to Luke's ears. 'A man can't be held a coward for his dreams.'

'I've an early start. I promised Minna I'd shoe Bess 'fore she left.'

His uncle said nothing, only sighed. Then he nodded.

'G'night, Luke. Sleep well, lad.'

I'll try, Luke thought as he turned his pillow to the cool side and closed his eyes. The shadow rose up, wavering and black, and he fought down the fear that gripped him. *You're not a child any more.* His fingers gripped the bedclothes. *You're a man. You will kill this witch and be done with it. She's a sixteen-year-old girl, for God's sake.*

And then? Back to the forge. Back to real life. Back to the hope of finding the other witch. The Black Witch.

The dawn light was still thin and grey as he made his way across the cobbled alley between the house and the forge. Ice crackled in the puddles of smut-black water and his breath made clouds of white in the frosty air, but people and children were already up and about, making their way to their places of work, running errands, emptying the night slops into the street. He could hear the carts

42

rumbling their way to Spitalfields market, or maybe to Smithfield's, or Billingsgate, or others, further afield. From close at hand he could hear the muffled bone-shaking *thump-badabadabada* as the drayman rolled his barrels of beer off the cart and across the cobbles into the cellar of the Cock Tavern.

London was awake. Spitalfields never really slept anyway.

Luke unlatched the door of the forge, rubbing the last of the sleep from his eyes with cold fingers, and turned to the fire, pulling out the clinker and building it up again from the grey ashes of the day before. As he picked up the coal shovel, he winced, feeling the throb of his wound and the pull of the dressing beneath his shirt.

The forge was hot and roaring, and he was in a muck sweat from the heat of the fire and the effort of working the bellows, when he heard the *clip-clop* of hooves, and he turned his head to see a skinny girl astride a large bay mare coming into the courtyard.

'Morning, Minna.'

'I've to be at the dairy by six,' Minna said without preamble. 'Can you get her done in time?'

'Yes, if you work the bellows.'

'But I'll get smuts on my dress! Who'll want milk from a girl what looks like she's bin up a chimbley?'

'Do you want her shod or not? There's an apron on the wall.'

Minna looked over at the stiff, dirty smith's apron

43

hanging by the door and gave a gusting sigh that blew the dark curls off her forehead. Then she rolled her eyes and pulled it down, winding the laces twice round her middle to make them meet.

'The things I do for you, Luke Lexton.'

'The thing I do for *you*, Minna Sykes. I could've been abed another hour if it weren't for Bess and her shoe.'

'It weren't my fault she threw it off,' Minna said pertly as she began to work the bellows.

'No?' Luke shoved the metal back into the heart of the blaze and watched it flicker from red to gold, then back. 'Whose fault was it then? You'll have to pump those bellows harder.'

'Oh for the love of . . .' Minna gritted her teeth and then winced. 'Ow.'

'Is that tooth still hurting you?'

'Yes. Lucy give me a teaspoon of laudanum last night and I slept, but it's back throbbing fit to bust today.'

'I wish you wouldn't take that stuff.'

'What – laudanum?' Minna's face showed her surprise. 'Don't be such an old woman, Luke. If it's good enough for Her Majesty it's good enough for me, ain't it?'

'It's not safe. Haven't you seen the opium addicts down at Limehouse?'

'A'course I've seen the opium addicts. But it's laudanum, Luke, practically no more than weak gin – they give it to babies!'

'And what happens when you can't afford it no more,

eh?' He pulled the horseshoe out of the fire and looked at it again. 'Nearly there.'

'Then I'll beg it off Lucy.'

'What happens if Lucy says no?'

'Then I'll go without! For gawd's sakes, Luke, stop fussing and shoe the bleeding mare.'

Luke said nothing. He pulled the shoe out of the fire and looked at it again.

'It's ready. You can stop.'

Minna gave a sigh of relief and came over to stand by Bess's head as Luke hammered and bent the shoe, curving it to fit the shape of the one Bess had thrown yesterday. The ringing sound of the hammer was clear and true, filling the small space, driving out the evil whispers of the night before. Minna said something and he cried, 'What?' above the din.

'I said,' she shouted, 'you'll be as deaf as William in a year or two!'

Luke only laughed and carried on. It was true, but he could think of worse fates than ending up like his uncle: hard of hand but soft of heart, and deaf from the constant hammering.

At last the shoe was close to the right shape and he stood, holding it in the big pincers.

'Let's try it against Bess's hoof. Come on now, old girl, come on.'

She was used to being shod and let him back her towards the forge and pull her hoof between his leg. But as he bent over to put the shoe to her foot, the wound on his shoulder gave a great stab, making him catch his breath and stop. Bess felt his pain and gave a little whinny, shaking her mane.

'Are you all right?' Minna asked curiously.

'Nothing.' He shook his head and bent again.

"What's that under your shirt? I can see something – have you hurt yourself?'

'I said, it's nothing,' he said shortly. Minna gave him a look, but subsided. Then the hot metal bit and the smell of burnt hoof filled the morning air. Bess gave a little protesting snicker at the sharp smell, but he lifted it away before she could feel the heat.

'It's good.' He plunged the shoe into barrel of rainwater, hearing the hiss and bubble as the hot shoe hit the cold water. 'But you shouldn't work her so hard, Minna. Her hooves are fit to split.'

'That's why I'm getting her shod, ain't it?' She stood, watching, as Luke fitted the shoe to Bess's hoof, hammering it on, turning the nails flat.

'She needs a holiday, poor old lady,' he said as he released the foot.

'I need a holiday an' all.' Minna pulled on the bridle and yanked Bess towards the waiting milk cart outside the gate. 'And I ain't going to get one, so less of the bleeding heart for the horse, thank you.'

He watched as she backed Bess between the shafts and hitched her up. Then she clicked her tongue.

'Thanks for shoeing her, Luke.' She put her hand towards her skirts where her purse hung. As she fingered it Luke could see from its lightness that it was empty, or near enough. He could have told that even without the way she chewed at her cold-chapped lips as she asked, 'How much do I owe you?'

'Another time.'

'I ain't taking no charity, Luke Lexton.'

'It's not charity.' He feigned irritation, showing his black hands, covered with soot from the forge and the hot metal. 'I want to get cleaned up. Pay me another time.'

She smiled, bright and wide, relieved.

'I owe you one.'

'You owe me more than one, Minna.'

'And I'll give it yer, one of these days. Bye, Luke.' She grinned, clicked her tongue to Bess and then they clip-clopped up the lane, towards the City and the dairy.

Luke was still standing, watching the lane, thinking, when he heard footsteps behind him and his uncle came through the gate.

'She works that horse too hard,' William said.

'I know.' Luke rubbed his hands on his apron and turned back to the yard, ready for the day's work. 'I told her. But she works herself too hard and all.'

'Did you charge her for the shoe?'

'She'll pay.'

'No she won't. You're too soft-hearted.'

'It's not her fault. How's she supposed to make a girl's

wage stretch to cover four mouths?'

'I know, I know.' William shook his head. 'And her dad's as useless as they come.'

'He's not long for this world, neither.' Luke thought of the last time he'd seen Mr Sykes, sitting in his own piss in a corner of the hovel Minna called home, with his youngest two running around his feet, noticed only when they came too close to knocking over his bottle.

'There's many a better man than Nick Sykes rotted their brain with moonshine,' William said. 'She should sell that horse, get a donkey, use the money for the little'uns.'

'She never will,' Luke said with certainty. 'You know Bess was her dad's, back when he were a drayman. In Minna's eyes she's just borrowing Bess until he's fit to work again.'

'And that'll be sometime west of never,' William Lexton said with a sigh. Then he turned to the forge. 'Come on now, enough gabbing. We've got work to do before I lose you.'

'Lose me?'

'Well, you can't work here and do your task for the Brotherhood, can you?'

'But—'

'It's not going to be easy, Luke. I tried to tell you last night, but you were too full of yourself to listen. No, no –' he held up a hand as Luke began to protest '– I know. And I would have been the same at your age. But these are no ordinary witches, Luke. John Leadingham's told me a bit about this family. The son's thick as thieves with Sebastian Knyvet. They went to school together, spent half their boyhood round at each other's houses, from what I can make out.'

'And who's this Knyvet bloke then?'

'Who's . . . ?' His uncle gave him a look that mingled surprise and irritation. 'Do you listen to anything I tell you? I tried to tell you all this last night. He's one of the Ealdwitan. And you know who they are, don't you?'

Yes. Luke knew who they were. The witch elite of England. The ruling council. If they only ruled the witches – that would be one thing. But their tentacles reached into every place of power in the land. Half the MPs in the House of Commons were Ealdwitan and a good measure of the peers in the House of Lords too. If there was a prospect of money or power they were there, to get their share of the pie, and more.

'Aloysius Knyvet is one of the Chairs who head the Ealdwitan. Sebastian's his eldest son. Now do you see why I said this was a fool's errand?'

'So they've got friends in high places.' Luke shrugged. 'They've still got skin that burns and flesh that bleeds, don't they?'

'Yes, but it's getting to that skin or that flesh. And that's easier said than done. At least you've got an advantage, though I don't know how far it'll help. You'll have to be careful not to let on. If you once show what you are, that you know what they are . . .'

Luke turned away. He hated being reminded of what he was. A witch-finder.

No one knew where the ability had come from. William thought he had been born with it, and that perhaps Luke's father had had the same ability but had never known it, or had kept it secret through fear. John Leadingham thought that it had been gifted to Luke the night he watched his parents die – that that one searing experience had burnt the gift into him, so that never again could he look on a witch and see an ordinary man or woman. Except, as Luke himself often wondered, he could not be the only person to have seen a witch, nor even the only person to have seen a witch kill. But he was, as far as he'd ever heard, the only person who saw them for what they were, as clear as others saw black from white. Even in the street he could see them, dressed like ordinary people, walking and talking like ordinary people but with their witchcraft shimmering and crackling around them, marking them out as clear as night from day.

Sometimes it was nothing but a faint gleam, soft as a dying ember. Other times it was bright; bright as a gas-lamp, bright as a flame. When they cast a spell the magic flared and waxed, as the candlelight guttered and waxed in the draught from the door. Then it waned, fading back, leaving them dimmer than before.

It had taken him a long while to understand that others did not see witches as he did. It had taken the Malleus even longer to believe what they had found – a child who could

50

see witchcraft – no need to test and prod and accuse. His word alone was enough.

'We'll have to get you inside the household somehow. A servant or summat. John Leadingham's looking into it.'

'I can't be a servant!' Luke said, horrified.

'What! Too proud to sweep a floor?'

'No! I don't mean that. I mean, I wouldn't know how! How could I be a footman in some great house? I wouldn't know the first thing about what to do – I'd get the sack before my feet had touched the ground.'

'A footman no, but there might be something else. You're too old for a boot-boy, but a garden hand maybe. I don't know about London, but John says they've got a great rambling place in the country with a hundred acres and more. There must be work for a man there.'

'What if they're not in the country? Don't the gentry come up to town in the autumn?'

'I don't know.' William shook his head. 'You're asking the wrong bloke, Luke. But where there's a will, there's a way. If there's a chink in their armour, John Leadingham's the man to find it. By fair means or foul, we'll get you into that house. And after that . . .'

After that, it would be up to Luke.

'I've got a plan.' John Leadingham tapped the side of his nose as they walked down the narrow alleys, tall warehouses towering either side of them, their top storeys disappearing into the shrouding murk. Luke could hear the lap of the

Thames on the mudflats and the bellow of a horn as a ship made its way downriver in the thick yellow fog.

'What is it?' Luke asked, but John shook his head.

'Ask me no questions, young Luke. You'll know soon enough, but for the moment I'm still working out some of the finer details. Now . . .' He stopped at one of the furthest warehouses – a tumbledown wooden structure that looked as if it might just slide into the Thames mud at any moment – and drew a key from his pocket. 'You're not squeamish of a little blood, are you?'

'No,' Luke said, but his stomach twisted, wondering what awaited him inside the warehouse. He thought of the nights when William came home with blood on his hands and shook his head, pale-faced, when Luke asked him questions about what he'd done. Would it be a witch, captive, awaiting trial?

The door swung wide and the stench of blood that flooded out made him take an involuntary step back, but John Leadingham strode inside as if he hadn't noticed.

Luke found himself standing tense, his muscles ready to fight or fly, as the gas-lights flared out across the warehouse. But then he laughed, the noise sounding strange and light with relief in his own ears.

'Pigs!'

Carcasses swung from hooks in the beams and there were bones stacked by the door out to the wharf. And not just pigs, he saw. There were sides of beef over the far side, and sheep too, stripped of their wool and skinned, with sharp grinning teeth and staring, round eyes.

'Well, what else did you expect? I'm a butcher, ain't I?' John swung the door shut with a dull thud of rotten wood and took off his coat. 'It's an abattoir.'

'Why've you brought me here?'

'Because I'm not sending a sheep to the slaughter – pardon the pun.' He pulled on a bloodstained apron and picked up a knife. 'You can fight, Luke, I've seen it. Even better if you've got a bit of beer in you. But you can't kill. That's a different skill completely – and one you need to learn, and fast. I'm not saying you should gut this girl like a stuck pig, of course not. I'm hoping you'll get the job done a good deal more subtly than that. But the fact is, you may find yourself in a tight corner, and carrying a knife and knowing where to stick it can take you a long way.'

He threw an apron at Luke and then a knife, hilt first. Luke fumbled the catch and cut himself across the palm, and John Leadingham grinned.

'Lesson one – make sure you end up on the right end. Now . . .' He pointed at the corpse of a pig, swinging gently on a butcher's hook driven in under its chin. 'This is a man. Where are you going to stick that thing?'

For the next three hours Luke worked harder than he'd done in a long time, and by the time Leadingham let him stop he was sweating, gasping and spattered with gore, the knife slipping in his bloodstained hand.

53

His head was spinning with all the new information – where to nick an artery, where to slice a tendon. What would incapacitate a witch, and what would merely slow him or her down while they healed themselves. And all the time, as John Leadingham barked out, 'Femoral artery, kidney, achilles,' Luke stabbed the pig and yanked out the knife.

'Don't think strength can help you. If they clock what you are – carotid artery – your best bet is to get their trust, get in close, then when they least expect it, strike. Spleen! Stick 'em as hard and fast as you can, and get out. Pulmonary artery! No, not there, you dolt. That won't do more than give them a nasty scar and they'll be up and at you before you can say "Spring-Heeled Jack". Here . . .' He stabbed the knife in between the ribs with a grunt and a crunch that made Luke's stomach turn. 'You've got to remember, a witch's magic lies in their strength, and their strength lies in their blood. Draw off enough blood and you'll weaken their magic too. Right kidney! Good, good man. Now, go for the tendons behind the knee – no, don't stab, slice. That's right. Brace their weight against yourself to get a purchase – and remember they'll likely be slippery with blood.'

At last he stopped and took Luke's shoulder, turning him panting and red-faced to look at him.

'This is easy enough with a dead pig that doesn't dodge or strike back or cry with pain. Now I want you to do the same thing, but imagine this pig is a girl – a girl who cries out as you come at her with the knife and tries to get away.'

'You want me to imagine this pig is a girl?' In spite of himself, Luke stifled a smile. His chest was rising and falling, and his limbs felt like glue, but the idea still made him want to laugh. 'How desperate d'you think I am?'

'Just try it.'

'If you say so.' It was hard to think of anything but the fat, bristly carcass swinging to and fro, but Luke shut his eyes and pictured a girl hanging where the pig was, a blonde maybe like Phoebe, her blue eyes wide with horror as he came towards her with the knife. 'All right, I'm picturing it.'

'All right then. Go. Aorta!'

Luke opened his eyes and lunged, knife outstretched, for the pig's throat – and behind him a voice screamed, 'No! Oh God, spare me!'

Luke stumbled, slipping in the blood, and the knife fell from his hand as he slammed against the pig, grabbing at its cold, clammy flanks to try to steady himself.

'What the hell?'

John took a step forward out of the shadows and his face was grim.

'That was all it took, was it? Me screaming like a girl – and a bloody poor imitation, if I do say so myself – and you were tripping over your own feet and turning to jelly?'

'Damn.' Luke could have kicked himself. *Damn.*

'You think you're a man, Luke, and you are – but it'll

take more than a man to kill this girl. It'll take a Brother. One of the Malleus. The test of the knife, the test of fire – they're nothing to this. Because with this you have to defeat yourself, as well as the witch, d'you understand? They'll use every weapon they can against you – they'll weep, they'll plead, just as they'll fight and lame and maim. If you're afraid—'

'I'm not afraid,' Luke broke in roughly. John put his hand on his shoulder.

'I didn't say you were, son. But if you *are* afraid, they'll see that and they'll turn your fear against you. And if you have a kind heart, they'll turn that against you too. So you must have no heart, understood? You must have no fear. You must be nothing but the hammer.'

4

'There's worse fates than marrying for money, Rose.' Clemency put a sugared plum in her mouth and smiled, her plump cheeks dimpling, her lips sticky with syrup. 'I should know. And better a rich wife than a poor spinster.'

Rosa sighed. Clemency put it gently, but the truth beneath her words was hard. What other fate was there for a girl of her class and education? She had no way of earning a living, she knew nothing. And what was the alternative? Living out her days as Alexis' unwanted spinster sister – despised by everyone and dependent on Alexis for everything from dress money right down to her food.

'But . . .' She bit her lip. She wanted to say: *But it's different for* you. But was it? She looked at the portrait of Clemency's father-in-law, Lionel Catesby, which hung between the two tall windows overlooking the park. The long golden beard, the red nose, the great belly like an aged Henry VIII. Philip was not his father – not yet. But he was halfway there and in a few years . . . Rosa looked at Clemency and tried to imagine Philip Catesby knocking on her door, climbing into her bed, kissing her with that great scratchy blond moustache and putting out a hand . . .

Heat rose up in her face and she fumbled and dropped her teacup.

'Oh, Clem!' She jumped up, dismayed, as the tea flooded out across the Turkey rug, soaking into the silk. 'I'm such a fool! Oh, where's my wretched handkerchief?'

'Don't be silly. Sit down, Rose, and stop flapping.' Clemency stretched out a hand to the bell and a moment later a maid came hurrying in.

'My cousin has spilt her tea,' Clemency said. 'Would you clear it up and refill the pot, please, Liza?'

'Yes, ma'am.' Liza curtseyed and then knelt, her hand outstretched over the stain as she whispered the words of a spell. Rosa watched, relief fighting with envy as the tea stain misted into the air and disappeared, leaving the rug clean and untouched. *If you married Sebastian, you could have a maid like Liza*, her treacherous subconscious whispered. *No more hiding and whispering and pretending to be what you're not. If you married Sebastian . . .*

'Penny for your thoughts?' Clemency asked lightly as Liza rose and left. There was a smile in her wide blue eyes. 'You're not worrying over that nasty old rug, are you? Philip's mother gave it to us when we married and personally I'd be delighted if the horrid thing went up in flames. So hopelessly old-fashioned! But, as she never fails to say when she comes for tea, there'll be forty years of wear in that rug. It'll probably outlast my marriage.'

'What!' Rosa looked up at Clemency, really shocked. Clemency just laughed, showing her pretty pink dimples.

'I didn't mean *that*. I just meant, well. You've seen the way Philip drinks and eats and rides. His father didn't make old bones, did he?'

Her voice was careless and something about her mocking expression made Rosa's heart twist and wring. Was this what awaited her? A marriage of convenience, where she could talk about her husband riding himself into an early grave with equanimity and barely even shudder?

'Clem, don't talk like that,' she said uncomfortably. 'What if Philip heard you?'

'It was a joke! Anyway, he won't be home from the Ealdwitan for hours. They're voting on an accord today. Something about use of magic in outwith workplaces.'

'Well – the servants then. You know what I mean.'

'Don't be so po-faced, Rose.' Clemency sat back in her armchair and looked across the table at Rosa, her eyes laughing. 'You know me, I'm just a tease. I always have been. I adore Philip. And what's turned you into Little Miss Prim all of a sudden?'

'Nothing.' Rosa twisted her handkerchief around her fingers, watching as the blood drained away and they grew pale and waxen. Then she let go and the pink flooded back in. 'Nothing. Just . . . thinking. What's it like being married, Clemmie?'

'Rosa! If you mean *that* then it's my turn to be shocked. Definitely *not* in front of the servants.'

'I didn't mean *that*!' Rosa said crossly, feeling her cheeks grow hot again. 'Or at least – well, not *just* that. The whole thing. Stop teasing me.'

Clemency looked at her, her blue eyes sparkling with mischief. The dimples came and went in her cheeks.

'Well, it's rather uncomfortable at first, and it certainly takes some time to get used to. But after a little while you grow to rather like it. Sometimes it can be positively pleasurable, even though his moustache certainly makes matters a little tickly. But then Sebastian is clean-shaven so that needn't worry you. Does that answer your question?'

'Clemmie!' Rosa couldn't stop herself laughing. She felt her own mouth turn upwards in a reluctant smile. 'You're incorrigible! I meant – what's it like to have breakfast every day with the same man, see him in his –' she lowered her voice, and whispered, '*nightshirt*. What's it like to know that you'll be with him every day until you're old and grey, both of you?'

'I might not be,' Clemency said, but the laughter had gone from her eyes and her face was serious. 'I don't know, Rosa. I can't answer all this. You're asking me to tell you what marriage to Sebastian would be like, and I can't do that. I'm glad I married Philip – he's a dear, even if he does clip his moustache on to my bedroom carpet and snore. It's a small price to pay for all this.' She waved her hand at the room they were sat in, the high French windows, the chandelier above their heads, and the Meissen cups on the silver tea tray between them. 'But Philip is not Sebastian, and Sebastian is not Philip.'

'No,' Rosa agreed. She thought of Sebastian, of his cool eyes, his mouth with its thin, sensitive lips smiling at her over the candelabra, of his hair, slicked to dark gold beneath his tall top hat, of the lean, deceptive strength of his shoulders beneath his beautifully cut tailcoat. No, Sebastian was *not* Philip.

Clemency was looking at her, her eyes lazy but thoughtful. Then, almost as if she were reading Rosa's mind, she said, 'He's handsome enough, so it can't be that. Rich *and* handsome: what more do you want?'

Kindness, Rosa thought. *Love*. But she didn't say it.

'I wish I'd been born a boy,' she said instead, 'so I could go and make my own fortune. Doesn't it rile you, Clemmie, that we have to always be the ones to wait, while they do the fighting and the adventuring?'

'Well, you weren't born a boy,' Clemency said pragmatically. 'And short of magicking sovereigns from the air, I don't see what you *can* do other than make a good marriage.'

'Maybe I should,' Rosa said mutinously. 'Make magic sovereigns, I mean.'

'If you started spending magicked gold the Ealdwitan would have you in irons under the Thames before you could say "traitor". There's no point in wishing things were different, Rose. You just have to play the hand you're dealt.

Anyway . . .' She looked at her watch. 'It's nearly three. The dressmaker will be here soon for the final fitting. When she's finished, why don't I walk you across the park and I can meet Philip at the headquarters.'

'I thought women weren't allowed inside?'

'They've introduced a ladies' room. I know – imagine the scandal. Philip said that when the vote was passed Augustus Rokewood nearly shouted himself into an apoplexy. *And*, even worse, wives are now permitted in the green dining room. Not in the main one though – *that* really would cause an outcry. Where would all the men go to hide?'

'Only wives?' Rosa asked.

'Well, I expect they'd stretch a point for sisters,' Clemency said, folding her napkin. 'And fiancées,' she added, with a sly sideways look. 'But I think that would be the outer limit. Otherwise, Philip says, all the wives would rise up in fury imagining their husbands' mistresses running amok over the vichyssoise.' She nodded at Rosa's cup. 'Have you finished?'

'Yes, thank you.'

'Well then, I shall ring for Liza to clear before the dressmaker gets here.'

'Clemmie . . .' Rosa said desperately as Clemency stretched her hand towards the bell. The words came rushing quick before she could think better of them, regret them. 'Clemmie, isn't there anything Philip could do for Alexis? He does *so* want a post and I know—'

'I can ask,' Clemency said, but her eyes were sad. 'But I wouldn't hold your breath, Rose. You know I love you, and I know we're cousins, but it's not a strong link compared to the bonds that tie the Ealdwitan together. It's not easy to break into their ranks. You need a close connection, really. A first-hand relationship, either by blood or . . .'

She trailed off. She didn't have to finish. Rosa knew. Or by marriage.

She swallowed.

'Would *you* do it?' Her voice was low and caught in her throat. 'Would *you* marry him?'

'It's not as simple as that, is it?' Clemency looked at her pragmatically. She pressed the bell and the chime rang out deep in the bowels of the house. 'He hasn't asked you, after all. Sebastian Knyvet is no boy to be had for the asking, you know. He's brought back more than wealth and trinkets from the East, he's brought a reputation too, and not entirely the good kind. I dare say you've not heard the rumours, but I'm a married woman – I hear more. He has broken hearts, and more than hearts. You won't ensnare him by batting your eyelashes and lowering your fan. Unless I'm very wrong, he's looking for something more than a bread-and-butter school miss.'

'Is that what you think I am?' Rosa stood. She felt her magic crackle across her skin, like a prickle of anger. Clemency shook her head.

'Don't be a fool, Rose. You're my cousin and my friend

– my sister in all but name. Sebastian is intrigued, I can see that. But he'll want a woman who can meet him halfway, match him strength for strength.'

I have strength, Rosa thought. Her fists clenched inside her kid gloves.

'You will have to play this very carefully if you want him. *Do* you want him?'

Do I want him? Rosa thought. She bit her lip, staring into Clemency's wide blue eyes.

'Do you want him?' Clemency repeated, impatiently this time. 'Do you want to save Matchenham and give your brother a future, yes or no?'

It was as if a hand had closed around Rosa's heart, crushing it. She felt as if she were drowning in the blue of Clemency's gaze.

'Yes,' she said in a whisper. 'Yes . . . yes I want to save them.'

'Good. Then the first step is to get you a habit that doesn't look like it was fitted on a badly stuffed scarecrow.'

'I like my habit,' Rosa said mutinously. 'It was good enough for hunting at Matchenham.'

'Hunting at Matchenham won't win you any suitors other than fat, red farmers. You look good on a horse; no, you look *devastating* on a horse. If we're to make him fall in love with you . . .'

'We?' Rosa said tartly. Clemmie opened her eyes even wider than nature had made them.

'I can see if I leave this up to you you'll be more likely

to end up a bride of God before you're a bride of Sebastian Knyvet.'

'I am not a damn nun!' Rosa cried hotly. 'Will everyone stop going on as if I'm training for a convent?'

'Clearly not with that language!' Clemency said, her face shocked. But her blue eyes were laughing above the primly pursed mouth. 'No, Rose, you are not in training for a convent. But you will have to tread a very fine line with Sebastian Knyvet, between virtue and allure. And something tells me you may find it easier to navigate on horseback.'

It was dark when Rosa got home and as she hurried up the stairs, the clock struck six. She would have to dress for dinner straight away.

In her room she unpinned her hat and then rang the bell for Ellen. As she pulled off her gloves she saw that the left-hand one was split, probably from where she'd clenched her fists at Clemency. Rosa sighed, thinking of what Mama would say when she found new kid gloves on her bill at the milliner's. The bill for the riding habit was going to be painful enough. She glanced guiltily at the doorway and then muttered a spell under her breath.

'You rang, Miss Rosamund?' Ellen's voice cut across her whisper. Rosa jumped convulsively and put the gloves behind her back, but the rent had already begun to knit.

'Oh! Ellen, thank you. That was quick.' Her face flamed. She could see it in the mirror, the pink flush of her cheeks clashing horribly with her dark-red hair. Every thought had gone out of her head, except for the guilty knowledge of that tear, mending itself behind her back. Please God Ellen didn't ask her what she was holding . . .

'Yes, miss?' Ellen repeated, a trifle impatiently. She'd probably been in the middle of fetching something for Mama. Rosa took a breath.

'Oh, um. Could you . . . I'm about to dress for dinner. Could you bring me up some hot water and I'll ring the bell to be laced in about twenty minutes?'

'Yes, Miss.'

'Oh, and for tomorrow . . .' Her heart gave a little leap against her ribs, a half-thrilling, half-sickening feeling, like taking a fence too fast and seeing the ditch on the other side a hoof-beat too late. 'Tomorrow the dressmaker is sending across my new habit. Would you tell Fred Welling to look out the side-saddle?'

'I'm sorry, Miss Rosa, but Fred's not here.'

'Not here? What do you mean?'

'He's broken his arm and collarbone, miss. Set upon by footpads.'

'Footpads!' Rosa almost laughed, it sounded so melodramatic. Then she recollected herself. It wasn't as though footpads were unheard of in London. Why, Alexis had been set upon and beaten crossing the Heath one night. It was only a swift (and extremely illegal) spell which had saved his purse and probably his life. And Fred would have had no such resources to fall back on. 'I'm very sorry. Poor Fred. Will he be all right?'

'I dare say, Miss Rosa.' Ellen tossed her head, and Rosa remembered that Ellen was said to be sweet on Fred, and that they walked out together sometimes on Ellen's afternoon off. 'But he can't manage the horses until the bones have set.'

'So – so what will happen?'

'I don't know,' Ellen said, and for all her worry about Fred, there was something a little pleasurable in the way she said it, relishing the drama. 'I'm sure I don't know. Fred says he has a cousin who wants to be a stableboy or something – some lad from Spitalfields, I heard tell. We'll all be murdered in our beds, I shouldn't wonder.'

'Ellen!' Rosa snorted. She unpinned her hair and began to brush out the plaits. 'Don't be so melodramatic. Nobody will be murdered. Spitalfields or not, I'm sure his cousin will be a thoroughly nice boy and look after the horses very well. And as long as he's kind to Cherry and can put on a side-saddle, I really don't care where he was born.'

5

'I'll have the law on you!'

A man, red with anger, burst into the forge. His arm was bound up in a sling. The door banged against the wall with a sound like a gunshot as he entered and William looked up, his face drenched with sweat from the fire.

'Are you Luke Lexton?' the man demanded.

'No, I'm his uncle.' William set the hammer to one side and nodded at Luke, where he stood working the bellows, the sweat running down the hollows of his chest and pooling at the waistband of his shirt. 'That's him. Luke, leave the bellows be for a moment and come here.'

Luke stopped pumping and wiped his arm across his forehead.

'So you're Luke Lexton?' The red-faced man looked Luke up and down, sizing him up, and seemed to subside a little. Luke was not a fighter, but he'd been hammering metal and pumping the bellows since the age of twelve, and he had the muscles of one. He also had a good eight or ten inches on the red-faced man.

'Yes,' he said. 'What of it?'

'I'll have the law on you,' the red-faced man said stubbornly. 'He never said nothing about breaking it for real. Nothing was said about that.'

'Oh for gawd's sakes, man,' William spoke impatiently. 'What did you think they'd do? Did you think your mistress would take your word for it that you felt a little poorly and send you off with calf's foot jelly and her good wishes on your word as a gentleman? Don't be soft! Of course they had to break it – you can't fake a broken arm, nor a mugging neither. But here, I've got your purse.' And he flung a shabby purse of money across the smithy. The man caught it awkwardly with his good hand.

'I shall count it!' he said defiantly. 'I shall count every last penny and if there's but one missing—'

'Yes, yes, you'll have the law on us,' William finished testily. 'Listen, lad, you were paid well for this. What did you think our six guineas was buying? And John Leadingham could've broken your arm without your leave – and where would you have been then? Still out of a job for the time being and not one guinea the better for it.'

Six guineas? Luke felt almost sick as the man opened the purse and peered inside, picking over the coins. *Six guineas!* That was – that was more money than he'd make in a month of Sundays, as an apprentice. Enough to feed Minna and her whole family for a year. How had they got such a sum? He thought of the good Brothers of the Malleus, pinching and scraping, and the weight of it pressed down on him until he felt near faint with it.

The man pulled out a coin and bit it. Then he closed the purse with a snap.

'It's my good word'll get your man in there,' he said sulkily. 'And I could still withhold it.'

'You do that,' William said dangerously, 'and you'll find that other arm broken, and maybe your legs too, and there will be no money to pay for either. Understood?'

'What's going on?' Luke asked, looking from the purse to William, and then back to the little man.

'What? Doesn't he know?' the man said, jerking his head at Luke. He began to laugh. 'What kind of a green 'un are you sending in there?'

'He knows enough,' William said. 'More than you do, which is not to say much.'

'Oi, you, I'll have none of that. Not when I've had my arm broken for your precious nephew's convenience. I'm Fred Welling. I am – I *was* – groom for the Greenwoods. No more, thanks to you and your mates. Six guineas they promised me, "You'll be laid off for a month," they said, "That's all it'll take," they said. "We'll arrange everything, all expenses paid. All you need do is recommend our man, no questions asked." Nothing was said about breaking arms.'

'It'll heal,' William grunted. He began hammering again, the blows ringing out like clear chimes in the evening air.

'What if it heals crooked? Or short?'

'It was a clean break and it's only an arm,' William said shortly between blows. 'It won't stop you riding or tending the horses.'

'How many horses?' Luke asked. Something shivered inside him. Was it fear? Or excitement that at last his task was to begin?

'Four,' the man said grumpily. Then he seemed to soften. 'Two hacks for the carriage, fit mostly for cats' meat. A nice Arab for Mr Alexis, name of Brimstone. And a pretty little strawberry roan called Cherry. She belongs to the daughter, Miss Rosamund – Rosa, they call her.'

Rosamund Greenwood. He shut his eyes, picturing her: a spoilt society bitch, one who'd never found a thing that couldn't be bought by money or magic, or some combination of the two.

'What's she like?' His voice was hoarse, almost to the point of being inaudible, and he swallowed and repeated. 'The girl, what's she like?'

'Pretty. A redhead, like her horse.' Welling gave a grin. 'Aye, she's a pretty lass.'

'Pretty? Do you know what she is?' Luke asked incredulously. A small spark of fury kindled in his chest and he felt anger begin to smoulder there.

'Leave it.' His uncle's voice came across the forge. 'Leave it, Luke.'

'*What* she is?' Welling looked from one to another as if he'd suddenly divined something was going on under the

71

surface. 'What do you mean, *what* she is? I thought you was casing the place for a robbery or something. What's really going on?'

'Never you mind.' William was across the forge in three strides. 'You've made a mistake by coming here. The agreement was we sent the purse, not that you come for it. Get out.'

The man didn't move, he just stood, looking from one to the other. Then, as William raised his hammer, he shrugged and sauntered across the yard. At the door he stopped, spat on the ground and left.

As his footsteps faded down the lane, Luke felt all the anger go out of him and he let out a great shuddering breath.

'Idiot,' William grunted. 'Coming here, whining about his arm.'

'They broke his arm?' Luke said. 'Who?'

'Who d'you think? One of the Brothers. Hey—!' He held up a hand. 'Don't give me that look, Luke. He was well paid, and whatever he thought was going on, he must have known you don't earn six guineas just by taking the odd sick day. It's half a year's wages for him. It had to look real, it had to *be* real, for his sake and yours.'

'Six guineas.' Luke felt the sickness rise in him again as he thought of the enormous responsibility of that sum. 'Where did they get money like that?'

'Never you mind. That's for John to worry about.'

'And so, what – I've got a position as a groom?'

'Yes. You're Luke Welling, Fred Welling's cousin. You live in Spitalfields, son to a drayman. We thought it best to keep it as close to the truth as possible, less chance of a slip that way. They know you've got no experience as a groom, but the story is that you know your way around horses and you're prepared to fill in for your cousin for no pay for a month, while his arm heals.'

'No pay?' Luke felt his lip twist. 'So they've laid their own groom off and they'd rather have an untrained lad for free than pay someone who knows his business?'

'Apparently, yes,' William said drily. 'You come with Fred's recommendation, don't forget. He's told them what we said to pass on – that you're wanting a position as a groom and hope to get some experience and a good reference from this, and that's pay enough.'

'They must be soft. For all they know I'll steal the silver and leave their horses lame and full of foot-rot.'

'God willing, you'll leave them with worse than that. But this is not going to be easy, Luke. I can't pretend it is. You'll have to be very, very sharp. It must be quick and clean, no way for them to fight back. Understood?'

'Understood,' Luke said. He returned to the bellows, watching as the forge roared louder, and the metal in its heart grew white and hot. And the thought came to him, that he was like that metal, about to be plunged into a fire hotter and more savage than any in nature, one that would test and temper him beyond anything he'd known.

* * *

They were waiting for him in the kitchen as he came down the stairs the next day, bag in hand, muffler pulled high.

'Luke, lad!' John Leadingham clapped him on the back, a buffet that made Luke stagger and grin.

'Watch out! You'll have me over.'

'It'd take more than that to knock you down, young Luke. I've seen brick outhouses built less sturdy than you.' John Leadingham's face wrinkled in a grin that made him look like a boy and Luke found himself grinning back, in spite of the nerves that griped at his guts. So. This was it. The beginning.

'Got the tools of the trade?' John asked intently. Luke nodded.

'Wrapped in paper under me clothes.'

'Good luck, boy,' Benjamin West said. He pushed his glasses up his nose, peering short-sightedly at Luke through the misty lenses. 'Take care of yeself.'

'Luke . . .' was all William said. He shook his head, as if the words were there, but stuck in his throat. 'Luke.'

'Goodbye, Uncle.'

'You take care, hear me?' He gripped Luke's shoulders, looking at him, his grip so hard it was all Luke could do not to wince away from it. 'Hear me?'

'I hear you. I'll take care of myself, I promise. I'll be back within the full moon.'

'And don't underestimate her. She may look like just a girl, but she's *not* just a girl, remember?'

'I'll remember.'

Of course he'd remember. How could he forget?

He looked around the little room, at the faces of the men he'd known all his life, good men, with hands and faces marked by hard work and hard lives, hands that'd sliced meat and hammered metal and carved wood, but hands too that had curved around a tankard in the warmth of an inn, held a woman, dandled a baby and wiped away tears. And hands that had killed a witch – each of them, every man in the room. Suddenly he wanted, desperately, to ask how it had been for them – was the witch old or young, man or woman? Had the witch begged, at the last, or wept? Had their heart misgiven them as they drove the blow home, or did their hand never falter?

But it was the one question he could never ask, never discuss. It was the rule: outside the masked anonymity of the meetings, all hands were clean of blood. And he was not a Brother yet.

He turned to go.

'Wait.' William put out a hand to stop him and he paused. His uncle dug in his pocket and pulled out two gold sovereigns. He held them out to Luke. 'Take these.'

'No!' Luke was shocked. 'No, I can't. I don't need it.'

'*Take them.*' His uncle pressed the coins into his limp hand and Luke stood, feeling the dense weight of gold in his palm, growing warm against his skin. 'I'd rather you had money if you need it. There's not much I can do to help, but this I can do. Apart from that, you're on your own, lad.'

Luke nodded and pocketed the coins reluctantly, feeling the truth of his uncle's words sink into his skin and bone. *Apart from that, you're on your own.*

He had never felt so alone.

Then he turned and walked into the rain.

'Who're you?' The man looking down at Luke was no taller than him, but he stood at the top of the flight of stone steps and Luke was at the bottom. Luke had the feeling that even if they'd been on level ground, something about his mud-spattered boots and rain-soaked coat would have left him at a disadvantage. The rain had stopped, but only a few minutes before, and his hair still dripped down his nose and the back of his neck. He looked up at the tall, white house towering above him, at the huge black door with its brass knocker, and then storey after storey of long windows glittering with raindrops.

'I'm Luke L—' he stumbled, and bit his lip. Dammit. The very first thing to come from his lips, and he'd nearly slipped up already. 'Luke Welling. Fred Welling's cousin. I've come to look after the horses.'

'Hmm.' The man at the top of the steps looked down his nose. 'I'm Mr James, the butler. You'll be reporting to me.'

Luke said nothing, but nodded, and shifted his heavy carpet-bag from one hand to another. It felt like it had absorbed several pints of rainwater on the walk across London.

It had been a long walk, from Spitalfields to

Knightsbridge, through the City, along Fleet Street, buzzing with newspaper men, a cut through Covent Garden, full of the debris of the morning market, and then Piccadilly, flash as you like, full of swells and nobs admiring the windows full of fancy fabric and furniture, books and hats – anything you could think of, London could sell you, from gutter pickings to the finest French wines.

And then, at last, Knightsbridge, tucked beneath the green jewel of Hyde Park, a great white oasis of pristine houses so tall and fine, and so different from the grey, crumbling, sooty slums of Spitalfields that he could hardly bear to look at them. Even the rain had stopped as he came into Osborne Crescent, as if this part of London even had different skies.

'Cat got your tongue?' Mr James snorted. 'What kind of manners did they teach you in Spitalfields? "Yes, Mr James", is what you'll reply when you're told something.'

'Yes, Mr James.'

'You'll sleep over the stable at the back of the house and take your meals in the kitchen. You go round by the mews, horses or not. Do *not* under any circumstances use the front door – it's the back entrance only for you, understood? Muddy boots get left at the kitchen door, and you'll be expected to wash at the pump before you come in from the yard. Mrs Ramsbottom won't take kindly to horse muck being traipsed over her clean tiles. Dinner is in one hour.'

Luke nodded and then, recollecting himself, said 'Yes, Mr James.' He eased the carpet-bag back into his other hand, wishing he could set it down, but something told him putting his wet bag on the whitewashed steps would be badly received.

Mr James nodded stiffly, then he looked Luke up and down, taking in his rain-soaked boots and clothes.

'You walked from Spitalfields?'

'Yes. I mean, yes, Mr James.'

'Hmph.' He seemed to soften slightly. 'Well, you'll be glad of dinner, I dare say. I'll call Becky to show you to your quarters.'

'There's no gas to the stable block.' Becky's voice floated ahead as Luke trudged wearily after her and up the stairs above the stable and carriage house. 'So it's candles. And you've not to waste them. Mrs Ramsbottom will count 'em, and if you go over more than what's reasonable she'll tell Mr James to dock it from your wages.'

'What's reasonable?' Luke asked.

Becky shrugged.

'That depends. She had a soft spot for Fred. He got away with murder.'

She'd have a hard time docking his wages anyway, Luke reflected, as Becky opened the door to the little room above the stable block. It was small and low ceilinged, barely more than a whitewashed attic, but it looked clean.

'The servants' lavvy is by the back door. You'll have to wash at the pump in the yard, but Fred used to beg Mrs Ramsbottom for a can of hot water in winter. Pick your moment though. The bed's clean; I changed the sheets myself. I can't speak for the rest – he wasn't exactly a model housekeeper, your cousin.'

'Thanks.' Luke let his carpet-bag slip to the floor with a squelching thud. Becky looked at him appraisingly from under her lashes as he peeled off his coat, taking him in from his travel-stained boots to his rain-drenched hair. His shirt was so wet it was plastered to his chest.

'Your afternoon off's Wednesday.' She twined a curl of sandy hair around her finger, where it had escaped from beneath her cap. 'Same as mine.'

'Right.' Luke turned to peer out of the narrow sooty window, across the smoke-stained chimney stacks of the stable mews.

'What's happened to your shoulder?' Becky asked curiously from behind him. Luke glanced reflexively and then bit his lip. The dressing stood out clear beneath the wet material.

'None of your business,' he said curtly.

'Well!' Becky gave a little huff of annoyance. 'Some'd say a civil question deserves a civil answer. Dinner's in three-quarters of an hour. Don't be late.' And with that, she turned on her heel, her apron strings fluttering as she stalked down the stairs.

Luke sighed and then sank on to the bed and put his head in his hands. He couldn't afford to get off on the wrong foot with everyone. There was every chance he'd need the help of the other servants, albeit unknowingly, if he were going to do what needed to be done. And Becky would have been a good place to start. He wasn't a fool; he'd seen the interest in her eyes as she took him in. And now he'd have to work twice as hard to bring her round.

So this was Fred Welling's domain. He looked around the little room, taking in the small windows, the low-beamed ceiling. He'd have to be careful not to bump his head going to bed. There was a stub of a candle on the saucer by the bed, so at least he was one candle in credit with Mrs Ramsbottom. A Bible on the washstand – it didn't look like it had been read very much. A rag rug on the floor and a metal bedstead with a chipped chamberpot beneath. And that was it, except for a few pieces of rickety furniture that looked like cast-offs from the house. Not exactly the lap of luxury, but not bad. It was a room of his own, which was better than many servants had, and bigger than his room at home.

Home. He thought of William and Minna and the sights and smells of Spitalfields and for a moment his heart ached and he wished he could put his head down on the flat limp pillow, close his eyes and *rest*. His whole body cried out for it.

Then he clenched his jaw and stood, wiping the last of the rain off his face with his sleeve.

He was here to do a job, and he'd do it, and get back home to where he belonged. That was all. And then – *then* – he'd tackle the Black Witch. Time enough for rest after that.

He began to unpack his bag. It was heavier than it looked, certainly too heavy for the meagre clothes he took out first. It was the other stuff, what John Leadingham called *the tools of the trade* that had made the bag so heavy to carry across London, all shoved down beneath his clothes and covered in a piece of newspaper. The long knife. The iron gag. The garotte, the blindfold and the syringe. The bottle, wrapped tight in a dirty rag.

'For God's sakes, don't breathe the fumes,' Leadingham had said. 'And don't, whatever you do, break the bottle or the witch won't be the only one in trouble.'

Now Luke cast about for a hiding space. A loose board beneath the bed caught his eye, but when he prised it up the space was already occupied by a bottle and a stash of postcards. Luke pulled them out. The bottle was whisky, by the smell of it. And the postcards were photographs of women, everything from buxom matrons to slim young girls, all without a stitch on them. So . . . Fred Welling had had more than his Bible to pass the time up here of an evening. They'd be a good camouflage at least, if anyone did remove the board.

He put his tools into the space beneath the floor, then fitted the bottle and the cards back into the opening, masking the bundle of newspaper behind them. Then he replaced the loose board and began to unbutton his wet shirt.

* * *

The clock over the stable was striking quarter to as he hurried down into the yard, tucking his clean shirt in as he went. Fifteen minutes before dinner. He had just enough time to put his head round the stable door.

He paused for a moment with his hand on the latch, smelling the good smells of clean hay and warm horse, and then he lifted it and entered the warmth of the stable.

Inside the horses lifted their heads from their hay. Closest to the door were two big bays with large gentle eyes, presumably the two 'hacks' Fred Welling had mentioned. Furthest away was a beautiful Arab who tossed his head and snorted down his nose as Luke entered.

In between was a little strawberry roan who whickered gently as Luke came level with her stall.

'You must be Cherry.' He leant over her rail and patted her shoulder, and she nuzzled him with the side of her head. 'Ain't you a beauty?'

He wished Minna were here. If Bess had a place like this to feed and sleep and rest . . . But there was no point in sighing over might-have-beens. 'If wishes were horses, then beggars'd ride,' as Minna would say. Bess was safe from the knacker's and the glue factory, for today at least. That was more than could be said for many horses. And if her belly wasn't always full, well, the same could be said for Minna's brother and sister. She was no worse off than them.

Luke pulled a wisp of hay from the bale for Cherry and she took it fastidiously between her teeth.

'Time to go in and face the others,' he said. 'Wish they was all as friendly as you.'

'Who're *you*?'

He jumped and swung round, his heart pounding.

A girl was standing in the doorway, her hands on her hips, staring at him with angry, dark eyes. Her cheeks were flushed and the low evening light shone on the dark-red hair gathered into heavy loops at the back of her head, making her seem to glow like an ember in the warm dark of the stables. She could not have been more than sixteen or seventeen, and she was a witch, Luke could see it in her every bone, in the magic that crackled and spat around her like a halo of fire.

For a minute he couldn't speak; it was as if she'd robbed him of his tongue. All he could think was that this must be her, the girl he'd come to kill. It *must* be. And she was standing in front of him, defenceless, her slim white throat bare to his knife – if only he'd had it. He'd never been so close to a witch, close enough to strike . . . He thought of the knife under the floorboards upstairs, of the quiet sound it would make as it plunged into the soft white skin, where the vein beat so close beneath – and his fingers closed on the rail of Cherry's stall, clutching the wood so hard that splinters dug into his fingers. His heart was beating so hard and fast that he felt sick.

'Who *are* you?' she repeated angrily. She took a step forward into the stable, her skirts swishing on the flags, and he saw that her small white hands were clenched

83

into fists. 'Who are you and what are you doing with my horse?'

'I'm . . . I'm Luke, miss. Luke Le—' He caught himself, snarling inwardly at his stupidity. For Christ's sakes, if he couldn't get even the simplest thing right, what hope was there of his ever meeting or besting the Black Witch? 'Luke Welling. I'm Fred's cousin.'

'Oh.' She flushed, and bit her lip. A lock of dark-red hair had escaped its coils and she tucked it behind her ear. 'I'm sorry, I didn't know you were arriving today. That was very kind of you to fill in so quickly. How is he?'

Much you care, bitch, Luke thought. Aloud he said, 'He's doing all right, miss. The doctor says his arm'll heal.' Although not if he turned up at the forge again, looking for more money.

'Oh good, I'm glad to hear it.' There was a little frown line between her narrow dark brows, and her brown eyes looked . . . well – worried, or a bloody good impression of it. 'I was so sorry to hear about the attack. It sounds terrifying. Please tell him we all wish him a quick recovery.'

'I will, miss.' He licked his lips again, and then said, 'I – if I might ask, are you Miss Greenwood? Miss Rosamund Greenwood?'

'That's right. You've met my brother Alexis, I suppose?'

'Not yet, miss.'

'Oh.' There was something in her face; he couldn't put his finger on it – some reserve in her dark eyes. 'Well, you've that pleasure still to come then.'

84

'Um . . .' He twisted the hay between his fingers, unsure how to answer. Then he remembered what William had said: *When in doubt, just agree with them. Yes, sir. No, sir. You can't go far wrong with that.* 'Yes, miss.'

She gave him a look, that same odd look, and then tossed her head in a gesture so like the little mare that he might have laughed if she'd been just an ordinary girl and he an ordinary lad.

'You'd better go in,' she said. 'The clock struck the hour a few minutes ago. Mrs Ramsbottom's very strict about meal times.'

Then she turned and was gone, leaving him holding the rail of the stall for support, trying to catch his breath.

So this was her. The witch he was to kill.

6

Rosa hurried back into the house, her cheeks hot with embarrassment as she relived the scene in the stable – the door opening, the strange man standing there, with his arm slung across Cherry's back, *her* horse, and Cherry nuzzling his hand as if she'd known him for ever.

What a fool she'd been. Of course she should have realized who he was – Ellen had only told her the night before. But Ellen had spoken as if his arrival was days, weeks away. And she'd screamed at him like a fishwife – no wonder the poor man had been struck dumb. He probably wasn't used to the daughter of the house shrieking at him on his first day.

He looked nothing like Fred, that was all she could think as she ran up the back stairs, hoping to avoid Mama. Fred was small and fair and pink, with thin little bones like a jockey. This cousin was tall and dark, with hazel eyes and hair the colour of wet straw. He looked more like – like a *navvy* than anything else. When Ellen had said *stableboy* she'd imagined a little skinny thing, with raw red knees and homesick eyes. The man she'd met in the stable had to be eighteen if he was a day, and looked as if he rode at least twelve or fourteen stone, and his dark eyes showed not homesickness, but a tense wariness she couldn't account for.

Well, it was no crime to be unlike your cousin. She had little enough in common with Alexis and he was her brother.

Suddenly, as if she'd conjured him from thin air just by thinking of him, she heard his voice.

'So, sister. How goes the hunt?'

'What?' She swung round, and there he was, standing in the dark at the top of the back stairs, for all the world as if he'd been waiting for her.

'You heard me,' he said. His face was shadowed, but there was something ugly in his stance. '*Sebastian*. What are you doing to get yourself blooded?'

'Ugh.' She turned her face away from him. 'Must you be so vulgar?'

'Must *you* be such a prude?'

She tried to push past, but he grabbed her wrist, painfully hard.

'Don't you walk away from me when I'm speaking to you. I *am* the master of this house, Rosa, and you will listen and obey when I speak, do you understand?'

'I will listen,' she hissed between her teeth, trying not to let the pain in her wrist show on her face. 'But as to whether I will obey or not, that lies with my own conscience. I won't be whored out to your friends for your profit.'

Alexis lifted his free hand and struck her, brutally, across the face. Rosa staggered and would have fallen if he hadn't hauled her back to her feet by the wrist he was still holding.

'You brute.' She put her free hand to her cheek. It was throbbing and swelling, and would be green and blue by tomorrow. 'You – you *bastard.*'

'Never speak to me that way again, do you understand?' he snarled. 'And wash your filthy mouth out with soap. Tomorrow, Sebastian rides out in the Row. You *will* meet him, and you *will* charm him, and God help you if there's the least trace of a bruise on your prim little face. Understood?'

Rosa stood for a moment, gasping. Alexis' grip on her wrist throbbed in time with the pain in her cheek. Then she closed her eyes, feeling her hatred well and boil inside her like molten lead, twining with her power into a hot, explosive bitterness.

'*Fýrgnást!*' she hissed.

Alexis stumbled back with a cry of agony, wringing his hand as if he'd had an electrical shock. He stared down at his palm. In the centre was a charred and blackened spot, still smoking a little.

'You little bitch!'

'Touch me again,' Rosa said, her voice very low and

shaking, 'and you'll get the same thing somewhere even more painful.'

'Go to your room.' Alexis' face was like thunder and he wrung his hand as if he could wipe her smouldering curse off it, but it was burnt deep into his flesh. Rosa smiled, in spite of the pain in her face, and Alexis roared, 'Get to your room, you hell-cat! If I see you again before breakfast you'll regret it, understood?'

'Quite.'

Rosa kept her head high and her spine straight as she walked along the corridor to her room, though her face throbbed and her wrist was red from Alexis' grip.

She held it together until the door closed behind her, but the sound of it clicking shut was like the lifting of a spell. She had not wept since Papa died, but she felt very close to it now – closer than when she had fallen from her horse and limped home on a twisted ankle, closer than when Mama had slapped her for riding astride in Alexis' cast-off trousers.

'Bastard.' She leant against the door, her forehead against the wood, as if he were only just the other side. The words were mangled and torn by her shaking, sobbing breath. Her face felt hot, her forehead burning against the cool wood. 'I hate you. I *hate* you.'

Only silence answered her. Alexis had gone – back to the library, back to his brandy. Or out to his club.

At last she made her way across to the mirror, to look at her swollen face. Her right cheek was twice the size of the left, her right eye pink and swelling shut. It would serve Alexis right if she *did* turn up in the Row with her face like this. See what Sebastian thought of her then, and see what Alexis' friends thought of him.

But the thought came to her, as she stared at her battered face, that whatever marriage to Sebastian would be like, it couldn't be much worse than life here. Once she was married, she would be out from under Alexis' thumb. In fact, if she married Sebastian, the tables would be turned. Alexis would be in *her* power.

The thought hung there, cold and heavy in the silence. At last Rosa risked turning the door knob and peering out. The corridor was empty and she made her way cautiously down to the study, where the grimoire was kept. Inside it was cold and dark, and she lit a lamp with hands that shook, the match flame trembling as she touched it to the wick.

The grimoire lay on the desk, its brass lock shut tight, and she whispered the word her mother had taught her as a little girl.

'Ætýne!'

The lock sprang open with a chink and Rosa opened the pages, feeling the magic swirl and shimmer beneath her fingers as she leafed through the pages, stopping here and there to check for possibilities. At last she came to a page marked with a ribbon, for easier reference.

A charme to heal a Bruise, Swellyng or Bloe: Binde in a

clene Kerchief a freʃh Kydny or a pece of Lamb's Liver.
If Nonne can be found, let the Kerchief be wette with
clene ʃpring Wattere, or Teares. Presse itte to the
Swellynge and speke these words: Gelácne áblávunge,
geháliged be, May the Bloode of the Lamb take my
Payne from me.

Someone had written in pencil beneath: *This charm never fails, though I have kidney only rarely to hand, and lamb's liver never, and generally use nothing more than a wetted handkerchief. It has been of great service in my marriage, alas.*

Rosa felt rage at the violence of men bubble up in her as she read the words. Rage at Alexis, with his cold words and hot fury. Rage at that unknown ancestor of hers, who had caused his wife to mark the spell for all her descendants' use. Rage at her father for dying and leaving her here at Alexis' mercy. Rage at them all – even the blameless ones: Sebastian, Philip Catesby, even at that poor outwith stable-hand.

She had no clean spring water and she would not waste her tears on Alexis.

Instead she looked out at the iron-grey clouds scattered across the sky, drawing them towards her in her mind, gathering them into a dark, sodden mass of unshed tears in the sky. The first drops of rain began to spatter against the window pane. She opened the casement and leant out, letting it fall on her clean white handkerchief. Even the rain was grey and filled with soot and smog. She thought of

Matchenham, of the clear soft rain that fell on the woods and pastures, and washed everything clean and new. London rain did not clean – it only soiled.

I want to go home.

Luke knocked at the kitchen door, waited, and then came awkwardly into the room, wiping his boots on the mat.

For a long moment he just stood, watching as they bustled around him. Hot tureens were steaming on the table, Becky was laying out spoons and knives, a big red-faced woman at the range was ladling potatoes from one dish into another. Luke stood, dazed at the thought that all this was for the service of just three people: a girl, a boy, and a woman. It didn't seem possible. He and his uncle ate well – but there was more food here than they would eat in a week, and more meat than Minna's family saw in a month, perhaps in a *year*.

Then a boy sitting in the corner with a pile of dirty shoes looked up.

'Who's he?'

Every head in the room turned to look at him and Luke felt the flush rise up his neck.

'*He* is Luke Welling,' Becky said pertly. 'Fred's cousin. And you'll keep a civil tongue in your head, young Jack, and get those boots cleaned before supper or I'll tell Mr James to take a penny off your wages.'

'I only arst,' the boy said mildly, and went back to scraping the boots on to a newspaper.

'Luke, this is Mrs Ramsbottom, the cook,' Becky continued. 'And this is Ellen; she's maid to Mrs Greenwood and Miss Rosa.'

'Please to meet you, I'm sure,' Ellen said, looking Luke up and down as if she wasn't sure what the cat had dragged in. 'You don't look much like Fred, I must say.'

'No,' Luke agreed. It seemed safer not to offer explanations.

'How're you related again?' Ellen asked.

'Cousins,' Luke said. He was beginning to dislike this tall, haughty girl with her blonde hair swept under a lace cap.

'Through his mother's side, I suppose? Is it his aunt Mary or Mabel?'

'Through Mabel,' Luke said at random. The kitchen was warm after the cold of the yard, and he felt sweat pool in the small of his back. 'But we're not first cousins. It's complicated.'

'Hmm.' She looked at him long and hard, then a bell went over the doorway and she gave a cross tut. 'Drat, that's the mistress's bell. Mrs Ramsbottom, I should be down in two ticks but will you put my plate on the warmer if I'm kept?'

The cook gave no answer, but a jerky nod seemed to indicate that she'd heard and Ellen ran swiftly up the narrow stairs and disappeared.

'Well, Luke . . .' Mr James appeared from a back pantry, holding a bottle in his hand. 'I can see from your *derrière*

93

that you've acquainted yourself with the horses.'

Luke looked down at himself and then plucked sheepishly at the strands of hay still sticking to the back of his trousers. He must have brushed a bale on leaving the stables.

'Mr Alexis Greenwood has sent word down to say that he and Miss Rosa will be riding in the Row tomorrow, so please have Brimstone and Cherry saddled and ready for ten o'clock, understood?'

'Yes,' Luke said, then hastily added, 'sir,' as he saw Mr James's raised eyebrow.

'Now, let's be seated. We won't wait for Ellen.'

'Luke, you're next to me,' Becky whispered. He looked down to see her hand stroking the seat of the wooden chair beside her.

'Dear Lord . . .' Mr James intoned as they all sat. Luke folded his hands. 'Dear Lord, help us to remember our good fortune in our lot and in this food on our plates. For all the tasks that we have to accomplish, lend us Your strength and may our work sharpen our appetites for the feast. Amen.'

'Amen,' Luke said. But far from whetting his appetite, there was a coldness in the pit of his belly as he put his fork to his lips. One full moon he had for his task. And he had no idea how to accomplish it.

That night, tossing and turning on the thin pillow, Luke thought he'd never sleep. His head was too full of everything that had happened in the day: trying to play the part of Luke Welling, trying to keep up with his new job, and trying all the while to work out the lay of the land for his mission.

But he did sleep. He must have done, for he woke in the night sweating and crying and with the image of the Black Witch in front of his eyes in the darkness. His hand shook as he reached out and struck a match, the flame wavering high in his trembling fingers.

The wick caught and he sank back, curled on his side, hating himself. He was one of the Brotherhood now, or almost – he'd undergone trial by knife and trial by fire and accepted the trial of the hammer. So why did he still wake night after night, his body drenched with sweat and his face wet with tears?

He lay, staring into the candle flame, trying to quiet his thudding heart and chase away the image of the Black Witch and that white, creeping hand crawling across the floor towards his trembling leg. And as the flame waxed and flickered, red and gold, an image came into his head; a girl, her hair like a halo of fire around her head, glowing like an ember in the dark. He closed his eyes, but the fire burnt against his closed lids, long after he'd shut his eyes.

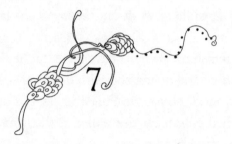

7

'Will you be able to ride like that, miss?' Ellen stood back and looked at Rosa, buttoned into the tight new habit, the black skirt swishing the rug as she paraded in front of the fly-spotted bedroom mirror. The skirts were much longer and heavier than she was accustomed to. Belle followed at her heels as she paced and turned. 'Your stays are awful tight.'

'I think so.' Rosa took an experimental deep breath, feeling the whalebone cutting into her middle, and then let it out. In her head she could hear Alexis' bitter hissing voice: *You look like a scrawny boy,* and she despised herself for caring. This was not her – this girl who primped and laced and brushed her hair until it shone. The real her was the girl who rode bareback through the woods at Matchenham, with her skirts pulled up so she could sit astride, and her hair tangled by the wind. But where was that girl now? It was as if London had killed her.

'You look beautiful, Miss Rosa.' Ellen spoke as if she could hear Rosa's thoughts. 'Mr Knyvet would have to have a heart of stone not to—'

'Ellen!' Rosa cut across her, blushing furiously. 'Mr Knyvet has nothing to do with this.'

'Yes, miss,' Ellen said, but the dimples in her cheeks told Rosa she did not believe her.

'How's the new stableboy?' she said curtly, changing the subject. 'Settling in?'

'Well!' Ellen tossed her head and began tidying the brushes on the dressing table crossly. 'He's not much of a boy for all that. *I* think there's something rather pushing and forward about him, if you ask me.'

'Really?' Rosa picked up Belle, nuzzling her warm forehead. 'He seemed just the opposite when I met him in the stables. Positively tongue-tied.'

She remembered his deep voice, his East End accent, the way his consonants blurred together, like wooden blocks shaken together until the edges wore blunt.

'Oh he's quiet, miss, but that's not what I meant. He's *too* quiet. It's – it's like he doesn't *care*, somehow, but . . .' Ellen stopped, struggling to put her finger on what she meant, but Rosa thought she knew. He had the quietness not of self-doubt, but of someone holding themselves back, keeping themselves apart. And the reserve in his eyes wasn't born of inadequacy but of something else, something she couldn't quite identify. As if . . . the words came to her suddenly, as if someone had whispered them in her ear: *as if he were trying to hide the wolf inside.*

She shivered suddenly. What nonsense. Just because he was quiet and didn't tug his forelock and look nervy enough for Ellen. Anyway, it was natural enough for Ellen to dislike him; he'd pushed out her sweetheart, hadn't he? Usurped his place.

Except . . . except wasn't he supposed to be Fred's cousin? So why would Ellen resent someone who was doing Fred a good turn, keeping his place for him until he was well enough to work again?

Never try to understand servants or outwith, Alexis' dismissive voice spoke inside her head. *They're a law to themselves – as nervy as animals and half the sense.*

'I'd better go down,' she said to Ellen. 'I mustn't keep Alexis waiting. He wants to be in the Row by eleven. Goodbye, Belle darling.' She dropped a kiss on Belle's warm twitching back and then set her gently on the window seat. 'Keep my seat warm. And wish me luck.'

'You have to admit, Rose, this ain't half bad,' Alexis called across the narrow strip of path between them.

Rosa looked down at Cherry's back and up at the blue sky, bright and sunny for once, all trace of last night's fog and rain clouds chased away by the winter sun. Only the smoke from London's thousands of chimneys drifted across the sky, deceptively clean and white against the stark blue.

Then she looked across at Alexis, his top hat gleaming

in the morning sun. She hated to agree with Alexis, but he was right. It wasn't like riding at Matchenham, full gallop across the dew-wet fields, with her hair loose like a gypsy and full of twigs and the smell of damp leaves, but there was something very pleasant about the ordered ranks of riders with their gleaming horses, the men so handsome in their top hats and riding coats, the women in their stocks and habits, hair swept up and shining in the sun. The brass on the carriages glittered like gold, the grass to either side was manicured into a soft green carpet scattered with golden leaves, and she could hear the bells from Brompton Oratory and St James's floating across on the fresh morning breeze. And even the pinching of her stays and the ache in her cheekbone could not take away from the bubbling delight of being on horseback again, the pommel of the side-saddle firm against her thigh.

Beneath her, Cherry whickered excitedly and Rosa knew that she felt it too.

'I'm sorry,' she whispered, putting her hand down to stroke Cherry's warm neck. 'I know I've neglected you.'

Behind them came Castor's plodding step and she thought of the stableboy and the look in his eyes as he'd handed her up on to Cherry's back. The way his gaze had gone to her cheek and stayed there, so that her hand had crept almost unconsciously to cover it.

'What?' she'd snapped. 'What is it?'

'Nothing, miss,' he'd said, his face impassive, and turned away.

She knew, she *knew* there could not possibly be a mark there – she'd checked in the glass this morning and the spell had worked. Not even the faintest purple. He could not have known. There was no way he could have known. But still – his eyes and the shadow of a frown between his brows . . .

She shook herself. *You're getting foolish. You've been living too long with outwith servants, living with deception.*

Luke watched Rosa as she rode, watched her reach down and pet Cherry, whispering something to the horse, and he thought again of the moment he'd handed her up into the saddle. Something about her face had caught his eye, the shadow of something around her cheekbone, almost as if the remains of a spell lingered there, shimmering in the morning sun.

He'd stared like a fool, like the idiot he was – unable to tear his eyes from it – and it was only when her hand had gone nervously to her face and she'd said, 'What? What is it?' with a catch in her voice, that he realized he'd frozen, the saddle girth slack in his hand, his eyes fixed on her.

'Nothing,' he'd choked out, and carried on tightening Cherry's girth for her. 'Nothing, miss.' Then he'd turned away, trying to hide his disquiet.

It was one thing to imagine himself living among

witches, entwined with their magic, at the mercy of any spell – it was quite another to find himself there in reality. He was here – just feet away from them – and they were riding in the Row just like all the other men and women, but reeking of magic so strongly he could not understand how the other riders didn't flinch away. And not just one witch either, but two – that Judas-haired brother of hers, Alexis. He might be a beef-fed bully with a seat like a sack of potatoes, but he was still a witch. His power shimmered around him like a miasma, though the day was clear.

He, Luke, was outnumbered. Even with the knife in his boot, it was an uncomfortable thought.

He was so wrapped in his thoughts that he almost didn't notice the third rider coming across and, when Rosa and Alexis reined in, he was caught by surprise. His horse, Castor, stumbled, barging Brimstone's hind quarter with his shoulder.

'Damnation!' Alexis snapped, as Brimstone jumped and sidled beneath him. 'Can't you control your horse, you clumsy oaf?'

'Sorry, sir,' Luke muttered. He looked over, to see a tall man in immaculately tailored riding clothes reining in a magnificent Arab that gleamed like polished mahogany, the sheen on its burnished coat second only to the polish on the man's tall leather boots. It would be impertinence to stare, but Luke's quick glance took in everything from the man's high top hat to the wicked-looking spurs that glinted at his heels. A little dog ran at his feet, jumping and chasing its own tail for the sheer joy of being alive, a strange contrast to the contained stillness and power of the man on horseback. The whole group, man, horse and dog, were wreathed around and about in spells, bound and twisted in a fog of power so thick that it was almost palpable – Luke barely repressed a shudder as he turned his eyes to the ground.

'Sorry, Knyvet,' Alexis was saying. 'New stableboy. Our usual chap broke his arm and got himself laid up for a month, so we've got his sot of a cousin filling in.'

'He's not a sot, Alex,' Rosa said stiffly. 'He's just new. Give him a chance. Anyway, Mr Knyvet doesn't want to hear our domestic troubles, do you, sir?'

'*Au contraire.*' The man bent over Rosa's hand, his horse stamping and sidling as he kissed her gloved knuckles. 'Everything about you is charming to me, Miss Greenwood. What a delightful . . . surprise to see you both here.'

'Oh . . .' Luke saw a flush on Rosa's cheek. 'As Mama said, I – I love to ride.'

'I remember that from Matchenham. Although, as I recall,' he looked at her from beneath his lashes, his blue eyes veiled and lazy, 'as a little girl you were happier bareback. But what I meant was, what brings you to the Row? I've never seen you before.' There was something in his expression that Luke couldn't quite place, something teasing, speculative, not quite pleasant, as if Rosa were a moth beneath a pin and he was not going to let her go easily.

'I don't think Mama would permit me to ride bareback these days,' Rosa said lightly, skirting his question, although the flush remained on her cheek, high and angry. The man, Knyvet, smiled, and was about to say something when his dog leapt up exuberantly at Rosa's skirts.

'Down, Pointer!' Knyvet snapped, and he kicked the little dog with his shining boot, sending it tumbling over the rutted surface of the row.

'Sebastian!' Rosa cried, and the little creature whimpered with pain and cowered back at its master's heel.

'Oh don't mind Rosa,' Alexis said with a sneering laugh. 'Her heart bleeds for anything on four legs. She's not quite so bothered about the chaps on two.'

'I've no use for disobedience,' Knyvet said. 'Be it in dogs, horses or servants. If they cannot learn to obey of their own volition they must have it beaten into them.' Then he gave a short laugh. 'But enough of this; let's speak of lighter things. Since we've met so serendipitously' – a smile creased his cheek – 'won't you allow me to escort you across the park? I'm on my way to the headquarters, so our paths lie in the same direction.'

'I'd be delighted,' Rosa said slowly. Her eyes went back to the little dog trotting in Knyvet's shadow, its tail firmly between its legs.

As they set off, Alexis hung back.

'Don't wait for me,' he called. 'I've a fancy Brimstone's

limping. I'll get the boy to take a look at his shoe and catch you up.'

Obediently Luke slid from Castor and pulled up the leg Alexis indicated with his whip. It looked sound enough. The shoe was firm and there was no swelling and no stone in the hoof, or none that he could see.

'I can't see nothing, sir,' he said. 'Do you want me to check the other leg?'

'Of course not, there's nothing wrong, you fool.' Alexis' voice was low and full of contempt. 'Just dig at it with your knife or whatever you do. Make it look realistic and try not to be more of an idiot than your mother made you.'

Luke gritted his teeth and drew out his pick, pretending to pull out an imaginary stone from Brimstone's shoe, but all the while following Rosa and Knyvet with his eyes. They rode like a matched pair, as they trotted down the Row, Rosa so slim and straight in her black habit that it looked as if he could break her in two, Knyvet tall and erect in the saddle beside her, his top hat making him look even taller, their magic crackling around them both like a cloud of light and storm. So this was the plan, was it? Marry her off to the tall arrogant bastard of a witch, to create more witch babies to wreak more misery on the world? Well, not if he could help it.

His fingers tightened unconsciously on the pick and Brimstone gave a whinny and flinched, pulling his foot away from Luke's grip.

'Hi, you fool!' Alexis snapped. 'You don't need to carve the poor brute's hoof out. Make it look realistic, I said, not stick him to the quick.'

'Sorry, sir,' Luke muttered. He stood, shading his eyes, watching Knyvet leaning into Rosa, saying something close to her ear. She laughed at his remark, her magic shimmering like a halo of ghostly fire in the winter sunlight.

'Come on,' Alexis said impatiently. 'We've given 'em long enough. Any more and it'll start to look obvious.'

Luke swung himself back into the saddle and they both cantered down the last length of the Row, to where Kynvet and Rosa had stopped beneath a tree. As they came up the last few yards separating them, Rosa laughed again and said something to the little dog, putting her hand down towards it. It yipped out a bark, jumping joyfully towards her hand, and then leapt back towards Knyvet. He kicked it away and it gave a whine. Knyvet said something to Rosa and she shook her head and clicked to Cherry, but as she did the pup leapt up again. There was an ominous rending sound and Rosa gave a cry.

'Dammit, Rose!' Alexis pointed with his crop at the hanging triangle of black fabric. 'The brute's torn your skirt!'

'It's nothing,' Rosa said quickly. She bent, pressing her handkerchief to her calf, and Luke saw, with a feeling of foreboding, that it came away red.

'God-damn it.' Knyvet flung down his reins. The little dog wagged its tail joyfully at the sight of his master dismounting, but then Knyvet grabbed its collar and it

105

squealed in pain. He picked up his riding crop.

'Sebastian!' Rosa cried. He ignored her and lifted the whip, and the little dog screamed as it came smacking down. He lifted it again, and again it bit, and the pup let out a squealing wail. Luke turned his face away.

'*Sebastian!*' Rosa shouted. There was a scrambling sound and Luke turned back to see her slide from the pommel of the side-saddle in an ungainly slither. She fell to her hands and knees on the ground but scrambled up. 'Sebastian, stop! For God's sake, stop!'

Knyvet didn't seem to have even heard. He was labouring the little dog again and again with all his strength. The creature had stopped crying and lay limp in his grip, only the force of Knyvet's blows making its body jerk.

'Sebastian!' Rosa sobbed. She grabbed at his arm, but he threw her off without even turning his head and she staggered back.

Luke swallowed. His fists were clenched. He felt a fierce desire to grab Knyvet by the collar and beat him like he was beating the dog, beat him until he squealed like the defenceless pup. But it would be suicide to strike a witch and, worse, suicide to his mission. He would be sacked, thrown from the house, and then where would he be? He had barely three weeks left – there would be no time for another plan, no time to do anything but crawl back with his tail between his legs. And then he would be dead himself, at the hand of the Malleus, as all men were who failed in their task.

'Sebastian!' Rosa's voice was hoarse and cracked on the last syllable of his name. '*Please.*'

Luke's hands were clenched on the reins so that the tendons stood out. He concentrated on his hands, on the burns and smelts left there by years of work in the forge. Concentrated on holding in Castor, holding him steady, when all he wanted to do was turn the horse for home and gallop far away from this place.

At last the sound of thrashing ceased and, in the silence that followed, he heard Rosa's low sobbing breath. Sebastian seemed to hear it too, for he looked up, his face splashed with blood, but impassive. His eyes were very blue, the cold pale blue of the winter sky above.

'For God's sake, Rosa,' he said. 'It was only a dog – and a damned disobedient one at that.' And then he kicked the corpse into the bushes at the side of the Row and mounted his horse in one swing, his spurs flashing in the sun.

'Good day to you both.' His voice was quite level and pleasant. Only the rise and fall of his chest and the flecks of blood across his cheekbones and the bridge of his nose betrayed what he'd just done. 'Miss Greenwood, please allow me to apologize for the damage to your habit.' He gave a bow, raised his top hat and then turned to Alexis. 'Alex, shall I see you at Raffles tonight?'

'Certainly,' Alexis said. He raised his own hat and Sebastian cantered off.

Luke watched him go, disappearing into the throng of

107

well-dressed ladies and men, his magic a pitch-black swirl of smoke dispersing into the bright sunshine and red-gold leaves of the autumn trees.

He was still staring after Knyvet's departing shadow when he heard Alexis' voice behind him.

'Come on, Rose, for God's sake. Get up and stop acting like a Shakespearean tragedy. It was only a dog.'

Luke turned. Rosa was sitting, collapsed against the tree trunk, her face in her hands. When she raised her eyes they were filled with grief and bitter accusation.

'Look,' Alexis said uncomfortably, 'I'm not saying he was right to beat it but—'

'He whipped it to death, Alex. In the *park*.'

'It ripped your skirt! Look, a disobedient dog is a recipe for disaster. You can never eradicate bad blood. A dog who won't obey commands has only itself to blame. Next it would have been going after sheep and snapping at children. Seb had no choice.'

'He had a choice,' Rosa said. Her voice was cold and bitter. 'Of course he had a choice.'

'Rose!' Alexis said, his voice impatient. 'It was a dog. A *dog*. What do you want? Black ostrich plumes and a hearse? Get back on Cherry and stop acting like he beat your first-born child to death.'

'I will not.' Rosa's voice shook. Alexis' lip curled in contempt.

'Suit yourself.' He kicked at Brimstone's flanks and yanked the horse's head viciously around. 'I'm going.'

'What?' Rosa's head jerked up.

'I've had enough of your histrionics,' Alexis yelled over his shoulder. 'See yourself home. The sot can take you.'

And he cantered away across the park.

8

Rosa was silent as they rode home. Luke kept back, watching her as she sat very straight, her hands rigid on the reins.

In the yard he jumped down and stepped forward to help her dismount. He had never helped a lady dismount before, let alone a witch, and he was painfully aware of it as he steadied the horse and readied himself to take her weight. As she stepped down he fumbled it, missing her step so that they both staggered, and his arms went around her, stopping her from falling to the muddy cobbles of the yard before he'd even thought of it.

'I'm so sorry, miss!' He felt a burning flush run from his throat to his forehead and his hands were all wrong, all in the wrong place – he couldn't let her stumble to the ground, but anyone might look out of the rear window of the house and see him with his hands around her waist.

'It's perfectly all right,' she said bitterly, but her voice broke on the last word, as if she were barely keeping the tears in check.

'Miss Greenwood – please, please don't cry.'

'I'm not crying,' she said stonily. He didn't say anything, but let his hands drop. She led Cherry into the stable. Luke stood for a moment, full of fury at himself, at her for putting him in this position, at that damned Knyvet. Then he took a breath and followed her with Castor. She was in the stall, rubbing Cherry with a handful of straw, her shoulders bowed with misery.

Luke stood helplessly, watching her as she groomed the horse, who whickered comfortingly, as if she knew something was wrong, but not what or how to mend it.

'Go away,' Rosa said hoarsely, without looking up. Luke felt frustration rise in him.

'Miss, I—'

'Please, just go away.'

'How can I?' he burst out. 'I have to clean and groom Castor! What do you want me to do, go into the kitchen and say that I've left this horse in a muck sweat because you're having a tantrum in the stables? I'll be sacked!'

'A tantrum?' She swung round, her face swollen with angry tears. 'A tantrum? Did you see what Sebastian did?'

'Yes, I saw what he did. And I was disgusted too – but I've seen worse, ten times worse. I've seen a man beat his *wife* that way. Your brother's right, it was a dog, no more, and I'm not losing my job over it.'

'You wouldn't understand,' she spat, and turned back to Cherry. 'Go back to the kitchen. Leave me alone.'

'And say what?' Luke said impatiently. He shut Castor into his stall and came to stand beside her. 'Tell 'em I've left the lady of the house doing my work?'

'No – yes – oh I don't care!'

She ripped off her hat, her hair tumbling out of its pins, buried her face against Cherry's side and began to sob, hopelessly, helplessly, her shoulders heaving so that her red hair shivered like flames in the wind.

'Miss . . . Rosa . . .' Luke stood awkwardly, twisting his hands together. He put his hand towards her and then stopped, suddenly sick at the thought of touching her again, feeling her magic silk-soft against his skin. But the sight of her wrenching sobs was too much and he couldn't stop himself from touching her shoulder, very lightly, the lightest possible brush.

The sound she made at his touch was so grievous, so like the puppy's whimper, that before he could think he'd put his arm around her shoulders, just as if she were Minna, and he just another boy, not mistress and stable-hand.

'Hey there, don't take on so,' he said, his voice low. She shook her head, her eyes closed, the lashes wet with tears, and he pulled her to him, shushing her and gentling her as he gentled Minna's little sisters when they fell and hurt their knee, as his father had used to comfort him when he was small.

They stood for a long moment in the warmth and quiet

of the stable, the horses breathing on their backs and whickering in gentle sympathy. Rosa fell quiet, the huge shaking sobs slowly subsiding until she was still and silent in his arms, limp in the exhausted aftermath of grief. And as they stood, locked together in the warm silence, it came to Luke like a cold chill draught, how impossibly, horribly wrong this was. She was not just a girl, she was his employer – and a witch. The witch he was sent to kill.

He realized suddenly that his hand was on the back of her neck, the fine red-gold hairs tickling his fingers, and that the skin there was so soft and white he could hardly bear it.

I could tighten my grip, he thought. *How hard would it be?*

For a moment he imagined it – he'd hold her closer, and closer, until he had her so tight that she would never breathe again. There'd be a moment's struggle, a cry smothered with a hand, or pressed into the cotton of his shirt. And then . . . nothing – just her body, limp and slack in his arms.

Her neck felt so slim and fragile – how hard would it be to snap it like the chickens John Leadingham despatched in a trice? It would take just the slightest shift of his grip – he could move his fingers up to twine into her hair, hold her skull, as gentle as a lover, and twist until . . .

There was a crack in the yard, as if someone had trodden on a stick, and Rosa seemed suddenly to realize who and where she was. She leapt back, out of his arms, her face ghost-white, her eyes wide and dark. Then she began scrabbling her hair back into its pins.

'I'm sorry.' She was whispering under her breath. 'I'm so sorry – I don't know – I can't think . . .'

And then she ran, leaving Luke standing like a fool, his arms empty, the stable his own domain again.

Rosa flung herself on to her bed, her face burning with a mix of anger and shame and something else, something that made her writhe into the pillows, unable to believe what she'd done.

What had she been thinking? Sobbing on the shoulder of a *stable-hand*! Thank God no one had seen. And he – what had *he* been thinking? If Alexis or her mother had seen them, she would have been whipped and Luke would have been sacked for gross impertinence, and it would be no more than he deserved, putting his arms around her as if – as if . . .

And yet, as Rosa's face cooled, she thought that perhaps it wasn't that, not really. There had been nothing impertinent about his expression as he looked down at her, nor about the way his hand had rested on the nape of her neck, on the tender slip of skin between her riding stock and her hair. It was as if . . . it was as if he thought for a moment they might have been – friends.

He wasn't a servant, of course. At least, not in the sense that Fred Welling or James were. They were born and bred to it, trained to service from their childhood. From what Ellen had said Luke was the son of a drayman, expected to

114

become a drayman like his father, mixing only with others of his class and sphere and never thinking to so much as speak to a lady from one year's end to another. So perhaps it was no wonder that he wasn't used to mixing with his betters and acted so strangely ignorant of the gulf that separated them both.

Rosa had no such excuse. She knew every inch of the great social chasm that yawned between them. And, too, she knew what he did not, *could* not. For they were separated by more than class, by a gulf just as unbridgeable: magic.

That at least, she reflected, as she flung herself on to her back and put her pillow over her cooling face, was one comfort. If he ever showed any signs of getting above himself or taking liberties, she could sort him out with a few words of a spell, as Alexis had done with Becky time and time again. A few kisses on the landing, a few squeezes in the library, and the girl was batting her eyelashes over the morning tea and making veiled threats about presents and payrises. Each time it happened she sealed her own doom and the next day she would be clearing at breakfast just as blank and respectful as if the whole thing had never happened – which indeed, as far as she was concerned, it had not.

The thought of Alexis was like a splash of cold water. He would be angry, very angry. And he would want her to make it up to Sebastian. The only question was how.

* * *

'Is this true, Rosa?' Mama looked from Rosa to Alexis and back again. They were waiting in the drawing room, where Rosa had been summoned to give an account of her actions. Mama was sitting on the chaise longue, her needlepoint spread across her lap, and the needle stabbed in and out of the silk as if she were stabbing an enemy.

'Well?' Alexis turned from where he was warming himself in front of the glowing remains of the fire and smoothed down his coat tails. 'Cat got your tongue, Rosa? Or should I say, dog?'

Rosa's hand crept nervously to her locket and then she snatched it away, before Alexis had time to notice. Instead she picked up Belle, who was shadowing anxiously at her heels as if she sensed the gathering storm.

'Yes,' she said. She was proud of the way her voice was steady, in spite of Alexis' barely contained fury and Mama's smouldering anger. 'Yes, it's true.'

'You are telling me . . .' Mama's voice was dangerously low and she stabbed the needle into the hoop with a violence that made Rosa wince. 'You are telling me, that you stood in Hyde Park and screamed at Sebastian Knyvet like a fishwife, berating him for beating his own dog in *your* defence? And for this you dared call him a brute?'

'Yes.' Rosa made herself stand straight. Belle cowered against her shoulder.

Mama turned to Alexis and some silent communication passed between them, Rosa could see the flicker of it in their eyes. She turned away deliberately. Let them have their magical whispers. If they were too ashamed to say the words in front of her, she didn't want to hear them anyway.

'Rosa.' Mama's voice broke in on her thoughts. 'We have not finished with this. For tonight you will go to bed without any supper. Tomorrow you will get up without any breakfast. However you *will* ride out, you *will* meet with and speak to Mr Knyvet and you *will* apologize to him for your disgraceful behaviour. Is that quite understood?'

'But—' Rosa began. Mama hissed the words of a spell and Rosa's throat suddenly tightened and closed. The words she had been about to speak strangled before they reached her lips. Only when she tried again did two misshapen, mangled sounds come out: 'Yes, Mama.'

'Good.' Mama's lips smiled, but her eyes were still cold and angry. 'Now, listen to me, Rosa. Sebastian has the power in the palm of his hand to repair our fortune, to secure Alexis' future and to save your family home, and you throw all that away over a disobedient dog and your own love of histrionics. What do you think Papa would think of your abominable selfishness?'

Rosa shut her eyes. She would not cry. Not in front of Mama.

'The mortgages are up on Matchenham in two months.' Mama picked up a sheaf of papers from the desk and threw them at Rosa's feet. 'Two months. If you wish to see your father's home sold to the highest bidder then you are going the right way about it. Now, go to your room.

117

I do not wish to see you again tonight, do you understand?'

Any words of protest died in Rosa's throat. Instead she just nodded. Then she turned and left, still holding Belle. As she climbed the stairs to her room she felt the first stirrings of hunger in the pit of her stomach.

It was nearly midnight before Luke finished grooming the horses and cleaning the tack. Late in the evening Alexis had sent word downstairs that he and Rosa would be riding again tomorrow, and that the horses were to be immaculate, and the tack and brasswork too.

When Luke finally made it up the stairs to his little room, he lay on the hard, narrow bed with his arm flung over his face as if to hide from the world. What had he been thinking, there in the stable? He'd risked everything – and for what? To comfort a girl who was his mortal enemy, who would be dead at his hand within a few days. And instead of plotting her death, he'd risked his job and his mission to comfort her over the death of a worthless pup.

For God's sake, lad, what's wrong with you?

It was John Leadingham's accusing voice that rang in his ears. But it was William's face he saw when he squeezed his lids tight shut – William's face, filled with disgust and grief at his betrayal.

Suddenly he couldn't bear his own thoughts any longer. He sat up and walked to the window, as if the cold night air could chase away his hot shame. He leant on the sill, resting his forehead against the breath-misted glass, and stared into the night. Knightsbridge was not like Spitalfields. Instead of the dark, crowded slums punctuated with burning street braziers, it was bright with gas street lights, there were candles at every window, stretching away and away into the distance, even the odd house that blazed with electric light. He looked up, above the roofs, hoping to see the stars. They at least would be proof that however far away home felt, he walked under the same skies as William and Minna and John and all the other friends he'd left behind. But the night was dark, with thick sooty clouds that shut out the sky.

He sighed and was about to turn to go to bed when a movement at the window across the yard caught his eye. A window was alight in the big house. It was lit with a single candle, and someone was sitting there, staring into the darkness. In the soft candlelight all he could see was a face and a flicker of white nightgown. But as the figure moved slightly he saw the blazing river of hair that fell to her waist, a stream of molten iron that caught the light of the frail candle flame and threw it back as fire.

Rosa.

No, God damn her, not Rosa. The witch. He must stop thinking of her as a girl, for she was *not* a girl. She was a witch – damned in the sight of God and condemned by man and by the word of the Bible. Condemned to—

The breath caught in his throat and he wrenched his gaze away from her and threw himself back into his hard narrow bed, his fists clenched in cold self-hatred.

She must die. That was all there was to it. He had pricked her name with his pin – fate had chosen her, not him. If he didn't return of news of her death within the month then it would be his blood spilt, not hers.

Within the month. How long, exactly? Luke began to count back to the night in Fournier Street, and his heart became colder and colder with each backward step. It was more than a week ago, ten days, in fact. He had just eighteen days left. Eighteen days to kill her and return with the news to the Brotherhood.

But he didn't need eighteen days. It only took a moment to kill – he just needed an opportunity. A plan that would not leave him swinging from the gallows or gutted by a spell.

And suddenly a way of doing it came into his head – and it was so simple he could have almost laughed. Only, it all depended on whether she would ride out tomorrow to meet Sebastian Knyvet. Would she?

Luke slept badly that night, torn between thinking of all the ways that his plan could go wrong and the chance that it would not happen at all. Would she really ride out to meet Knyvet, after all that had happened yesterday?

But the message came down after breakfast: Cherry and Brimstone to be saddled and ready in ten minutes, Mr Greenwood's orders.

He took a deep breath and made his way out to the stables.

He'd only just finished saddling Brimstone when he heard the sound of boots on the cobbles and looked up to see Alexis striding across the yard, Rosa walking behind him, her face white and pale.

'Is Brimstone ready?' Alexis demanded. Luke nodded.

'Yes, sir. But not Cherry, I've still got to saddle her up.'

'Dammit, I said ten minutes. Seb'll be waiting.'

'I'm sorry, sir,' Luke tried to keep his face impassive. He bit back the words he really wanted to say: *You try grooming and saddling two horses in ten minutes, you fat slob.*

'Well, I'm not waiting on the convenience of a lazy stable-hand.' He swung his leg up and called, 'Rosa, I'm heading out. Come and find me with the boy. I'll be near the north end, I suppose. Don't take all day.'

Rosa said nothing but only nodded.

'Cat got your tongue?' Alexis said, and there was something unpleasant in his voice, a needling laugh.

Rosa looked up at him and her gold-brown eyes were suddenly dark with hatred, her lips pressed together until they were completely bloodless. Her whole face, white beneath the stark black hat, seemed nothing but blazing eyes, full of fury. But she said nothing, only jerked her head towards the gate.

'See you in the Row,' Alexis said. 'I'll leave you with the sot.' And with that he yanked on Brimstone's curb and

121

nudged him into a canter out of the yard and down the mews.

As the sound of Brimstone's hooves faded into the distance Rosa let out a shaky breath and seemed to find her voice.

'I'm sorry.' Her voice was hoarse, as if she hadn't spoken in a long time. 'He shouldn't be so rude to you – it's unforgiveable.'

'Me?' Luke said surprised. 'I don't give a d—' He stopped himself short, just in time and bit back the word. 'I don't mind what he chooses to call me,' he finished gruffly.

She didn't answer, but just sank on to a hay bale while he adjusted the buckles. His fingers were sweating and his heart was beating fast – this was the moment. If she looked up now, he was sunk. His fingers slipped on the cold metal of the buckle. But she didn't. Her head was bowed between her knees, almost as if she were faint, and she was not looking at him or Cherry, but down at the voluminous folds of her jet-black habit.

It was done. He patted Cherry's side, feeling his flesh prickle cold and hot with sweat. Then he turned to Rosa.

'Ready, Miss Greenwood,' he said. Then he stopped awkwardly. 'Is something wrong?'

'I – I missed breakfast,' she said wearily.

Luke looked down at himself, then brushed the straw from his britches.

'Wait here.'

* * *

122

Becky was folding linen when Luke put his head cautiously round the kitchen door and whispered, 'Hey. Hey – Becky.'

'Oh!' Becky jumped and dropped a pile of napkins and then swore crossly. 'Oh, Luke Welling! You'll be the death of me. What are you doing creeping round?'

'I'm in me boots – I don't want Mrs Ramsbottom to catch me. Listen, is there a piece of bread I can beg?'

'So we're not feeding you enough now, are we?' She put her hands on her hips. 'A small vat of porridge and a piece of bread and butter the size of my head not good enough for you at breakfast?'

'Not for me – for Miss Rosa.'

'Miss Rosa?' Her face was blank with astonishment. 'Why are you begging food for her? Is she sickening for summat?'

'No, but she missed breakfast.'

Becky frowned and began thoughtfully refolding the linen she'd dropped.

'Now I come to think of it, she weren't at dinner last night, neither. It's no wonder she's famished if she's had nothing but tea and water since lunchtime yesterday. But what a ninny to refuse her meals and then beg scraps from the kitchen! Think she's banting for her young man?'

'Banting?' Luke said blankly.

'Oh you men!' Becky got up crossly and went to the bread crock in the corner. 'You know – missing meals to lose weight. Still, she wouldn't be the first to go silly over a man. And goodness knows, her family need her to catch a fat fish – and her bait's precious small. Pretty looks and a slim waist don't count for much in high society – it's a nice fat dowry wins Prince Charming these days. Mind you, she's skinny enough already. Hardly a pick of spare flesh on her. And some men like a girl with a bit of flesh on her. How about you?' She looked at him under her lashes as she began to slice bread and then took a piece of ham from the shelf. 'Do you like your meat fat or lean, Luke Welling?'

'Look, she's waiting in the yard,' Luke said, trying to keep the impatience from his voice. 'Don't worry about wrapping it, just give me the piece.'

'And your hands all dirt from the yard?' Becky cried. 'Lord love us, it'd be as much as my place is worth if I gave one of the family a dirty sandwich. Here, take this.' She thrust a sheet of greaseproof paper at him and he snatched it impatiently and took the sandwich back out to where Rosa was waiting.

She was sitting on the bale where he'd left her and her head had sunk even lower, as if she were a plant wilting without water. Cherry nuzzled at her neck, but she barely looked up.

'Miss Greenwood,' Luke said awkwardly. He held out the sandwich, wrapped in its paper, and Rosa's face broke into a smile.

'Thank you, Luke.' She began to tear into the sandwich, gulping it down so fast that he laughed.

'Hey, hey, gently now. You'll do yourself a mischief.'

As he said the words he felt cold at his own hypocrisy. What was he doing? Fussing like a nursemaid over her when all the time . . .

You're gaining her trust, he thought bitterly. *Isn't that what John Leadingham said? Get their trust, get in close. Then when they least expect it . . .*

'Thank you.' She spoke around a mouthful of ham and then leant back, her eyes closed as if she could hardly bear how good it tasted. 'Thank you. This is . . . It's incredible. Delicious.'

A kind of hatred rose up in him.

'Thank Becky, not me,' he said curtly and turned away, but not before he saw the surprise and hurt flicker across her face. Of course she didn't understand. How could she? And if she did know what was in his head, he wouldn't be standing here. He'd be melted to a puddle of tar on the floor, or smeared around the walls like dog meat.

'Luke?' she said uncertainly, but he couldn't answer. He only stood with his back to her, his hand on Cherry's halter, as much to steady himself as the horse.

She scrambled up from the bale of hay and from the corner of her eye he could see bewilderment in her face. Then she seemed to stiffen. She straightened her spine and spoke haughtily.

'It's time we were getting on. Help me mount, please.'

'I'll get the mounting block, miss,' he said tonelessly.

'No, don't bother. We're late. Just give me a leg.'

125

For a moment he didn't think he could – it was not just the thought of touching her, with the magic swirling and crackling through her skin. It was everything. The slim firmness of her waist, the scent of her hair so close to his face, the heat of her, the sheer vitality of her life so light in his hands – everything. A kind of dizziness rose up in him and he found his breath was coming fast and hard.

'Luke,' she said impatiently. And then, as he didn't move, '*Luke*.'

He took a step forwards, shut his eyes, pretending she were just Minna, just another girl. The firm weight of her narrow boot in his hands, the flurry of her skirts . . . and she was up on Cherry's back and he stepped backwards, his heart pounding like a hammer.

'Come on,' she said shortly. He hauled himself up on Castor's back and by the time he'd gathered the horse together she had trotted out of the yard.

Luke's heart was thumping as he watched her ride down the Row, her spine very straight, the heavy coils of dark-red hair at the base of her neck shining flame-red in the thin winter sunlight. The light eclipsed as she rode beneath a tree, then blazed out again as she came out of its shadow into the sun.

Far in the distance he could see Alexis talking to a group of men. One of them was Knyvet. He raised his hat as he saw Rosa approaching and Luke saw her hand clench on the reins and Cherry's decorous trot falter to a walk. She said something under her breath.

'I'm sorry, miss?' he called across.

'I said, I can't do it.' Her face beneath the severe black hat was very pale. 'I can't go up to him and pretend yesterday never happened. I can't.'

She pulled Cherry's head around.

'Rosa,' Alexis called warningly. There was a note in his voice that made Castor throw up his head and snort in alarm.

But if Rosa heard, she gave no sign. She was urging Cherry into a canter, the opposite way up the Row, back towards home. Luke's heart began to beat. If it happened, it would be now. He heard the blood roaring in his ears, his heart thudding in time with Cherry's pounding hooves as Rosa urged her along the Row, away from the group of men.

'Rose!' Alexis shouted. Rosa gripped the reins tighter.

There was a sudden snapping sound. Rosa gave a cry and Cherry shied and whinnied in alarm.

Suddenly she was falling, the side-saddle sliding round Cherry's back, Rosa slithering to the ground in a confusion of black skirts, kicked-up dust and autumn leaves. But her foot was caught in the stirrup and Cherry carried on in a panicked canter, not slowing, but quickening almost to a gallop, Rosa's body tossed and dragged beneath the pounding hooves.

There were screams from the women in the carriages

either side, shouts from men and grooms on horseback, cries of alarm from the walkers on the footpath.

Knyvet began to gallop, his horse's hooves striking dust from the path.

'Rosa!' he bellowed. Luke saw that his face, beneath the black top hat, was white.

The blood roared in Luke's ears, cold sweat prickling across his spine, and he wanted nothing more than to turn tail with Castor and run. Back to the stable, back to Spitalfields – not to have to see this horrible thing to the end.

Coward.

Instead he put his whip to Castor and urged him into a gallop too.

'*Ábíeteaþ!*' Knyvet shouted. His magic blazed like a dark fire and Luke almost lost his grip on Castor's reins. The horse stumbled and it was only with a huge effort that Luke gathered him back together.

'*Ábíeteaþ!*' Knyvet shouted again, his magic almost blinding in its dark intensity.

Then the girth snapped completely and Cherry was cantering free and Rose lay crumpled on the dirt, like a blackbird with a broken wing.

Knyvet skidded to a halt next to Rosa's body, slid from his saddle and knelt in the dust beside her.

'Rosa?' he said. He was panting, his voice ragged between breaths. 'Rose? Can you hear me, darling?'

For a minute Luke's heart hammered fit to burst in his

chest. Everything. *Everything*, depended on the answer.

'I'm . . . I'm all right.' Her voice came, croaky and shaken. But it was all he needed to know. She was alive. She was alive.

He closed his eyes, feeling heat and then icy cold wash over him in succession. It was all over. He had failed. She was alive.

9

'Oh, Rosa . . .' Sebastian closed his eyes and Rosa saw his face was white as his snowy stock, spots of hectic colour standing clear on his cheekbones. His fist was clenched around his crop. 'Don't ever, *ever* do that to me again.'

He put his arm around her and helped her to sit, very gently, as if she were made of china and might break.

'Is anything broken?' His voice was rough and she realized that he had been truly afraid. Something strange seemed to be happening inside her – as if all her insides were pummelled and bruised by the fall: melting, turning liquid with relief and this strange, unaccountable new Sebastian.

'I don't think so,' she managed. 'But my ankle hurts. Is Cherry all right?'

'Damn Cherry, it's you I'm worried about. Your foot was trapped in the stirrup. Let me look.'

'I don't think Mama—'

'This is no time for propriety.' He pulled off his gloves impatiently and began tugging at the buttons of her boot. 'If it's sprained we need to get the boot off as quick as possible. Tell me if I hurt you.'

Rosa couldn't suppress a little gasp of pain as he pulled off her boot – and his face went rigid.

'I'm sorry. Let me . . .' His fingers pressed gently against the bone and then manipulated her foot. 'It's not broken, just bruised.' He lowered his voice and cast a quick glance over his shoulder at the passers-by. 'I could heal you – but not here. I've already compromised us with that spell to snap the girths.'

'It's all right.' Rosa's heart was beating quick and shallow. She was not sure if it was the aftermath of the fall or the strange disquieting sensation of Sebastian's hand cradling her foot. For a minute she shut her eyes and felt again the snap of the girth and herself sliding inexorably to the rough ground and the tangle of pounding hooves . . . If it hadn't been for Sebastian's spell she would be dead. Perhaps it was the strange realization that on some level she owed him her life.

She pulled her foot gently out of his grip. 'I can heal it myself. There's no need for chivalry.'

'You need to rest.' He looked at her sternly. 'You shouldn't be casting spells. If you won't let me, then ask your mother. Or Alexis.'

Rosa shuddered at the thought of Alexis healing her and Sebastian shook his head.

'You're cold. It's the shock. Can you stand?'

'I'm not cold,' Rosa protested. But she let Sebastian help her to her feet and then bent to put her foot back in the boot.

'Don't,' Sebastian said. 'If it swells you might not be able to get the boot off. Leave it off and I'll send for my carriage to take you home.'

'No, no,' Rosa begged. 'Please, Luke can go home and get the governess cart; it will do quite well. Truly – don't send for your carriage. There's no need.'

'What in God's name happened, Rose?' Alexis came up behind Sebastian's shoulder. 'Did you fall?'

'A girth snapped by the look of it, I'd say,' Sebastian said shortly. 'Where's the horse and where's that damn stableboy?'

'Here, sir,' Luke said expressionlessly. Rosa looked and saw him trotting slowly up behind Sebastian, holding Cherry's reins, the missing side-saddle across his lap.

'Is Cherry hurt?' Rosa asked anxiously.

'Let's take a look.' Alexis slid from Brimstone's back. He took the side-saddle from Luke, examining it suspiciously. 'Girths look all right . . . No, wait, this buckle. It's mangled – the pin's worn right through. How did you not notice this?'

He stared accusingly at Luke. Rosa, watching his face, saw him close his eyes and swallow. He was pale, stubble shadowing his cheeks.

'I can't explain it, sir,' he said at last. 'I must have missed it.'

132

'Dammit, do you think that's in any way good enough?' Alexis tapped his crop against his thigh, full of righteous bullying anger. 'Look at me when I'm speaking to you!'

Luke opened his eyes and looked steadily at Alexis.

'No, sir. It's not good enough.'

'It certainly is not.' Alexis' face was nearly as red as his hair, the freckles seeming almost pale against the flush. 'Pack your bags. You can leave in the morning. Without a character.'

'No!' Rosa spoke without thinking, but the words died in her throat when their faces turned to her, Alexis' red and angry, Sebastian's pale, one eyebrow raised in enquiry. Only Luke did not look at her. His eyes were on the ground, as if in resignation.

'I beg your pardon?' Alexis' crop twitched against his thigh again, only this time his anger was not at Luke. 'How dare you contradict me in front of a servant?'

'I didn't . . .' Rosa twisted her fingers together. 'I mean, I wasn't – I only thought—'

'What you thought doesn't interest me,' Alexis snarled.

'Greenwood.' Sebastian cut across him, his voice like a whip. 'Please have the courtesy to let your sister speak.'

Rosa would not have thought it possible for Alexis to turn any redder, but he seemed to manage, a tide of fury flooding from his throat to his hairline. But he said nothing. He gave a stiff nod towards Rosa, inviting her to speak, and Rosa swallowed.

'I'm sorry, Alexis,' she managed. 'It was only that – I should have said . . .' Inspiration came and she stood up straighter in spite of the pain in her foot, taking courage from the lie, and from Sebastian's hand supporting her elbow. 'I should have said, *I* adjusted Cherry's girth, not Luke. It's my fault.'

'How does that explain him overlooking the broken buckle?' Alexis exploded. 'He's in charge of the tack. If he didn't properly examine it—'

'*I* broke the buckle. Cherry stepped on it while I was adjusting the straps, but I thought it would be all right. I – I was in a hurry to catch up.' She hung her head. The blush that coloured her cheeks was real, lending credence to the lie. 'I thought it would wait. I meant to tell Luke later.'

For a long moment Alex said nothing. He just stood, his crop tapping against his thigh, his breath coming quick and angry. Then he turned on his heel and swung himself back into the saddle.

'Well. Then you have only yourself to blame,' he hissed at Rosa. 'And you . . .' He pointed his crop at Luke. 'You're on your final warning. Consider yourself lucky I'm not sacking you anyway for allowing a woman to fiddle with the tack.'

He gave Brimstone a crack with his crop that made the horse jump and whinny. And then he was off across the park at a gallop, the riders scattering before him, and Rosa and Sebastian looked at one another.

'I'm sorry,' Rosa said. She wasn't sure if she was apologizing for herself or for Alexis. She let her eyes flick towards Luke, sitting motionless on Castor. His face was blank, unreadable. 'I'm sorry.'

'Don't be silly.' Sebastian gave a short laugh. 'Alexis is a fool and a boor. That's no fault of yours.'

'Then why are you friends with him?' she shot back, before she could consider the wisdom of the question. Sebastian only looked at her, his blue eyes pale and cool as the winter sky. For a minute he held her gaze. Then he looked away.

'I leave you to decide that for yourself.'

In the silence that followed, Rosa groped for a remark but found nothing. She only stood, searching, trying to find the perfect riposte and failing.

Then Sebastian broke in.

'I'm so sorry, Rosa. Why am I leaving you standing around on your bad ankle like a fool? We must get you home. The only question is how. Is your carriage at home ready?'

He looked at Luke.

'No, sir,' Luke said. Rosa breathed a sigh of relief. The carriage was in perilous need of repair and hardly used, and Mama would be out in the governess trap.

'Please, Sebastian.' She put her hand on his arm. 'I can ride, honestly I can.'

'Ride? With a broken buckle?' Sebastian said shortly. 'Don't be foolish, Rosa.'

'Well then, I'll walk.'

'Nonsense. We'll send for my phaeton . . . You.' He spoke to Luke. 'D'you know where Hanington Square is?'

'No, sir.' Luke shook his head. His eyes were on the rutted surface of the Row. 'I'm sorry, sir. I've never been up west before.'

Sebastian clicked his tongue and Rosa stiffened, almost expecting another flash of cold rage. But when he spoke his voice was calm and even; preoccupied, but no hint of that dangerous icy fury that had consumed him before.

'There's nothing for it, I'll have to go for mine. Stay here,' he said to Rosa. 'Your man will look after you.'

'Sebastian . . .' Rosa felt exasperation rise in her. 'Truly, there's no need. I can walk, I promise you.' She thought of all the times she'd fallen or been thrown at Matchenham and limped home, sore and bleeding. No carriage then. She was lucky if she got a bowl of hot water and a healing spell.

'I'm going,' Sebastian said firmly. He swung himself back up on to his horse, tipped his hat to her and cantered off down the row.

Rosa sank on to a bench and let out a tremulous breath. In truth her ankle was hurting and the idea of walking home on it was not pleasant. But the idea of being driven in Sebastian Knyvet's carriage was somehow even more disquieting.

She watched him galloping across the park, his horse's shining coat flickering between the trees. And a strange feeling rose up in her – a mixture of excitement and fear. He wanted her – she'd known it from that first moment his eyes met hers in the candlelit drawing room, but now she was sure. Sebastian, who could have had any girl in London or Delhi for the asking and their dowry too, wanted *her*, Rosa Greenwood, a girl without two shillings to rub together. She was no longer the pursuer – she was the pursued. The thought made her shiver.

But as she watched him disappear into the throng by the gate, an image came into her mind: it was the image of a fox, a little vixen she'd seen at Matchenham, chased by a hound.

Luke slid from the horse on to legs that felt like they would give way any second. His limbs felt like they had the time he'd had the influenza – weak and shaky, with joints made of jelly, not bone. His heart was beating in his throat so that he felt almost like throwing up. For a minute there it had been all over – and she'd saved him. Why? *Why?*

His guts griped and for a moment he thought he was actually going to be sick – right there, in the Row, amid the glossy horses and shiny boots.

'Luke . . .' He heard Rosa's voice as if from a long way off. 'Luke. Are you all right?'

'Shouldn't I be asking you that?' he said hoarsely, and turned to face her, forcing down the weakness. *Get it together*, he raged at himself. *Get it together, you god-damned yellow-belly.*

'You had a shock too.' Her eyes were huge in her pale face. She'd lost half her hairpins with the fall and fiery tendrils had escaped from beneath her hat and twined around her white throat and the stark black collar of her habit.

'Why did you do it?' he demanded suddenly. He knew he should have been grateful and that his voice was full of an anger he couldn't suppress and didn't understand. 'Why? It was my fault! Why did you tell them it was you?'

'It wasn't your fault,' she said softly.

He wanted her to rage, damn him for being impertinent and ungrateful and irresponsible – and instead she was watching him with those wide dark eyes, her face unguarded and full of concern for *him*.

'It *was* my fault.' The words tore out of him like they were edged with thorns. Good God – not his fault? If she only knew . . . For a crazy second the truth hovered on the tip of his tongue and the urge to blurt it all out was overwhelming – he imagined spitting it out, like a gobbet of poison on the clean sawdust of the Row. She stood and her magic swirled and shimmered around them both. He felt it reach out, insinuating itself into him, trying to soothe and comfort and calm.

No! he wanted to bellow. He raised his hands to press them against his forehead, pressing back the confused desperation that was boiling up inside him. The dressing on his shoulder gave a great throb, as if infected, and for a second he thought he might fall – it was only his grip on Cherry's reins that kept him upright.

Then Castor nuzzled his shoulder as if to steady him and somehow – somehow – he got it together enough to mutter, 'It *was* my fault. I should have checked the buckle. But you still haven't said why – why did you save me?'

'Because I couldn't bear to see you sacked over a stupid buckle!' she burst out. 'And Alexis would have done it, you know – he would have sent you packing back to Spitalfields tomorrow without any notice and without a character – and then where would it be, your dream of being a groom?'

He almost laughed. The cover story seemed so thin and transparently stupid, like a tale a child might have dreamt up.

'I never wanted to be a groom,' he found himself saying bitterly.

'What?' Her brow furrowed. 'Then what are you doing here?'

Don't tell her! The urge to spit out the truth was almost overpowering. Had she bewitched him? Was this crazy urge to tell her everything part of some truth-telling charm? But he didn't feel as if it was he could feel no spells coming from her other than that first soothing, gentling warmth that he'd shaken off without effort.

'It was my uncle's idea,' he said. It was the truth – and the words slipped out without him even thinking about them. 'Not mine. I wanted – I want – to be a farrier like him, a blacksmith. I always have.'

'It's a good trade,' she said quietly. 'There'll always be horses needing to be shod.'

'My uncle says it's a fool's game. He says you end up scarred from your mistakes, and deaf from the hammering, and that no one wants to pay for proper smithing any more, they want cheap factory-made metal that any fool can break and bend.'

That was true too. The relief of speaking the truth for once – of not dissembling and deceiving – was so great he felt like weeping. Why was it so hard to lie to this girl? No – *not* a girl. A witch. She was a witch and an abomination in the sight of man and God. So why was it so hard to pay her in her own coin, with deceit and trickery and betrayal?

'And what about you?' she asked. 'What do you think?'

'I think . . .' He stopped. What could he say? *I've never wanted anything else but a forge of my own, and a couple of horses, and a woman to come home to of a night and maybe make a child with, one day.*

But that was not the truth. Or not all the truth. Because there was something else he wanted more. Revenge. Justice for his father and mother. To be able to close his eyes at night and know that he was not a coward, that he had avenged his parents' memory at last.

'I think sometimes we can't get what we want,' he said slowly, picking his way between the truth and the lies, like he walked the streets of Spitalfields of an evening, picking his way between the putrid fruit and the thin-running streams of shit and rubbish. 'Leastways, not all of it. Not at the same time.'

She looked away at that, as if the words hit very near to home, but said nothing.

'And I think that my uncle wants to see me succeed. And so do I.'

'So you're an ambitious man, Luke Welling?'

'I suppose so,' he said shortly. Then, in an effort to change the subject on to less dangerous ground, 'But you should be sitting, miss. Mr Knyvet won't thank me if he comes back to find you standing around on the leg we're supposed to be sparing. Please. Sit down. Save me a ticking off.'

'All right.' She looked at the bench and then nodded. 'But only if you sit too.'

'I couldn't,' he said automatically, his fingers tightening on the reins. 'Castor – Cherry . . .'

'Nonsense,' she said, and smiled. 'The horses are tired. They'll stand. Loop their reins over the post if you're worried.'

She was right. He looped the reins over the end of the bench and sat, stiff as a post, and as far away from her as he possibly could. For a moment she looked at him, puzzled, and then she seemed to shake her head and sit back, enjoying the rare winter sun.

Luke sat back too, feeling the thin sunshine soak into his limbs, through his thin, worn jacket and into his exhausted muscles and aching bones, into his shoulders

141

where the brand-mark still ached and throbbed.

He felt tired, so tired he could have lain down his head right there on the hard bench. He had failed. The girl was alive. And the thought of starting all over again made him want to weep.

Rosa couldn't help wincing as Sebastian lifted her into the phaeton. It was high and built for racing, not for transporting ladies.

'I'm sorry,' he said, seeing the look on her face, and the way she gritted her teeth against the pain. 'I wanted the carriage, but my father had taken it. This was the only thing available.'

'Truly, don't apologize,' Rosa said. 'It doesn't hurt now.' It wasn't true. During the long wait on the bench her foot had swelled painfully and now it throbbed every time the carriage lurched on its springs. She couldn't wait to get home where she could heal it, behind closed doors, where the servants couldn't see. She would just have to remember to fake a limp a little, at breakfast, until she could plausibly be better.

Sebastian seated himself beside her and arranged a rug over her knees, then clicked to the horses.

'You look pale,' he said as they began to pick up speed. 'I don't believe it doesn't hurt.'

'Distract me,' Rosa said with a forced smile. 'Tell me about India.'

'India? It's a strange place, of great wealth and great

poverty. The maharajahs have almost unimaginable wealth – you can't conceive of their fortunes, their diamonds and rubies and the servants they have. On the other hand the beggars are beyond anything we have in London. The heat. The stench. The flies and the sickness . . .'

He trailed off.

'Though we have plenty of sickness and poverty in London,' Rosa ventured. Sebastian nodded.

'Yes. That's true. Have you ever been to Limehouse and Spitalfields and the like?'

'No, never. What's it like?'

'Stinking. A different stink from India, but worse in a way. The river has picked up all the foul, foetid material all the way along its journey through London, and in Spitalfields and Wapping and Limehouse it dumps all this filth on the banks of the Thames. There are children who go through the mud, scavenging for coins and objects they can sell. And the streets themselves are no better, strewn with beggars huddling round their fires and women touting their wares.'

Rosa thought of Luke. He didn't seem to fit with the picture Sebastian was painting. But she had seen enough of London to know that prosperity and great poverty could live side by side, cheek by jowl, sometimes even in the same street.

'You know it well?' she asked. 'East London?'

'My father has factories there, just off Brick Lane. Some criticize him for basing his operations there. They claim that it's the cheap labour that draws him. But I think, why not operate in a way that helps both the rich man *and* the poor? For it's the poverty which breeds misery – men and women without work or hope of finding it. At least with honest employment men and women can hope to better themselves and keep their families fed and clothed. For those who don't work, of course, there's little hope.'

'But surely there are those who *cannot* work?'

'Some, yes. And for those my father has a soup kitchen attached to one of his factories. The truly deserving get a hot meal, at least, and perhaps a job if they are fit enough. But there are many more who *will* not work, through idleness or by making themselves unfit for work through their own folly.'

'Drink, do you mean?' Rosa thought of Alexis, pouring brandy down his throat until he lay slumped and snoring on the chaise longue in front of the fire. Once he had drunk until he wet his drawers and James had had to carry him to bed and strip him down.

'Drink, yes. Or worse.'

'Worse?'

'Opium,' Sebastian said shortly. Then he laughed, a short mirthless laugh. 'But we should not be talking like this, Miss Greenwood. Your mother would be shocked to hear me speaking of such things to her innocent daughter. So would mine.'

'Ignorance is not innocence,' Rosa said slowly. 'I wish there was something I could do.'

144

'If you wish, and your mother permits, I will take you to visit the factories one of these days.' Sebastian looked at her very seriously. 'But I warn you, the East End is not for shrinking violets.'

'I know. And I'm no shrinking violet.'

'No.' His hands on the reins were steady and he looked at her, his eyes shadowed by the top hat. 'No. I can see that. You are very far from that, Miss Greenwood.'

'Rosa,' she said suddenly, impulsively.

Sebastian smiled and he flicked his whip at the horse so that their pace quickened to a jolly, rollicking trot.

'Rosa.'

'Whew.' Becky put her head around the stable door as Luke finished brushing down Cherry. 'What happened out in the Row then?'

'Nothing,' Luke said curtly. He couldn't bear to relive it all again – the sickening crack of the girth, Rosa's body dragged along in the dirt like a rag doll . . .

'Nothing!' Becky put her hands on her hips, her apron strings fluttering in the breeze. 'Nothing, he says, when you come home with two horses and a face like thunder, and Miss Rosa gets brought home in state in Mr Knyvet's carriage? If that's your idea of nothing, Luke Welling, I'd like to see what you'd call "something".'

'I meant all's well that ends well,' he said. 'She's all right, in't she? So nothing happened.'

'From the look on Mr Knyvet's face I'd say something happened all right. And maybe that something will end in a proposal if our miss plays her cards right.'

146

'Don't be so common, Becky.' Ellen's voice rang out across the courtyard and Becky jumped and swung round, her face a mix of annoyance and guilt.

'What? It's a free country, ain't it?'

'Not while you're in employment under Mrs Ramsbottom. If she heard you talking like that . . . not to mention flirting with the stable-hands.' She shot a look at Luke.

'You're one to talk.' Becky tossed her head. 'Anyhow, it's Wednesday. I'm on me afternoon off. So's Luke.' She turned back to Luke. 'What about it then, Luke? When I've changed my apron, d'you fancy a stroll across the park? Show the swells we can enjoy a sunny afternoon as good as them?'

Afternoon off. The relief washed over him like a wave. The chance to get away from all this. Away from it all.

'I can't,' he found himself saying. 'I've to get back to my uncle's. Family business.'

'All the way to Spitalfields?' Becky's lips made a pout. 'Are you sure? You don't want to waste your afternoon traipsing across London and back.'

'I have to. What time have I got to be back?'

'The curfew's nine o'clock.' Ellen gave a marked glance up at the stable clock, which showed three already. 'And Mr James locks up the kitchen door at ten past, sharp, so woe betide any maids who're late. But the stable's got its own entrance.'

'So what does that mean?' Luke asked impatiently.

'It means, don't get caught.' Ellen raised one eyebrow.

147

Luke was already shrugging into his coat.

'Ain't you going to scrape your boots and brush the straw off yerself?' Becky asked, shocked. Luke shook his head. Time enough for that when he got to the forge – and William wouldn't care anyway.

'No. I'm off. Tell Mrs Ramsbottom I'll not be back for supper.'

'Suit yourself,' Becky said, her face a little doleful as Luke walked out of the stable yard and into the Knightsbridge throng without a backward glance.

It was getting dark as he finally made his way into Spitalfields. The market was long shut up, but there were small children scavenging in the piles of rubbish for scraps to take home for their dinner and the beggar men were huddled around piles of burning packing to keep warm. The sky had stayed clear and now the night was turning cold, with a bite to it like a bad-tempered dog.

Luke's breath was white in the air and he clapped his arms around himself as he walked, to try to keep from shivering. He wished he hadn't left his muffler in the room above the stable.

As he passed the Cock Tavern the door flung open and a figure came stumbling out into the road, nearly hitting Luke full in the chest before sprawling on his knees in the road.

'And stay out, you good-for-nothing drunkard!' the landlord yelled. Then he slammed the door shut, leaving Luke to help the man to his feet.

It was Nick Sykes, Minna's dad. He looked up at Luke with bleary eyes.

'Got a penny, mister?'

Luke turned his face away from his reeking breath and tried not to breathe in.

'No,' he said, unable to keep the disgust from his voice. If he'd had money to spare it would be for Minna, not for her worthless dad to spend on more rot-gut gin.

'Ha'penny then, kind mister?' Nick Sykes whined. There was no trace of recognition in his slumped, blotchy face.

'I said, no,' Luke snarled. He let go of Sykes's jacket and the man stumbled to the ground. Luke wiped his hands against his shirt and carried on, into the cold night.

He heard the forge before he saw it, the clear bell-like ring of William's hammer on hot metal. And then he saw the smoke and sparks from the chimney disappearing into the night sky.

Man is born unto trouble as the sparks fly upward. The words came to him unbidden and he shivered as he turned the corner into the lane.

Even on this cold night the door to the forge stood open, trying to relieve the intense heat inside. But Luke could have crawled inside and shut the door and lain like a salamander, soaking up the good, clean fiery heat of the force and the fire, the heat and the roar of the bellow and the clang of the hammer driving out all the hatred and fear in his heart.

He walked the last few yards across the cobbles, thinking

about whether William would be glad to see him, and what he would say when he was asked about his task and how he was faring.

And then, without warning, there was a cracking sound and something huge and heavy flew through the air, just missing his head, and smacked into the wall of the alley with a sound like a thunderclap.

There was silence from the forge and then the sound of William swearing, long and low. He came out into the yard, wiping his hands on his leather apron. His face was full of weary irritation – and then he saw Luke and it changed to a kind of blank surprise and then, just as swiftly, a huge smile.

'Luke!' He lumbered across the cobbles to clap him on the back. 'Luke, lad! Is it done?'

'No.' Luke shook his head, and his uncle's face fell a little. 'No, it's just my afternoon off.'

'Well, I'm right glad to see you, lad. But is it wise to leave so soon, do you think? The full moon's halfway gone.'

'I know!' Luke snapped angrily. And then he felt wretched for taking his fury out on William. 'I'm sorry, Uncle. I know. I know I've not got much time, but I couldn't take it one more day. It's all, it's just . . .' He stopped, horrified to find treacherous tears rising in his throat, threatening to choke him. He turned away, pretending to cough.

'Never mind,' William said kindly. 'Never mind, lad. I've finished for the day anyway. That were my good hammer flew past your head just then.' He bent and picked it up from the lane, looking at it with exasperation. 'The shaft just split clean off in my hand.'

'How did that happen?' Luke asked, more as a way to swallow away the tears than for really wanting to know. His uncle gave a short laugh.

'Who knows. It just went – a sign I've been working too long, I dare say. Never work hot metal when you're tired, or you'll end up burnt, that's what I've always said, and it's a good motto. But without you here it's a struggle to get through the work. I won't deny I'll be right glad to see you back, Luke.' He stood for a moment, the broken hammer loose in his hand, and then clapped Luke on the back again, his face full of weary smiles.

'Come on, lad. Let's get some supper into both of us. You look half clemmed yourself. Ain't they feeding you at that place?'

For a long time there were no words, just Luke and William side by side at the table, spooning the good hot broth into their mouths and tearing off hunks of bread to dip into the soup. At last, when his spoon had scraped the bowl clean for the second time, Luke spoke.

'I saw Nick Sykes being chucked out the Cock earlier. How's Minna?'

'Bad.' William wiped out his bowl with a piece of bread. His face was troubled. 'She's got laid off at the dairy.'

'Laid off?' Luke put down his spoon. 'What happened?'

'Her horse is sick. She can't do the round without Bess. I told her she should have sold the nag while the going was good. Now she's stuck with a sick horse and no money to pay for its keep.'

'What'll she do?'

'Lord knows. I'm afraid it'll be the streets. Or the match factories. I don't know which is worse for a young girl like her.'

Luke thought of it, chewing mechanically on a mouthful of bread that seemed suddenly dry and tasteless as chalk. He thought of Phoebe and Miriam touting themselves outside the Cock, and the idea of Minna dressed in scarlet petticoats, selling herself to any passing stranger for a few pennies, made him flush hot with rage. But William was right – what was the alternative? The match factories: where the young girls worked hour after hour after hour, until their faces rotted from the phosphorus and they died in agonies, their brains eaten away by the dreaded phossy jaw, unable even to speak.

'Come on, lad, don't take on.' William was watching his face. 'Bess has been sick before, she'll pull through. Anyway, that's not what was eating you before this, was it?'

'What d'you mean?' Luke swallowed the dry bread and kept his eyes on his plate, afraid of what he might see reflected back at him in William's gaze.

'Whatever brought you back here. It's not Minna that's been troubling you since you walked through that door, you didn't know about her until ten minutes ago. What is it, lad? You look like a dog that's been whipped.'

'I . . .' Suddenly it was a relief to let it out and the words came tumbling. 'Oh God, Uncle, I tried to do it. I weakened the buckle on her girth and it snapped, but she wasn't going fast enough. She fell, but she wasn't killed, or even hurt bad. I risked everything and I screwed it up like a fool.' He put his fist against his forehead, grinding the knuckles against bone.

'Hey, hey.' William put his hand on Luke's arm. 'Don't take on. It was a first attempt. There'll be others.'

There'll be others.

Yes. He would try again. He would *have* to try again.

He swallowed.

'I didn't think . . . I didn't know . . .'

'What?'

But how could he say it? That he didn't think she would be a girl? He didn't know she would have red hair that twined in curls at the nape of her neck? That he didn't think she would have a dusting of nutmeg freckles across her nose, or that her eyes would be golden-brown, or her wrist small enough to encompass with his hand?

'I didn't think she'd be kind,' he said. He heard his own voice crack and despised himself for his weakness. 'She looks so . . . so innocent.'

'She's *not* kind,' William said. His voice was steady but his eyes were troubled. 'And she's not innocent. You know the truth of it, Luke. She's a witch – and she's learnt to dissemble and twist and deceive from her cradle. This is all

153

part of the test. But you must hold fast to your faith, just as you held fast to the hilt of the knife when you drove it into your own side. You didn't flinch then, did you? Though you *knew* yourself to be innocent and you knew it would be your own death to push the knife home. Well then – don't flinch now. Drive the knife home. Don't worry about guilt or innocence; let God and the Malleus deal with the consequences.'

'I'm not a killer,' he found himself saying. 'I wish I could be – but—'

'You are *not* a killer,' his uncle said firmly. 'Listen to me, Luke. You are not the hand here, you are the hammer. Remember that. You're just an instrument. It's for God and the Malleus to guide you, show you where to strike. You're no more guilty of murder than the hammer itself.'

Be the hammer.

Luke swallowed. And then he found himself asking the question, the unthinkable, the unaskable.

'Who was your first, Uncle?'

William didn't need to ask 'First what?' He just sighed.

'You know I can't tell you that, not outside the meeting house. Not until you're a Brother.'

If I'm a Brother, Luke thought. *I must make it. I must.*

'I'm sorry,' he said aloud. 'I shouldn't have asked.'

There was a long silence while the fire crackled and shifted in the grate. Luke stared at it until his eyes hurt. At its heart it was pure white gold, the colour of iron when you'd overheated it, almost to the point of melting. Above it flickered little orange flames, the same colour as metal when it was forging heat and ripe for working. And at the outside, a smoky, guttering, deep red that flickered and shimmered in the draught from the window. It was so exactly the colour of Rosa's hair that he closed his eyes, trying to shut it out, shut out the memory of the first time he'd seen her, standing in the stable like an avenging angel, a halo of fire around her head.

It was into this darkness that William spoke unexpectedly, his voice quiet but quite clear above the crackles of the fire.

'It was an old woman. She'd been selling potions to young girls, spells to rid them of their babies. Sometimes they worked, killed the child. Sometimes they killed the girl. What she didn't say was that even if the girl lived, her womb was poison. Nothing could live there. The old witch-woman didn't just take the unwanted babe, she took them all, all the children those girls might have had and loved. I asked her to stop and she laughed at me. Said she'd see me dead along with all the others and my loins as dried up as those girls' wombs.'

'She didn't kill you though,' Luke said. William shook his head, staring into the flames of the fire.

'No. I killed her. With a rag over her face, full of that chemical stuff that John brews. She didn't get more than two words of the spell out her mouth before she fell in a heap like a pile of rags.' Then he sighed. 'But I never did father a child.'

Something inside Luke went cold and still, and the hairs on his arms and neck shivered in spite of the warmth of the fire.

'When did it happen?' he asked, very low.

'Near fifteen years ago, I suppose it must be. I joined the Malleus right after your parents were killed.'

'Is that why . . .' Luke stopped and swallowed, and started again. 'Is that why you took me in then? Because you couldn't have a son of your own?'

'No.' William put his big, heavy hand on Luke's shoulder and turned him around, forcing Luke to look him in the face. 'No, Luke. Never think that. I took you in because you were my brother's son, and I loved him, and I kept you because as you grew I loved you too, and you were mine. The thing with the witch – it's completely separate. And who knows,' he gave a laugh, one without real mirth, 'maybe I never had it in me anyway. There's many a man never fathers a child, and witchcraft nothing to do with it.'

'But you never married?'

'No.' William let his hand drop and took up his pipe from the mantelpiece. He knocked it out, packed the bowl very carefully with tobacco, then struck a match on his boot and lit the pipe with a hand that was almost steady. Then he threw the match into the fire and watched it dwindle to nothing. 'No. There was a girl I might have married. But I didn't think it was fair to the lass. All girls want a baby of their own, don't they?'

'You could have given her the choice . . .' Luke began. But William was shaking his head.

'No. What kind of choice is that? Give me up, or give up the babe you'll never have? That's no choice. That's asking for one sacrifice over another, and neither of them fair for a woman who'd done nothing wrong herself. Why should she suffer for my sins? No. This way the sacrifice was mine, as it should be. I gave *her* up.'

Silence fell in the little room and Luke watched the fire and listened to the suck and pull of William's pipe. Blue smoke wreathed in the rafters.

'Can you stay the night?' William asked, as the church clock tolled ten. He rose and put his pipe on the mantelpiece.

'I'm supposed to be back tonight. But I sleep over the stables, so there's no one to see me come and go. If I start before four, I can be back before the rest of the house wakes.'

'Good.' William put his hand on Luke's shoulder as they turned to the stairs. 'It'll be good to have you under your own roof, even if it's just for the one night. It'll give you heart for the task, heart for what you need to do.'

What I need to do . . .

'It was a good plan, lad. Don't blame yourself. And maybe it didn't work, but you walked away in one piece, didn't you? There'll be another chance. Providence will give you a chance.'

'Maybe,' Luke said. He tried to smile.

'Goodnight, lad. Sleep well.'

As Luke shut the door to his room behind him, he knew that he should feel full of zeal and determination, galvanized by William's words. He was a fighter, a member of an elite band of warriors, fighting against the devil's work. But he didn't feel any of that. He felt only weariness and dread and a kind of sickness at the thought of going back to his task.

He sat on his own familiar bed and unbuttoned his shirt. As he pulled it off it chafed at the bandage over his shoulder and, in a fit of impatience, he tore at it, ripping off the dressing. There was a sharp jolt of pain as it stuck and then it peeled off, crusted and bloody, and he spat on his fingers and rubbed at the dried blood beneath. The mark was smaller than he'd thought, not much bigger than a sovereign, but it flamed like an angry sore and the skin around the burn was raised and red.

Still, there was no pus on the bandage, no infection to be seen. He threw the bloody dressing in the grate and lay down between the cold sheets, feeling weary to the bone.

He would go back.

He would go back and he would kill the witch. Because there was no way out of this, save one: death. Hers . . . or his.

'Where have you *been*?' Becky hissed as Luke ran through the open back door, smoothing his rumpled hair and trying to stifle his panting breath.

'I overslept. Had to run all the way from Spitalfields. Did anyone notice?' Luke gasped. The clock chimed seven as he slid into the chair. He was sweating in spite of the cold, frosty morning and he needed a shave.

'Mrs Ramsbottom was asking where you was at breakfast, but I said you were held up in the stables. Lucky for you, we're all at sixes and sevens. An invitation arrived last night, *if* you please, and sent the whole house into a spin.'

'An invitation?' Luke poured himself tea from the enormous pot on the table and bit into a piece of Mrs Ramsbottom's soda bread. The tea was lukewarm, but the bread was hot and very good.

'It seems that Mr Knyvet enjoyed playing the gallant knight on horseback to our Miss's damsel in distress.' Becky was enjoying the moment of power, spinning out the information as long as she could. 'He's only invited Miss Rosa and Mr Alexis to his house in the country for a hunting party.'

'Miss Rosa?' Luke said, startled. 'But how can she ride?'

'Seems her ankle's made a miraculous recovery overnight. Must be love. Or magic.'

Luke said nothing.

'They'll want the horses, of course. I don't know whether they'll go down by the same train or an earlier one.'

'Horses? By train?' Luke put his cup down.

'Yes, ninny.' Ellen came sweeping into the kitchen, her skirts rustling. 'How else did you think they'd get there? You can hardly ride two horses all the way to Sussex, can you?'

'Me?'

'Well, you're the stable-hand, or so they say.' She banged down the tea tray she was carrying. 'The horses won't look after themselves on the journey.'

'When are we leaving?'

'Tomorrow. So you'd best look sharp and see that everything's in order. Now, I can't be standing here gabbing, I've got trunks to pack and dresses to mend and stockings to darn. Becky, I'll need you to give me a hand with things when you've finished the beds, so no shilly-shallying, please.' She swept out.

'Hark at her!' Becky said crossly. 'Who's died and made

her queen? As if I spend my days shilly-shallying. I'd like to see her do twelve grates in . . .'

Luke chewed his mouthful mechanically, barely listening as Becky listed her grievances against Ellen. His mind was racing, wondering what this delay would mean for his plans, and how he could possibly accomplish the mission so far from home.

Rosa sat in the window seat, Belle in her lap and her sketch book in her hand. Every so often she touched her pencil to the page, but she wasn't really drawing, she was thinking. Thinking about Sebastian, about that unexpected invitation and what it meant. A strange tangle of feelings twisted inside her. Some parts of it she could pick out, like unravelling snarled-up skeins of embroidery threads – there was pleasure at the prospect of hunting and a sickness at the thought of her old threadbare dresses. The invitation had mentioned a ball. She had no ball dress.

But mixed in were other feelings that she could not unravel – and knotting them all together was a fizzing, nervy thrill that could have been anything from excitement to fear. What was it? It was tangled up with Sebastian, with the way he looked at her, with the sound of his crop on his puppy's back, and the sound of his voice calling her his darling. How could one man be so strange and contradictory? Which was the real Sebastian – the man who had saved her life, who had run to her and helped her tenderly into his

161

carriage, or the one who had beaten his pup to death in front of her eyes?

She was afraid of him – although she could not say exactly why. But she was drawn to him too. He represented everything that was missing from her life – luxury, excitement, even tenderness. It was a long time since anyone had called her their darling – not since Papa had died, perhaps.

But most of all, he represented an escape.

The sketch book fell from her hand and Belle whined and jumped as the spine dug into her side.

'I'm sorry.' Rosa picked it up and stroked Belle's warm, panting side, feeling the thrum of her heart beneath her fingers. 'Oh, Belle. What's wrong with me? I don't know what I want. I don't know what I don't want. I wish I could be like Clemency; she's so happy with Philip.'

She pulled back the lace curtain and looked out of the window, down to the yard. The back door opened and out came a figure. It was Luke. For a moment he just stood in the courtyard, his head down, his neck bowed. Then he seemed to shake himself and he walked across to the pump and stripped off his shirt, sticking his head under the faucet. Rosa shivered in sympathy as the icy water gushed down, soaking his hair and spilling over his shoulders and back. He stood, shuddering, rubbing his wet face with his shirt, trying to chafe some warmth into his body. His skin was raw with cold, the muscles on his back and shoulders hard and taut as he shivered.

As he scrubbed his damp hair with his shirt she noticed the dressing was gone. In its place was a blurry scar on his shoulder, red as fire from the cold and the chafing. The door opened again and Becky came out.

Luke stopped stock-still, his shirt in his hand. Then he dragged the wet shirt over his head and almost ran to the stable block.

'Luke!' Becky's cry filtered faint through the closed window. 'Luke! Wait!'

'Can't stop,' he shouted back. Then the door to his room slammed shut. Becky stood for a moment, the ribbons on her cap blowing in the wind. Then she turned on her heel and went back into the house.

'Miss Rosa.'

Rosa jumped and dropped her book heavily on to Belle, who squealed and ran under the bed in a huff at this final injustice. Ellen was standing in the doorway, hands on her hips.

'Ellen! You almost gave me an apoplexy.'

'I'll thank you to make yourself scarce, Miss Rosa, for I've your drawers to turn out and your trunk to pack.'

'Oh, Ellen . . .' Rosa felt her face fall. 'Must we do this now?'

'Tell me when you'd like me to do it, Miss Rosa?' Ellen opened Rosa's chemise drawer, pulled out a handful of white lawn and then shut it with a resounding thump that made the brushes on top of the chest clatter in sympathy. 'Because I have to have all your belongings laundered, darned, pressed and packed by this time tomorrow.'

'Never mind.'

Rosa picked up her book and went downstairs to the drawing room, but she knew she'd made a mistake as soon as she opened the door and the smell of Alexis' cigar filtered out.

'What?' He turned as she peered in and his face over the top of the chaise longue turned red and ugly. 'Oh it's *you*.'

He had been drinking already. The brandy decanter was open on the table beside him.

'I'll go.'

'Yes, do.'

She backed out and shut the door and then laid her forehead on the silky wood, feeling that she did not belong here. Matchenham was her home – it always had been. If she were at Matchenham she could saddle up Cherry and go for a gallop across the fields, letting the cold clear air and the fierce exhilaration of the ride chase away all her fears, along with the headache that was making her skull feel as if an iron band were closing around her head.

I want to go home, she thought, feeling the tears rise inside her. But she could not.

There was only one place in this house where she did not feel harried and miserable. One place where she belonged. The stables.

* * *

Luke paused from his mucking out to wipe the sweat from his forehead and for a moment stood, leaning on the pitchfork, looking out across the yard. The manure heap steamed in the cold air and he was hot and tired. In the big house he could hear the clatter of washing up in the kitchen and the sound of Mr James lecturing the boot-boy about work ethics and elbow grease. In Rosa's window he could see Ellen traipsing to and fro across the bedroom, shaking out frocks and linen, her crossness palpable even at this distance.

But his work wasn't finished and, if he were going to get the stable clean and swept before supper, he needed to get on. He picked up the fork again.

'Luke!' It was a whisper, nothing more. He stood for a moment, looking about, and then shrugged. His tired mind was playing tricks.

'*Luke!*'

There it was again – no mistake this time. A girl's voice, hoarse and low. It seemed to come from the lane behind the yard. He put down the fork and strode to the gate, looking up and down the lane. He almost missed her, even so, a pile of huddled rags pressed against the wall to the stable block. It was only when a familiar voice said hoarsely, 'Luke, thank gawd it's you!' that he turned and looked.

'Minna!'

She'd been crying, clean tracks across her dusty face.

'Minna, what's wrong?'

'It's Bess, Luke. She's dying.'

'Minna, no.' He put his arm around her awkwardly, and she gave a great sob, pressing her small, skinny, snot-nosed face into his shirt. 'I'm . . . Isn't there something we could do?'

'What? I took 'er to Billy Bones. He says she won't last the week.'

'Billy's no horse doctor. You need to take her to a vet, Minna. A real one, not a quack like Billy.'

'And where am I going to get the money for a bleeding horse doctor?' Her small face looked up at him, fury mixed with misery. 'I ain't even got enough to feed the kids, let alone get some ponce to look at Bess and tell me she'll be feeding hounds in a week. I need a job, Luke. I came to ask – d'you think they'd take me on here?'

He looked at her, at her bare, dirty feet, her tangled hair, her pinched face covered in tears and snot and the dust of the streets.

He shook his head.

'I'm sorry, Minna. They're no better than paupers themselves. I'm working for nothing.'

'For nothing?' Her face was aghast. 'Why in hell would you want to work for nothing?'

'Long story. But they're not going to be taking on new staff, trust me. And I wouldn't want you here even if they were.' Luke rubbed his hand over his face. Then he remembered something. 'Wait here.' He disentangled himself from Minna. 'Right here, understand? I won't be a tick.'

Upstairs in his room he stood for a minute, looking at himself in the mirror, thinking about William's sacrifices and all he'd done for him. Then he pulled up the loose board, took out the two sovereigns and shoved them in the pocket of his work trousers.

Luke clattered back downstairs and out into the yard – and stopped dead. Minna was in the centre of the courtyard, right in front of the stables. And she was not alone.

'Rosa . . . Miss . . . What . . . ?' he stammered. Damn Minna. Damn *her*.

Next to Minna she looked like a rare exotic bird, her hair glowing like fire in the winter sun, her golden-brown eyes wide, her magic glowing and shimmering around her like a heat haze on this chilly day. In a strange way they were so alike – both of them young, both of them small and slim – skinny you might have called it – eyes large and dark in their faces, personalities too big for them. But Rosa was simply built like that; you could see it in her narrow bones and long slim fingers, in the shape of her face. Minna was half starved, skinny by force rather than nature, and that was the difference. Next to her Rosa seemed to glow.

'I met your friend,' Rosa said. Her face was troubled. 'She says she's walked all the way from Spitalfields looking for work.'

Dammit. His fingers clenched on the sovereigns in his pocket.

'Yes, miss.'

'I'm so sorry. I wish we could offer her something here.'

167

I'm not, he thought. Not for anything would he have had Minna mixed up with this, with the witchcraft and deception and the blood that would follow soon enough.

'But I was just telling her about Mr Knyvet. His family runs soup kitchens and factories in the East End. Here.' She took out a pen and scribbled on a bit of card. 'This is the name of the street where the soup kitchen is. If you go there and show them my card, tell them I sent you, they'll give you a hot meal – maybe even a job, if they've got one in the factory.'

'Thank you, miss.' Minna smiled, the skin stretched tight over her bones. When had she last eaten a hot meal?

Behind Rosa's back Luke shook his head, willing Minna with his eyes not to take the card, not to get mixed up in this, with Knyvet, with everything else. But Minna bobbed a curtsey and put the card in her pocket.

'Did you want something, miss?' Luke said, his voice expressionless, but trying to tell Rosa without words that she was not wanted here, that this was not her place, but his.

'I . . .' For the first time she faltered. 'I – I just wanted to see Cherry.'

'She's fine, miss. No need for you to worry. I looked her over after yesterday and you wouldn't know anything had happened.'

'It wasn't . . .' She stopped and then seemed to fold, turning her face away so that he could not see her expression. 'Thank you. Never mind.'

As she turned to go back into the house she looked very small and Luke had the strangest impression that she was steeling herself to go back in.

After she'd gone he turned back to Minna.

'Don't go to the factory, Minna.'

'What? Why ever not?'

'Because . . .'

Because Knyvet was a bastard – and a man he wouldn't trust with a dog, let alone a friend. Because he was a witch.

'I can't explain. But you don't want to be mixed up with Knyvet. He's a bad lot.'

'Who cares about his morals?' Her face was blank with astonishment. 'Lord's sakes, Luke, it's not like he'll be hanging round the place, is it? And if it's a job – well . . .'

'I came to give you this.' He pulled the sovereigns out of his pocket and held them out. But Minna was shaking her head before she'd even seen the coins.

'No. No, Luke. I can't take it. I won't.'

'Minna, take the money.'

'Jesus, Luke! It's two sovereigns. Where d'ya get these?'

'Just take them.'

'How will I pay you back?'

'I don't care about that. Get Bess better and then pay me back. Or, if you have to, sell her, buy a donkey, and pay me back out of the spare. Anything's better than letting her waste away and losing your job.'

'I . . .' Her hand hovered over the coins and he could see she was wavering.

169

'Take it. Please. I don't care how long you take to pay me back.' She never would, he knew that, but the pretence was the only thing that would allow her to accept his charity.

'Oh, Luke. Thank you.' She took the coins and flung up her arms to kiss him, and he kissed her back, her cheek too thin and gaunt beneath his lips. There was something strange on her breath and he pulled back.

'Minna, have you been on the laudanum again?'

'No,' she snapped. But he knew by her face that she was lying.

'Stop it, Minna,' he said warningly. 'Stop it now while you still can.'

'I'll stop it when me bleeding tooth stops hurting! Don't be such a fussy old woman.' She shoved the coins in her pocket, all her smiles turned sour from his scolding.

'Minna—'

'What's all this?' A voice boomed out behind them both, making Luke turn sharply and Minna jump like a cat.

It was Mr James, standing in the stable yard, his arms folded.

'What's all this?' He spoke to Luke rather than Minna, jerking his thumb at her as if she were no better than she should be. 'I will not have loose women hanging around the stable yard in full daylight, Luke Welling.'

'Full daylight – so would it be all right at midnight?' Minna said pertly, recovered from her fright. 'And who's Luke Welling when he's at home?' She shot Luke a look

170

that said, *I'll have this out of you later*. Luke glared back, fury in every nerve and bone, willing her to shut her smart-alec mouth before she got herself a clip round the head and him fired.

'Be quiet!' thundered Mr James. 'And get out of my yard, young woman.'

'Try to stop me,' Minna shot back. She turned on her heel. 'Bye, Luke.'

He didn't return the farewell, didn't say anything, just stood with his neck bowed and the fury and fear running through his veins like acid.

'Good riddance!' Mr James bellowed, and clapped the gate to the mews shut with a sound like thunder. Then he turned to Luke. 'What in God's name is going on out here? Consorting with women in full view of the house? What were you thinking?'

'I'm sorry, sir.' Luke kept his voice as even as he could, kept his eyes on his boots, kept his fists clenched. 'She just came in off the street. I've no idea who she is. Was.'

'Hmph.' Mr James looked at him from beneath glowering black brows, still suspicious. 'How did she know your name then?'

'She didn't, did she?' Inspiration flushed over him. 'She said, "Who's Luke Welling when he's at home?"' Thank God for Minna and her smart mouth.

'She said goodbye to you,' James countered.

'Only after you said my name. She must have heard you. It was just sauce.'

'Well then, what were you giving her when I came across the yard? I saw you put something into her hand.'

'It was a bit of lucky heather.' He'd never thought of himself as a good liar; usually he stammered and tied himself in knots. Now it made him sick, how easily the lies came. He was growing used to deception. It was living side by side with the vile witches, their deceit rubbing off on him. 'She tried to make me buy it. I said no. I was giving it back.'

Mr James said nothing, only stood with his arms folded across his waistcoat. Then he seemed to make up his mind.

'Very well, Luke Welling. But if I see her around here again, I'll give you notice. Now, get yourself upstairs and get packing for the hunting party. I want you ready for the train at six tomorrow. Understood?'

'Understood,' Luke said, and then added bitterly, 'sir.'

12

The trunks stacked in the hall were painted with *GREENWOOD* in white capital letters, and the labels said *Southing*. The horses had already left. James was out in the road, blowing the whistle for a hansom cab. Rosa stood in the hallway, buttoning her gloves, and thinking of Cherry shut into the narrow railway carriage, tossing her head nervously as the engine whistled and the speed picked up. She hoped Luke would remember her nosebag and give her a sugar lump when the train started off.

Just then Ellen came down the stairs, her face even grimmer than usual. She was not wearing her coat.

'What's the matter? Why aren't you dressed? We'll miss our train,' Rosa said. 'Where's Mama and Alexis?'

'Your brother's ready. He's in the library finishing his business.' Finishing his brandy was what Ellen meant, and they both knew it. 'But your Mama . . .' She paused.

'What?' Rosa asked.

173

'Your Mama's not coming.'

'*What?*'

'You'd best go up and see her. She's in bed.'

Rosa didn't wait. She picked up her skirts and took the stairs two at a time.

Mama was in bed with a cold flannel on her forehead and her eyes closed, but she opened them as Rosa came in.

'Mama? What's going on?'

'I'm unwell.' She looked it – her face in the dim light was blanched and drawn. 'I cannot travel.'

'What? But – but . . .' Rosa was lost for words. She clenched her hands, feeling the kid strain across her knuckles. 'How can I go to Southing unchaperoned?'

'You'll have Alexis. He will have to do.'

'And my dress,' Rosa cried. 'What about my dress, Mama?'

'I'm sure you can think of something,' Mama said faintly. Rosa drew a breath, trying to keep calm, trying not to give way to the fury with angry words.

'How, precisely, Mama? It's one thing to take out a stain or change the colour of a skirt. It's quite another to magic myself up a dress out of thin air. I couldn't do it any more than I could sew one! And even if I could, you *know* what Sebastian would think if he saw me at his ball in a dress spun from charms and air. Do you *want* me to advertise the fact that we are too poor to afford a real ball gown? Because—'

'Rosamund, that is enough.' Mama sat up, her face suddenly angry. 'I have had enough of your selfishness. Now – all this arguing is making my headache worse. Go. And make sure Alexis doesn't miss the train.'

It was dark when the train drew into Southing station.

'Southing!' bellowed the stationmaster. 'Anyone for Southing alight here.'

'Wake up!' Rosa shook Alex's shoulder and they stumbled out of the first-class carriage and on to the station platform. For a moment Rosa could see nothing but steam and smoke, just lights twinkling through the white drifting clouds. Then the train gave a *wheesh* and a whistle and was off, and the platform began to clear.

'Mr and Miss Greenwood?' enquired a voice from behind them and Rosa swung round. A groom in neat livery was standing beside the exit, a porter next to him, with their trunks piled on his trolley.

'Yes,' she said.

'Come this way, please – miss, sir. My name is Cummings. Mr Sebastian regrets he couldn't come himself, but asked me to convey his warmest welcome.'

Outside the carriage stood a boy holding the horses' heads. The groom handed them up, tipped a coin to the boy and the porter, and then clicked to the horses. At last, with a jerk and a clatter of hooves, they were off.

Rosa sank into the velvet-upholstered cushions and looked about her at the polished walnut gleaming in the light from the carriage lamps, the silk drapes, the hot bricks at her feet. Then she looked down at her skirts, so drab against the raspberry-coloured velvet of the seat. Alexis was not too bad, at least not in the low lamplight of the carriage interior. His boots were irreproachable, his coat well cut and not too worn, and his top hat was new. But his clothes had always been the first priority and he had been full grown when Papa died.

Rosa had long since grown out of the clothes bought in their prosperity and after Alexis' new suits and clothes were paid for there had somehow never been enough left to pay for extras for her. She hadn't minded – there seemed little point in new frocks to wear at Matchenham, with only the horses and Mama to mind whether the hems of her skirts were let out and her pinafores frayed. But now, in the luxurious interior of the carriage she saw, more clearly than ever, the worn patches on her thin, cheap cloak and the stains on her skirt. She whispered a spell under her breath and scrutinized the threadbare material, praying to God that the enchantment would hold, in spite of her tiredness, and that Sebastian would not notice the cheap deception. Most men could be relied upon not to see the small charms of vanity – the smoothing of wrinkles, the patching of a frock, the enchantment of grey hairs. But Sebastian was not most men.

'How far is the house?' she whispered to Alexis as the coachman tipped his whip to the horses.

'Oh, not far. Twenty minutes perhaps. Most of it's Seb's

drive, to be honest. But you've been to Southing before, haven't you?'

'I don't think so.' She looked out of the window at the unfamiliar cottages and the shapes of the hills. The village houses were built of Sussex flint, like those round Matchenham, so they looked homely, but she was sure she had never seen them before. 'I was never allowed to come when you went for holidays. Perhaps I came with Mama and Papa when I was very small – but I don't remember if so.'

'Huh. Perhaps you're right.' He turned up his collar and closed his eyes. 'Hope the sot has made it all right with the horses. Think he knows which end of a train is which?'

'Don't be hateful.' Rosa turned her face to the window, watching the dark countryside flash past. Rain speckled at the windows and in the far-off distance she heard the scream of the train as it disappeared into the night. 'Does Sebastian know we're bringing him?'

'Well, I don't suppose he thinks we've packed the horses in our trunks,' Alexis drawled.

'No, that we're bringing an . . .' She lowered her voice, even though the coachman was outside the box and could not possibly hear. 'An *outwith*.'

'He knows. We won't be the only people with an outwith servant. I don't suppose the Southing servants will be very pleased, but they'll be used to it. He'll be out in the stables anyway, so he won't interfere with the house servants.

Now, shut up, do. I've a hell of a headache and your chatter isn't helping.'

Rosa was about to snap back a retort, but there was a sudden rumble as they passed over a cattle grid and then two huge gateposts and a gatekeeper's cottage loomed out of the darkness. She pressed her face to the glass, her anger forgotten as she peered into the night.

The drive wound through woods and fields, and she realized that Alexis had not been joking when he said that most of the twenty-minute drive was within the grounds of Southing. She caught glimpses between the trees: tall chimneys, glinting golden lights. But the architect who had built Southing had seated it in the landscape so that you never saw the house itself until the last possible moment – and then suddenly it was there, in one breathtaking sweep, as the carriage rounded the last curve of the drive.

'Oh . . .' Rosa breathed. Her breath frosted the glass, making golden halos of the lamps that lit the carriage drive and the tall pillared porch.

A footman stepped forward to open the carriage and she stepped, as if in a dream, into the cold country night, lit by a horned moon, a thousand stars, and the golden light that streamed from the windows of Southing.

'Miss Greenwood.'

For a minute she couldn't work out where the voice was coming from, who would be calling her name in this strange place. There was someone coming down the steps, but the light streamed out from the tall doorway, dazzling her eyes. Then she saw. Sebastian.

'Mr Knyvet.'

He was dressed in evening dress, with a faultless white shirt and tie, and holding a tiny cheroot with a gold-wrapped tip which he threw away as he descended the steps towards her. His head was bare and the lamps shone on his dark-golden hair as he bent over her hand.

'Miss Greenwood. I am so very, very pleased to welcome you to Southing,' he said, in his soft, hoarse voice. And he smiled – not his usual sardonic twist of a smile, but a true, wide smile that changed his whole face and made him look more like a boy than a man.

He opened his palm and in his hand was a single rose, made of frost and ice and magic.

'Se— Mr Knyvet . . .' Rosa stammered. She looked over her shoulder reflexively, looking for the footman but Sebastian only smiled.

'Don't worry, he's one of us. Take it. I made it for you.'

'Thank you.' She took it from his hand. It was perfect – down to every frozen stamen. Even the thorns were sharp enough to prick. She looked down at it, marvelling as it melted, its beauty slipping away through her gloved fingers.

'Seb!' There was a squeak of carriage springs and a crunch of gravel as Alexis heaved himself out of the carriage and on to the drive. 'What ho! Game for a hand of baccarat tonight?'

Rosa looked up and then back down to where the frozen rose had lain. There was nothing left but water.

The elderly white-haired groom was a witch. It was all Luke could think of as he followed in the man's footsteps, trying desperately to concentrate on everything the man was saying. This stall for Cherry, this for Brimstone, over there was the tack room, but here was where to put the saddles for cleaning. He knew this information was what he'd need to survive – but the man was a witch. Not a very good one – his magic was a fragile will-o'-the-wisp in the night air. But a witch, nonetheless. And it made it impossible to concentrate on what he was saying.

'Eh, are you listening?'

'Sorry.' Luke stumbled. He rubbed his face, feeling his stubble rasp across his palm. He needed a shave and a wash, but most of all a good night's sleep. 'What did you say?'

'I said, now the horses are settled, I'll show ee to tha room. Where's tha traps, boy?'

'My traps?' Luke echoed stupidly. The old man's country burr was hard to understand.

'Tha traps – bags, kit. What do ee call 'em in Lunnon?'

'Oh.' Luke shook himself. He'd got so used in London to the servants' hall being a refuge away from their kind, it was doubly strange to find one of them here, on what felt like safe ground. 'Sorry. I left 'em in the yard.'

'Come on then, laddie, pick 'em up, and we'll get ee

settled afore supper. Ye'll be clemmed, I shouldn't wonder.'

He stumped off across the yard and Luke followed.

'When will the hunt start?'

'Oh, they'll be hunting tomorrer,' the old man said. 'Mr Sebastian was never one to let the grass grow. He's been cooped up in Lunnon these long months and in India afore that. He's half mad to get wet pasture under his horse's hooves agin.'

'I've never been hunting,' Luke said as he picked up his case. He didn't try to hide his nerves. No use pretending he wasn't as green as they came for this – he would take any information this old man could give him, and welcome. 'Anything I should know for tomorrow?'

'Well, I seed your master and miss only brought the one 'orse each, so I dare say Mr Sebastian will lend ee one o' his father's hacks. Bumblebee most likely. It'll be your job to get your master and Miss's 'orses ready on the day. And o' course you've to make sure Miss Greenwood doesn't go killing of herself.'

Luke nearly dropped his case, cold with horror that the man had reached inside his thoughts so simply, but then the man laughed, a loud raucous belly laugh, and Luke realized it was a joke.

'Sounds simple enough,' the old man wheezed, 'but it's them young ladies you've to keep your eye on, 'specially if she doesn't know the lie of the land. Make sure now she doesn't go leaping no treacherous ditches, nor taking no 'edges too high for her. And keep her away from Bishop's

Ford,' he added, his face suddenly serious. 'That bridge won't last the season.'

'Bishop's Ford?' Luke asked. 'Where's that?'

'Old ford to the east; you'll know it by the wooden bridge and the two oak trees either side. The bridge looks sound enough but there's a strut gone and it won't bear an 'orse. I've said time and agin they should take it down, but the telegraph boys use it for their round. It's safe enough on foot, leastways until the winter. But not for an 'orse and rider. If you want to cross on horseback you mun' go farther upstream, towards Barham. There's a good bridge there; that's the one the hunters will take, if they're heading for Thatcher's Covert.'

'I'll remember,' Luke said numbly. He hardly noticed as the old man handed him to a maid at the back door, nor as she led him through a warren of subterranean passages and rooms to a back staircase, chattering all the while. As he trudged after her, up the narrow staircase towards the attic room that was to be his for the weekend, there was only one thought in his head, and it sang through him, like metal singing from the clean blows of a hammer: *Bishop's Ford*.

It was as William had said: providence had handed him a gift straight from God. Now it was up to him not to waste it.

As she descended the great stairs, the hubbub of voices hit Rosa first, followed by the heat as she entered the drawing room. It was a huge, long room with tall windows, panelled walls and a ceiling frosted and frilled like a wedding cake. The heat came from the fireplaces at each end, great cavernous things banked with giant logs the size of small trees, burning so briskly that the ladies nearby had retreated behind fire screens and fans. Rosa felt her face flush warm in the glow and she thought of how her pink skin must clash with her hair. She tugged at the green dress, wishing it were not so shabby and so tight, wishing the bodice were not so low, wishing it were not the dress Sebastian had seen her wear last time he came. She prayed that he wouldn't notice. She prayed that if he did, he didn't realize the truth: that it was almost the only presentable dress she possessed.

There was no one there that she knew. Alexis must have retreated to the smoking room with his cronies, where she could not follow. She scanned the crowd, looking for Sebastian, but knowing even if she saw him, she would not have the courage to stride up and claim him. She was just considering turning tail and running when she felt a touch on her arm and a soft voice spoke.

'Are you Miss Greenwood?'

Rosa turned. A white-haired girl with piercingly beautiful blue eyes stood at her shoulder. She was perhaps a year or two younger than Rosa herself, her hair hanging in a long plait down her back.

Her eyes were clear and lucent as a summer sky, a startlingly true blue, quite different from the arctic paleness of Sebastian's gaze, and yet there was enough similarity in their faces for Rosa to ask, 'Are you Sebastian's sister?'

'Yes.' She smiled. 'My name is Cassandra. Sebastian has told me a great deal about you.'

'Oh.' Rosa blushed furiously. 'I . . .' She found she was stammering, tongue-tied.

'All very pleasant. And proper.'

Her words should have reassured. But it was somehow disquieting that Cassandra felt Rosa might be in doubt.

'I'm delighted to meet you,' Rosa said, putting out her hand, and Cassandra took it, smiling warmly. 'But please, call me Rosa.'

'Rosa, then, and you must call me Cassie.'

'Cassie,' Rosa said, and smiled back. 'But tell me, are your father and mother here? I haven't yet paid them my respects.'

'My father has been called to the Ealdwitan on urgent business,' Cassie said. 'He hopes to return on Monday.'

'And your mother?'

'My mother . . .' She hesitated. 'My mother is . . . not well. She does not enjoy company. She will not be joining us this evening.'

For a moment Rosa was taken aback. A hostess not to come down to dinner on the first night of a house party? Then she recovered her manners.

'Well – well then, I shall hope to see her tomorrow. Will you be hunting?'

'I?' Cassie's face was surprised for a moment, then she

broke into a laugh. 'No. Not I.' Before Rosa had time to wonder why, she added, 'I'm blind.'

'Oh!' Rosa flushed. 'I'm sorry,' she said meaninglessly, and then winced, wondering if that was the right thing to say.

'Don't be,' the girl said lightly. 'It has its compensations.'

'What do you mean?'

'I don't have to do embroidery,' she said with a laugh. 'There are other things too – I can see more, perhaps, than you.'

'More? What do you mean?'

But just then a huge gong rang out and everyone stood.

'Dinner,' said Cassie. 'Will you walk in with me?'

'No,' said a voice at her elbow. 'Miss Greenwood walks in with me.'

Rosa turned and looked up into Sebastian's clear blue eyes, a winter blue above his snowy-white cravat, and he smiled, a wicked, teasing flash that twisted in her gut and her heart. He held out an arm and two impulses fought inside her – the desire to take his arm, his protection, and walk into dinner with the most eligible bachelor in the room, perhaps in the entire county. And the desire to shake her head, prick his arrogance, and give her arm to Cassandra.

She was still standing like a fool, looking up at Sebastian when Cassie spoke.

'Ah, Rosa, I'm so sorry. I had forgotten that I was supposed to accompany Lord Grieves' son.' She smiled, her

185

blue eyes full of summer warmth. Rosa smiled back, forgetting that Cassie couldn't see her.

'Good,' Sebastian said very softly in her ear as they turned to walk into dinner. 'I want you all to myself.'

His lips were warm against her ear and Rosa shivered as his breath tickled the soft hairs against her neck. Her grip tightened on his arm and she felt the iron hardness of the muscles beneath his dinner jacket, so different from Alexis, soft from drink and lassitude.

'What are you thinking?' he asked as they passed through the double doors into the dining room. The panelled walls were studded with the heads of stags mounted on wooden blocks, their antlers casting strange shadows in the candlelight. Between the heads were savagely beautiful fans of glittering swords, pistols and daggers. And beneath it all was the long table, aglow with candles reflecting off the crystal glasses and silver cutlery arrayed to each side of the plates, dazzling against the faultless snowy cloth.

I was thinking you are as contradictory as this room, Rosa thought. *Beautiful and savage and urbane, all at the same time.*

But she only shook her head and passed under the arc of swords to take her place at the glittering table.

13

Luke woke very early and for a minute he had no idea where he was. He lay in the darkness, listening to the strange sounds – the soft insistent hoot of an owl, the wind in the trees. And the sound of breathing in the bed across the other side of the room – not William, but a stranger.

Then he remembered.

He was at Southing. The man in the bed opposite was another groom and, thank God, an ordinary man like himself. He was not sure he could have borne to sleep in the same room as a witch. And he had just nine days left to complete his task.

He sat up, rubbing the sleep from his eyes. Then, with a glance to make sure the man in the bed opposite was sound asleep, he pulled down the neck of his shirt and twisted to look at the scar on his shoulder. It was all but healed and beneath the angry red swelling you could just see the faint shape of a hammer.

He shrugged his shirt back on and then swung his legs out of bed, feeling his head spin with tiredness. The other man had a watch hanging from his bedpost and Luke padded across and looked at it, yawning. Half past five, read the dial. Good.

He ran down the back stairs in his stockinged feet, pulling his boots on at the last moment. The door to the gardens was bolted, but when he pulled back the latch he was relieved to find it was not locked. The country air hit him as he walked out into the pre-dawn gloaming. It smelt so different from London – cold and clear as spring water, the soft aromatic scent of wood smoke in place of the sharpness of coal, the dampness of grass instead of the smell of wet cobbles.

The stable smelt reassuringly the same – of hay and manure and warm horse. The horses were still asleep, and Cherry chuntered crossly and tossed her head as he pulled on the bridle.

'Hey,' he whispered. 'None of your sauce, miss.' There was a sugar lump in his pocket and he held it out, her soft, whiskery lips gentle on his palm as she took it. She crunched it delicately like a lady as he saddled her up, but he led, rather than rode her out of the yard, choosing the quietest parts of the cobbles, so that the sound of her hooves was muffled by grass and drifts of straw. The maids would be getting up soon and he did not want the household to know what he was about.

Out of the yard he put his foot in the stirrup and hauled

himself up. Cherry gave a little whicker of delight, her bad mood forgotten, and Luke patted her neck.

'You're a sweetheart, you are, aren't you.'

She tossed her head, her skin warm and silky beneath his hand and together they quickened their pace to a trot. The dawn light was turning the sky to pink as he turned out of the gate towards the pale glimmer of the rising winter sun.

It was the oak trees that Luke saw first, two of them, standing sentinels beside the river, like gateposts. He reined Cherry in and turned her head towards them.

There it was. Bishop's Ford. He could see why the old man had warned against it – from up here the bridge looked sound, but when he slid from Cherry's back and scrambled down the bank to the fast-flowing river, you could see the rotten planks and the missing struts beneath.

It was deadly. It was perfect. So why could he feel no joy in it at all?

Cherry whickered softly up in the field above and the sound gave him a wrenching stab of guilt at the thought of what he was about to do.

As he climbed the bank and hauled himself back into the saddle he couldn't bear to meet her trusting brown eyes, though she turned her head to him and butted him affectionately.

'I'm sorry, girl,' he said, his throat stiff and hoarse. 'If there was another way I'd take it, you know I would.'

He knew what John Leadingham would say: *What's the life of one horse against the misery wrought by a witch?*

He thought of the pigs and cows in John's slaughterhouse – animals sent to their death for the good of mankind – so that people might eat and cook and have candles to burn and shoes to wear. What difference was there in this? None, really. So why didn't it feel the same?

One simple truth beat inside him, in time with Cherry's hoof-beats as she galloped across the turf. Him or the witch. Him or the witch. Him or the witch. This was his cross to bear – Cherry's death would be the price he had to pay, the price they all had to pay.

He put his head down, close to her mane, and the wind in his face brought tears to his eyes.

'I'm sorry,' he whispered. 'Oh my God, I'm so sorry. Please forgive me.'

He did not know who he was asking forgiveness from: God, Cherry, himself – or someone else completely?

It's God's work that you're doing, lad; John Leadingham's hoarse croak in his head.

God's work. So why didn't he feel exalted? Why did he feel like a murderer?

He arrived back in the stable just in time to shut Cherry into her stall before the other grooms arrived. She was not sweating; he had not galloped her hard enough for that. She was cool and full of energy, and she whickered softly as Luke filled the bucket with water and poured a handful of oats into her feeding tray.

There was much to do before the hunt gathered – feed Brimstone, saddle him up, and put the side-saddle on Cherry. He had to find this borrowed horse and saddle him up too, then he had to wash and change into a clean shirt. He knew he should make time to eat his own breakfast, for it would be a long, hard ride before the hunters stopped for food, but he didn't know if he could force down the food.

But there was just one more thing he had to do before he started.

He searched the floor of the stables, looking for a likely stone. He discarded one as too large, and another as too sharp, before he found one that was just right: small and round as a pea. Then he took his pick and drove the stone deep beneath the horseshoe, where it was invisible to the eye. When Cherry put her foot down there was the slightest hint of hesitation, the slightest wince, but only if you looked for it. It would take a few miles with a rider on her back before she began to limp.

'I'm sorry, girl,' he said again. There was a catch in his voice and he hated himself for it.

Rosa took a deep breath, drinking in the cool sweet autumn air. It was country air – so clean you could taste the sweetness on your tongue, and so different from London's sooty bitter atmosphere it was like drinking spring water

191

after salt. Southing was very different from Matchenham, but it felt like home. The fields stretched out below the house, mile after mile of sweet short Sussex turf. Down to the right were the copses and coverts where they would go to flush out the fox, the river winding between the trees, glinting in the pale autumn sun.

She had not felt so happy since leaving Matchenham and when she turned to smile at Sebastian she knew that her face was radiant with delight, flushed with the cold and the pleasure of being on horseback again, that her waist was laced down to a trim silhouette, that her habit was faultless and that all this – her delight, her red hair and clear skin against the stark black of her hat and habit – all this made her look better than she had ever looked in his presence before.

He smiled back, his teeth flashing white in his tanned face, his pupils pricks of black in his ice-blue eyes, and she looked out across the sea of riders in their scarlet and black coats, the hunt master calling to his officials, the huntsman blowing his horn to encourage stragglers, the dogs baying excitedly as they raced up and down the drive in full voice.

'Were you a centaur in a previous life, madam?' asked another rider with a laugh. 'You are magnificent on that animal – you have the best seat I've ever seen in a woman.'

'Thank you!' Rosa called back. Usually she would have flushed and muttered something deprecating; this morning she knew it to be true. Beneath her, Cherry curvetted and snorted, excited by the sound of the hounds and the sight of pasture in front of her.

Luke was somewhere behind her, on a horse belonging to the house, a hunter called Bumblebee. She tried to catch his eye, but his head was down.

'I warn you,' Sebastian said as the hunt gathered, ready to depart, 'I ride hard. I'll be with the first field or die in the attempt. Can you keep up?'

'I'll keep up,' Rosa said, nettled. Cherry could jump as well as any horse on the field.

'We're heading over to Tushing Woods.' He indicated a small copse on the ridge of the hill. 'See if we can flush out a fox from there.'

'Really, sir?' Luke's head came up sharply. Rosa was surprised; she had not thought he was even listening. Now he was tense, his big hands gripping the reins tightly. 'That's to say – I was told the place to go was Thatcham's?'

'No, Farquharson tells me he was up there last week and there was no sign of a fox,' Sebastian said indifferently. 'Tushing is a better bet.'

Luke said nothing, but his grip was still tight on the reins and Rosa saw a vein beating in his temple. She was puzzled – what could it possibly matter which way they went? Then the horn sounded again, Cherry snorting and stamping and curvetting beneath her, and they were off.

* * *

'View halloo!' cried a voice far up the field, its pitch almost a scream with excitement, and Rosa gathered Cherry together and leapt the ditch. She landed perfectly, like a cat, but then stumbled infinitesimally as if one of her hooves misgave her. Behind her Rosa heard the heavy thunder of Luke's horse and the heave and thump as he took it over the ditch, but she didn't stop to look. She was intent on the pack ahead and Sebastian's lithe, narrow back in its scarlet coat, urging his horse on, and on. Alexis was somewhere to the left of the field, Brimstone already sweating beneath his bulk. The horse would be tired out within the hour unless Alex rode him more sensibly. By contrast, Sebastian's beautiful thoroughbred looked like he could go for ever.

And then suddenly she saw it – the fox – a red-brown streak crossing the emerald grass with the hounds shrieking and baying in pursuit. The horn sounded again and the whole field surged after it, mud flying, the clods of turf scattering as they tore up the field.

'Come on!' Rosa begged Cherry. Alexis was already using his hunting crop freely on Brimstone, labouring the poor beast's hind quarters like a racing jockey. She felt her own crop tight beneath her arm, but she never beat Cherry – she never needed to. Cherry would give her all without punishment.

They were heading uphill, the horses sweating and snorting, when suddenly the fox broke its line, darting back down towards the river, the hounds in hot pursuit.

The hunt wheeled after it, like a flock of scarlet birds in an emerald sky, and began to pound down the bank towards the river.

'Come on!' Rosa screamed to Luke. There was mud on her face and her breath was tearing in her chest. And then she felt Cherry falter beneath her, even as Luke hollered back,

'She's limping, miss.'

Dammit. Rosa slowed, just a little, and felt the truth of it. Cherry was favouring one foot.

'Was it the jump?' she shouted across to Luke. 'I felt her stumble.'

'Could be, miss. Or could be a stone.'

They slowed, and Rosa watched as the rest of the field tore away from her, down towards the river where the fox had already forded and plunged into the undergrowth.

'Damn,' she swore, as Luke slid from Bumblebee and pulled out his knife. 'We'll never catch up. Please, make it quick if you can, Luke.'

She shaded her eyes, watching the riders as they crossed the river. It was too deep to ford, but the dogs paddled across somehow. The men jumped, by and large, the ladies making for a bridge further upstream in the direction of Barham. It was a strange route to choose, she thought. The fox was clearly going to go downstream, downhill where the going was easier for it, and the sparse trees thickened to wood. There must be no bridge further down.

'It was a stone, miss.' She heard Luke's voice over her shoulder. 'I've got it.'

Sure enough the field had curved downwards and were beating their way through the trees with the hounds baying and shrieking.

'We'll never catch up,' Rosa said despairingly as Luke scrambled back into the saddle. 'The river's too wide to jump downstream. If only there were a bridge . . .'

'There is,' Luke said. At first she couldn't understand him – his voice was hoarse and cracked. He coughed and spat, and then spoke again. 'There is. Look. By those two oaks.'

He pointed – and sure enough, between the trees, beside the two sentinel oaks, she saw a patch of darkness where the river's glitter was cut by something broad and black, something with handrails.

Rosa felt a huge smile split her mud-spattered face.

'Luke, I could kiss you.'

She pulled Cherry together, feeling the horse's headlong excitement, and together they thundered down the pasture, towards the waiting oak trees and the patch of dark water.

'Come on!' she shouted over her shoulder at Luke. 'Come on, what are you waiting for?'

Far across the river there was another blast of the horn – the fox had broken out of the scrubby trees by the river bank, making for the hill on the far side. The riders were urging their horses up the slope and she saw Sebastian turn half around, calling something to Alexis, gesturing back down towards the river, towards Rosa.

Rosa gripped the pommel of the side-saddle between her thighs, feeling the thunder of Cherry's hooves beneath her, feeling the wind in her face so hard that tears came to her eyes. Behind her she could hear Luke pounding, pounding after her.

'Wait!' she heard his voice, his cry almost lost in the wind and the thumping hooves. 'Miss, Rosa, wait!'

'Hurry!' she shouted back. If she could cross the river fast enough she could catch up with the first field, she *knew* she could. If Luke couldn't keep up, that was his lookout.

She and Cherry tore down the soft pasture and into the shadow of the trees by the bridge. The oaks flashed past. She heard the hollow boom of Cherry's hooves on the wooden slats of the bridge – and then something else, a dreadful tearing scream of breaking wood.

Cherry reared and she screamed too, a sound such as Rosa had never heard – not a whinny, but a shriek of pure terror.

'Rosa!' She heard Luke's desperate bellow behind her.

And then she was falling and Cherry was falling too – a mass of screaming horse and flying mane, a tangle of hooves and bridle and skirts – her feet still in the stirrups, the broken shafts of the bridge murderous pikes in the river bed.

There was no time to think of a spell.

There was no time to shout an incantation or cast a shield.

Together she and Cherry hit the water with a splash that knocked all the breath out of her body. Water filled her eyes and ears and mouth. The river roared above her and around her, and there was nothing but tumbling horse and bone and hooves and terror.

And then there was nothing at all.

14

Luke was near enough to hear the crack of the wood as it gave and the scream of the horse.

'Rosa!' he shouted desperately.

There was a flurry of black skirts, like a bird shot in flight, and Rosa's magic blazed out bright as a flame, as she fought to save them both. And then she was gone.

Luke skidded to a halt on Bumblebee, scrambling from the saddle almost before the horse had stopped. His whole body was shaking as he ran to the river bank and began sliding down the muddy chute towards the rushing waters. Oh Christ, what had he done?

He saw, before he even reached the water's edge.

Cherry lay in the stream, impaled on one of the broken shafts of the bridge. It had gone clean through her ribcage and she was dead already, Luke could see it in the way she lay, limp, unresisting, and the way the stream below her had turned scarlet with the gushing blood.

'Oh God.'

He knew, suddenly and certainly, that he'd done a terrible, terrible thing.

'Rosa!' he shouted. No answer came but the roar of the waters. Then he saw something, a red-gold flame beneath Cherry's dappled back. She was there, pinned beneath the horse.

'Help me!' he roared, slipping and sliding down into the water. The hunt was not that far away; he could hear the sound of the horn and the baying of the hounds. 'For God's sake, someone help me!'

He could not swim. He'd never learnt. But he struck out anyway into the middle of the river, grabbing on to the beams of the bridge to try to keep his footing, clutching at anything – the pikes, Cherry's bridle, even her mane.

In the middle of the stream he hooked his arm around a wooden pile and pushed with all his strength at the horse, putting his shoulders and every muscle into shifting its bulk just an inch or two higher up the wooden shaft. His fingers groped beneath the creaming water, feeling for Rosa's body. She was there. But he could not move her.

'Cherry,' he gasped, heaving at the horse's unresisting bulk until his joints cracked and his muscles tore and screamed with protest. And all the time the waters tugged and tugged at him, trying to pull his feet from under him and sweep him away to drown too.

'God damn you, Rosa!' His breath sobbed in his chest.

His face was wet with river water and sweat and tears. 'You'll not die. Hear me? You're not to die!'

He braced his feet against a rock in the torrent and heaved again at Cherry's warm, dead weight, her blood running down over his shoulders and swirling into the water in a crimson slick.

She shifted – or maybe it was the pike in the river bed. Something gave a minute amount, and when he felt under the water for Rosa's body, it didn't come free but it moved.

Heat flooded back into his numb fingers and he heaved again at Cherry's side, bracing his shoulders against her ribs and scrabbling for Rosa beneath the churning red water.

She moved again, an inch or two further from beneath Cherry's hind quarters. One more heave – and she slid free with a rush so that he stumbled and almost fell into the current. Only his grip on Cherry's bridle saved them both, and then he struck out for the bank, hauling Rosa in his wake, a drowned black rat.

At the bank he pulled her on to the muddy shore, heaving her clear of the tugging waters, and leant her body gently against the twisted roots of a tree. She lay there, painfully still, painfully white, her head at a strange, unnatural angle. But when he put his ear to her breast he could hear a beat and a wet gurgle – or thought he could. He willed her to cough – but she didn't. He would have given anything for a thimbleful of witchcraft. No matter if it damned him to hell for all eternity, he would have paid the price if it meant he could save her. But he was powerless – and so was she.

For a moment Luke stood frozen in indecision. Then he began scrambling up the bank towards the bridge. At the top he shaded his eyes, looking after the riders. They were almost gone. Only one rider and horse stood in silhouette on the ridge: Sebastian. He would have known that beautiful thoroughbred anywhere and the arrogant set of the rider's shoulders. Sebastian could save her. He was a witch, wasn't he?

'Knyvet!' he bellowed, the words whipped and torn by the autumn breeze. Sebastian turned his head as if he'd heard something, but wasn't sure what. 'Knyvet!' Luke shouted again, his voice cracking with the effort. 'Come back! There's been an accident. Rosa – she's dying!'

For a moment he thought Sebastian had heard him. His horse took two steps downhill, towards the river.

'*Knyvet!*' he screamed, the words tearing in his throat. 'For God's sake, help!'

But then the horn sounded from the other side of the ridge, its long note drifting in the breeze, and Sebastian's head turned to its siren call. Luke almost saw the shrug of his shoulders inside the beautifully cut jacket. And then he was off, away over the brow of the hill, and far out of reach.

Luke buried his face in his hands. They were covered in mud and Cherry's blood.

He was completely alone. He couldn't go after the riders – they were on the other side of the river and he had no way to cross it. And by the time he had galloped back to the house to fetch someone she would be dead – if she wasn't already.

It was up to him.

He slid back down the bank, his fingers grabbing at roots and branches to stop his fall, and stumbled on to the little muddy shore where Rosa's body lay. Her face was utterly, starkly white. Her hat had gone and her wet red hair straggled loose across her shoulders, its fire doused.

'Rosa,' he said very softly, his voice hoarse and broken from his efforts to call Sebastian. 'Rosa, can you hear me?'

She said nothing – or nothing he could hear above the roar of the stream. But he thought he saw her ribcage move, and when he put his ear close to her face he realized she was breathing, or trying to. It was a horrible wet, bubbling sound, and as he drew back he saw there was blood on her lips.

'Oh Jesus.' He had never felt so helpless. He'd once watched a man drown in his own blood like this – a shiv between his ribs after a pub fight. And he'd felt a kind of detached sorrow. But it was nothing like this. The man had entered the fight of his own free will and lost. It was nothing to do with Luke. This – this was different. This was Rosa, dying in his arms, because of his actions.

Her breath bubbled again, poppy-red spatters on her blue lips.

What could he do? He searched his memory frantically – and a memory came – of Phoebe fainting in the bar one night and Miriam loosening her corsets to let her breathe.

He began to tear at Rosa's habit. It buttoned up the front – hundreds of damn slippery bone buttons that his cold fingers fumbled and lost. But at last he had it open – and as he peeled back the wet black layers his heart seemed to stop.

The snowy-white stock beneath was scarlet with blood.

Where was it coming from? He ripped at her blouse, his fingers wet now with her blood, small mother-of-pearl discs scattering into the mud. There was a silver locket, slick with blood and he pushed it roughly aside. Beneath her blouse was some kind of chemise – God damn it – why so many layers? At last beneath that was her corset. It fastened with hooks and eyes and tied at the top with a pitiful pink ribbon. The bow was soaked in blood.

He put his hand to the laces, ready to tug it apart – then he stopped. Somehow he couldn't bring himself to undo it. Her small white breasts rose and fell above the stiff edge, as she struggled painfully for breath, that horrible gargling sound bubbling inside her lungs. But all he could think of was her nakedness beneath – the violation of tearing apart her clothes as she died beneath his hands.

Don't be stupid, a voice snarled in his head. *Much she'll care about her virtue when she's as dead as her horse.*

He set his hands to the fastenings and wrenched them savagely apart.

What was beneath brought bile to the back of his throat and sent a cold rush of horror prickling across the back of his skull and down his spine. For a moment his vision seemed to fracture and break and he swallowed. The force of the fall had snapped one of the whalebones in her corset, and the sharp edge had stabbed clean through the fabric, puncturing the pink tender skin beneath, sliding between her ribs and into her lung.

As he watched, Rosa dragged another breath and blood and air bubbled from the wound.

This was completely beyond him. She was drowning in her own blood – and there was nothing he could do.

What have I done?

You did what you had to do, lad. And now it's over.

But it was not over. Not as long as she dragged breath after painful breath. Not as long as the blood bubbled at her lips.

He could finish it here. He could drive the whalebone home up into her heart. Then he could take the body back, his face wet with tears, and sob out his explanation: he told her not to go for the bridge, she wouldn't listen, she was mad to catch up . . .

But he couldn't. Crumpled white at his feet, her red hair trampled in the mud, she was no longer a witch but just a girl – a girl whose life was ebbing away as he watched.

He couldn't kill her – not now, not ever. He'd known that from the moment he plunged into the river in a desperate attempt to undo what he'd done. Perhaps even before that, in his heart of hearts. He'd pushed this far in spite of himself, in spite of his misgivings, in spite of the weight around his heart every time he thought of his task and her death.

He should have felt even heavier now – for if she did not die, then he must. If he saved her life he was only betraying his Brothers and condemning himself to death. He should have felt full of dread and horror at what was to come as he watched her chest rise and fall with every painful breath.

But he did not. He felt only a fierce determination that she would *not* die, not if his actions could save her.

'Rosa,' he said, though he did not know if she could hear. His voice was hoarse with tears and shouting. 'Rosa, can you hear me? This is going to hurt, but I'll get you out of here, I promise. And someone at the house'll be able to heal you.'

He put his hands beneath her armpits, the black habit gaping, and he heaved.

As her body slithered up the bank she gave a rattling gasp that might have been pain, or shock, or just the mechanical effect of her ribcage lifting with the pull.

'I'm sorry.' He gritted his teeth and pulled again, her body slipping up the rutted, muddy bank, her boots knocking against tree roots and stones. 'I'm sorry.'

At the top he laid her on the grass bank and put his forehead against hers, her cold flesh chill against his hot sweating skin.

For a minute he knelt there, feeling his heart pounding,

and the weak pointless tears scratching at the back of his eyes.

Then he put his arms around her, beneath her armpits and her knees, and very carefully, as carefully as he could, he picked her up, holding her against his chest, trying not to disturb the piece of whalebone sticking out of her lung. She was not heavy, in spite of the soaked habit that trailed on the grass. Without the drag of her soaked clothing she would have been no burden at all.

He began to walk, stumbling over tussocks and molehills.

'Don't die,' he found himself whispering in time with his trudging steps and thumping heart. 'Don't die. Don't die. Don't die.' Then, as he stumbled again, '*Damn.*'

What had he *done*?

Her cheek was cold against his chest – and he could not tell if her body was cooling, or if it was just the contrast with his own body, hot from toiling across the rutted field. He turned through the gap in the hedge into the lane where the going was easier, but he was panting now, his breath coming hoarse and hard, and Rosa felt twice as heavy as when he first pulled her into his arms.

'Don't die.'

Was she still breathing? There was fresh blood on her lips but that might just have dribbled out as he carried her. His heart was thumping so hard he could not feel any pulse from her.

'Don't die.'

Saints in heaven – how could he ever have thought she was light? His arms were ready to tear from their sockets. His legs felt like wool. He almost tripped as a rutted puddle barred the way across the road and the cold water soaked his legs, but he pushed on grimly. There was nothing else he could do.

'Don't die.'

At last – the gate into the Southing drive. He stumbled on to the gravel, crunching across the wide expanse in front of the house with legs that trembled and staggered up the steps to the drawing-room French windows, the closest entrance to the house. He had no hand free to pound on the glass so he kicked with his boots instead, pounding at the frame so that the doors shook against the wood.

'Let me in!' he bellowed. 'There's been an accident; she's dying.'

There was no answer. He had a sudden, horrible realization – the whole house was out hunting. The servants had all been despatched to take the hunt breakfast to the spinney. What if there was no one here?

'Open up!' Luke roared in despair. 'For the love of God, please, please somebody come and help me.'

And then he saw a figure making its way slowly across the drawing room.

'Open up!' he shouted. 'Hurry!'

It was a girl – one of the servants or one of the family, he couldn't tell, but why in God's name was she moving so slowly, so deliberately? She was picking her way through the furniture as if she was walking in a mist.

'Are you deaf?' he cried, his voice close to a sob. 'Open up, I said. It's Miss Greenwood, she's dying.'

'I'm not deaf.' He heard the voice through the glass as the girl reached him, her beautiful cornflower-blue eyes looking up at him as she struggled with the lock. 'I'm blind.'

The door gave and he stumbled into the room, muddy boots and bloody clothes leaving a trail of filth and blood on the Persian rug.

'What's happened to her?' the girl asked, her voice sharp. 'I can feel she's nearly gone.'

'She had—' Luke's voice stuck in his throat. How could he say *an accident*, when it was anything but?

He put Rosa down carefully on the chaise, her body a crumpled rag, her magic a thin wisp of flame so slight he could hardly tell it was there. The girl knelt beside the chair, her head bowed. Her fingers hovered over Rosa's face, touching her bruised blue skin, and then trailed down to where the whalebone stuck like a stiletto dagger between her ribs.

'Don't!' he gasped, as her fingers reached it, but she didn't falter, didn't jerk it or knock it, just felt very delicately around the wound, a frown between her narrow silver brows.

'This is very bad,' she said at last. 'It's beyond me. But the others are all out. The hunt . . .'

'I know,' he snapped. 'How d'you think this happened?'

209

The girl frowned again, then she seemed to make up her mind.

'There's nothing for it,' she said. 'I'll have to fetch Mama.'

The wait seemed endless. Luke knelt beside Rosa's body, listening to the water dripping slowly from her habit and the slow gasp and bubble of her breath. Each time she let go another painful breath he felt sure that it must be the last. No one could keep fighting against the inevitable like this. Each time the silence stretched a little longer. But every time, just as the despair rose in his chest, her ribs heaved up and another gurgling rasp came from her lips.

If he closed his eyes he could see the flame of her magic against his lids – like a candle in the darkness. It was low – so low he could hardly see it any longer. In his mind he cupped his hands around it, nursing it as he would have nursed an ember in the forge fire, blowing gently, keeping it from harm, until it had the power to flare up into the consuming blaze he knew it could be.

Another gasp.

And wait.

Another gasp.

And wait. And wait. And wait . . .

His fingers found hers, clenching them, willing her to keep going.

Her hand was cold.

Another gasp.

And then the door opened.

'Come inside, Mama,' he heard. 'You're quite safe.'

'No! I mustn't!' It was a hoarse, gasping whimper. 'Sebastian . . . Your father . . .'

'You're quite safe, Papa's not here. Nor is Sebastian – he's hunting.'

'They said I must not . . . They will take me back . . .'

'No they won't. I will have you back in your room and they will never know. Come now, just a few paces more. And look – here is the girl. You remember? The girl I told you about. She needs your help.'

Luke looked up. A woman was standing in the middle of the room. She was in her forties, perhaps. If this was Sebastian's mother she must have been a child when she had him – no older than Rosa. She was wearing a white nightgown spattered with the faint shadow of stains, carefully laundered but not quite removed. There were burn marks on her hands and arms, as if she'd held them over a candle, or scalded herself on a hot grate. Her black hair was wild and matted and hung round her thin white face. She must have been very beautiful once – she had the clear blue eyes of Sebastian and the blind girl.

Her magic was terrifying. A wild black blaze of hate.

'No . . .' She was shaking her head, even as the girl led her coaxingly across the floor. 'No, no, no, no, no . . .'

And then she saw Rosa and she stopped.

'See?' the girl said. 'This is why. You must heal her, Mama.'

Luke was shaking his head before he could stop himself, in an echo of the witch-woman's frightened repetitive denial. Nothing good could come from this woman – there was darkness in her face and in her magic.

'Listen . . .' He touched the girl's arm. 'This can't be right . . . Can't you—'

'No,' the girl said firmly. 'That's not my gift. I'm sorry. But I can see – I can see she will live. Mama will heal her. Mama . . .' She stroked her hands over her mother's hair and Luke saw the magic pouring from her fingers, soothing and gentling and coaxing along with her words. 'Mama, you can do this. Please. Please.'

'Did he do this?' the woman asked, her eyes wide and full of fear. For a moment Luke's heart froze – had she seen inside him so easily, read his mind? But the girl was shaking her head.

'It wasn't Sebastian, Mama. It was nothing to do with him. Just an accident. But please, Mama, hurry . . .'

The woman said nothing and Luke felt his fists clench. To have this power – and to refuse to use it . . .

'Please,' he said roughly.

He wasn't sure if she even heard him. She did not turn to look at him.

But then she spoke.

'*Lig biseach di.*'

The words were strange and hot and full of power – rolling off her tongue like boiling metal in the forge.

'*Lig di bheith ar aon léi féin.*'

Luke did not understand them – but he felt their heat as they passed, the scorching blaze of their power.

'*Lig biseach di.*'

The witch-woman put out her hands towards Rosa and he saw the power flooding out of her, like a river of dark fire. Rosa seemed bathed in it, consumed by it, burnt up by its brilliance.

The woman took a step forwards and then, with one swift horrible movement, she yanked at the whalebone, pulling the shard out from between Rosa's ribs so that the blood sprayed across the room in a shower of scarlet flame.

'*Suaimhneas ort!*' she screamed.

She staggered back, falling to the Persian rug, her hands over her face.

She's failed, Luke thought dully. *She's mad. She doesn't know what she's doing.*

And then . . . and then Rosa opened her eyes.

15

Luke stared down at her. She was lying on her back, the habit gaping open, and where the whalebone had been the skin was white and whole. Her ribs were streaked with blood, but there was no sign of the gaping bloody hole that had split the skin just a minute before.

For a minute Rosa looked from one face to another as if she were quite bewildered.

Her eyes dilated almost to black and then back to golden brown as they adjusted to the light in the room.

Then she coughed, spitting up blood on to the back of her hand.

'Cassie?' she managed croakily.

'Hello, Rosa.' Cassie smiled, her serious face suddenly transformed.

'Wh-who's this?' Rosa's eyes went from Cassie to the wild witch-woman and back.

'My mother,' Cassie said.

'Your *mother*?' Rosa pulled herself to sitting on the chaise. Then she looked down at herself and her pale skin flushed scarlet. 'Oh!'

For a moment she struggled, ineffectually trying to pull the two halves of her butchered corset back together. Then, as if a spell were broken, Luke remembered his manners and where he was and who he was supposed to be.

'H-here,' he stammered. 'Here, Miss G-Greenwood. Take my jacket.'

She took his jacket and clutched it to her breast, her cheeks flaming as red as her hair.

'You had an accident,' Cassie said. 'This man saved you – he carried you up to the house.'

'I remember . . .' Rosa said slowly. She put her hand to her head. 'I remember . . . We were on the bridge . . . the river . . . there was a cracking sound . . .' Then her hand flew to her mouth. 'Cherry!' She looked up at Luke and her eyes were wide and full of fear. 'Luke, where's Cherry? Is she all right?'

'I'm sorry . . .' His voice broke and he couldn't find the words to say anything else. He could only repeat the words, pathetically, pointlessly. 'I'm sorry. I'm sorry.'

She said nothing. But her eyes filled with tears.

'No . . .' was all she said. 'No.'

'I'm sorry, Rosa.' Cassie knelt by her side and took Rosa's muddy, bloodstained hand in her small white one. 'But you are alive – and you have Luke to thank for that.'

But Rosa was crying, great gulping sobs that seemed to be tearing her up from inside.

'I know I should be grateful,' she wept. 'I *am* grateful – but oh, Cherry!' She buried her face in her hands and he turned away. Luke swallowed, his throat sore and dry. It was more than he could bear.

A low moan came from behind him and he turned. It was the witch-woman, Cassie's mother. Cassie was on her feet and at her side in an instant.

'Mama?'

'Take me away . . . They're coming back.'

'Not yet, Mama.'

'Take me back upstairs!' Her voice rose to a kind of scream and Cassie jumped and turned her head nervously, as if listening out for servants or horses.

'All right, Mama, I'll take you.' She turned to Rosa. 'Can you manage for a moment, Rosa? My mother is not well, as you see.'

'Don't do it,' the witch-woman cried as Cassie led her from the room. 'I can see it in your heart – you will regret it for ever. Take the other path – that one will break you.'

Luke stared after her. Was she talking to him or Rosa?

Rosa watched her go too, her tear-stained face turned to the door long after Cassie and her mother had left. Then she turned back to Luke.

'How did she die?'

'One of the broken struts of the bridge through the heart,' he managed, though his throat was sore with grief. 'It was quick. She knew nothing.'

She pressed her lips together. Her face was very pale, the nutmeg dust freckles standing out against her skin. She closed her eyes, her lashes making dark circles against her cheeks, the tears squeezing out from beneath. Luke fought against the crazed impulse to take her in his arms as he had that night in the stable. But he had no right to comfort her – not just because of who he was, but because of what he'd done.

'P-perhaps it's b-better this way,' she managed at last. 'My first pony, Willowherb, when she grew old Alexis had her sold to the knacker's yard, to make meat for dogs. I wouldn't have wanted that for Cherry.'

'No,' he said. His voice was as rough and hoarse as hers, though his tears were unshed. 'No. She died quick. She died happy.'

Happy? He remembered Cherry's scream as she felt the boards going out from under her and he shut his own eyes, though nothing could shut out the memory of her skewered body and that terrible, whinnying shriek.

'She died happy,' he repeated, his voice hard with anger at himself, at the lies.

'You'd better see to your horse,' Rosa said. Luke looked out of the open French doors, to where Bumblebee was nibbling the Virginia creeper that twined around the windows. He must have followed them home. Luke should

217

have been relieved to see him, relieved that at least Bumblebee's safety wasn't on his conscience too. But he could feel no relief at all.

'Yes.' He rubbed his face. 'All right. And Brimstone'll be back by now, I shouldn't wonder. Mr Greenwood will be wondering where I am.'

'I wonder how long it will take him to notice his sister's absence,' Rosa said bitterly.

'Miss Greenwood . . .' he started. He didn't know what he was about to say. That she deserved better. That she didn't have to live this life, trapped by her mother's rapacious ambition and her brother's greed, despised by both of them. But it was not true. There was no escape for her, any more than for him. They were both trapped, each in their own cage.

'Yes?' She looked up at him from the sofa, her small, pale face spattered with mud and blood. Her golden-brown eyes were dull.

'Nothing.'

He turned to go.

'Wait.'

She had dragged herself to sitting. He stopped, his chest rising and falling as hers was too, beneath his wet, bloodstained coat.

'Yes?' he said, more harshly than he meant.

'I-I . . .' she stammered, and then stopped.

'What?'

He ought to be sacked for speaking to his mistress like

that – he would be, if anyone else heard. But she only shook her head angrily.

'Nothing.'

Then as he turned again to go, 'No, Luke, wait.'

She grabbed his shirt at his shoulder, pulling him down to her height, and he felt her lips, shockingly soft and warm against his cheek, and the slim strength of her arm around his neck in a fierce, almost angry embrace.

'Thank you,' she whispered, her breath hot against his ear. 'Thank you. I owe you my life. I will never forget that.'

She let go and he was left gasping, hot with desire and shame.

For witchcraft comes from lust, that carnal desire which in women is insatiable. He heard the words inside his head, as clear as if John Leadingham had spoken them, as he turned and stumbled out of the French doors and across the gravel drive.

Whose lust?

He thought of himself ripping open Rosa's clothes, trying not to look, yet looking even as he tried to turn away. Even as he retched at the sight of the whalebone slicing between her ribs, he had looked. He had not been able to help himself.

He did not look back to see if she were still watching him. He could not look back. He grabbed at Bumblebee's reins, and led him away.

Rosa watched Luke go and then she sank back on the sofa,

her head in her hands. She was tired to the bone. Every part of her ached with weariness. Somewhere beneath the exhaustion she knew that her clothes were covered in blood, that her good corset was butchered, that beneath Luke's jacket her breasts were bare. But she did not know if she had the energy to do anything about it. Now that Luke had gone none of it seemed to matter.

She knew she should feel shame at the thought of him pulling her from the river, pulling apart her clothes. But she didn't. She would be dead if he hadn't. So – he had seen her naked. That was the least of it. He had seen Sebastian's mother, full of madness. And he had watched her heal Rosa's wound in front of him. An outwith. And he had seen their power.

What had she done?

'Rosa?' The voice was soft.

Rosa's head jerked up. Cassandra was standing in the doorway, her face worried.

'Rosa, are you quite well?'

Rosa laughed. It sounded bitter in her own ears.

'Quite well. Quite well unless you count almost drowning beneath my horse. Quite well apart from being cold, wet and bloodstained.'

She shivered, and Cassie came across and took her hand.

'Your fingers are like ice.' She touched Rosa's forehead. 'Heavens! You have a fever. Let's get you upstairs and into bed.'

Rosa found she was very tired. Her legs shook as she stood.

'Yes please,' she said. Her voice was strange and far away. 'I would like that very much.'

'Rosa . . .' Cassie's voice was urgent in her ear as she helped Rosa stand. 'Rosa, you must never, never speak of what my mother did. Do you understand?'

'I . . .' Rosa found her head was swimming. This strangeness was too much. 'Why – why not?'

'Especially not to Sebastian. You must promise me you will never mention that you have seen her.'

'I promise.' Her head was aching and her knees shook as she stood upright. 'But, Cassie, why?'

But Cassie said nothing, and Rosa found that it took all her strength and concentration to put one foot in front of the other.

It was only later, much later, in her room that she closed her eyes on the pillow, and that strange gaunt face floated in front of her vision again. What was wrong with Cassie's mother? Was Sebastian so ashamed that he could not bear to have her talked about?

She was too exhausted to think about it for long. Instead she drifted into a troubled sleep, with dreams haunted by pounding hooves, Luke's sobbing pleas, and a strange wild-haired witch with Sebastian's eyes.

Luke was walking slowly back from the stables when he heard horses' hooves. He looked up. Alexis and Sebastian were trotting into the yard. When they saw Luke both changed direction to come across to him. Alexis had his crop in his hand, twitching against his thigh. Sebastian had a bloody fox foot dangling from his saddlebag. They were both keyed up from the hunt, full of triumph and arrogance and a sense of their own potency. Luke felt suddenly very weary with the knowledge of what was about to happen.

Every part of him hurt. His shoulder ached from where he had wrenched it trying to heave Cherry off Rosa's body. His back ached from carrying her all that long trek up to the house. Most of all his heart ached, at the knowledge of what he'd done, what he faced back in London . . .

He did not feel fear at the sight of Alexis and Sebastian – he felt only an intense weariness at the unjustness of it all. He could have killed Alexis. He could have killed him in cold blood and felt he'd done the world a service. He could have killed Sebastian – not with joy, but with a grim sense of right. Why couldn't he have drawn *their* names? Why Rosa and not them?

He turned away.

'Hi!' Alexis' shout rang across the yard. 'You. Where d'you think you're going, eh?'

Luke kept walking.

'I said *stop!*' Alexis bellowed furiously and, to his shock and fury, Luke felt his feet drag on the ground, as if invisible weights had suddenly attached themselves to his boots. He gritted his teeth and pulled against the heaviness – but

222

before he could free himself he heard Sebastian's low, angry, 'For God's sake, Greenwood.'

The pull loosed abruptly, but he would not give them the satisfaction of seeing him flee. Not now. He shoved his hands in his pockets and turned to face them.

'What the hell are you playing at?' Alexis snarled as Brimstone came level with Luke. He flicked out with his whip, catching Luke painfully across the ear. 'First you disappear from the hunt and then saunter back here like I've nothing better to do than wait on your convenience. Where the hell were you?' Luke bit his lip, and Alexis shouted out, '*Answer me,* damn you!' The crop flicked again and Luke felt a sting on his cheek. When he put his hand up there was blood.

'Saving your sister's life,' he ground out, hating them both with every ounce of flesh and blood and bone in his body.

'*What?*' It was Sebastian, not Alexis, who slid off his horse to stand level with Luke. 'What did you say?'

'You heard me. And you heard me on the ridge, didn't you? Calling?'

Sebastian went very still, as still as stone.

'That's right,' Luke said. 'I was calling for help. The bridge gave way. Cherry fell. She's dead, impaled on one of the bridge posts. Rosa was underneath when she fell.'

'My God.' There was no trace of emotion in Sebastian's face, his eyes were as dead and cold as ever they had been. But his face had gone white, with two spots of colour high

223

on the cheekbones. A splatter of mud stood out black against his pale skin. 'Is this true?'

'What d'you mean, saved her life?' Alexis blustered. 'Stood by while she scrambled out, I'll warrant. And she's Miss Greenwood to you, you lying—'

'Shut up,' Luke snarled. He didn't care if he was sacked. His mission was over. Everything was over. 'Speak to her yourself if you don't believe me.'

Then he walked away, trying to keep his breathing even and his fury inside. He half expected to hear hooves behind him and turn to meet Alexis' crop, or his fist. He half *wanted* to. It would have been a relief to draw back his fist and let fly – there would have been a grim satisfaction in hearing the smack of bone against bone.

But there was no sound. Only the crunch of gravel beneath his own feet until he reached the side door and was able to slip inside, out of sight. He walked slowly up the back stairs to his little room. Thank God it was empty. He lay face down on the thin horsehair mattress and the tears came at last.

Rosa opened her eyes. There was a tapping coming from somewhere. For a moment she was disoriented – quite unable to work out where she was. The room was warm and dim, full of looming shadows. Thick velvet drapes shut out the day and the only light was from the flicker of a log fire. There were goosefeather pillows beneath her cheek and a satin eiderdown across the bed.

Then she remembered. She was at Southing. Sebastian's house. Cherry was dead. And Luke had seen things no outwith should ever have witnessed.

She closed her eyes, shutting out the sight of Luke as she had left him, white and exhausted and shocked by all that had happened.

Then the tap came again.

'Come in,' she called.

The door opened and a small, pale face peered round.

'Cassie!' Rosa jumped out of bed and ran across the room. 'Thank you – oh, thank you. I never had the chance to say. Is your mother—'

'I haven't much time.' Cassie spoke quickly and quietly. 'I'm supposed to be practising the piano with my governess. It's about your groom . . .'

'Yes.'

'He's an outwith.' She said it flatly, not a question but a statement.

Rosa nodded, forgetting Cassandra couldn't see and then said hastily, 'I mean, yes. Yes he is.'

'And he saw Mama.'

'Yes.'

'Rosa – I wouldn't ask this if it were someone else – but Mama, she . . . she's not well.' She stopped, twisting a handkerchief in her small white fingers. 'No one must know what she did. No one must *ever* know – least of all Sebastian. We need to make Luke forget.'

Rosa said nothing. She bit her lip, thinking of Alexis and

Becky, thinking of the power they held over the outwiths who shared their lives.

'Do you understand what I'm saying?' Cassie asked.

'Yes,' Rosa said reluctantly. 'Yes, I understand. But, Cassie – what's wrong with her? Why mustn't Sebastian know?'

'She's mad. She's always been mad, since I was born. Since before, perhaps. They say she's dangerous – that she must be confined for her own safety. Father would be terribly angry if he knew that she had come down. Believe me, Rosa, you do not want to encounter my father's anger.'

Rosa bit her lip. She had seen Sebastian's fury. She could imagine his father's.

'But it's not just Mama,' Cassie pressed on. 'It's all of us. He knows. He has to un-know.'

'Yes,' Rosa whispered. It was not fair. Luke had saved her life and this was his reward – for her to reach inside his head and steal her memories. She had never wiped a memory before, but she had watched Alexis do it to Becky often enough. A cup of wine, steeped with rosemary for remembrance. The victim drank the wine, while you told them what you wanted them to forget, then whispered the incantation and burnt the herbs, burning away the memories.

'If Sebastian finds out what Luke saw – well, Luke's life wouldn't be worth a farthing. I have the wine,' she pulled a bottle out from a pocket in her skirts, 'but without sight I can't find him in the stables – and I doubt he would drink wine from a strange witch anyway.'

'No,' Rosa said. She gave a sigh as heavy as her heart. 'It must be me. I can see that.'

'And it must be tonight,' Cassie said. 'Are you strong enough?'

She didn't know.

It was dark when Rosa let herself out into the yard. She had waited until the house party was having dinner, the time when all guests and most of the servants would be safely occupied. A maid had bought her up a tray of suitably invalid food – creamed chicken, white bread, beef tea. It had taken only a moment to choke it down, put a locking spell on the door and creep out into the night with her oldest cloak covering her nightgown and her tell-tale hair.

Now, as she tiptoed across the moonlit stable yard, she wondered what she would do if Luke were not in the stables, if he had gone up to his room already, or into dinner. How would she find him in this huge, rambling warren of a house?

But when she opened the door to the stables he was there, wearily sweeping out Cherry's empty stall by the light of a storm-lantern hanging from the wall.

The sight brought tears rushing to the back of her throat and eyes, but she blinked them away angrily. She could not grieve for Cherry – not yet. When this was over, when she was back in London and could think again, perhaps. But not now.

'Luke,' she whispered.

He looked up and, for an instant, his expression was bewildered. Then he saw her looking round the stable door and his face became hard. He glanced left and right and hurried across.

'What are you doing here?' His voice was low and angry.

'I – I came to thank you.' It was true. It was not the whole truth. 'Can you talk?'

'No.' He glanced over his shoulder. 'You shouldn't be here, Miss Greenwood.'

'Please. I only want a moment. Come outside.'

He bit his lip and then gave a curt nod.

'Only for a moment.'

He took her wrist and they hurried out into the yard and round the corner of the stable block, where a row of disused pigsties sheltered them from view and cast a thick black shadow in the moonlight. They huddled against the wall at the back of the stables and Luke said, 'What? What is it? You know it'd be more than my place is worth if I were found here.'

'*Your* place?' Rosa found herself snapping. '*My* reputation, you mean. You're not the only one risking disgrace here.' Then she bit her lip. This was not how she had meant it to be. She had planned the conversation in her room – her whispered thanks, his manly protestations, the drink, the whispered words of the spell. Instead – acrimony and anger. She clenched the damp rosemary twigs in her left hand, the bottle in the other.

'I'm sorry,' she said. 'I . . . You saved my life. I couldn't just let you . . .'

'You couldn't let me be?' he said. His face in the moonlight was hard as stone. Why was he so angry?

'I couldn't let you walk away. What you did . . .' She swallowed. Why was this going so wrong? He stood silent, his arms crossed across his body, refusing to help her.

'I bought you this, to say thank you,' she said at last. She held out the bottle.

'What is it?' He took it, his face suspicious.

'Just wine. Wine and herbs. It's meant to stave off a cold.' The lies felt miserable and dark on her tongue. He had saved her life and she was repaying him with deception and spells. 'All that time in the river – I didn't want you to become ill on my account.'

He took it. Something in his expression softened slightly.

'Please,' she said. The deceit twisted inside her, like cramp. 'Please, won't you try it? I made it for you.'

He put his lips to the bottle. She held her breath. Then she saw his Adam's apple move as he swallowed, and she began to speak, the words tumbling over themselves.

'Luke, what you saw – Sebastian's mother, the way she healed me. You should never have seen that. I'm sorry – you were never meant to know. Please, forget it. Just forget it. I . . .'

She stopped. He had pulled the bottle away from his

lips, his eyes aghast. He looked down at the bottle and then back up at her.

'This is a spell, isn't it?'

'I—'

'You bitch.' He looked from the bottle in his shaking hand, up to her face.

'I – Luke—'

'Please.' He let the bottle fall to the ground with a smash and grabbed her with both hands, his fingers hard on the soft muscles of her upper arm. There was something desperate in his face. '*Please*, I'm begging you, don't do this.'

'Luke—'

'Rosa, *please*, if you've any gratitude at all, if you really meant one word of those thanks, *please* don't cast that spell. Don't take away my memories – you don't understand, you'll be condemning me to death.'

His grip on her was fierce, frantic. Rosa opened her mouth, but no words came. The smell of wine and rosemary on his breath and on the cobbles rose up, making her head swim. His grip was so tight it hurt. It came to her that they were alone, that no one would hear if she screamed. That she was weak from her near-death in the river, her magic a thin, poor thing against his strength. That men had killed for far, far less than this . . .

'Rosa?'

'All right,' she gasped. He let her go and she stumbled back against the wall, her breath coming fast.

'Thank you,' he said. He closed his eyes. His face in the moonlight was all shadows – unreadable in the darkness – but there was no mistaking the heartfelt gasping relief in his voice. 'Thank you, *thank you.*'

'But you must promise never to tell anyone, do you understand? It would mean my disgrace and perhaps your life, if they found out that you still knew.'

'I promise,' he said hoarsely. He slid down against the wall until he sat on the cobbled floor of the yard, his back against the soft crumbling brick of the stable wall. She sat down next to him in the deep shadow, feeling the warmth of his arm and shoulder close to hers and the chill of the night air on her other side. In the darkness she could hear his breathing above the quiet sounds of the night. It was fast and shaky, still recovering from his intense fear and panic. Then something struck her.

'Luke, how did you know?'

'Know what?'

'Know that the bottle was a spell.'

There was a long silence. Rosa began to wonder if he would answer her at all and whether she had been very stupid. Her fingers clenched around the rosemary twigs. It was not too late. If she burnt them now, spoke the incantation, she could still complete the spell. She could still take those memories . . .

'Because I see witches,' he said at last, his voice as low as if he were confessing a murder. 'I've always known. I can see magic, feel it, hear it.'

Shock rippled through her, hot and then cold. It was not possible. It was *not* possible.

'What do you mean?' She turned to face him in the darkness and conjured a frail witchlight on her palm to read his face. It took almost all her remaining magic, but she *had* to see him, to read his face. 'You mean you knew? You knew when you came to work for us that you were walking into a houseful of . . .' She paused, the word like a curse on her tongue.

'Witches? Yes.' His face in the witchlight was pale and tired, but his hazel eyes were dark. She stared at him. His eyes met hers and she finally understood. Understood his strange reticence, his wariness, his sense of holding himself apart. He *was* apart – he was neither witch nor outwith, but something in between.

'How?' she said at last. 'How did you know?'

'I can see,' he said simply. 'I can see the magic coming out of you.' He put his hand out, towards her face, and she thought for a moment that he would touch her but his fingers stopped, just inches from her skin, as if he was afraid she would burn him. 'They're all different. Every witch. Your brother's is green like his eyes, yellow when he's afraid. Knyvet's is black, like smoke.'

'And . . . and mine?'

'It's like a flame.' He let his hand drop and she fought the urge to reach out, run her fingers down the bridge of his nose, the curve of his cheekbone, touch the soft roughness of his beard. 'It's red-gold, like your hair. Like a halo. It's more beautiful than I could ever describe.'

Rosa swallowed. She tried to think straight.

'You know – you know there are those of my kind who'd kill you if they knew this.'

'I know.'

'So you have my secret . . . and I have yours.'

'Yes,' he said softly. His deep voice was low. 'We're equal.'

The clock struck with shocking suddenness in the still night air – nine loud chimes. Rosa stood up, her heart thudding hard.

'I must go. They will be coming out from dinner. I'm supposed to be in bed, convalescing from the fall.'

'Rosa . . .' He caught her wrist. 'Thank you.'

'No, thank you,' she whispered.

For a moment she stood, feeling his fingers on her wrist. His skin was as rough and hard as his grip was gentle. Then she tugged her wrist free and ran, pulling the cloak over her head. Two grooms were coming out of the stable block as she passed but neither cast a glance at the fleeing girl in the shabby cloak. She could have been a maid, or an errand girl, or a ghost.

16

Luke shivered in the shadows long after she was gone. The smell of the spilt wine filled the air, the stench of magic mingling with the fumes of alcohol and rosemary. He felt hot and cold with fear at the thought of all that she could have taken. Not just the memory of the river – but more, perhaps. The memory of why he was here. The memory of his task. And he would have known nothing until the Malleus came for him one night, with a knife between his ribs.

The thought was like a cold hand round his heart.

He could not kill Rosa. He knew that now. He was a coward, through and through.

One of them must die – but he could not kill her. It was as simple and as wretched as that. Which left – only him.

And so – what now? Back to Spitalfields?

It was unthinkable. What could he say when they asked him about his mission? I've decided not to do it. The girl was young and pretty. I didn't feel like it. I didn't have the guts.

How would they kill him? Would it be quick and kind or long and slow? Would it be a knife in a dark alley, like a thief in the night, or face to face in the meeting house, like an execution?

Without warning a picture came to him – of John Leadingham's abattoir, the bloodstained hooks and the hissing lamps. And himself, swinging from a hook, naked and gutted like a pig. He closed his eyes.

He had nowhere to go. He could not go home. He could not stay here. His first mission, and he had failed. He had betrayed the Brotherhood and failed in his oath. It was all her fault. He should hate her for it. And he could not.

Back in her room Rosa ripped off the cloak and stuffed it into the carved mahogany wardrobe. The hem of her nightgown was spattered with mud. She could not leave it like that for the maid to notice in the morning.

'*Ápierre!*' she whispered, rubbing her finger across the mud. Nothing happened. Her heart was too full of turmoil over what she had done, what she had not done. '*Ápierre!*' she hissed again, more forcefully. If only she had the grimoire, a proper spell instead of these half-remembered charms from her childhood. '*Ápierre! Bescréade!*'

She peered at the stains in the candlelight. Perhaps they looked a little better. Not perfect, but better. She climbed into bed and lay there, stiff and shivering beneath the starched sheets.

There was a gust of male laughter from some far distant corridor – Sebastian and his friends going to drink port or play billiards, no doubt.

Before she doused the candle she stared at the rosemary, lying soft and wine-draggled across her fingers. It was Luke's memories she held in the palm of her hand. What had made him so terrified to lose these last few weeks? She heard his voice again, the naked desperation as unmistakeable as his accent: *Don't take away my memories – you don't understand, you'll be condemning me to death.* He was telling the truth – she did not need a sooth-spell to be sure of that. But what could he possibly have done that would mean life or death?

The answer *must* be tangled up with the astonishing revelation he had made. A man who could see witchcraft, who could not just sense their power, but physically *see* it. She had never heard of *anyone* who could do this – let alone an outwith. Even the possibility was unthinkable – and she knew what Alexis would say if she told him. First he would not believe her, but if she eventually managed to convince him, Luke's life would not be worth a farthing.

She thought of the day she had first seen him, in the stables, with the setting sun streaming through the door and turning the dust motes and scraps of straw to flecks of gold that landed on the tanned skin of his arms, and the freckles on his face, and his gold-dark hair, illuminating them with glory.

She thought of him sitting next to her in the dark shadow of the pigsty, his face white and drawn in the thin, pale gleam of witchlight, his clear hazel eyes grown dark and afraid.

She could not betray him – even though her conscience told her that her loyalty should be to Alexis, Sebastian and her own kind. Even though he was just an outwith. Even though he was perhaps more dangerous than anyone could possibly know. She could still not betray him.

Rosa awoke to the sound of the breakfast gong, but for a few moments she just lay with her eyes closed, listening to the sounds of the house while the memories came slowly back.

Cherry.

The river.

Cassandra's mother.

Luke. *Luke.*

She opened her eyes. The rosemary twigs were still clutched in her hand, damp and limp with sweat. Carefully she uncurled her stiff fingers and laid the bundle on the polished wood of the bedside table. Then she swung her legs out of bed and found a handkerchief in the drawer of the dressing table by the window. She wrapped the twigs carefully in its linen folds and tucked it back in the drawer, between the layers of woollen stockings and petticoats. She would have to decide what to do with it.

Then the gong went again, the second bell, and she began pulling on her clothes. She was just doing up the last button on her boots when there was a tap on the door.

'Come in,' Rosa said.

It was a maid with a teapot on a tray.

'Oh, Miss Greenwood!' she cried as she saw Rosa bending to finish the last of her boot buttons. 'You shouldn't be up and about – I was to bring you up breakfast in bed.'

'Breakfast in bed!' Rosa nearly laughed. She had never had a breakfast tray in her life, except once when she was laid up with scarlet fever, and then it was only a bowl of gruel as befitted an invalid. Mama had breakfast in bed, of course, and had done for as long as Rosa could remember. But such luxuries were not for girls.

'Of course, Miss Cassandra told us about the accident and said you'd likely not be fit to come down until lunchtime, perhaps not then.'

'Well, I'm up now,' Rosa said. 'So never mind. I'll go down to the morning room with the others.'

'I only came up to see if you were awake yet and bring you your tea if you were. Oh, and to tell you there's a parcel arrived for you.'

'A parcel?' Rosa frowned. Who would be sending her a parcel, here? 'What kind of parcel?'

'A big one, miss. With a London postmark.'

'Do you think there's time for you to bring it up before the last breakfast gong?'

'Oh, bless you, miss, yes. The breakfast things will be out for an hour or more yet. Mr Sebastian never makes it down before ten, and we don't expect the house guests to tumble out of bed like ninepins. I'll bring it up in a trice and you can open it comfortably before you go down.'

Rosa had finished her tea by the time the girl came back with the parcel. It was, as she'd said, a big one. The box was too wide to go through the door sideways so the girl had to turn it on end. Then she laid it on the bed.

'Are you sure you wouldn't like to have a little something on a tray, Miss Greenwood? Some buttered toast, perhaps, or a soft-boiled egg.'

A soft-boiled egg? Rosa thought of the magnificent spread on the first morning – hot chafing dishes full of sausages, devilled kidneys and crisp bacon, scalding porridge with cream, piles of golden potato cakes and hot mushrooms swimming in butter and juice.

'No thank you, honestly—' She scrabbled for the girl's name but it didn't come. 'I'd just as soon go down. I promise I'll tell Miss Cassandra it was my own choice.'

'Very well, miss.' The girl bobbed a curtsey and left, and Rosa turned with greedy curiosity to the big box.

It was wrapped in brown paper and string, and sealed with red wax, but there was no sealing mark – just blobs on the knots – and the postmark was Piccadilly, which could have meant everything and nothing.

But as she tore back the paper a piece of card fell out. She picked it up, and letters began to appear, scrawling across the thick card in Clemency's large, looping hand.

From your fairy godmother, darling. You SHALL go to the ball.

Rosa held her breath as she pulled back the lid of the box. Beneath the ivory cardboard was more ivory, masses of it, like a frothing snowy sea. As she pulled it out the folds fell away and in her arms was a dress – not just a dress, the most beautiful dress she could have imagined. It was made of ivory silk embroidered with hundreds of tiny green leaves, twining and wreathing up the bodice, looping around the narrow waist, trailing in garlands down the flowing train.

'Oh, Clemmie!' Rosa whispered. She held the dress to her bosom. It was too beautiful to be hers. Writing began scrawling across the piece of card.

My dressmaker had your measurements from the habit and I couldn't resist – I knew when Philip mentioned a ball on the last night what your predicament would be. Please don't be angry! You can pay me back after you're married. Yours, with impudence and love, Clemmie.

P.S. Bonne chasse!

As she watched, the ink faded into the paper and the card was blank. Only the dress remained.

Rosa knew she should be angry with Clemency. And part of her was. But beneath that was a frothing, bubbling excitement. She *could* go to the ball. And with this dress, she need not spend all night trying to hold her gloves to cover the shabby, worn places, and stand to hide the spell-patched stains. In this dress she could dance, she could flirt. She could match any other woman in the room.

Bonne chasse, Clemency had written. Good hunting. Oh, Cherry . . .

'I told 'em,' the old man said sadly.

'What?' Luke raised his head and turned from scrubbing down Cherry's empty stall. His head felt dull and thick, as if he'd drunk too much gin the night before and overslept. In fact he'd drunk nothing but the mouthful of spell-soaked wine, and hardly slept at all.

'I told 'em about that bridge. And now a good 'orse is dead. How come ee didn't warn the lassie, eh? I tried to tell ee.'

Luke rubbed his face, trying to clear his head. He'd been expecting the question. Thank God the old man had chosen to ask it when they were alone in the stables.

'I did tell her,' he said, the lie black and bitter on his tongue. 'I called out. But she was ahead of me and I couldn't make her hear.'

The old man sighed and shook his head.

'Ah, that sounds right enough. These young ladies, 'eadstrong they is. Not like in my day. You wouldn'ta caught a young lady hunting back then. They're not strong enough for it. Well, thank the blessed Lord twas only a horse died, and not the young lady. Back to Lunnon town tomorrer, eh? You'll be glad to be back on your own turf again, I'll be bound.'

Luke nodded, but his heart felt anything but glad. He had spent the night trying to think of a way out of this trap. He could not go back to Spitalfields – not without Rosa's blood on his hands. Could he stay in Knightsbridge, with the family, somehow? But the Malleus would come looking for him; he would be found and killed.

Which left only one option: flight. He would have to run away, never to see Spitalfields again. Never to see William, or Minna, or any of his friends. Never to be a Brother in the Malleus. He would spend his life on the road looking behind him, over his shoulder, waiting for the knife, the rope, the hand in the dark.

And Rosa. She would stay. Would they come for her too? He didn't know. Her name had been chosen, which meant that she had to die. The thought gave him a strange cold pang deep in his chest. *She's a witch*, he told himself savagely. *She can take care of herself.*

But the picture that floated before his eyes in the dim warmth of the stable was just a girl, a girl with no inkling that she was doomed.

'Best look sharp now,' the old man was saying. 'The first of the carridges'll be arriving soon and they'll be wanting that stall.'

'Carriages?' Luke said stupidly. 'What carriages?'

'What carridges!' The old man laughed, but kindly. 'What carridges, he arsts, as if he's been in Timbuktoo the

242

great while. Why, there's a ball tonight. The Knyvets allus throw a great ball the last night of the house party, and then they returns to London for the rest of the season. It's the finest thing for miles around, and the great lords and ladies come from all over the county, aye, and from London too.'

'They're saying summat else too, tonight,' came a voice from over their shoulders, and turning Luke saw a tall cheerful lad that he half recognized from the servants' hall. He searched his memory for a name; it didn't come, but he remembered who the lad was: Knyvet's groom.

'Wassat then, young Wilkes?' said the old man.

'They're saying in the servants' hall as there'll be an engagement announced.'

'An engagement?' Luke said sharply. He didn't know why the suggestion hurt like a hot coal.

'Aye. Seemingly Mr Sebastian sent down to the safe for his grandmother's engagement ring. An' I don't suppose he wants it for his own finger.'

They laughed together, Wilkes and the old man, companionable and low.

'Who's it for?' Luke's grip was hard on the shaft of the broom, until he felt it might snap between his fingers.

'Who's the lucky girl, you mean?' Wilkes said. The laughter was still in his eyes as he answered. 'Well, that'd be telling. But there's nothing like a scrape with the hereafter to make a chap realize how much he values a lady.'

243

'And who says she'll say yes?' Luke demanded. He knew that his voice was full of an anger they'd never understand, that his face was stiff with a fury he had no right and no reason to feel.

'Who says she'll accept?' Wilkes' round pleasant face was astonished. 'Well, man, I dare say your young miss is very pretty an' all, but you don't have to be the sharpest tool in the box to see that her family's on its uppers. Why d'you think she's been sent here like a bait on a string, if not to catch a fish?'

Something welled up inside Luke, hot as molten iron, scalding inside his chest and his gullet and his skull, until he felt he'd run mad with it.

He tried to speak, but no words came. Instead he let the broom fall to the floor and ran from the stable.

'*How* tight did you say you laced, miss?' the maid asked again.

'Eighteen inches,' Rosa said. Mary shook her head.

'Well, I'm sorry, miss, but the dress won't fasten. It must have been made for seventeen.'

Damn it. Damn Clemency and her fashionable notions. She *must* squeeze into the dress. She had no other.

'Very well. Seventeen.'

She shrugged her way out of the dress and Mary undid the corset laces and began to pull again. Rosa shut her eyes.

'Hold on to the bedpost, miss.'

Rosa gripped the polished mahogany, feeling the

intricate carvings dig into her fingers as she clutched the post for support. She held her breath, feeling the bones dig, and dig . . . Her rib where the corset bone had gone in gave a sharp twinge and she almost cried out.

Then Mary gave an exclamation and let go.

'It's done.' She put a tape around Rosa's waist and said with satisfaction, 'Seventeen and one eighth. Will you try the dress again, miss?'

Rosa stepped into it and stood before the glass, feeling Mary's fingers at her spine as she fastened the dozens and dozens of tiny buttons, one after another.

'Perfect,' Mary breathed at last, and Rosa looked down at herself and then into the mirror.

She hardly recognized herself. The dress fell away in stiff folds that made her look taller, and above the full flowing mass of ivory and green her waist looked impossibly small, even smaller than she would have believed herself, in spite of the pain in her hips and ribs. The neckline was demure – but it dipped ever so slightly in the centre and her breasts, compressed by the tight corset, swelled above, looking whiter than white against the ivory silk and dark-green embroidery.

Mary had put her hair up and dressed it with real leaves – ivy and yew, the same deep winter green as the embroidered vines on her dress.

'And what about your jewels, miss? That locket's pretty enough but . . .'

'I have none,' she said honestly. Mary smiled over her

245

shoulder at Rosa's reflection in the mirror.

'For another young lady I should say, what a shame, but for you, miss, tonight, you have no need of them.'

'Thank you,' Rosa whispered. She swallowed.

'And anyway,' Mary lowered her voice, and her eyes were suddenly alight with mischief, 'if the gossip in the servants' hall is right, after tonight, you may have one jewel at least.'

'What do you mean?' Rosa turned to frown at her. 'What kind of jewel?'

'A ring,' Mary said. Her cheeks dimpled in a smile and then she bobbed a curtsey. 'Now, if you'll excuse me, miss, I've still to see Miss Cassandra and Miss Restorick up the corridor. Will there be anything else?'

For a moment Rosa could not find her voice; she only stood, with her hand gripped on the locket, her thoughts whirling and tumbling like a flock of crows in the sky. Then she remembered the maid's question.

'No, thank you, Mary,' she said. Her voice was low.

After Mary left, Rosa sank to the bed. Her face in the tall glass was white as chalk, her eyes dark and huge against the pale skin. For a moment she could hardly breathe – she thought she might faint, and she almost pulled the bell to call Mary back to loosen her corset and give her some air.

Then her hammering heart began to slow and the colour crept back into her cheeks.

Was it true? *Could* it be true?

Tonight. Everything Mama and Alexis had fought for –

everything could be achieved, tonight, if Sebastian asked just one simple question and she said one single word in reply: yes.

Suddenly she knew she was about to be sick. She ran to the washstand and stood, her hands splayed on the wood either side of the basin, her forehead prickling and wet with sweat. Her stomach heaved against the tight constriction of the corset and she choked, but nothing came up. It was hours since she had eaten. There was nothing to vomit.

The mirror above the washstand reflected back a stranger with dark, frightened eyes.

She knew what Mama would say: *This is normal. It's normal to feel nervous. This is the biggest decision of a woman's life.*

Perhaps it was normal to feel nervous. But was it normal to feel afraid?

17

'Miss Rosa Greenwood!' The announcement rang out across the crowded ballroom, but no heads turned. Rosa swallowed and looked out across the throng.

She had never seen so many fashionable men and women in one room. They made a sea of bodies – the men dark as crows in their evening dress, the women kingfisher-bright in silk and satin. Jewels flashed in the light from the chandeliers: diamonds, rubies, emeralds; the thousand candles making white shoulders and throats seem whiter still.

Then she heard the doors open behind her – another couple was about to be announced. She could not stand here on the steps all day, waiting for a miracle, waiting for the courage to go down alone and unchaperoned into the melee.

The band struck up again. Rosa drew a deep breath, touched her fingers to her locket, and began to descend the marble steps.

At the bottom she stood for a moment, hesitating, listening to the ebb and sway of the music, and the butler calling out 'Lord and Lady Hellingdon!'

There was the sound of shoes on the steps behind her.

What should she do? There were girls crowding around the tables to her left, champagne glasses in gloved hands, laughing and chatting. They all seemed to know each other. To the right were a group of bachelors coming in from the terrace, still smelling of cigar smoke. In the middle of the room couples swayed and turned with faultless elegance and Rosa realized with a sinking feeling that she did not know the dances. Papa had waltzed her around the drawing room as a little girl, but that was different – nursery dancing, just the two of them as he hummed the music through his moustache and she stood on his feet and clutched at his waistcoat and watch-chain. This rigidly correct synchronicity was something quite different – dozens of couples moving as one in time to a tune she did not recognize.

Her stays felt suddenly painfully tight. She could not breathe. She closed her eyes, counting to ten. *One. Two. When I open them it will be all right. Three. Four. Five. It will be quite all right. Six. Seven. Eight. Pull yourself together. Nine—*

'Miss Greenwood!'

She opened her eyes. For a moment the blaze of light from the chandeliers dazzled and she blinked. Then her eyes adjusted and she recognized the young man standing before her: it was the rider who had complimented her on the morning of the hunt, who had compared her to a centaur and said she had the best seat he had ever seen.

He looked different out of his hunting clothes – younger, his face pale against the dark tailcoat, his eyes so dark the pupils and iris merged into one.

'Miss Greenwood, you look pale. Are you quite well? Do you need me to escort you to a seat?'

'No, no.' Rosa took a deep breath. 'I was just – it was a moment's foolishness. But forgive me, I don't believe I know your name.'

'Rokewood. Abelard Rokewood.'

'Mr Rokewood. I'm so pleased to meet you again.'

'If you are sure that you are quite well—'

'I'm sure,' she cut in hastily.

'Then won't you grant me this dance?' He held out a hand to her. Rosa lifted her own gloved fingers to his and smiled.

'I would be—'

'I regret,' a voice cut in, and they both turned, 'that will not be possible. Miss Greenwood is promised to me.'

It was Sebastian. Her heart gave a strange little skipping beat at the sight of him. If Mr Rokewood looked younger in evening clothes, then Sebastian looked older. Perhaps she had grown used to the Sebastian she encountered out riding – this Sebastian was different. His face above the snowy-white cravat and coal-black tailcoat was severely handsome, and his eyes looked bluer than ever, blazingly blue, the pupils pricks of darkness in their arctic cold. His dark-blond hair had been cropped close to his skull.

Mr Rokewood let his hand drop and Sebastian put out his own, and took Rosa's outstretched fingers. He bowed his head, kissing her gloved knuckles and, as before, she felt his fingers graze the soft naked skin at the inside of her wrist, where the glove button gaped. The touch sent a shiver through her, a mingled coldness and heat that went deep inside, to her core. When his eyes met hers, she could not look away.

'Rosa, may I have this dance?'

'I . . .' She swallowed. It was hot in the ballroom and her cheeks flushed. She felt fierce and afraid all at the same time. 'Mr Rokewood . . .'

'Not at all.' The young man gave a rueful laugh and shook his head. 'Had I known you were promised for this dance I would never have presumed. Perhaps later, Miss Greenwood?'

'Miss Greenwood has promised *all* her dances to me, is that not right?' Sebastian looked at her, and his lips curved in a perfect smile, his rare true smile that could pierce to the heart.

'I . . .' Rosa said again.

Mr Rokewood gave a bow.

'In that case there is nothing for me to do but beg your pardon, Miss Greenwood. And congratulate Mr Knyvet on his good fortune, of course.'

'I'm sorry,' Rosa said. But he was already gone, disappearing into the thick crowd, one tall dark stranger among a hundred others.

Sebastian took her hand.

'Rosa, I'm sorry for being so high-handed. But I couldn't help myself. Perhaps it was realizing how close I came to losing you at the hunt. Will you grant me this dance?'

She hesitated. In her head she could hear Mama and Clemency and Alexis all hissing *Yes!* like a ghostly chorus.

And then she thought of kind Mr Rokewood, with his rueful smile and soft dark eyes.

Another voice inside her, she was not sure whose, whispered, *How dare Sebastian?*

Perhaps Sebastian read the struggle in her eyes, for his face softened and he said, very humbly, 'Please, Rosa?'

She felt again that strange, pummelled, tumbled feeling that Sebastian gave her, as if she had been battered tender by a great fall, as if her bones and muscles had been shaken sore and soft.

'Yes,' she said at last.

He nodded, but he did not lead her on to the dance floor. Instead he stood, searching her face with his eyes, as if looking for something.

'What is it?' she asked at last. There was something discomforting about his gaze. It made her feel exposed, almost dissected.

'I heard what happened.'

'Cherry is dead.' Rosa felt the grief rise in her throat, choking her, but she swallowed it back. She would not cry – not here, not in front of Sebastian.

'I don't give a damn about Cherry. *You*.' His fingers tightened on hers, fingers that could curb a horse, restrain a dog, that could hurt as well as caress. 'I blame myself. I should have seen you had a proper escort, not that fool of an outwith.'

'It wasn't his fault—'

'No. It was mine. You should have had someone who knew the lie of the land, knew that bridge wasn't safe, someone with the power to protect you.'

'Luke rescued me—'

'It was sheer luck! What if it had been worse? What if you'd been seriously hurt? What could he have done without magic, without any power to help?'

Rosa bit her lip.

'Sebastian, you're hurting me.'

'I'm sorry.' He released his grip. 'I was just . . . *Please* be more careful, Rosa. You ride as if you were immortal. Don't you fear anything?'

'Of course I do!' The words came before she had considered them.

'Really? What?'

A thousand answers hovered on Rosa's tongue. Alex in a temper. The flat of Mama's hand. Losing Matchenham. Being alone.

You, she thought.

Instead the words came unbidden to her tongue, almost a surprise to herself, even as her hand went to touch the locket at her throat.

'Losing the ones I love.'

'And who do you love?'

'Cherry. My father.'

'They are gone,' he said, his voice brutal in its casual statement of the truth. 'Who do you love now?'

She knew she should say Mama, Alexis . . . She set her jaw.

'I love them still.'

'You cannot cling to the past, to death.'

They were at the edge of the dance floor and, as the first notes of the next dance rang out, he took her hand, guiding it to his shoulder, and touched her, very lightly, at the waist.

'Sebastian – I don't know the steps.'

'This is a waltz. You *must* know how to waltz, don't you?'

'I've never learnt,' she said desperately.

'Don't worry, I'll guide you. Follow my lead.'

He was as good as his word. As the music swelled out, Rosa felt him grip her, with that lean deceptive strength hidden beneath his faultlessly tailored evening dress. And his magic gripped her too.

'What are you doing?' she whispered as she felt her feet begin to move, irresistibly, in time with the music.

'They are all our kind,' he whispered back. 'Not an

outwith in the room, I promise. Stop fighting me, Rosa. Trust yourself to me.'

She thought of Luke, of his rough cockney voice, close to her in the darkness, describing Sebastian's magic.

Knyvet's is black, like smoke.

She imagined his magic swirling around, encompassing them both, twisting her and turning her to the sound of the music, mingling with her own red-gold fire into a blaze that would engulf her.

'Rosa, you are magnificent.' Sebastian's voice, close to her ear. His hand on her waist, guiding her, until she could almost believe him. She *could* do this. She could.

She closed her eye and let the music consume her along with his will, giving herself to the dance and Sebastian's arms.

As the waltz ended on a last triumphant chord he pulled her close and she felt the lean, hard strength of his muscles beneath the evening jacket. His lapel was silk-smooth against her cheek and she breathed the scent of him – the spice of cologne and the bitterness of smoke. The last strains of the music faded and she waited for the hubbub of voices to take its place – but there was nothing, only the sound of her own fast breathing and Sebastian's heart.

Rosa opened her eyes, wondering how the room had become so silent, so fast.

They were not in the ballroom.

They were in the conservatory at the back of the house. There was no way they could have danced there. Sebastian must have used his magic to take them there and she had not even noticed. Rosa pulled back from his grip. She shivered at the sudden realization of his power.

'Why are we here?' she whispered. Her voice was loud in the silence, echoing off the vaulted glass ceiling. 'Why have you brought me here?'

The room was in darkness, save for the light from the stars above them showing through the glass roof and the cold white moonlight. The moon was almost full, and its beam made strange shadows of the palms and exotic plants, turning the stone-flagged floor into a maze of black and white stripes and shards. They were quite alone. Faint, faint strains of music drifted from the faraway ballroom. There was no one who would hear her if she cried out.

'Don't look so frightened,' Sebastian said. His face was pale in the darkness, the shadows beneath his cheekbones sharp and stark. He smiled. 'You look at me as if I were a wolf sometimes, Rosa, and you Little Red Riding Hood. I won't eat you, you know.'

His fingers were cold and very strong.

'Rosa, I brought you here because something happened this weekend. When I heard news of your accident I realized – I couldn't . . .' He stopped and swallowed. Rosa held her breath. This was not the Sebastian she knew, the smooth, polished Sebastian carved of marble. It was a strange, new, hesitant Sebastian, whose fingers gripped hers with painful intensity.

'I love you, Rosa,' he said. He looked up at her, his blue

eyes almost as pale as his face. 'I realize that now. I cannot lose you. I *will* not lose you. Rosa . . .'

He knelt on the stone flags. His hair in the moonlight was almost white, ash white. Rosa's heart began to beat very hard and very fast. *This is it*, she thought. *Dear God.*

'Rosa Greenwood, will you marry me?'

For better.

For worse.

Matchenham.

Freedom.

Oh God.

Silence. Silence apart from her beating heart and shuddering breath. Sebastian said nothing, he only knelt, his head bowed submissively, waiting for her answer. Rosa hoped for him to say something – as if his reaction would give her a clue about what to do. But he said nothing. There was no way out.

'I . . .' Rosa whispered. 'I don't – I . . .'

Sebastian did not move. She clenched her hands, trying to stop herself from trembling. She had no idea what to say – no idea what to do.

Then she heard a voice, her own voice. It shook.

'Yes.' Her lips were numb, stiff. 'Yes, I will marry you.'

He rose up, his arms around her. His face was fierce and pale and, for a moment, she was afraid that her fear was so obvious that it had angered him, that he knew the battle that had been raging inside her and was hurt, or furious.

Then he kissed her with a fierce delight, his lips burning

against hers, and she realized that it was *because* of her hesitancy that he wanted her so, that it was her fear and reluctance that excited him, that her uncertainty only made his determination stronger. *There is no chase if the fox does not run.*

She had said yes. She had said *yes*.

The word pounded inside her and she felt her mouth open to his. His hands were hard and strong against her waist and the back of her skull, holding her so that she could not turn away from him, so that her mouth and body was crushed against his.

'Oh, Rosa, my darling.'

He was stronger than her. Far, far stronger.

His lips against hers, his teeth.

Oh God, what had she done?

A cloud drifted across the moon and they were alone, in darkness, his hands upon her body, around her waist. She felt his fingers graze the nape of her neck where the skin was bare and she shivered with something that could have been desire, or fear. Was this love? How could she know? She thought of kisses in novels, how the girls grew weak and shook with longing. She felt weak. She felt powerless. But it did not feel like love.

At last he pulled back, his blue eyes blazing with a fierce, cold desire.

'We will tell them tonight. Let's go and announce it now.'

He took her wrist and turned for the door.

'No!' she blurted, without stopping to think of a reason. It was only when he stopped and turned, one eyebrow raised, his expression hard as stone, that she groped for an excuse. 'I – I have to tell Mama first. Please. It, it wouldn't be right to announce it like this, before she knew.'

Sebastian only stood, his face impassive, like a statue in the moonlight. What was he thinking? She couldn't read him – Alexis was like a book, his moods written on his face in shades of scarlet and puce. Sebastian was a mystery – as cold as ice. She saw only her own panic reflected in his pale eyes.

At last he spoke.

'You're right of course.' He kissed her gloved hand. 'But I don't know how I will wait. You're mine now, and I want to shout it from the rooftops. Is that so wrong?'

He smiled, but there was no answering warmth in Rosa's heart.

I am not yours, she thought. *I am my own.*

But of course that was not true. Married women were barely people at all – by law she would become one with Sebastian; all her property and money, would pass to him, even the least of her possessions. Everything that she had would become his. Nothing would belong to her, except by his gift. Not even her own body.

You have nothing anyway. No property. No assets. Mama said it herself – you have nothing but breeding and beauty. And what are those worth to you? Nothing. You are nothing.

Rosa felt her breathing become quick and shallow, and

there were spots of flaming light in her vision, bright pin-pricks in the darkness.

'Excuse me,' she gasped. She groped for a bench and sat, her head bowed towards her lap as Mama had taught her, waiting for the moment to pass.

'Rosa, darling.' Sebastian sat solicitously beside her. 'Can I fetch you anything? Water? Brandy? There will be salts somewhere; let me ring for a maid.'

'No, please!' she managed. 'It's nothing, truly.' She raised her head and tried to smile, tried to act like a girl who had just got engaged.

'You are pale as death. A white rose, not the red one I have grown to love.' He touched her cheek gently. 'But wait – there's one thing you must let me do.'

From his pocket, Sebastian took a handkerchief and unwrapped it, slowly. For a moment Rosa couldn't think what he was about to do – wipe her eyes? She wasn't crying. She had cried for Papa, and Cherry. But she would not cry for this. Not in front of Sebastian.

Then a flash of fire told her what was to come and her heart seemed to clench and miss a beat.

'This was my grandmother's . . .' Sebastian held it out, a great ruby, its smouldering heart like a dying ember, its fire dimmed but not quite extinguished by the cold glimmering moonlight. 'May I?'

She nodded and he pulled off her glove, leaving her skin bare to his touch, and slid the ring on to the third finger of her left hand. It hung loose for a moment, until

Sebastian whispered a charm. Then it tightened, tightened, and then just as Rosa was about to panic and rip it from her finger, it stopped. She felt the cold metal digging into her skin.

Sebastian touched it gently, twisting it around her finger until the jewel was centred.

'*Léohtfœtels-ábíed*,' he whispered, and a bright witchlight ignited in his palm, making the ruby's fire blaze out in the darkness.

'It's beautiful,' he said, and he kissed her hand and then her arm, her throat, the soft hollow beneath her ear, the dip of her collarbone where the silver chain of the locket pooled. 'As beautiful as you. And as full of fire.'

She did not feel full of fire. She felt cold, as cold as his lips, tracing across her skin, making her heart race.

'Sebastian . . .' she said huskily.

'I love my name on your lips.' His lips dipped to the edge of her corset, where her breasts swelled above the stiff boards. 'It sounds like a plea.'

Suddenly she could bear it no longer.

'Stop!' She pulled free and stood, her heart beating sickeningly fast, her breath coming quick. 'Please, if someone saw . . .'

'What?' A smile quirked his pale lips, paler still in the witchlight's glow. 'I would have to marry you?'

'Please, Sebastian.'

'I'm sorry.' He took her hand, pressed his lips to her ungloved knuckles and the ring. 'Your innocence is part of

261

what I love about you, but I forget you're only sixteen. Shall we go back to the ballroom?'

'N-no. I need . . .' She stopped. Her breath was coming quick and shallow, her chest rising and falling above the corset. 'I'm sorry, Sebastian. I need . . .' She searched for an escape. Inspiration came at last. 'I must get a wrap. I'm cold.'

'Let me send a maid.' He stood and moved towards the bell.

'No, truly.' She moved quickly to the exit, putting herself between him and the bell. 'I'd prefer to go myself. Anyway, in truth I need a moment to recover. It's not every day . . .' The coldness washed over her again, threatening to overwhelm her, but she forced herself on. 'It's not every day one gets engaged. I will come back, I promise. But I need a moment to myself. And I'd like to write to Mama. Please?'

He looked at her for a moment, quietly, speculatively, and she realized that, without intending to, she had asked for his permission and in doing so she had given him the right to refuse.

She opened her mouth. The word *please* hovered once more on her lips.

I will not beg.

'Of course,' he said at last, with just enough pause to force home the fact that he could have said no. 'Of course, my darling. Only, don't be too long. I can't bear to be apart from you for too long. Not tonight.'

'I will hurry back,' she promised. 'You go, back to the ballroom. People will be wondering where you are. Our absence mustn't cause talk – not yet.'

'Very well. But I shall expect you at the supper table and I shall come to find you if you're not back by then.' He kissed her again, softly, tenderly, and then closed his fingers, extinguishing the witchlight in his palm, and turned to leave.

The darkness drifted back.

The smell of smoke hung in the air long after he was gone.

18

The night air was cold as Luke walked across the darkened yard and so fresh he could taste its clearness on his tongue, like water. Above him the sky was speckled with an impossible number of stars; not the few dozen that managed to pierce the London smog on clear nights, but a hundred thousand more, like a drift of white sparks dwindling into the darkness. They were myriad, uncountable. How had he not known they were there, behind the smoke and clouds?

And yet he missed London – in all its sooty, dirty glory. Here there was nothing *but* the stars, and the moon like a great white lantern. In London the moon would have been a sickly yellow thing, if its light had pierced the smog, but there were other lights to guide you. The flaming warmth of braziers at street corners, roasting chestnuts and apples. The packing fires lit by the homeless drunks, too debauched for the workhouse, who clustered around the markets, scrounging the rotten food and the waste to make a life in the narrow streets and homes in the sooty arches beneath the railway.

Where there was life and people there was light and warmth – even in the meanest hovel. Somehow they would find the means for a fire, the tallow for a candle. Here there was nothing but the cold, dead light of stars and moon and, bright though it was, there was no life at all in its beam, and no warmth either.

He sighed, his breath a cloud of white in the moonlight. He had come out here to clear his head, to try to think what to do, away from the clamour of the servants' hall and the good-natured teasing of the other stable-hands and the housemaids' chatter. But he was no closer to deciding. If there was an answer, it was not out here, in the darkness. Perhaps it lay back in London. Well, if so, he'd find out tomorrow, for better or for worse.

He turned, intending to cut back past the stable block and in by the side door, slip away to his room before anyone could draw him back into the throng. But then he heard a sound coming from the stable block. It sounded like a sob.

For a moment he hesitated. It was none of his business. Whoever was there had chosen to be alone. But then came a low whinny and it sounded like Brimstone. He turned back. He'd just check that whoever was there wasn't harming the horses, just peer through the door, and then he'd leave them alone.

The door was ajar and he stood outside for a moment,

holding his breath and letting his eyes adjust to the darkness within. At first he could see nothing and then he caught sight of a white shape, like a ghost, huddled on the floor of Cherry's stall. It was a girl. Her hands were over her face, but he would have known her anywhere, by the wild red hair that tangled down her throat and the glowing flame of her magic, hot with agony.

He must have made a sound – perhaps the door creaked – because all of a sudden she leapt up, her face wild and white with fear, and then she saw him and it changed to something like fury.

'What are you doing here? Were you spying?'

'Spying?' He was taken aback by her anger, but he took a step forwards into the darkness of the stall. 'No, I was coming to check on the horses. What are *you* doing here? Why are you crying?'

'Leave me alone.' She went to push past him towards the door, her ungloved hand against his chest, and suddenly he saw it, a flash of fire in the darkness. Before he could think, he'd caught her wrist.

'What's this?' He turned her knuckles to the light. The ring glowed like an ember on the third finger of her left hand and a great wash of coldness came over him. She'd done it, she'd accepted him, she was lost. 'Rosa . . .' It was like a pain in his chest, as if something were twisting, bending, breaking. 'Rosa, *no.*'

'What business is it of yours?' She wrenched back her hand, her face pale with anger. 'How dare you!'

'You're marrying a man you hate and fear.'

'It's nothing to do with you.'

'I saved your life!' There was a catch in his voice and he hated himself for it. 'Doesn't that mean anything?'

'Of course it does.' Her voice was low and he heard the shake in it. 'But it doesn't give you the right to dictate what I do.'

'No. You're giving that right to Knyvet instead. For God's sake, Rosa, don't do it. He'll break you.'

Take the other path – that one will break you. He heard it again in the witch-woman's mad shrieking voice.

'Do you understand?' He touched her hand, where the ruby burnt. 'He will beat you and break you like he beats his dogs and his horses.'

'You don't know anything about it.' She looked up at him and her eyes were full of a weary self-hatred that made him flinch. 'There's no other way. If I don't accept him, my life won't be worth living anyway. Mama and Alexis will make sure of that. I was sent here to snare him – he can save Matchenham and get Alexis a place at the Ealdwitan—'

'Why should you care about Alexis?' Luke cried. 'He's a man! He can make his own way in the world – what kind of man sells his own sister to buy himself a short-cut?'

She didn't answer that, but set her jaw.

'I will not see Matchenham sold. I *can't*. It would break my heart.'

'It's just a house, Rosa. As long as you've a roof over

your head and food on the table, what does it matter where it is?'

'It matters to me!' she cried. 'Everything I ever loved, anyone who ever loved me – Cherry, Papa – they were all there. And they've gone, and all I have left is Papa's house, the bricks and stones and timbers. What kind of daughter would I be if I let it all go when I could save it?'

'But if Knyvet buys it back for you, it won't be yours, it will be *his*. And so will you.'

'I know,' she said, her voice suddenly quiet. 'I know. And I know that when I marry him, there will be no way out, only death. Mine or his.'

The words sent a shiver through Luke. They were so close to his own thoughts just a moment ago.

'Rosa,' he said desperately. There were tears in his eyes, and in his voice. 'There *are* other people who love you. There must be.'

'Really? Who? Don't say Mama, for you know it's not true. Nor Alexis. My nanny who brought me up from a child went away when she got a better offer from another family. No one has ever loved me, no one has ever wanted to marry me, no one has ever even wanted to kiss me, before Sebastian. Forgive me if—'

Luke took hold of her shoulders, more roughly than he meant.

'That's not true.'

She turned her face up to his. Her eyes were wet. Her lips were parted in surprise, mid-sentence. Luke felt her magic around them, flooding him with its fire.

He knew what he was about to do was very, very stupid. But he had nothing left to lose. And he had never wanted anything more.

He bent and kissed her.

For a minute she did nothing, just stood, limp in his arms, her lips soft and unresisting beneath his. Luke knew, suddenly, that he had made a terrible mistake. He was no better than Knyvet, forcing himself on her – except that she could blast him through the stable wall behind him, if she chose.

He began to pull away.

'I'm s-sorry . . .' he stammered.

And then her arms went around his neck, in a grip so fierce he gasped and almost stumbled. Her lips against his were firm and hot, her fingers in his hair, gripping him so that he could not have pulled back, even if he wanted to.

'Rosa . . .' he tried, but his words were lost in her kiss – and then his mouth was on her jaw and her throat, kissing her as he had never kissed a girl before, as he had wanted to for so long. She was light and fierce in his arms, her magic a cloud of flame around them, consuming him, burning him up from the inside.

'*What. Is. This?*'

The words came from behind them, hissed low, but shockingly loud in the silence of the stable.

They sprang apart, Luke's heart beating hard in his chest. He reached for Rosa's hand, but she was not there.

She had taken a step forwards, towards the man. He was nothing but a black silhouette in the moonlight, but Luke knew who it was before Rosa said, 'Sebastian, it's not what it looks like—'

'*Be quiet.*'

'Seba—'

She never got to finish. Knyvet threw out a blast of magic that sent her flying backwards, sprawling across the stone floor to crash into the stable wall with a force that made Brimstone give a neigh of alarm. He reared up, his hooves beating against the partition between the stalls.

Luke felt the blow as if it was a punch to his own gut. For a minute he couldn't speak, he was so choked with shock and fury that Knyvet would treat her like this.

Then somehow the words roared out of him, almost of their own volition.

'Leave her alone!'

'Be *quiet*,' Knyvet snarled, and something whip-tight curled around Luke's shoulders like a rope. He staggered and nearly fell.

'Please, Sebastian,' Rosa sobbed.

Another binding, a ring of steel tightening around his chest.

'Knyvet . . .' he gasped. He could hardly breathe.

'God, you really won't be told, will you?' Sebastian sighed. He pointed and Luke felt his lips seal together as if they were one piece of flesh. He screamed, not silently, but through his nose, so that it came out more like a moan; a

270

sound so muffled and pathetic it barely reached the door, let alone beyond. Why hadn't he shouted when he had the chance?

'*Tówierpe!*' Knyvet spat, and Luke was flung backwards, to slam into one of the oak pillars holding up the stable roof. His head cracked against the wood so hard he would have gasped, if he could have. He drew painful shuddering breaths through his nose and heard his own breath whimper at the back of his throat.

Fight me like a man, you damned coward, he thought. But the words would not come.

Sebastian pulled a coil of cord behind the door and now he began to tie Luke to the post.

'Just in case,' he said pleasantly, as he pulled the knots tight, the ropes cutting into Luke's skin. 'I wouldn't want the spell to slip while my attention was elsewhere.'

Kill him, Luke pleaded Rosa with his eyes. *You're a witch – do something. Split his skull. Save us both.*

But she only stared at him with wide, horrified eyes as if she couldn't believe what was happening.

When Sebastian was satisfied that the knots were tight enough to hold Luke, even if the spells failed, he turned his back and looked at Rosa.

'At least you know how to hold your tongue.' He walked across to her and touched her gently on the cheek that had smacked into the wall. 'I like that in a woman. What I don't like,' he helped her to her feet, 'is infidelity. Unless, of course, it was not your fault.'

Rosa said nothing, she only looked at him, her eyes huge and dark in her white face.

'Tell me,' Sebastian twisted her arm. 'Tell me that he forced himself on you. That you couldn't fight back. That his attentions were unwanted. Tell me, and I will kill him and spare you.'

Luke shut his eyes. *Her death, or yours.*

His heartbeat sounded in his ears, waiting for her response, and when she spoke it was almost too low for him to hear the words. Almost.

'I'm sorry,' she said quietly. 'But I can't lie.'

The blow was so fast Luke missed it. At the vicious crack and Rosa's cry, his eyes flew open, but she was already lying on the floor. There was blood coming from her nose. Sebastian shook his hand, as if he'd knocked it against a door handle in passing. His face was pained, but calm.

'Tell me again,' he whispered. 'My darling.' He pulled her to her feet and wiped the blood tenderly from her cheek with his fingers. 'Come, my darling. You can tell me. He's only an outwith from the slums. Spare yourself, my darling. Oh my God, I love you so. I don't want to hurt you. Don't make me hit you again.'

Rosa shook her head, not in denial, but thickly, as if she were trying to clear away confusion. Sebastian and Luke waited.

At last she looked up.

'I kissed him,' she said, through bloodied lips.

This time Luke saw the blow as well as heard it, saw Knyvet's hand meet her face, saw her flung back on to the stone flags, heard the thud as her body hit the floor. Blood was flowing freely down her white dress.

Fight back! Luke begged her in his mind. Why was she lying there when she was a witch as powerful in her own way as Knyvet? Her magic swirled and boiled around her in red-gold flames, and she wouldn't use it. Why not? *Why not?*

Fight back, he pleaded silently. *Denounce me. Anything.* Anything had to be better than this silence.

But she only lay, still and unmoving on the cold stone floor. Her head was flung back and he could see the damage Knyvet had done.

He wanted to scream. But his lips were sealed.

Beneath the white silk Rosa's ribs still rose and fell in slow, ragged breaths. Knyvet had been careful, in his own way. Rosa's beauty was not ruined, only marred for a while. He had not gone for the spleen, or the kidneys, or anywhere that might kill.

But he had done it sober. In cold blood.

As Luke watched, Knyvet wound his hand in her hair and pulled her limp body up from the floor, her limbs lolling. He kissed her bloodstained lips, then let her unresisting body drop, with a thud, back to the flags.

'Goodnight, my darling. Sleep well.'

He turned to Luke.

'As for you . . .' He moved towards the pillar. Luke

knew that he should feel fear, terror even. He had escaped death at the hands of one witch – he could not expect to be so lucky a second time. 'As for you, outwith, I won't waste my magic on scum like you.'

He put his hand out, grabbed a fistful of Luke's hair, and yanked his head as far forward as it would go. Then he banged it back, hard, against the oak pillar. Luke felt a white-hot blaze of pain explode across the back of his skull. Then nothing.

19

When Luke woke he was in bed. There was a bandage on the back of his head and he had the worst headache he could remember in a long time. He groaned and opened his eyes blearily. A pair of bright-blue eyes were staring into his, with a concerned expression.

'You're awake!' It was the groom who shared his room. He was dressed in his uniform and smelt of the stables. He grinned, relieved. 'Mr Warren said to let you sleep so I didn't wake you first thing, but I was worried you'd've copped it, so I came up to see if you was all right. When they brought you in I wasn't sure you'd be here in the morning. How'd you manage to get a kick like that?'

A kick? Luke licked dry lips and tried to speak, but the words wouldn't come.

'We've all done it,' the groom carried on. 'Frisky horse, it's easy enough to let yer attention slip for a moment. But blow me, he musta caught you quite a clip with his hoof. You've got a headache fit to kill, I reckon?'

Luke nodded, setting small fires of pain ablaze in the back of his skull. They fizzled out and he lay trying to collect his thoughts. Had he really had a kick from a horse? He didn't remember it.

'I heard as you're going back to London today,' the other groom said. 'You be all right on the train with two horses?'

Two horses . . . A memory flickered . . . Cherry.

'One horse,' Luke managed.

'Oh, a'course.' The young groom slapped his forehead. 'I'd forgotten it was your young miss what had the fall off the bridge. Blimey, it's been bad luck for you, this journey, ain't it? You'll be glad to see the back of Southing, I shouldn't wonder.'

Southing.

Rosa.

Something came back, a memory of Rosa's face, covered in blood. But why – he'd had the fall . . . He lay still while the groom chatted on, wishing the man'd be silent just for a minute so he could grope his thoughts back together.

'Well, every cloud and all that, eh?' the man continued cheerily. 'At least if you've earned yourself a bang on the head and your miss lost her horse, she's gained a husband – and right plum too, so my mistress was saying. Are they announcing it when they're back in London, you reckon?'

Luke couldn't answer. His limbs were suddenly cold beneath the thin, scratchy blanket.

A ring, flashing with fire, on Rosa's finger.

Her face, streaming with blood.

Knyvet . . .

'I've got to get up,' he managed hoarsely, and he swung his legs out of bed, his arms trembling as he pushed against the hard, flat mattress.

'Eh, mate, you're in no state to go mucking out. I'll do yer horses if you tell me which ones. Wait a while . . .'

'I can't.'

He began to drag his clothes on, his head pounding. As he dressed he tried to think. He *had* to see Rosa. But how? A groom couldn't go marching into the young ladies' bedrooms. He didn't even know where she was, in this great maze of a house.

Rose! he thought desperately, pleading with her to hear. She was a witch, wasn't she? Surely they could read minds, *something*.

Then it came to him. The ladies' maids.

Luke burst into the servants' hall so fast that the door thumped against the wall. There was only one maid there, sitting at the table doing some darning.

'Lordy love us!' She looked up. 'Who tied a firework to your tail?'

'I need to get a message to – to my mistress. How can I do it? Could you take her a note?'

277

The girl laughed comfortably, tied off her darning and bit off the end of the thread. Luke wanted to strangle her for her slowness.

'Well?'

'Well yourself! Who's your mistress when she's at home?'

'Miss Greenwood. Rosa Greenwood.'

'Well, Mr Well, you're out of luck. They've left. Didn't they tell you?'

'*Left?*'

'Yes, she caught the early train back to London this morning with her brother. I expect you're to follow with the horses. Why Lordy, what's the matter with you? You've gone quite pale. Here, sit down.'

She shoved a chair at him and Luke groped his way to it and sat, feeling the blood pound in his head.

'Had a bang on the head, did you?' She looked sympathetically at the bandage and he managed to nod.

'Nasty things, horses. I never did like them. My dad was an ostler and his father too, but it skipped a generation with me. To me they're just nasty great beasts what'd step on your foot any day of the week and never say sorry. Here,' she pushed a huge brown teapot at him, and took a cup from a shelf, 'have a cuppa, and I'll run out to the yard and see if the head groom knows what you're to do.'

'Thanks,' Luke said hoarsely.

'Miss Greenwood,' the girl said slowly as she filled up

his cup. 'She's that lass what's just got engaged to Mr Sebastian, right?'

Luke nodded, dully, the pain in his head throbbing until he thought he might be sick.

'Well, isn't that nice,' she beamed. 'Nothing like a wedding in the family to cheer things up. We'll be seeing a fair bit of you round here, I dare say.'

After she left Luke put his head in his hands. He didn't feel like tea – he felt sick and faint, and full of dread-soaked questions. What would happen when he got back to London? Would he be sacked? Why had Knyvet allowed him to live, after what he'd seen? And, most importantly of all, why did everyone think Rosa was still engaged to Knyvet?

Rosa was sitting in her bedroom, staring blindly out across the roofs, when she heard the slow, weary clop of hooves in the mews alleyway behind the house. When she looked down, through the gathering fog, she could see the dark shape of a horse and rider approaching. Only one rider and only one horse. *Cherry* . . .

For a minute her eyes pricked with tears and she thought that she would give way to one of the helpless fits of weeping that had taken her since she'd arrived back in London. But she drew a deep, shuddering breath and pressed her lips firmly together, pushing the tears back down where they belonged. She would not give in. Not to this. Not now.

The rider turned in at the gate and then dismounted. Through the thick yellow fog she could see only the outline, but it was Luke, she would have known his silhouette anywhere, the slow deliberation of his movements as he unbuckled Brimstone's harness and led him into the stall, next to Cherry's empty one.

He looked bone-weary, his movements slow and dragging. She watched him until he was gone from sight, inside the stable, and then turned her eyes back to the rooftops, to the spiky chimneys and the circling starlings, looking for a place to roost. The sparrows and pigeons were long gone, to wherever they sheltered, and a thin sickly moon was on the rise, its light a sulphurous yellow through the swirling fog. How could London be so beautiful and so filthy at the same time? She thought of the wide gleaming lawns at Matchenham, at the soft golden stone of the house in the winter sun, and the tears rose inside her again, a trapped grief trying to get free.

'Rosamund,' came a voice from the doorway, and Rosa turned, her heart beating fast. It was Mama. She stood in the doorway, her emerald-green silk skirts rustling against the threadbare carpet as she came into the room.

'You know what you must do.' Her expression was unsmiling.

Rosa closed her eyes. Yes, she knew.

'Come.' Mama put a cold hand on Rosa's cheek, against the worse of the purple bruising. Rosa steeled herself, forcing herself not to flinch away. 'It's not pleasant, I know,

280

but it must be done. You've done well; don't falter at the last fence.'

She nodded.

'Go now, before he goes into the kitchen.'

'Yes, Mama.'

She looked at the carpet, refusing to meet Mama's eyes. She could not bear the reflection of herself that she would see there.

Mama turned and left, and Rosa stood, letting the blood come back into her stiff limbs. Before she left the room she turned, quite deliberately, to the mirror over the dressing table. For the journey back to London she had worn a veil, for there were limits to what magic could heal. She had done her best – the bruises were purple, not black and blue. Her eyes were bloodshot but the bones in her nose had started to knit. The kink would remain, a broken ridge to remind her, always, of Sebastian's power.

A fall out riding, Mama had told Ellen. Most unfortunate. Miss Rosa will keep to her room for a few days while the bruises heal.

But she would not hide herself from Luke. He had seen the worst already.

Her own eyes met her in the mirror, gold-brown and red-rimmed.

It was time.

Luke was sweeping Cherry's empty stall as Rosa entered the stable and did not immediately hear her above the slow rhythmic swish of the brush. She stood in the shadows, watching him, wanting to remember this moment always. A single lamp burn in the window and the light glinted from his straw-coloured hair, catching the small golden stubble on his cheek and at his jaw as he turned. His shirt sleeves were rolled up and she could see the muscles in his arms move and flex as he methodically worked his way across the small space. Brimstone nuzzled at his shoulder as he came close, more trusting and affectionate than she had ever seen him with Alex. A lump rose in her throat and she stepped forward into the light, before she could think better of this.

He turned as he heard her footsteps and his breath caught in his throat.

They stood, neither of them saying anything, and then he crossed the stall to her and took her shoulders, turning her face to the light.

'My God.' She could feel him shaking. 'I'll testify against him if you want to prosecute. I'll speak for you in court, tell 'em what he did.'

She would have laughed if she hadn't felt so like crying. Testify! He would never even get to the court. It would be his death.

'I came to tell you . . .' She tried to make herself hard, cold, as Mama would be. 'I came to tell you . . .'

She couldn't finish. The words stuck in her throat, choking her.

'Rose . . .' he began. There were tears in his hazel eyes.

She could not bear it. Then his gaze went to her finger, where she was still wearing the ring. The colour left his face. 'Why . . . ?'

'I'm sorry,' she said stupidly. It was not what she had meant to say. This was turning out all wrong. 'Luke, oh Luke, I'm so, so sorry.'

'Take it off.'

'I can't.' It was true. The ring had shrunk, the metal band biting into her finger until it could not be removed.

'What?' He took her hand and his eyes widened. 'We'll get pliers – nippers. I'll get it off, I promise.'

'That's not what I meant.' She swallowed. 'I'm not . . . I'm not *going* to take it off.'

'*What?*' He gripped her very hard and she fought against the stupid treacherous tears. 'Rose, don't do this – there must be another way. Are you afraid of him?'

'Yes,' she said. At that one word, as if he couldn't help it, he pulled her into his arms. They stood for a long moment, clinging together, her face against his chest, listening to the frantic pounding of his heart. She could feel him trying to form words, trying to speak, and she knew that she must speak first, before he broke her resolve. She rested her cheek against the soft roughness of his shirt and drew a breath.

Like this, not looking at him, she could do it.

'Listen, Luke, there's no way out for me. I *have* to do this – for Mama, for Alexis, for Matchenham.' *For you*, she added silently in her head. She swallowed, trying to make him understand. 'I have no choice – there's no escape except through him.'

'He's no escape, Rosa, can't you see that? He's just another prison and a worse one. Please . . .' His arms tightened around her. 'Come away with me. We'll start again.'

'Can't you see, it's impossible? The difference between us . . .' She couldn't finish, but it hovered there, the impossible chasm of identity and class and magic that lay between them. He was a stable-hand and, worse, an outwith.

'So that's it? That's what it comes down to, he has money and I don't?' He pushed her away and she heard the crack in his voice as he turned, as if he couldn't look at her. 'You're selling yourself for a house, Rosa.'

I'm selling myself for you, she cried in her heart. *If I don't do this, they will kill you – do you understand that? I can't save myself – but I can save you.*

But she could not tell him that.

She only nodded, and swallowed against the pain in her throat.

'I want you to go away, forget me.'

'How can I forget you?' He turned, his face full of anger, but she was not afraid, not like she had been at the sight of Sebastian's fury. Luke might hate her, for a while, but he would never hurt her, she knew that. He would hurt himself, first. 'How can you ask me that? I love you.'

The words were spoken almost before she had time to realize what they meant. There was silence in the stable as

284

the words hung between them, like a spell. His eyes held her. She could not look away.

She moved across the space between them and put her hand on his cheek, feeling the rough stubble of his beard beneath her fingers, drinking in his clear hazel eyes, the way his brows were dipped in anger or incomprehension, the lines at the corner of his mouth and eyes, the dusting of straw fragments in his hair and on his shirt.

With her other hand she took his collar and pulled him down to meet her. His lips were soft against her bruised ones and he kissed her gently, carefully, as if afraid to cause her any more pain.

'Don't worry,' she whispered. 'I'm tough.'

His lips on hers, his hands around her waist, lifting her up, holding her to him. She never wanted him to let go. Her hands were in his hair, caressing his face, smoothing away the lines and the dust and the pain . . .

Then she steeled herself and pulled away.

'You have to forget me.'

'I will *never* forget you,' he said fiercely.

'Oh!' She put her hands to her face, pressing against her eyes, feeling the bruises that Sebastian had left flare with pain. 'I wish that were true.'

She moved across to the lamp standing in the window, high above the straw, and opened the tiny glass door that shielded the flame. Luke watched her for a moment, puzzled, and she took out the rosemary from her skirt and began put it to the burning wick.

As it flared up his face changed.

'What are you doing?'

'I want you to forget, Luke. Forget everything that happened. Forget my family. Forget Sebastian and Southing and this house. Forget everything you ever knew about witches, forget—' She stumbled and choked, and forced herself on. 'Forget *me*.'

'No!' Luke's face was full of a blank horror. For a minute he stood, frozen, too horrified to move. Then as the rosemary twigs flared up he seemed to come to his senses and leapt across the few feet between them, his hands outstretched, reaching desperately for the lamp and the burning sticks.

'*Opstille!*' Rosa screamed before he could reach her, and Luke dropped like a felled tree, his head hitting the flags with a crack that made her cry out.

He lay very still and for a moment she could only stand, her breath sobbing between her teeth as the rosemary twigs burnt. At last the flame died away and there was nothing but ashes left.

'Luke?'

He lay face down, unmoving, but when she put her hand to his back she could feel he was breathing, his shoulder moving almost imperceptibly beneath her palm. There was fresh blood soaking the white bandage across the back of his head. Brimstone gave a whicker of concern and shifted uneasily in his stall.

'Luke?' Rosa asked again. He didn't answer. She knelt

286

on the cold stone floor and kissed him, once, very gently on the cheek. 'Goodbye, Luke. Be happy. I hope you get your forge.'

Her throat swelled suddenly with unshed tears and she straightened and turned to go.

'Two days? I don't care if there's only two *hours* to go, he's not well!' William's angry voice filtered up the stairs to where Luke was lying in his narrow bed, his face to the wall.

'He promised, William.' John Leadingham's croaking rasp. 'In a few days it'll be out of my hands. I'll have to pass the matter up to the Inquisitor and he ain't likely to be—'

'I don't. Bloody. Care!' William spat, his voice rising on the last word. 'I'm telling you, the lad barely knows his own name, let alone who he's supposed to be killing. There's a clot on the back of his head the size of a potato – Phoebe Fairbrother found him in the gutter outside the market at chucking-out time, did she tell you that? Lying in a pool of filth in the clothes he went away in. She hardly recognized him and he was too far gone to recognize her. He's been in that room for three days and nights and he's yet to manage more than "Yes, Uncle" and "No, Uncle". He doesn't remember anything of the last month, not even the meeting. What do you want me to do? Turn him out in the street with a knife and tell him to get on with the task?'

'Listen, Brothers . . .' It was Benjamin West, his voice placating. 'Who's to say he hasn't done it, eh? He can't tell us himself, but perhaps that's how he got isself into this state. Perhaps it were the girl's dying curse, like.'

'I don't know . . .' Leadingham's voice was doubtful. 'It don't sound likely to me. Who would've taken him to the market, if she was dead? It doesn't make sense. But I'm willing to postpone judgement until we know for sure.'

'But it don't make sense either way,' West said plaintively. 'What's the alternative – they found him out? Why's he not dead then, answer me that?'

There was a silence, a long uncomfortable silence, as the men turned the question over in their minds. Then William spoke, his voice flat and hard.

'None of it makes sense. But I'll not see the lad dragged before the council in the state he's in, and there's an end to it. If you can't find the girl alive then Luke's job is done, as far as I'm concerned. Now, leave him alone.'

Luke heard their muffled voices as they took their leave, and then the house fell silent. He sighed, tracing with his gaze the familiar cracks in the bedroom wall, as he'd done on sleepless nights ever since he was a small boy. The years were still there, stretching back in his memory, but there were gaps, like the cracks in the wall. A gap around his parents' death and his coming to live with William. Where they had died there should have been memories – and pain. He could feel the shape of its absence, but try as he might, the memory itself was gone. And gaps, too, throughout the years, things he could not remember, gatherings with men he knew, faces he remembered, but whose reason he could not recall. And worst of all was that great aching gap of the last month, like a hole punched in his mind. He could remember nothing. Nothing. What had he done? Who was the girl they had been talking of, downstairs? Had he killed someone, was that what they meant?

He sat up and put his hand to the wound on the back of his head. It was healing, slowly. William had cropped his hair short to help stop infection and he felt the unaccustomed bristles against his palm as he rubbed his hand across the back of his skull. It was closed up enough not to need a bandage now, although it seeped sometimes at night, a clear pink fluid that stained his sheets. His skull was in one piece and that was something. William said it was concussion and the memories would come back in a day or two. He had said that yesterday and the day before. Luke no longer believed him. This was not concussion, this was permanent, as if his memories had been burnt away, cauterized like an infectious lesion of the brain.

He swung his legs over the side of the bed, shivering at the cold on his bare skin, and began to dress, pulling on the clothes his uncle had laid out for him two days ago in the hope that he might get up. As he buttoned his shirt he felt the skin on the back of his shoulder pull tight, as if there was a new-healed scar there, but he had no recollection of a wound. He twisted his head to look. There was a mark, the flesh turned thick and shiny where it had healed. He could not quite see what it was, but it looked like – a hammer, perhaps? He had never seen it before and it chilled him. Here was something else that had fallen into the cracks in his mind, lost for ever. What had he cared about so deeply that he had let it be branded into his skin? Whatever it was, he had forgotten it, along with everything else.

He made his way slowly down the stairs, half hoping to find his uncle already gone to the forge. But he was there.

'Luke!' William turned, his mouth open with astonishment. Then he pulled a chair out from the table. 'Luke, lad, I didn't think to see you down today. Sit down, sit down.'

'I'm all right,' Luke said gruffly, but he sat and allowed William to put a bowl of broth in front of him, and half a pint of ale. William watched anxiously as Luke tried to eat the soup.

'Come on, lad,' he said at last. 'You're not going to mend by picking like a fussy maid.'

'I'm sorry, Uncle. I can't, I've got no heart for it.' He laid down the spoon. 'I heard them, downstairs. What was John Leadingham on about? What task?'

'Never you mind,' his uncle said fiercely. 'John Leadingham's an officious fool. I'll not have him bothering you. It's . . . business stuff. Nowt to do with you.'

'It didn't sound like business,' Luke said warily. 'And it seemed to be a lot to do with me. What were they on about? What girl? And what killing?'

'Never you mind,' William snarled, so fiercely that Luke only sighed and picked up his ale.

After a long draught he spoke again.

'I thought I might call past the dairy after work, see how Minna's doing.'

William looked uncomfortable at that and he pushed his chair out from the table and walked to the window, to look out into the cobbled lane.

'Well . . . as to that . . .'

Luke looked up. There was something in his uncle's voice, something uneasy. 'As to what, Uncle? Is Minna all right?'

'I suppose there's no use beating round the bush,' William said heavily. He came back to sit at the table and clasped his hands. 'She's gone, Luke. D'you remember Bess got sick?'

Luke strained his memory and then shook his head angrily.

'Well, she did. If I told her once, I told her a thousand times, she should've sold the mare while the going was good, got a donkey, put the money in the mouths of those kids. But she wouldn't. And then Bess got ill and Minna poured good money after bad taking the nag to a horse doctor who told her the case was hopeless and took her shillings all the same.'

'Where's she gone?' There was a feeling of fear, bordering on panic, rising in Luke's gullet. He knew, he *knew*, somehow, that this was connected with the great gaping void in his memory – and yet the memories wouldn't come. The more he grasped at them, the more insubstantial they became.

'We don't know. She went for a factory job, that's all we heard. Nick Sykes couldn't tell us where or who; she had a card, that's all he knew, but he didn't see it. He can't read anyhow.'

'And she never came back?'

'No. She sent back two shillings by a messenger boy and promised more the next week, but it never came.'

'Who's looking after the kids?'

'They've gone to the workhouse two days ago. Don't look at me like that, Luke. What could we do? I've not got the time nor space to house those kids; neither have any of our friends. Times are hard. We did what we could – whipped round to give them a square meal, sent money and clothes, but you could see the way it was going, Nick Sykes took the money and drank it away, and the food and clothes he sold. There was nothing for it. They're in the workhouse orphanage until Nick mends his ways or Minna comes back.'

He did not say what he was thinking, but Luke knew

293

his uncle well enough to read it in the sadness in his eyes: the one was as unlikely as the other.

The engagement was not supposed to be announced until the spring, but somehow all London seemed to know, and overnight the Greenwood name was good for credit at the drapers' and dressmakers'. Alexis found his application for a secretaryship at the Ealdwitan miraculously approved and when Rosa's face healed she spent her days trailing miserably round department stores, milliners' and haberdashers' after Mama and Clemency, watching her trousseau grow ever larger, second only in magnificence to Mama's own wardrobe.

She knew that Mama was growing impatient with her misery, but Sebastian, strangely, did not seem to mind her reluctance to talk about their wedding, her refusal to set a date. In fact she had hardly seen him since they had become engaged. His father had died, unexpectedly, and he was very busy at the Ealdwitan and at Southing, trying to sort out the endless tangles of legacies and entailments and death duties. Rosa was ashamed that her first feeling on hearing the news had been not sorrow for Sebastian but relief, that here was a reason to postpone the wedding – a reason that even Mama could not possibly object to, nor blame on Rosa.

She saw Cassandra, once, in town. They were waiting under the canopy at Fortnum's for the carriage to come round, when a voice spoke at her elbow.

'Rosa? I'm not mistaken, am I?'

Rosa turned and saw Cassandra's small white face at her elbow, her deep-blue eyes as wide and startling in London as they had been at Southing.

'Cassie! What are you doing here?'

'I've come up to town with my governess.' She indicated a pinched, grey-faced woman who was standing by the road anxiously scanning the thoroughfare for a carriage. 'We are buying winter woollens. Are there any two more dreary words in the English language? I'm so glad we've met. I didn't have a chance to tell you how very glad I am that we are to be sisters.'

'*Are* you glad?' Rosa said doubtfully. 'I had the impression at Southing that you didn't approve.'

'I did not say I am glad you're marrying Sebastian,' Cassandra said gravely. She looked at Rosa with her penetrating blue eyes and Rosa had the impression once again that Cassie was seeing right through her, to her past and perhaps even future. 'Are you?'

'I'm sorry about your father,' Rosa said miserably. She wished she could have answered the question without evasion, but there was something about Cassie's clear gaze that made it very hard to lie.

'I'm not,' Cassie said bluntly. For a minute Rosa couldn't speak and before she could recover Cassie went on. 'He was a bully and a brute. He broke Mama and he broke Sebastian too, in a different way.'

'A-and you?'

'He never spoke to me. He pretended I did not exist. I think, perhaps, he was afraid of me, of my blindness, of what I *could* see.'

'I – I'm so sorry,' Rosa stammered. 'I lost my own father b-but . . .'

But he was a wonderful man, she wanted to say. *He was everything to me.* But she could not say it, it would have sounded like boasting after Cassie's confession. *He broke Mama . . . Sebastian too . . .*

'I wish,' she said slowly, 'I wish I'd had an opportunity to see your mother again. Before I left. I never had a chance to say thank you for what she did – I owe her my life. Would Sebastian—'

'No!' Cassie spoke urgently, cutting across Rosa's faltering words. She felt for Rosa's arm, her fingers closing painfully tight on Rosa's sleeve. 'No, for all our sakes, please – the best thing you can do for Mama is forget you ever saw her. And whatever you do please *never* mention to Sebastian what happened.'

'But why?' Rosa said. She matched her voice to Cassie's – not quite understanding why they were whispering, but Cassie's anxiety was contagious. 'I know madness in the family is considered a disgrace by some, but now we're engaged . . .'

Cassie only shook her head, the ribbons on her hat fluttering in the winter breeze. Her small face was determined, her chin set, and there was something almost like Sebastian's immutability in her expression.

Rosa opened her mouth to argue, but before she could go on, Cassandra's governess came hurrying up and Rosa had no choice but to join in the pleasantries as they took their leave, promising to meet soon, before Christmas, before the wedding for certain. The last thing Rosa saw was Cassie's pale little face in the window of the Knyvet carriage, above their coat of arms.

On the drive home she thought of Sebastian's mother, and of his father, who she had never met. And she thought of her own father, of his round jolly face, his soft beard, the way his eyes twinkled beneath his top hat when he came home on winter nights. He had loved her – he had made her feel safe. There were very few people she could say that about, in her life. Except, perhaps, Luke.

And now they were both gone.

'Tea!' Mama said to James as they climbed the last few weary steps to the front hall. 'And biscuits. And please tell the maid to see to the fire in the drawing room.'

'Begging your pardon, madam, the fire is banked already. Mr Knyvet is waiting in there.'

'Mr Knyvet?' Mama dropped her packages on the hall table and rushed to the mirror to pull off her hat and adjust her hair. Then she turned to Rosa. 'Oh, you're a disgrace, Rosa. Trying to tame your hair is like trying to comb an – an octopus. Or a hedgehog.'

'Mama!' Rosa shrugged away from her mother's pinching fingers. 'I'm sure Sebastian doesn't care about my hair.'

'Sebastian will no doubt expect his wife to be impeccably groomed, as he is himself,' Mama said sharply, but she let go and Rosa entered the drawing room.

Sebastian had his back to the door, staring into the roaring fire. Rosa felt its warmth on her face and wondered again at the change in their fortunes wrought overnight by that one simple word: yes. Where a few weeks ago there would have been meagre sticks and a few chips of coal, now the fire leapt and danced in the wide grate, its heat reaching every corner of the long room.

Her fingers hurt, the heat of the fire thawing them too fast for comfort, and she felt suddenly small and mean and full of self-hate. Sebastian's name had brought all this. The logs in the grate, the parcels in the hall, the joint they would eat tonight. And she could not love him for it.

'Sebastian,' she said softly, and he turned.

'My darling.' He came across the room and took her face in his hands, tilting it up so that he could kiss her mouth. Her lips were cold from the street and his mouth felt feverishly hot against hers. She felt his tongue against her teeth and pulled away, and his lips curved in a thin, lazy smile.

'Still playing the nun, Rosa?'

'We're not yet married. Mama is outside the door.'

'Your mama is so delighted with our engagement that she wouldn't care if I took you here on this rug.'

Rosa felt her face flush scarlet. For a minute she couldn't speak. It was not just the crudity, but the fact that it was so close to being true, that robbed her of the power to reply.

'Oh, Rosa!' He kissed her again, but paternally this time on the forehead. 'Your name was perfect – clairvoyant. You flush like a newly opened rose. I adore to shock you just to see the blush on your cheek – but you really shouldn't make it so easy. Sit down, my darling, you look exhausted. Have you been wedding shopping?'

'Yes,' she said mechanically. It was almost true, Mama and Clemency had been wedding shopping, after all. Then she remembered her manners. 'Sebastian, I was so sorry to hear about your father. What happened?'

'An accident.' Sebastian spoke shortly. 'He had been working on an experiment, a sort of . . . transfusion.'

'I don't understand.'

'Nor do I, completely. But it seems that there is a new machine that can extract –' he glanced at the doorway, checking that they were alone, and lowered his voice '– it can extract the magic from one person and inject it into another, giving them strength and power beyond their own abilities. They had refined the process using prisoners, condemned men, you understand. Their success was mixed but at last they came to believe they understood the matching process. It seems that they were wrong.'

'But was he mad?' Rosa sank on to on the sofa. 'What was he thinking, a Chair of the Ealdwitan to risk his life in an unproven experiment?'

'Perhaps he was mad, yes.' Sebastian's face was hard. 'The quest for power is a kind of madness of its own. My father was unsparing of others, but also of himself. He was not the only person to die in pursuit of this.'

'But why do it at all?'

'There are others, overseas, who are developing the same techniques. We cannot risk leaving this power in their hands alone.'

'God in Heaven.' Rosa put her face in her hands. When Clemency had shaken her head and refused to discuss Philip's work at the Ealdwitan she had thought it was because it must be boring, political. Not this. Not this mad quest for power and domination.

'So . . . what now?' she managed. 'Will you be Chair?'

'Yes. I'm afraid our wedding must be postponed until that is ratified. It means yet more delays, on top of my father's funeral. Do you mind?'

Mind? She almost laughed.

'No, I don't mind. I mean – I understand. This is more important.'

He took her hands and began pulling off her gloves and kissing her fingers one by one. At last he kissed the great stone that burnt on her left hand.

'I mind,' he said huskily, his soft, rough voice sending a shiver down her spine. 'I cannot wait until you are mine, in name and body, in every way imaginable.'

She did not answer, but only stared into the fire. There was a sound at the door and Mama entered. She laughed at the sight of Rosa's hand in Sebastian's, and Rosa snatched it away.

'Forgive me for disturbing you, my dear lovebirds, but I came to ask if you would stay for tea, or perhaps even dinner, Mr Knyvet? Please do not stand on ceremony here; we are all family now, or almost.'

'Alas, I cannot.' Sebastian stood and bowed. 'I have to go to Spitalfields, to try to sort matters out at the factory and the soup kitchen. You cannot imagine the mountain of administration my father's death has caused.'

Spitalfields. The word gave Rosa a pang, like a sudden stitch in her side. She shut her eyes for a moment, trying not to let Sebastian see.

'Then let me ask James to bring your hat and coat,' Mama was saying. She rang the bell and James appeared. As Mama gave the order, Rosa turned to Sebastian. She spoke quickly, before she could think better of it.

'Sebastian, won't you take me with you?'

'Where, darling?'

'To the East End.' She could not bring herself to say 'to Spitalfields'. It was too close to saying 'to Luke'. She would never see him, she knew it. The East End was teeming, sprawling, filled with London-born and immigrants, sailors and natives, merchants, manufacturers and itinerant labourers. There was no hope of finding one face among the throng – and he would not recognize her if they did meet. But at least it would be *something* – something more worthy than endlessly shopping with Clemency and Mama – that could be of real value to others. She thought of Luke's friend, the skinny girl with hungry eyes too large for

301

her face that she had sent to the Knyvets' soup kitchens. 'Listen, if I'm to become part of your family, I want to understand your businesses, your family's philanthropy. Please – take me to the factories, to the soup kitchens. Perhaps I can help in some way.'

'It is no place for a lady!' Mama exclaimed.

'That's not true! Think of Lady Burdett-Coutts, Mama! Think of all she has done for the poor.'

'Her interests are fallen women,' Mama said tartly. 'Hardly suitable for an unmarried girl of sixteen, Rosa!'

'Please . . .' Rosa turned to Sebastian, knowing it didn't matter what Mama thought – if Sebastian agreed, Mama would acquiesce. 'Please take me. I'm not cut out for a life of idleness and shopping. I want to do something, something to occupy myself. I know I can't do much now, as an unmarried girl, but if I understand your family's concerns then perhaps, after we are married . . . ?'

Sebastian took his coat and hat from James and put them on. He looked as if he were thinking. At last he spoke.

'Very well. Not today. But if your mother agrees, I will take you.'

'Tomorrow then?'

'You are persistent, Rosa,' he laughed.

'Tomorrow? Mama, do you agree?'

Her mother shrugged.

'If you are under Sebastian's protection, I can hardly object, I suppose.'

'Very well.' Sebastian nodded. 'Tomorrow. But I warn

you, Rosa, you may be shocked at what you see.'

'Tomorrow,' she nodded as they walked out to the hall. 'I will not be shocked, I promise. Thank you, Sebastian.'

He turned to leave, but then stopped.

'Oh, my cane. James, did I give you my cane?'

'I beg your pardon, sir.' James hurried forward with a black ebony cane with a carved silver head. 'I quite forgot.'

'Thank you.' Sebastian took it in his gloved hand. 'I would not lose it for the world. It was my father's.'

'It is beautiful workmanship,' Mama said. 'What does the head show? I cannot see.'

'It is a coiled snake.' Sebastian lifted his hand, showing them the silver. 'An ouroboros in figure eight form. It symbolizes the circle of life, the beginning and end, destruction and renewal.'

Rosa shivered. There was something disquieting about the snake's calm, methodical self-cannibalization. It had achieved the ultimate goal: immortality – and paid the ultimate price.

Sebastian noticed the shudder and kissed her cheek.

'You are cold. Don't wait to see me out; go back to the drawing room and the fire.'

'Very well. But you won't forget, will you? About tomorrow?'

'I will send my carriage for you at ten. Is that too early? But the nights draw in so quickly now, and the East End is no place for a woman when it gets dark.'

'Ten is perfect.'

She stood, watching as he disappeared into the fog, the silver head of his cane glinting in the gas-light.

'Goodnight, Rosa . . .' His voice floated back through the thick yellow murk. 'Until tomorrow.'

Until tomorrow. She closed the door against the chill and the moist darkness and went back inside.

'Beautiful day, miss,' the groom called down to Rosa from his seat. 'Nothing like a breeze to blow away the fog, eh?' She nodded, forgetting that he could not hear her, but she was too absorbed in looking out of the carriage windows. At first the streets had been familiar – Belgravia Square, Hyde Park Corner, Piccadilly. But as they made their way past Regent Street into the narrow maze of streets around Leicester Square and Covent Garden, she began to realize what a different London this was from the one she knew. Gone were the tall, grand vistas with their long, clean lines. In their place were crooked tumbledown houses backing on to cobbled alleys, little sooty squares where grubby children played, turning their faces in wonder as they saw the carriage pass.

'Best lock your door, miss,' the driver called down, and Rosa slid the bolt across, though she found it hard to believe anyone would attack them in full daylight. And in any case, these people looked poor but that did not make them thieves. She knew, now, that the poor could be more honourable than the rich.

As they drew near the East End, even the air changed. She caught glimpses of the Thames between buildings, running thick and yellow, foam and filth on its surface. The streets grew so narrow that only one carriage could pass and they stopped frequently, waiting for beggars and children to get out of the road, or for carts and draymen to move out of the way. There was a smell of decay – sweet and sharp with filth at the same time. Above the stink of the river and of a thousand night-soil buckets she could smell coal smoke and a rich, heavy odour like rotten beer.

'What's that smell?' she called up to the groom.

'Which one, miss?' he called back with a laugh. His voice was muffled and she saw that he had drawn his scarf across his face. 'But I think you mean the brewery, if you're not talking about the stink of Old Father Thames here. Strong, ain't it? But not unpleasant, like, and it helps to drown out the rest. Nearly there now.'

They passed a ragged queue of people – men, women and children – strung along the wall of one narrow street in a line that snaked away down a side alley so that she could not see the end of it. There were perhaps a hundred of them, all hollow-cheeked, even the quiet, listless babies. Many of them had scarfs and rags wound around their faces, but she was not surprised; it was very cold and a cruel wind came off the river.

At last the carriage turned a corner and drew to a halt outside a tall, forbidding building made of grey stone, with windows high in its walls. At street level there was only a huge double door and the groom leant down and banged on it smartly with a stick.

'Open up! Miss Rosa Greenwood, for Mr Knyvet.'

A small window opened in the top half of the door and a face peered out, then Rosa heard bolts being withdrawn and the door swung wide. The coach and horse rattled through and she peered out to see they were in a grey courtyard lined with windows and opening on to the river, where a boat was unloading huge pallets on to a wharf. There was almost silence from the buildings, no sound of voices or laughter, apart from the great rattling of some kind of machinery. Above their heads a tall chimney rose against the sky, adding a plume of smoke to the rest of the pollution.

The few men unloading the pallets carried on their business without taking any notice of the carriage, or of Rosa herself, and she was just wondering what to do when a voice came from the other side of the courtyard.

'Rosa!'

'Sebastian.'

He helped her from the carriage, his tanned face still bearing its Indian colour, incongruous against the smoke-stained grey of the building and the pale, drawn faces of the workmen unloading the barge.

'What are they doing?' she asked.

'Unloading the shipment of matchsticks. We don't split them here, that's done at another site. Here they are only dipped and packed for sale. Now, where shall we begin?'

He looked up and Rosa saw a giant clock fixed in the middle of the longest side of the courtyard. It read half past eleven.

'Perhaps with the soup kitchens, for they will be quiet at this time of day since they do not open until noon. If we wait until later the stench and crush will be unbearable. This way. Watch your step. The cobbles are rough, I'm afraid.'

He took her arm and led her carefully across the yard, skirting round the puddles in the cobbles and the drains. They were about to pass under an archway, through a door, when there was the sound of an altercation at the gate.

'You know the rules, Fishwick.' A man's voice raised in anger. 'Now, out, before I summon the guvnor.'

'Pleash, Mr Wyndham, shur.' The other's voice was thin and hopeless, and slurred as if he were missing teeth. 'My wife, she's very bad . . .'

'What's going on?' Sebastian strode across and the gatekeeper immediately pulled off his cap and knocked his stick against the other man's arm, who hastily pulled off his own. He too had a scarf around his face and jaw and Rosa noticed that his hand was missing three fingers and the last was cut short at the knuckle.

'Bill Fishwick, shir,' said the second man in a dull voice. 'Which I arsht pardon, milordship, sir, but it wan't idlenesh, truly. My wife took ill, I couldn't leave her . . .'

'Fishwick's late for work, Mr Knyvet, sir,' said the gatekeeper gruffly. 'For the second time this month. Which I told him, the first time was the warning, the second time the sacking.'

Sebastian looked at Fishwick, at his pinched face. There was no hope in the man's eyes – they looked dead and lifeless already.

He shook his head.

'You know the rules, Fishwick.'

'But—'

'See him out, Wyndham.'

'Please!' Rosa heard the man's desperate shouts from behind her, as Sebastian walked her away, still holding her arm. '*Please!*'

'I know what you'll say, Rosa,' Sebastian said calmly, as they passed under the arch and through a doorway. 'But they all have a sob story. And if I made an exception for him it would be grossly unfair to all the other workers – men, women and children – who struggle in with circumstances just as bad, or worse. There are a hundred workers for every vacancy, a hundred waiting in line for the soup kitchen. How is it fair to keep a worthless man in a job while conscientious workers wait in line for charity?'

She nodded numbly, trying not to let her feelings show in her face. He had said she would be shocked. She was determined not to be.

'Here is the soup kitchen.' Sebastian opened a door and

Rosa went inside an echoing hall, filled with close-packed trestles and benches. Three women were laying out cups and bowls at one end and just next door, through a serving hatch, Rosa could see a sweating cook stirring a huge steaming vat over a range. It smelt strongly of cabbage and something bitter that she did not recognize.

As Sebastian came in the women looked up and their eyes widened in shock, then one by one they dropped into stiff curtseys.

'Please don't worry.' Sebastian raised a hand. 'There is no need to stop work. My fiancée here,' he patted Rosa's arm, 'wanted a tour of the works. We shall not detain you.' He turned back to Rosa and explained, 'The facilities here are quite separate from the factory. Those two doors lead to the street; one is the entrance and the men and women queue there to be allowed entry.'

Rosa nodded. The ragged queue she had seen around the corner of the factory made sudden sense.

'If they are decent and not drunk, they are fed and then go out through the second door to the street. On the other hand, if we have work – and we try to provide as much employment as we can – they are taken out the way we came, through the third door, to sign on for a trial day. If they are any good, they are told to come back the next day to the factory gate for paid work, like all the others.'

'I see,' Rosa said. The smell from the range was beginning to make her feel ill, but she was determined not to let Sebastian see it. She put up her chin. 'Where now?'

'Now I will show you the factory.'

Rosa's head was spinning as he led her along a passageway, up some stairs and opened the door to a huge, long hall, painted dull workhouse grey. The windows were high; they let in a little light, but there was no view except grey clouds. Beneath, a great clattering conveyor belt transported a river of matches along in front of a row of bent women and girls, who scrabbled the matches into bundles and then packed them into boxes. There were dozens of them, perhaps a hundred, Rosa thought. Sebastian let her watch for a while, his eyes on her face as she took in the scene.

'Ready to move on?' he shouted over the roar of the machinery. 'Next the matches are bound into parcels.'

Rosa followed him into the next room. Again, the same ceaseless clatter, the conveyor belt with its load of boxes going round and round. Boys and girls, some of them barely ten or twelve, bound the boxes into parcels of twelve and stacked them on pallets. They worked in complete silence like automatons, their faces grey and expressionless. Many of them too had rags and scarves around their faces and Rosa wondered why – surely it was risky with the machinery so fast and near?

They are poor, Rosa told herself, trying not to give way to the horror she felt at the sight of their blank eyes and lifeless movements. *This is what the poor are like – isn't it?*

But Luke was not like this, nor his friend – what was her name? Minna? She remembered the girl's wicked, laughing face, bright with mischief. The women and children working the packing lines seemed to have had all spirit crushed out of them, leaving just the shell of their bodies working, working, working endlessly.

'They work from six in the morning until six at night,' Sebastian shouted in her ear, 'and would work longer if we let them; they need the money.'

Rosa saw a child dart until the conveyor belt to retrieve a fallen box of matches and she had to shut her eyes for a moment at the sight of the girl's plait so close to the roaring machinery. All it would take would be one slip . . . Her fingers clenched involuntarily on Sebastian's arm.

Sebastian saw her face and shook his head.

'I told you you would be shocked.'

'I wanted to come,' she managed. So this was where Sebastian's family made their money. The graceful beauty of Southing was sucked from the bodies of these men, women and children. The thought made her feel ill and she loathed herself for the weakness. Was this what Luke had gone back to? Was this what she had sent Minna to? She scanned the faces of the women on the packing line, but none of them had Minna's thin, sharp face and laughing eyes.

'Where next?' she asked, and she was proud that her voice remained steady. 'This is where the matches are packed – you said they are dipped here too?'

'Yes, but I won't take you there,' Sebastian said. 'The

dipping room is no place for a lady. The fumes are very unpleasant.'

'I want to see everything.'

'No.'

'Sebastian!'

'You know nothing about it and you will accept my authority on this.'

His voice was calm, but his blue eyes were colder and harder than she had ever seen. Rosa knew that she had lost.

'Let us have tea instead,' Sebastian said. It was a statement, not a question, and Rosa nodded: better to pretend to acquiesce than admit the fact that she had no choice in the matter at all.

He led her through more passages, an office crammed with clerks scratching figures into ledgers, and then opened the door into another world, a room panelled in walnut and lit with a softly fringed lamp. The door closed behind them and she might have been at Southing, or a gentlemen's club, or some other place where comfort and luxury reigned supreme.

'Please have a seat, my darling.' Sebastian showed her a silk-upholstered chair and she sank into it, her head still spinning with the faces and fumes. He moved to the fire and rang a bell; almost instantly a messenger appeared.

'Tea, please. For two.'

The boy hurried away and Sebastian came and sat next to her.

'It's shocking, I know. Even I was horrified the first time

I came here – and I was a child at the time, with a child's acceptance of the brutal realities of life. There is much that I would like to improve, but at least we provide honest employment – these are men and women who would otherwise be without means of sustaining themselves and would turn to crime or, in the case of the women . . .' He hesitated.

'Prostitution?' Rosa said bluntly. 'Is that what you mean?'

'Yes, though I don't like to hear the word on your lips.'

'But, Sebastian, would it be so hard to pay them a shilling more here or there? Or work them a little less hard?'

'What you see is not the effect of the work, Rosa. It's their upbringing. It is the fact that they have grown up in these poisoned, stifling streets without light or morality.'

'But that's not true!' She clenched her fists. 'I—'

'Yes?' Sebastian said. There was something dangerous, watchful in his eyes. Rosa held her breath. She had almost made the mistake of mentioning Luke's name. As if by agreement they had both avoided any mention of that terrible night at Southing, when she had kissed Luke. It was as if by pretending he did not exist, the whole horror could be wiped out of existence too.

'Nothing,' Rosa said miserably. 'But would it be so impossible to pay them a little more? Enough to move out of poverty, to somewhere with a little light and clean air?'

'They would take their filth with them,' Sebastian said softly. 'If you gave them a bath, they would not wash in it, for they have never been taught how. It is the people who

314

live here who create these neighbourhoods, not the other way around. Besides, what do you think would happen if I paid ten per cent more than our nearest rival? Our matches would cost ten per cent more, people would cease to buy them and the factory would end up having to close. Ten per cent of no wage is nothing.'

'But if you explained that the cost was in order to give a humane wage . . .' she tried despairingly. Sebastian only shook his head.

There was a rap at the door and Sebastian stood up.

'That will be the tea. Come in!'

But it was not the tea. It was a small messenger boy, stunted and anxious. He shook his head as Sebastian asked him for his message and beckoned him outside with a look at Rosa. Sebastian sighed, but followed him into the corridor and closed the door. When he came back inside, he was holding a tray.

'Rosa, there is a matter that requires my attention in the dipping room. I'm sorry to leave you, but it's urgent. Here is the tea . . .' He poured her a cup and added milk and a lump of sugar with silver tongs. 'When I come back I'll escort you down to the carriage.'

After he left, Rosa sank back in the chair. She felt numb. She knew she should drink the tea, that Sebastian would be angry if he came back and found she had not touched it, but she could not bear to think of consuming anything in this dark, poisoned place. He had not even asked her if she took sugar. Was this what her life would be like from now on, dictated to not by Mama's whims and Alexis' moods, but by Sebastian's instead?

She took a forced sip of tea. It was sickly sweet and she pushed the cup away.

Today should not have changed anything – everything she had found out about Sebastian's nature she had known already. She already knew that he was cold, that he was dictatorial, that there was a streak of brutality that frightened her.

But it had. It had changed everything.

She had been prepared to sacrifice herself. But she saw, clearly now, that it was not only her sacrifice. This factory had paid for Southing, its pastures wrung out of the suffering of men, women and children. Their happiness and health had paid for the bricks and stones and glass and paddocks. Every horse in the stable, warm and shining and well fed – how many matches did it represent? A thousand? A million? Each one whittled and dipped and packed by those desperate, grey-faced, blank-eyed workers.

She could not let them pay for Matchenham too.

She ripped off her glove and pulled at the ruby on her finger, yanking at the ring with all her strength. It was no use. The band dug cruelly into her finger and the more she pulled, the harder it bit. She spat on her knuckle and tried again, whispering spells under her breath to try to force it free, but the ring stayed firm, and when she stopped her finger was red and swelling, with blood beading scratches where the ornate setting had cut her skin.

Rosa let her hand drop. What was she planning to do – run away, leaving only the ring as the sign of her change of heart? No. That would be the coward's way out.

She would find Sebastian and tell him herself.

She stood, her heart beating suddenly hard and fast. She was more afraid that she had ever been in her life, more afraid than when the girth broke and she was dragged through the grit. More afraid than when Cherry had plunged to her death in the river.

In private she would be at Sebastian's mercy. She had to tell him now, in public, at the factory.

Outside the office she stood for a moment looking up and down the long, grey corridor. There was no one in sight, so she set off back the way they had come earlier, hoping to luck. As she turned a corner she bumped into a listless girl hurrying in the opposite direction.

'Excuse me,' she said. The girl didn't stop and Rosa put out a hand, grabbing her wrist and forcing her to halt. 'Excuse me!'

'Don't stop me, miss.' The girl's face was grey with fear. 'I daren't be late. I'll lose my post.'

'Then tell me quick, which way to the dipping room?'

'Visitors ain't allowed,' the girl said automatically. She tugged at her wrist, but Rosa held fast.

'Tell me and I'll let you go! No one will know it was you, but if you're late—'

'Straight ahead,' the girl said with a look of fear and fury. 'Take the third passage on the left and keep going past

317

the packing room. It's the last door on your right, marked "no entry". Now, let me go!'

'Thank you,' Rosa said as the girl tugged herself free. She watched her hurry away and then turned, her heart beating hard, the girl's directions ringing in her ears.

Straight ahead . . . third passage on the left . . . She passed one opening to her left, a dark room stacked with the packed-up matches. Someone had left a coat on the topmost pile. To Rosa's horror, it glowed in the dimness. She hurried on.

At last she came to the last door on her right and, sure enough, it was marked 'no entry'. She raised her hand, about to knock, and then something told her this would not be a good idea. Instead she grabbed the handle. It was locked and she whispered a charm, looking over her shoulder as she did.

The door gave way suddenly and she stumbled into the room.

The fumes hit her first, as physical and painful as a slap in the face. They were eye-watering, stinging not just her eyes, but her skin and the inside of her nose as she struggled for breath.

In the centre of the room were great boiling vats filled with chemicals, men and girls bending over them, working the dipping machines to coat the tips of the matches just so. The floor was covered with powdery residue and Rosa could see that it glowed in the dark corners.

But none of this was what made her stand in the doorway, gasping and struggling not to flee. It was the faces of the men and women.

Almost all were horribly swollen and deformed – with missing teeth, missing jaws even. Their skin was mottled from yellow, to red, to greenish black. She had never seen anything like it – it was as close to Hell as she could imagine, these walking, working zombies of death.

'Please . . .' she managed. She put her hand to the sleeve of the girl closest to her. 'What in God's name is wrong with your faces?'

The girl did not answer, she just continued to work, like a golem. Her eyes were dead and blank.

'What is wrong with you all?' Rosa shouted. 'Why won't you answer me? Why don't you stop work?'

They did not respond – and suddenly she understood. They were under an enchantment, all of them – like the men, women and children in the rest of the factory. Why else would they keep going, keep returning to this living Hell for the few shillings a week, while their faces and bodies slowly rotted away?

If she had stopped to look she would have seen it earlier; the air was thick with magic, putrid with it. But it was not directed at her and so she had not noticed. She had never looked.

'*Ætberstan!*' she sobbed, trying to feel her way through the thick web of spells wound around the machinery and the silent men and women. But it was far too strong. She did not have the strength to snap the enchantments. *'Ætberstan!'*

Who had created such an enormous machine of evil? Who would have had the strength? She remembered the Ealdwitan edicts that she had recited as a small child on her father's knee: *I shall let the outwith be, and so no harm will come to me, I shall not seek to bend his mind, but keep my spells to my own kind.*

Who would dare to go against that, the very first law that their kind were taught?

She knew. Even before she raised her eyes to the portrait of Aloysius Knyvet, Sebastian's father, hanging high above the doorway. He was seated in a carved mahogany chair and in his hand was his cane with the ebony shaft and the snake's head. The cane that was now Sebastian's.

Rosa dropped her eyes unseeingly to the vat in front of her, racing through possibilities. She could not free these men and women. She was not strong enough. Could she persuade Sebastian to do so? If only the outwith would trust her – if she could rouse them from their stupor long enough to fight against the enchantment, she might have a chance. But to them she would be just another witch.

Footsteps sounded in the corridor and she jumped. If Sebastian found her here . . .

She ran to the far end of the room and crouched down, close to where the great stove bubbled away, heating the chemicals to make the dipping mixture. Back here, in the shadows, she would be hidden . . .

The door opened and she saw Sebastian's face look in sharply. He glanced up and down the row of dippers and Rosa held her breath. The heat from the stove was almost unendurable and she longed to cast a spell to shield herself from the worst of it, but did not dare in case Sebastian caught the flare of magic. She felt the heat of the gas against her cheek and the stench of chemicals made her eyes water. She put her face in her skirts and prayed . . .

Then the door swung shut and she let out a great breath and stood up. The sudden movement made her head spin and she stumbled and almost fell, clutching at the girl next to her to save herself.

'Oi, watch yourself,' the girl said dully, but didn't break from the work. Something about her voice was familiar.

'Minna?' Rosa touched the girl's shoulder. 'Minna? Is that you?'

She would hardly have recognized her. In just a few short weeks she had become thin almost to the point of being skeletal and beneath her cap Rosa could see her hair was thinning.

'What of it?' the girl said huskily. With a shudder, Rosa saw that two of her teeth were missing.

'Minna, it's me – Rosa, Miss Greenwood. I gave you my card.'

'What of it?' Minna repeated dully. Her face looked almost stupefied, but her hands never faltered, moving swiftly, automatically, as unchangeable as the machinery of the factory itself.

'Please, come away with me,' Rosa begged. 'I was wrong to send you here.' She strained to snap the spells – if she could not save all the workers, perhaps she could at least save Minna. If only Minna would help her, trust her . . .

'I'm Luke's friend,' she said desperately. 'He sent me, with a message. He wants you to come away.'

'Luke Lexton?' Minna said, and something in her eyes seemed to flicker, a moment of recognition, like the moon breaking through the clouds. Then the haze closed over again and she shook her head. 'No, I can't stop. I must keep going.'

'Please, trust me!' Rosa begged, but Minna didn't even reply.

Frustration rose within her like a great sob. What had she done? What had she condemned Minna to?

Luke. It came to her like a breath of air in the foulness of the room. If Minna would not trust her, she would trust Luke.

'Minna, where can I find Luke?' she demanded, but Minna seemed to have sunk back into that terrible torpor and she did not answer, but only shook her head.

'I've to go and see a man about a set of gates,' William said, wiping his chin and putting down his fork. 'Can you manage?'

'Yes,' Luke said with a touch of irritation. He was growing weary of his uncle's anxiety. There might be a hole in his memories, but he wasn't ill and he was sick of being treated like an invalid.

'There shouldn't be anything too much, couple a horseshoes maybe, and there's that fireguard Mr Maddocks wants mending, if you have time. I shouldn't be more than an hour.'

'I'll manage,' Luke said shortly. Then he felt bad. 'I'll be all right, Uncle. Go. We need the work.'

It was true. In the weeks Luke had been missing, and since his return, William had let the forge slip and the work had dried up. No one wanted to bring a limping horse to the forge only to find the farrier busy or gone.

Now with Luke up and about they desperately needed new work and William was taking on anything he could find – blacksmith work and tinkers' stuff that he would usually have refused.

'All right.' William pulled on his cap and coat and went to the door. 'Remember, if you're feeling tired, there's no shame in stopping—'

'Go!' Luke said, more roughly than he meant. William sighed and shut the door behind him. Luke sighed too and put his head in his hands wishing, wishing that he could remember what lay in that great gulf in his mind. Once he had dreamt and there had been the smell of burning rosemary and a gold-red swirl, like forge-flames in the darkness. He had woken with a word on his lips, *rose* – but whatever it meant sank far away as he rose to consciousness and the memory, whatever it had been, had gone. The more he scrabbled for it, the further it retreated.

Now he got up slowly from the table and went out to the forge to blow the fire into life again.

'Luke Welling?' Rosa said again, desperately. There was a catch in her throat. The evening was drawing in and the streets of Spitalfields felt very dark and narrow. In her new silk dress, part of Mama's trousseau shopping, she stuck out like candle flame in a darkened room, all eyes turning to her as she picked her way through the filth-strewn streets.

Now she stood at a street corner, trying to ignore the

gales of ribald laughter coming from the public house in front of her, and asked the girl again, 'Are you sure you've never heard of him? His father's a drayman. He's about nineteen, twenty perhaps – he's lived here all his life.'

'I'm sorry, darlin',' said the girl. She eyed Rosa speculatively through her lashes and Rosa saw, to her shock, that the girl's lips and eyelids were painted. 'Someone's bin telling you porkies.'

'Porkies?' Rosa echoed stupidly. She felt close to tears.

'Pork pies – lies. Ain't you never heard of rhyming slang?' She made a face and laughed. Rosa felt her cheeks grow hot.

'I'm sorry. I won't waste your time any further.'

'Not to worry, darlin'. But if your boyfriend lived round here, I'da heard of him. There's not many men round here unacquainted with Phoebe Fairbrother.' She gave a raucous laugh.

'Would your friend know anything?' Rosa pleaded, nodding at the brunette seated in the tavern window. The girl shook her head, impatiently now, setting her brassy curls swinging.

'If I ain't heard of him, Miriam won't know 'im neither. I'm telling you, there ain't no Luke Welling round 'ere. The only Lukes what live in this district is Lucas Michaels, but he's fifty if he's a day, and Luke Lexton. Now, if you'll excuse me, I've got my customers to attend.'

She turned, but before she could go Rosa grabbed her arm.

325

'Wait. What did you say? Luke Lexton?'

'It's clear you ain't deaf anyhow.'

'I've heard that name. Oh, God, where have I heard it?' She shut her eyes, desperately scrabbling for the memory. She *had* heard it, recently too . . . It came to her suddenly – Minna, in the factory, asking 'Luke Lexton?' when she had mentioned Luke's name. And she hadn't even noticed.

'Luke Lexton!' she cried. 'Yes! That's it, I made a mistake. I should have said Luke Lexton, not Welling. Do you know where he is?'

'Made a mistake, didja?' The girl snorted disbelievingly, but there was a smile at the corner of her mouth. 'What do you want with Luke Lexton then? You'd need two more legs for him to take notice of you.'

'What?' Rosa said, too confused to be polite.

'He's sweeter on horses than women,' Phoebe said. 'Not that I wouldn't give him a ride, if he came asking.'

Rosa knew she should pretend to be shocked, but she didn't care.

'Where does he live?'

'At his uncle's forge, off Farrer's Lane. But his father's no drayman – he's dead.'

'Farrer's Lane – where's that? Can you – would you show me?'

'Why should I?' The girl folded her arms and Rosa felt desperate. 'I'm a working girl, darlin'. I get paid for my time.'

'I don't have any money!' She could force Phoebe to tell

326

her. That was dark magic, but she had seen the spells in the Grimoire, although Mama had told her never to look at those pages. If only she had a coin . . .

Phoebe looked her up and down appraisingly, her eyes hard. She seemed to come to a decision.

'Give me that locket.'

'What? No!' Rosa's hand closed around it reflexively. She felt its heavy warmth against her collarbone, where it had rested since Papa had given it to her on her tenth birthday. 'You don't understand . . .'

'I understand that you want a service and you're not prepared to pay for it. But I don't care, wander the streets of Spitalfields on your own; you'll soon find some kind fella prepared to take you under his wing, no doubt.' She gave a raucous laugh and Rosa bit her lip. She could well imagine what kind of fellows she might meet in the dark streets between here and Luke's uncle's forge. They were spilling out of the Cock Tavern now, amorous and angry by turns. One of them plucked at Phoebe's sleeve.

'Gi's a tumble, Phoebs, for old time's sake, eh?'

'Oh piss off, Nick Sykes, you old soak,' the girl snarled. She gave him a shove and he stumbled backwards, tumbling into the filth-filled gutter where he lay, laughing or sobbing, Rosa could not tell which. Phoebe turned back to Rosa. 'Well? Take it or leave it, I ain't got the time to be gabbing here.'

'I'll take it,' Rosa said, though her heart hurt as she fumbled for the catch of the locket. Phoebe reached for it,

327

greedily, and Rosa said, 'Wait!'

She opened it up and, using her nail, prised out the tiny pencil drawing of Papa. She saw now that it was crude, the work of a child. But it was all she had.

For a moment the locket hung from her fingers, still hers. Then she let it drop into Phoebe's outstretched palm.

Phoebe nodded.

'Come on then. Look slippy and don't talk to no one. You're like a fox in a hen house. No, hang about, that's the wrong way round. But there ain't no such thing as a fox house.'

But perhaps Phoebe had it right, Rosa thought, as she followed her down the first dark alleyway between two buildings. She was more dangerous, more predatory than any of the poor drunkards. She could gut them alive if she chose. She was aware, suddenly, horribly, of the power even the feeblest witch held over the outwith. No wonder their kind had been hated and feared for so long.

Phoebe was cheerful now, chatting as she led Rosa through stinking back alleys, where children played in spite of the filth and the darkness. They cut across the corner of a deserted market space, where a few beggars were rummaging in the cast-off boxes, and then up a street less forbidding than the rest, if only because it was emptier. The evening fog had begun to descend and Rosa shivered, wishing that she had not left her wrap in the carriage. What would the driver be thinking? Would Sebastian have noticed her absence?

Then suddenly Phoebe swung left through a low arch and into a cobbled yard. There was a roaring sound, as of a huge fire, coming from a low brick building to their right, and a shower of sparks flew up suddenly from the chimney.

'Luke,' Phoebe yelled. 'Gotta visitor.'

'Who is it?' The voice was so familiar that Rosa choked. She could not speak.

Phoebe stuck her head through the door to the forge.

'La-di-da type by the name of . . .' She looked back over her shoulder at Rosa. 'What was your name, darlin'?'

'Rosa,' she whispered. 'Rosa Greenwood.'

'Rosa Greenwood,' Phoebe repeated back. There was a reply that Rosa could not hear and Phoebe shrugged and turned back to Rosa.

'Says he's never heard of you. Well, there you are. Not my fault if you made a mistake. Anyway, I've done what I said. Tarra now.'

And with a swish of skirts and a flash of scarlet petticoat, she was gone.

Rosa took a deep breath and stepped forward into the forge. For a minute she almost didn't recognize the man working the bellows. He was stripped to the waist, sweating, his muscles standing out in the light from the fire, the flames flickering across his naked chest and shoulders. His head was down, his brows knit in effort or concentration.

Then he looked up and she saw his clear hazel eyes.

He wiped his brow with a cloth and then took a shirt from a peg by the door and pulled it over his head.

'Yes, miss,' he said as he tucked it in. His voice at least was familiar, the same low voice she remembered, though his East End accent sounded stronger than it had in Knightsbridge. 'What can I do for you? My uncle's not here, as you see.'

'Luke . . .' She didn't know where to begin, how to start. 'Luke, it's me, Rosa.'

Something flickered in his eyes, not recognition, but a kind of wariness.

'I've never seen you before,' he said flatly.

'That's not true.' What could she say? How could she convince him? She had taken *everything*, every memory of herself, of why he had come, of what had happened to him there. 'I know things about you.'

'Like what?'

'I know that you've lost your memory, that you can't remember anything for the last month back, maybe longer. I know that you have a scar on the back of your head, that you came back with a wound there, from a fight.'

'Anyone could know that,' he said hoarsely, though he looked uneasy. 'You could have talked to Phoebe.'

'I know that you have a mark on your shoulder.' She thought of him washing under the pump in the yard. 'A scar, like a brand.'

His hand went involuntarily to the place and then he shook his head.

'You saw it while I was dressing, just now.'

'Luke, why won't you believe me?' It was not what she wanted to ask; she wanted to shake him, ask why he'd come to Osborne House, why he had changed his name and lied about his father. Had it all been a lie? No – she thought of his confession, in the dark of the stable yard. His uncle and the forge – that had not been a lie. And she remembered his other confession. About what he could see.

'I know something else,' she whispered. 'I know that you – that you . . .' She swallowed. 'I know that you can see witches.'

He flinched, as if she had slapped him.

'It's true, isn't it?'

'How do you know?' he demanded. He was across the forge in an instant, grabbing her arms with a strength that almost frightened her, except that it was Luke, Luke who would never hurt her.

'I know b-because . . . I am one.'

She let her magic shine out, feeling it flicker across her skin like electricity, flow through her limbs and her fingers, crackling to the tips of her hair like static energy.

Luke let go of her as if she had burnt him. He was staring at her with a look of horror. His hand went again to the scar on his shoulder as if it hurt.

Rosa stretched out her hands, where the witchlight burnt, clear and bright in her palm.

'*Please*, Luke.' She tried to reach him, to heal his mind, pour back the memories she had ripped out of him by the roots. 'Don't you remember? You came to my house, you saved my life, you *kissed* me.'

'No!' he cried desperately. He put his hands to his head, as if it might explode, as if something might crack. She was not sure if he was trying to force the memories back in, or keep them away.

'It's true. I need your help – I've found your friend Minna—'

'Get out!' He cut her off.

'She's at the match factory, down by the Thames, where *I* sent her, Luke. It's horrible – the workers are under some kind of spell, they're dying, but they won't listen to me. Please, come and help—'

'Get out!' he roared. His face was suffused with blood.

'Please, just—'

'Help you?' he cried. There was something desperate in his eyes, as if he was breaking apart inside. 'How can I help you? I should kill you.'

'What?'

'Have you heard of the Malleus?' He took a step towards her and for the first time she noticed that he had something in his hand. A hammer.

'No,' she whispered.

'We're sworn to kill your kind.'

'*No!*'

'Yes. Now, get out.'

Rosa looked at him. *This is Luke*, she told herself. She tried not to tremble. *Luke!*

He raised the hammer above his head.

She ran.

Luke watched as the girl disappeared into the fog. He could see the bright red-gold flame of her hair dwindling as she ran and then at last even that was gone, swallowed up in the darkness of the narrow streets.

He let the hammer fall from his hand on to the stone floor of the forge.

The Malleus. How could he have forgotten the Malleus?

Images flickered through his mind like half-forgotten dreams – the feel of the knife in his side, the screaming heat of the brand on his shoulder . . . His hand went to the mark beneath his shirt and now he knew what it meant. The hammer. The hammer of witches.

That girl – Rosa – he had never seen her before and yet he knew every inch of her face, the softness of her skin beneath his touch, the feel of her waist between his hands . . . How did he know her? *Why?*

And how did she know him?

He thought of her words: *I know that you can see witches.*

The scar at the back of his head gave a great throbbing pang and he vomited on to the floor, heaving and choking until there was nothing left but bile in his gut and he was cold and sweating, and full of fear.

What had he done?

* * *

Rosa ran. She ran without looking where she was going, turning at random in the narrow twisting streets, the fog parting and then closing behind her, enveloping her in its strange, muffled world. She stumbled past taverns disgorging drunks on to the pavement, past beggars crowded round braziers, past girls hawking watercress, their eyes huge in the darkness. At last she stopped in a quiet alleyway, panting, her lungs screaming for air, fighting against the constriction of her choking stays. There were black spots in front of her vision, dancing against the sickly yellow swirl of the fog, and she thought she might faint, but she did not. After a while her breathing began to slow and she tried to consider what to do next.

Luke was a killer?

It didn't make sense.

And yet, in another horrible way, it did. It explained the way he had come so mysteriously with only Fred Welling's word and no experience. It explained why he'd been prepared to fill in for no money. It explained – she shut her eyes as the realization washed over her – it explained the broken buckle. The buckle that *she* had taken responsibility for, when Alexis wanted him sacked.

She put her hands over her face.

He had tried to kill her.

He saved your life.

He had betrayed her.

He told you he loved you.

The voices crowded in her head, screaming at each

other for domination.

Shut up – shut up! I can't think!

She put her hand up to the locket to feel its reassuring weight in her palm as she tried to think what to do. But it was gone.

It began to rain, a fine mist of drizzle that mingled with the fog, clinging to her skin and hair in fine droplets. Rosa shivered.

The factory. Whatever had happened with Luke, it changed nothing about the factory, about the fact that she had sent an innocent girl there to her death. That was her wrong, not his. It was hers to undo.

Luke would not help her. There was no one left to turn to. It was down to her alone to sort this out. There were only two options: undo the charms herself, or force Sebastian to do it. But how?

23

'I wish to see Mr Knyvet.'

The guard at the gate had changed and did not recognize her. He looked her up and down doubtfully and for the first time Rosa looked down at her stained and rain-soaked dress. There was a great patch of soot where she had crouched behind the gas burner in the dipping room, and in retracing her way back to the factory she had stumbled in the fog and fallen into the gutter. She did not look like Sebastian Kynvet's fiancée.

'Tell him,' she groped in her skirt pocket for a card and pressed it into the man's gloved hand, 'tell him it's Miss Greenwood. He will know who I am.'

'Very well, Miss . . . Oi, Joe.' He turned to a small boy crouched in the shelter of a brick arch and said a few words. The boy set off at a trot across the courtyard. Rosa waited, the rain trickling down her neck in slow droplets, feeling the guard's cold eye on her. After a few minutes the boy returned and whispered something into the man's ear. He stood up straighter.

'I beg your p-pardon, miss,' he stammered. 'I wasn't, that's to say—'

'It's quite all right.' She cut him off and turned to the boy. 'Can you take me now?'

The boy looked up at the guard, as if not trusting his own judgement, and the man nodded, sharply.

'Of course you can, you young fool. Cut along quick now, and keep a civil tongue in your head.'

'This way, miss,' the boy whispered, and she followed him through the brick archway and up the same sets of stairs as before. The clock struck seven as they climbed and Rosa wondered, bewildered, where the hours had gone. Had it really taken so long for her to find Luke? She felt suddenly, enormously tired. It had taken magic for her to find her way back to the factory in the fog, divination spells at every street corner, walking in circles as her powers waned.

As they passed the packing rooms she looked in. In spite of what Sebastian had said about stopping at six, the workers were still there, the conveyor belts still carrying their endless, relentless supply of matches. One girl looked up as Rosa passed and their eyes met: dark holes in a face as thin and white as a skull.

Sebastian was in his office. He looked up as she entered, his face blank with astonishment, and then hurried across the room.

'That will do, Joe, you can go,' he said to the boy. Then he turned to Rosa. 'What in God's name happened? I looked for you everywhere! I was beside myself. I can't imagine what your mother is thinking.'

Nothing, Rosa thought wearily.

'Your clothes! You're soaked to the bone.' He led her across to the fire and pushed her down on an armchair, crouching next to her as if she were a child. 'I'll ring for tea – and brandy if they have it, or you'll be ill.'

'I'm not ill,' she said huskily.

'But what were you thinking?' He took her chin in his fingers, turning her face towards him so that she was forced to meet his eyes. 'Rosa?'

She looked at him, at his cold, pale eyes, willing herself to find some spark of humanity there, *some* kind of conscience at least.

'Sebastian . . .' She drew a deep breath. 'Do you love me?'

'Of course.' He put his hand to her cheek, where the ache of his blows still dwelled. 'You cannot imagine how much.'

Rosa swallowed and took his hand in hers. It was cold, and very, very strong. Hands that could curb a horse, beat a dog. Or a woman.

'Sebastian,' she said softly, 'let them go.'

'What do you mean?' He did not take his hand out of hers, but instead closed his fingers around her wrist, hard enough to bruise. Rosa tried not to flinch.

'I saw the dipping room.'

'God damn it.' He said it quite low, without the black fury she had feared. But his grip didn't lessen.

'I'm not a fool. There is no way men and women would work willingly in those conditions, no way they *could* work. Sebastian, they're dying. They are rotting away as they work, eaten up by whatever poison is in those matches. You've chained them, haven't you? It's magic keeping them at their posts, day in, day out.'

'You know nothing about it,' he said. His voice was cold and flat as river ice, as cold as his eyes.

'What you're doing is illegal, *more* than illegal — it's inhumane, madness. Let them go.'

'And if I won't?'

Possibilities raced through her head: she would leave him, she would break off the engagement. Somehow, she thought, none of these would sway him.

'I will disgrace you,' she said flatly. 'I will tell everyone we know. I will denounce you to the Ealdwitan.'

'You think they will listen to you?' he sneered. 'A chit of a girl against the word of a Chair?'

'A woman,' she spat, 'giving evidence against her own fiancé. But in any event, it will not be a case of taking my word for it. If they come here, there will be no question. Their eyes will give them all the evidence they need. They will break you.'

'You ungrateful little wretch.'

He stood and began pacing the room. When Rosa stood

too, he wheeled round and screamed, 'Sit down, damn you!'

Rosa sat immediately and then a surge of anger shot through her and she jumped back up.

'No! Why should I?'

'You are to be my wife, and you *will* obey me.'

'I am *not* your wife and I never will be! I don't love you, I *never* loved you. I would rather marry—' A sob rose in her throat, choking her. 'I'd rather marry a – a stable-hand.'

'You are mine,' he said softly. 'And I will see you dead before I lose you to the arms of another man.'

Rosa opened her mouth to answer.

'*Tówierpe!*' he spat, and instead Rosa flew backwards into the chair, with a force that knocked all the breath from her body. Before she had time to recover he was across the room, crouching beside her with something in his hands. It was cord, the cord they used for tying up the bales of matchboxes.

She felt it bite into her wrists and began to struggle with all her strength.

'*Áhíewe!*' she screamed, and a blast of flame shot towards him. Sebastian howled, reeling back, clutching at his face. When he lifted his hands away Rosa saw that his lip was bleeding, his cheek slashed to the bone.

'You'll pay for that, you bitch.'

He pulled off his cravat and bound it round her mouth, silencing the half-worked spells on her lips. It didn't stop her kicking, but he soon had her bound hand and foot to

340

the chair. She felt the heat of the fire on the side of her face and looked at him, hoping he could read the hatred in her eyes.

But he only knelt in front of her, staring at her. His blue eyes, just inches away from hers, were bloodshot.

'Until death do us part, Rosa, my darling,' he said softly. Then he stood and left the room.

For a moment Rosa did nothing. She breathed through her nose, trying to calm her pounding heart and pull her magic together. The cords were biting painfully into her wrists and she strained at them, yanking uselessly. Nothing happened – only the pain in her wrists and ankles increased. Sebastian had bewitched the knots – these bindings would not break without magic. But she had none left. The long search for the factory and then the fight with Sebastian – it had taken her very last effort. And she could not speak anyway. She remembered Mama saying: *It's not the words on your lips that are important, Rosamund, it is the words in your head – try to grasp that, for heaven's sakes.* But there were no words in her head, just a silent scream of fear.

Far away she could hear sounds, crashes, as if machinery were falling to the ground. Cries of fear too. And then: the smell of smoke.

The heat of the forge blazed bright and Luke sweated as he hammered the red-hot metal, the sweat running in rivulets down his face and into his eyes like tears.

William wasn't back. No doubt he had met a friend and they were drinking. Another night Luke might have gone out himself to the Cock to find them. Not tonight. Tonight he was glad to be alone, hitting something as hard as he could.

But nothing – not even the hot, bright flames of the forge – could chase away the shadowy memories that seemed to be crowding into his skull.

A hand, creeping across the floor like a spider.

A girl's lips, so soft he could hardly bear it.

The sound of a fist meeting bone – and a girl's cry.

The feel of a brand in his shoulder.

And then, as he began to twist the hot metal into shape, something else. The shape of a coiled snake, silver bright, on top of an ebony cane.

He let the hammer drop, putting his hands to his head, as if he could keep out the horrors, but they forced their way, exploding in his head like fireworks. The crack of a bridge strut. The scream of a horse. Narrow brows furrowed, a coin in the sun. Blood on white skin. Hair like fire.

Minna.

Cherry.

Rosa.

Oh, God, Rosa.

The memories flooded back, his skull felt as if it would crack. And then he knew – he knew what he had to do.

* * *

The guard at the gate was a witch, although not a good one. The thin white wisp of his magic melded with the fog, disappearing into the night. Luke felt in his pocket for the bottle. The one he had taken to Knightsbridge was gone, probably still under the board in Fred Welling's room for all he knew, but a moment's search of William's room had revealed a rough bundle in his chest. Unwrapping it, Luke found a knife, a bottle, a rag.

Now they were in the pocket of Luke's jacket, the rag twisted round the bottle so that the knife would not chink and smash the glass.

His heart pounding, he pulled out the rag and the bottle, thankful for the meagre gas-light and the muffling fog. When he wrenched out the cork the fumes almost choked him, stinging his eyes and throat, but he splashed some on to the rag, stoppered up the bottle, and took a deep breath. Then he crept forward, hugging the wall.

The witch did not see him until the last moment and, when he did, his eyes widened and his mouth opened – to call for help, or shout a spell? Luke didn't wait to find out. He leapt at him, the rag clenched in his hand, and crushed it over the man's mouth and nose. He was a big man, matching every inch of Luke's six foot, but Luke had the advantage of surprise. The man clawed at Luke's fingers, scrabbling for a hold, but the stuff in the bottle was too strong. His struggles slackened, his kicks and snorting gasps turned to spasmodic twitches, and at last he hung from Luke's arms, limp as a sack of coal.

Luke dragged him into the shadow of an arch and there pulled off the man's greatcoat and cap. No point in sticking out more than he had to.

Dragging them on over his jacket, he stepped out into the courtyard. It was dark, but not as dark as it should have been. There were flames coming from an upper window.

Luke ran to the door and wrenched it open, a great wall of smoke coming out to meet him. He choked but, pulling his muffler over his face, he plunged in. In front of him was a hall, clearly empty, some kind of refectory. The sound of crackling and the smell of smoke was coming from upstairs. He took a deep breath and began to climb up towards the heat.

The first thing that met his eyes at the landing was a huge, long room filled with men, women and children working a vast conveyor belt. They were choking in the smoke, their eyes watering, but they worked on.

'What are you doing?' Luke bellowed at one of them, a girl of about ten. 'This place is burning down! Get out!'

She shook her head and carried on scrabbling the matches into stacks.

'Are you mad?' He pulled off the muffler, the better to shout, and choked against the smoke, but found the breath to shout again. 'Get out, all of you!'

They took no notice. Luke looked around him. There was a long iron pole behind the door, with a hook on the end, designed for opening windows too high to be reached with a ladder. He grabbed one end and brought it smashing down on the conveyor belt. There were cries of alarm from the workers and one of them, a girl with wispy pale hair, looked up, confusion in her eyes.

'Whatcha doing, mister?'

'Get out!' he bellowed again. She shook her head dully, and he raised the pole above his head and brought it down again. The conveyor belt juddered but didn't stop, and the girl reached, as if mesmerized, for another handful of matches. Luke could have screamed. Would they never stop work until the blasted belt stopped too?

Suddenly he had a thought.

Yanking the knife from his pocket, he scattered aside the handfuls of matches and began to saw at the thick India rubber of the conveyor belt. It was hard, almost impossible – as soon as he made one good cut the machine pulled the fabric from his hands, and he was faced with a fresh, undamaged stretch. He hacked and hacked, fighting against the hopelessness that threatened to overwhelm him. The crackle of flames sounded louder than ever.

Should he just give up? Leave them to it?

With one last effort he raised the knife above his head and stabbed it viciously through the material of the conveyor belt, deep into the wooden support beneath.

It held.

The relentless force of the conveyor belt pulled on, but now it was destroying itself, its whole force ripping against the knife in its guts. A long rent began to appear in the centre of the belt. Then, suddenly, it stuck. The knife had come up against a join in the belt, stitching too strong to slit. There was a shriek as the belt pulled tight, the metal gears bending and whirring. The whole roomful of workers had stopped, watching, hypnotized as the machine strained and screeched its protest. Then, with a deafening bang, the belt snapped, throwing matches high into the air, raining down like hail on their backs.

'Sweet Jesus!' gasped the pale-haired girl. 'What've you done?'

'Get out!' he roared at her. This time she blinked. And then she nodded and ran.

There were murmurs as the others watched her go – and Luke shouted, 'Well? What are you waiting for? D'you want to burn?'

It was as if his words burst a dam and one after another they began to stumble and then run towards the door, making for the courtyard and the relative safety of the Thames.

Luke pulled the knife out of the belt and started to run in the other direction, deeper into the factory.

Bodies pushed past him, making for the door, and he scanned every face that passed, looking for Minna – but she wasn't there.

'Minna!' he shouted above the noise of footsteps and the far-off crackle of flame. A girl, about his age, stumbled into him and he grabbed her arm. 'I'm looking for a friend, Minna Sykes. D'you know her?'

'Dipping room,' she gasped, and then pushed past him. 'And where's that?'

'Down the corridor, on yer right. Lemme go, mister.' She tore her arm out of his grip and ran.

The long, low room was almost empty now, but he could hear the roar of machines from next door and he ran in to find the workers still labouring in spite of the smoke, choking as they tied the matchboxes into parcels. Now he knew that the spell was bound up in the machines it was easier. He didn't waste time begging or trying to shake them out of their indifference, he just went straight for the belt with his knife. There was the same grinding, shrieking roar, like the dying screams of the machine, and then it snapped and the workers were dazed and staggering like new-woken drunks, the room ringing with his shouts as he harried them towards the stairs.

The smell of smoke was very strong now and he could hear the crackle of flames, but above it was another smell, something acrid that tore at his throat. And still he had not found Minna – or Rosa. Had she come back here? Back to Sebastian's waiting arms?

He tried to remember her parting words as he ran up the corridor, the muffler pulled high across his face to try to shut out the bitter, choking fumes, but he could not. All he could remember was the horror in her eyes as he raised that hammer and she ran.

Down the corridor. On your right.

There was a door. It was marked 'no entry'. There was

smoke and the red glow of flames coming from the crack beneath. Luke touched it with his hand and it was hot. He pulled off his muffler, wound it around his hand, and grabbed for the handle.

Inside, Hell met his eyes.

Wherever the fire had started, it was close to this room, and the flames were eating at the dividing wall and flickering up through the floorboards, attacking the joists beneath. But – impossibly – the workers still toiled, stirring at the great vats of chemicals that bubbled in the centre of the room, a white mist rising off the surface.

Luke stepped forward, ready to slash at the dipping racks, up-end tables, douse the stoves. He would free this last group and get out.

Then he stopped.

Standing between the vats was a man, his figure just a black outline against the smoke – but Luke did not need to see his face to recognize that tall silhouette. It was Sebastian Knyvet.

Luke swallowed. He thought about running – but what if Minna were here, in this last room? He couldn't fight his way through all this and then run without even freeing her. But if Knyvet saw him . . .

It seemed like an eternity as they both stood, frozen as the flames flickered around them. Could Knyvet see him? He couldn't tell. His shape was wreathed in smoke and flame, his face hidden.

And then Sebastian moved. He grabbed the lip of the

cauldron closest to him, seeming not even to notice the scalding metal on his bare hand, and heaved.

Toxic, boiling chemicals flooded across the floor, hissing and spitting, throwing up an acrid white smoke that made Luke gasp and retch and the workers fall back. A girl almost staggered into his arms and Luke caught her reflexively.

'Luke?' she gasped.

'Minna!'

It couldn't be the phossy jaw – not yet, surely? But it looked very like it. Her face was swollen and livid, and the tooth that had given her so much trouble was missing; where it should have been there was a bloody gap for the phosphorus to enter, rotting the bone from within.

'Get out,' he said urgently. Minna shook her head, looking back at the dipping racks with an expression almost like longing, and Luke wanted to slap her.

'Get out, Minna! There's no more dipping – this place is burning down – can't you see?'

The flames were licking at the dipping racks and the drying frames now, the dipped matches bursting into flames as the heat began to reach them. One of the racks collapsed in a shower of sparks and miniature explosions.

'Get out!' He took her shoulders and shook her, trying to reach her through the thick cloud of spell and stupor.

She opened her mouth – and then shut it again and nodded once. Then she stumbled from the room.

Luke watched her go and then turned back to try to

persuade the others. It was too late for some; there were bodies on the floor overcome by the smoke. But others were staggering out into the corridor, making for the stairs further from the inferno.

Another drying frame went up with a roar. The fire's heat was becoming intolerable. It had taken hold now – there was no hope for the factory. He had to get out, or burn with it.

Luke turned to go. As he did, he cast one last glance at Knyvet, wondering if the man was planning to burn.

He had turned. He was standing in the centre of the room, wreathed in flame and smoke. His head was bare and his pale hair was bright in the dancing flames. And there was something in his hand. Something that made Luke stop dead in his tracks.

An ebony shaft. A twist of silver. A shape that had dwelled in his nightmares for so long: a coiled snake.

The Black Witch.

No. He shook his head, the smoke swirling in his skull, making him numb and stupid. It was impossible. Sebastian was far too young to be the witch he'd seen.

But that cane – it was unmistakeable.

Then Knyvet spoke.

'So you came back for her.'

Luke felt frozen. His face was burning, but his hands were cold as ice. As cold as Knyvet's blue, blue eyes.

'You. Where did you get that cane?' he managed.

'You've come all this way to discuss gentlemen's

350

accessories?' Knyvet laughed. His smile was horrible to see; he had been slashed all across one side of his face, so that the bone gleamed through the flesh, pink and white in the burnt skin.

'*The cane!*' Luke snarled.

'Much as I'd like to discuss fashion with you,' Knyvet gave that horrible death's-head smile again, 'I fear I must leave.'

Luke looked behind them, at the stairs. The exit was gone, the stairwell filled with flames – a great hole where the landing should have been. Something shifted beneath their feet and a joist gave way with a groaning crash. Luke clutched at a table, but Knyvet turned towards the window, pointed his cane and shouted a spell in some kind of foreign tongue, words Luke didn't recognize. Glass and bricks flew outwards like an explosion, leaving a jagged hole in the wall, large enough to jump from, if you were a fool, or suicidal. The night air whistled in, fanning the flames higher.

'Goodbye,' Sebastian drawled. 'How lovely that you and Rosa can be together at the end. Such devotion.'

Luke went cold.

'Oh.' Sebastian began to laugh. 'You didn't know? She's having a little tea party upstairs – tied up, as you might say. Unfortunately our delightful afternoon was brought to a close by her announcement that she intended to expose my family's practices and bankrupt the factory. Not the act of a devoted fiancée, wouldn't you say?'

351

'What?' Luke tried to clear his head. He held on to the table, his fingers numb. The smoke was choking him, making him almost too dizzy to stand. His eyes were streaming. 'She threatened you?'

'Yes. I don't take kindly to blackmail – and it's never a good idea to give an ultimatum. You might find the person prefers a third option, one you didn't offer. You're welcome to her – what's left of her. I doubt it'll be much.'

And then he ran towards the jagged hole and leapt.

For a minute Luke held his breath, waiting for the smash on the cobbles below, the screams from the workers. It never came and he stumbled to the gap, feeling the cool wind on his face.

Knyvet was hovering in mid-air, high above the workers beneath. There was a smile on his face. Then he turned and skimmed above the rooftops, far out of sight.

Luke looked down, his heart in his mouth. It was a long drop – perhaps thirty feet – on to cobbles. But it was better than burning. And he had every reason to live. He thought of the cane in Knyvet's hand, the cane that held the answers to the mystery of his parents' death. Knyvet knew – even if he had not carried out their execution, he *must* know who had killed them, and why.

Luke could not take him on alone, but with the Malleus at his back . . . He looked at the sky. Far above the sluggish Thames, the moon was full. It was the last night of his task. If Rosa died tonight, he could live; live to fight side by side with William and John and the rest of the Malleus, live to kill Sebastian, live to avenge his father and mother.

He held on to the jagged bricks of the opening. *Jump, you coward.*

But . . . Rosa.

Jump.

Rosa.

Coward.

The words pounded inside him, in time with his pounding heart, like a hammer.

Rosa!

He did not jump.

He turned and ran back into the factory.

It was hot in the little office. Unbearably hot. And the room had begun to fill with smoke.

At first Rosa had screamed, or tried to, her throat growing raw and her lips bruised as she worked her mouth around the choking gag, until at last it was between her teeth like a bit and she could pant and shout, albeit muffled.

But no one came. Between cries she listened. She could make out the sound of smashing machinery and the far-off crackle of fire. At one point she thought she heard shouts and running footsteps, and she screamed again, louder, but whoever it was either couldn't hear her above the noise of the dying factory, or else didn't care enough to stop.

How could she ever have promised to marry Sebastian? Nothing would have been worth shackling herself to a man like him: not money, not her family – not even Matchenham. Now, so close to the end, it all seemed meaningless. Survival was no longer a matter of ball gowns and mortgages – it came down to very simple things: a rope; a flame; her heart pounding, pounding, pounding with the refusal not to give up, not to give in.

For one thing was true, powerfully and clearly true: she did not want to die. She was not *going* to die. She felt the same surge of rage that had swept through her when Sebastian had ordered her to sit down, and she disobeyed.

He wanted her to die, to burn.

She would not. She would *not* die.

But she had to be realistic. Sebastian was stronger than her, stronger physically and magically. She could not break the ropes by force and she could not break them with magic, his spells had ensured that.

Think, Rosa.

But she could not think. The ropes bit into her skin and the fire was coming closer. Closer.

A rope. A flame.

The smoke in the room was almost overpowering now, not woodsmoke, but an acrid chemical smoke, with the same harsh stench she had smelt in the dipping room.

Think!

A rope. A flame.

The fire down beneath was sucking in so much air that the chimney in the little office had started to smoke, the flames no longer dancing upward but gusting out into the room, pulled by the voracious hunger for air of the inferno beneath.

A rope. A flame.

The suddenly it came to her. Fire. If fire could destroy a factory, it could destroy a rope.

She yanked desperately at the chair, bracing with her feet, and it shuffled a few inches towards the fireplace. It wasn't nearly close enough, even with the flames flaring out into the grate.

She heaved again and the chair shifted another inch. Then another. Then another.

She was closer now, much closer. She pulled again. Nothing.

Rosa wriggled in her bindings, feeling the ropes bite, then she braced her feet more securely on the floor and pushed again. The chair rocked, but did not shift. Craning her head she could see she had hit the edge of the rug, where the braid made a raised hump. It would take an almighty shove to get the chair over that lip.

She took a deep breath, braced her feet on the floor, and then she put all her strength and her magic into one massive kick.

The chair toppled backwards with a crash, landing sideways on the slate hearth, one wing hard against the marble surround and one side almost in the grate itself.

Rosa screamed. The flames were scorching against her arm. She smelt burning silk and did not know if it was the chair, or her sleeve, or both. Her arm felt as if it was roasting. She racked her brains for a spell, but she was unable to think for pain. 'Stop!' she wept. 'Please, oh God, please stop hurting!'

The flames didn't die away, but the pain went from unendurable to a dull agony. Rosa lay, sobbing, turning her face as far from the blaze as she could. She could smell the wood of the chair beginning to burn now. She pulled against the bindings. They no longer hurt – the small pain of the rope's bite subsumed into the scorching heat of the flames eating at her skin.

Pictures went through her head: Papa kissing her goodnight, his spells filling her room with stars and fairies. Cherry's warm neck, the smell of her mane, the heat of her skin in the sun. Matchenham in the evening, with the summer sun setting. Luke. Luke with his hand on her cheek. Luke's lips, soft against hers. Luke, his eyes filled with hate as he raised the hammer.

Luke.

There was a sudden snap and she fell sideways out of the chair, one wrist free. It was enough. With one hand unbound she made a superhuman stretch and grabbed a paperknife off the desk. It was not very sharp, but it was enough. A minute of frantic, panicked sawing and her other wrist was free, then her ankles, and at last she was free to crawl away to a cool corner of the room and examine her wounds.

They were not as bad as she'd thought. One sleeve was charred and smoking and the skin beneath was hot and tender, swelling in fat white blisters, and there were red weeping welts on her wrists and ankles, but it was nothing that she couldn't heal, given time. The most important thing was that she could walk.

She climbed painfully to her feet and went to the window. It was shut and barred, and beyond there was nothing but a tiny yard, bordered on four sides by grey concrete walls stretching upwards. Could she scrape together enough magic to force open the window? Then what?

Perhaps the door would be better. She could hear the sound of flames but they didn't seem to be right outside. She opened it and peered out.

The corridor was dark but she could hear the hiss of the gas-lamps. They must have been turned on without lighting, by someone trying to flood the place with gas. It was only a matter of time before the gas met the flames down below, or the ones in the grate in the office, and the whole place went up. But why? *Why?* Why would he destroy the factory, rather than set the workers free?

The answer came to her at once: insurance. Undoing the spells was risky and expensive, and it left the central problem still there: the fact that she, Rosa, knew what had happened.

Sebastian didn't care about the buildings, he didn't care about the workers, he didn't care about *her*. What he cared about was money and his family's reputation. Burning down the factory solved all his problems. This way,

Sebastian could walk away with a suitcase full of insurance money, free to start again in new premises, with no one the wiser.

She had to get out.

But how? Which way? She thought of the design of the factory – the high, windowless outer walls. There was no escape outwards; she had to go inwards, towards the central courtyard. She began to run down the corridor, feeling the heat grow as she came nearer to the source of the fire.

At last she turned a corner – and came to a dead end. The corridor carried on – but there was no floor, only a blazing inferno where it should have been. But something was moving across the gap. A figure – tall and muffled – a dim black shape behind the scarlet blaze. For a moment her heart seemed to stop. *Sebastian?*

She raised her hand, shaking, ready to strike with what little magic she had left.

Then a hoarse, breaking voice shouted, 'Rosa? Rosa, where are you? *Rosa!*'

It was Luke.

24

'Rosa!'

Luke was close to giving up. The heat was becoming unbearable and the floor seemed to rock and groan beneath him.

But he could not. If only he had come when she asked him. He thought of all it must have cost her – to betray her kind, betray Sebastian, betray her own family – and he had sent her away with a curse and a raised hammer.

There was no future for him, if she lived. But he could not let her die.

'Rosa!' he called again, turning a corner. 'Where are you?'

But there was nothing there – no corridor – no floor – just a mass of burning flames. The floor beneath his feet shuddered and he could feel the heat striking through his boots. He thanked God for the guard's greatcoat – the thick densely woven wool keeping off the sparks and the heat of the flames.

'Rosa!' he yelled again, his voice cracking and breaking. He was hoarse from shouting, hoarse from the smoke. There was no answer, just the endless crackling roar of the flames, and he turned to go back, try another passage.

As he did there was a screaming roar and another section of floor suddenly gave way behind him, flames and sparks shooting into the air like fireworks. Luke looked down. He was standing on maybe three joists, each being eaten away by the flames. He was going to die. The realization came quite suddenly, quite calmly. There was no way out. There was no point in fighting any more.

He wished he had said goodbye to William.

He shut his eyes.

Then he heard a voice.

'*Luke!*'

She was standing on the other side of the burning chasm in the floor. Her white face was smudged with soot and ashes, but her eyes were bright, and her hair blazed like a crown of flames in the dark, firelit corridor.

'Rosa?' He was so hoarse it came out as a croaking whisper.

'Luke! I'm so sorry! You shouldn't have come. Sebastian, he's flooded the place with gas; the workers are all going to die . . .'

'They're out,' he shouted back hoarsely. 'Most of them, anyway. The ones who could walk.'

'Then why are you still here?'

'For you,' he said, his voice so low he didn't know if she

would hear, across the roar of the flames. She did. He could see it in the stricken look of – almost *grief*, on her face. She didn't speak. Just put her hands to her face. She was shaking her head.

'No, no!' He could hear her low moan across the gulf between them. 'Luke, no! If you die because of me—'

'I don't deserve to live.'

'What? No!'

'I tried to kill you, Rosa. That's why I came to your house. I was sent there, to kill you.'

'Luke—' she began, but whatever she might have said was drowned in the sudden scream of breaking wood, the roar of the fire, and Luke felt the floor beneath his feet shiver and begin to tip. For a second he stood frozen, and then he gave a great, hopeless leap, scrambling for the far side of the divide, where Rosa stood.

She leant out, across the flames, her slim arm bare to the blaze, but he knew, even as he reached for her hand, that she could never hold him. His fingers brushed hers, wet with sweat – she screamed something unintelligible – and then, like a miracle, she was holding him.

It was not possible. He hung above the furnace below, feeling the agonizing heat of the fire on his legs. Rosa lay on the floor, her bare arm hanging down into the burning chasm. Luke could only stare up at her, at her white face, at her wrist and hand holding his – impossibly small. There was no way she should have had the strength to even hold him, let alone catch him as he fell.

She had her eyes closed and her face was sheened with sweat.

'Rosa!' he gasped.

'Shut. Up.'

He felt her nails digging into him. He could see her lips moving in some inaudible exhortation.

Slowly, slowly, she was dragging him back from the edge, pulling herself backwards along the floor, her lips constantly moving with a low litany. Her magic blazed around her, a fierce flaming gold, and suddenly he understood. Witchcraft. She was holding him by witchcraft.

He knew he should struggle. He knew what William and John and all the Brothers would say – that this was devil's work. That it would be better to burn in life than be saved by such unholy means and burn in death. But he no longer cared. He no longer cared about anything except the unbearable heat of the fire on his smouldering boots, the stench of burning wool from his great coat, the flames eating away at the joists below Rosa, minute by minute.

He was almost there. He was almost to the edge. In another moment he would be able to swing his leg up, pull himself to safety . . .

But just as Rosa gave one last superhuman effort, the veins in her forehead standing out in desperation, her hair wet with sweat – there was a massive earth-shaking *BOOM!*

A roar, like a river bursting its banks.

An explosion that rocked the building to its foundation. Concrete and bricks and burning beams tumbling around him – and he was falling. He felt Rosa's magic wrap around him in a fierce embrace.

And then nothing.

When Luke opened his eyes he could see sky. It was not quite dawn, but there was a thin yellow light at the horizon, as if the sun could barely penetrate the river fog. He was lying on the cold ground with a beam digging into his spine and there were bricks and masonry scattered all around. His leg felt as if it might be broken. He couldn't feel his arm at all and, when he tried to lift it, it wouldn't move.

With difficulty he turned his head to see what was pinning it and his heart gave a great leap of hope and despair.

It was Rosa. She was lying on his arm. Her head was flung back, her white throat bare to the sky. Her hair was loose and straggled all around.

Her face, beneath the soot and blood and muck, was white – and her hand, when he touched it, was cold. There was not a single spark of magic around her.

A great sob forced its way up from his gut.

'Rosa.' He pulled her up, pulling her against him. 'Rosa, what have you done? What did you do?'

He began to cry there, crouched in the deserted ruins of the factory. Her death solved everything. He was free. And he would have given anything to undo it.

'I'm so sorry . . .' He put his cheek against hers. 'I'm so

sorry. I don't care what the Brotherhood says, I will burn for what I did to you.'

'We nearly did burn.' Her voice was soft by his ear – and then she coughed and pulled back.

'Rosa?' He clutched her, hardly able to believe she was alive, and she cried out, pulling her arm from his grip.

'My arm!' She held it up ruefully, looking at the weeping skin and broken blisters. 'God, for a bit of magic to take the edge off . . .'

'But – but you were cold!'

'I *am* cold.' She rubbed her hands and then touched his. 'So are you.' She shivered and then winced again. 'Oh, my arm . . .'

'Why can't you heal it?'

'I'm spent. Magic's like . . . it's like strength, in a way. If you asked me to lift that beam now, I doubt I could. My muscles are like wet wool. It'll come back, but for now – I couldn't conjure so much as a witchlight.'

She looked down at her scorched and blistered palm and Luke remembered the stable, the frail white glow in her hand . . .

'You saved me,' he said slowly. 'I tried to kill you – and you saved me. Why? I deserve to burn for what I tried to do to you.'

'You came back for me,' she said simply.

For a long time they said nothing, just sat side by side in the ruins of Sebastian's factory, looking out to the river and the boats drifting past. It was still early, the sky pale in

364

the east, but Luke could hear the cries from the waterfront drifting downriver and he knew that the East End never really slept.

'We must get going.' He stood, painfully, feeling his exhausted muscles complaining and his stiff joints cracking. His hurt leg screamed as he stood, but it was not broken – just stiff and sprained. He put out a hand and Rosa scrambled to her feet and stood brushing down her charred silk gown with a rueful face. 'Where will you go?' he asked.

'I don't know.'

'Well, we can't stay here.' Luke looked at the sky and then the river. 'The police will come soon. And Knyvet will be back.'

Rosa shivered.

'He has everything now: Southing, the factories, the Chair . . . But not me. And he would kill me for that, if he found out I was still alive. I cannot go home. Can we go back to your uncle's? To the forge?'

'No.' Luke shook his head. 'I told you, I was sent to kill you – the price for failing was death. My death.'

'So, your people are as barbaric as mine,' she said softly.

'Not William,' Luke said. He swallowed against the pain in his smoke-scorched throat. 'William loves me. But I can't – I can't make him choose between me and the Brotherhood. I must go my own way, alone now.'

'So must I.' She took his hand and a faint prickle of magic, like a flame, lit her face for a moment, like a ray of warmth in this dreary fog-muted dawn. 'So we are not alone.'

Luke nodded.

They turned, and together they began to walk towards the rising sun.

Acknowledgements

My thanks for all the help with *Witch Finder* and The Winter Trilogy would fill a chapter if not a book, but I will try to keep this brief!

First, thank you to the fabulous people at Hodder, in particular Naomi, Victoria, Laure, Anne, Michelle and the ever-marvellous Sales and Rights teams.

Also to my agent, Eve, and the redoubtable Jack for everything!

Love always to my first readers – Meg, Eleanor, Kate and Alice (particular horsey thanks to the latter two).

Carriages at Eight by Frank E. Huggett (Lutterworth Press) was enormously helpful with details of the world of Victorian carriages and stable-hands. *The Victorian House* by Judith Flanders (Harper Perennial) helped with details of servants and practical details, and the *Victorian Family* trilogy of memoirs by M V Hughes was a wonderful evocation of everyday life in the 1880s from the perspective of a young woman.

I must also record a huge debt of gratitude to Paul Binns, blacksmith, for his invaluable technical help with the details of a Victorian forge. I only wish I had been able to cram in more historical detail! Needless to say, any errors are mine, and I hope blacksmiths and farriers will forgive any dramatic licence I've taken with details.

Finally, thank you to everyone who supported, bought, read, reviewed and loved The Winter Trilogy. I quite literally couldn't have done it without you.

The story
continues
in

WITCH
HUNT

Turn the
page for a
sneak peek...

The forge was still in darkness, no sparks coming from the chimney, as they walked quietly up the lane. Luke lifted his arm from Rosa's shoulders and put his finger to his lips as he lifted the latch of the gate and pulled it ajar, holding its weight so that the hinges wouldn't squeal out and wake William.

Rosa slipped through the gap into the cobbled yard, and Luke pulled it shut behind her, latching it so that no one would see the open gate and think the forge open. The snow was still falling and the cobbles were slick with ice as they crossed them carefully, silently. Luke glanced up at his uncle's window as they passed, but it was still dark. He had no watch, but it must be gone seven, and even when he was sleeping off a hangover William rarely slept past eight.

Inside the forge he pulled the door shut against the cold and stood looking at William's tools. He laid them out on the bench – a rasp, nippers, the smallest hacksaw . . . He and Rosa stood looking at them, and he could see the fear in Rosa's face. He felt it himself, looking from the huge heavy tools down at her small hand, bloodied and dusted with soot.

'It's not going to work,' he said at last. 'William's got nothing small enough. We need a goldsmith's tools, not these.'

'Try,' she said. 'At least try.'

With a sick heart he picked up the nippers and tried to angle them to pinch just the gold band of the ring, keeping clear of the skin of her finger – but it was nearly impossible; they were too large and too heavy, and the ring dug so tightly into Rosa's finger that it was impossible to get a purchase on the metal without pinching her flesh. At last he thought he had it, and began to tighten, gently, and then harder.

'Stop!' she screamed suddenly, and he let the nippers clatter to the floor. There was sweat on her forehead, sticking the red-gold hair to her face. She closed her eyes. Blood was running down her finger. 'No, take no notice of me,' she said, her voice shaking. 'Try again.'

'No,' Luke felt sickness rise in his throat, the sight of her blood turning his stomach. 'No I won't.'

'Coward,' she said bitterly, and Luke felt his stomach clench as if he'd been punched.

'*What* did you say?' His voice came out louder and more dangerous than he'd meant. 'If you were a man, I'd—'

He broke off, suddenly hot with shame. Had it come to

this? So afraid of his own cowardice that he was reduced to shouting threats at an injured girl? Not just a coward, but a bully too. At least Knyvet, loathsome though he was, was brave in his own way.

'I'm sorry.' He couldn't bear to look at her as he walked back to the tool rack to put them away. 'I didn't mean—'

'It's tightened,' she said in a small voice, breaking into his stumbling apology. 'That was why I screamed. It wasn't the cut – I could have stood that. But the ring – when you tried to clip it off, it tightened.'

'What?' He moved across the forge and snatched up her hand. She was right. The ring, previously just too narrow to get past her knuckle but loose enough to turn, was now so tight he couldn't move it, though her skin was slick with blood. 'Are you sure? Couldn't it just be that your finger's swollen?'

She shook her head.

'My finger's been swollen ever since I tried to take it off yesterday. That's not it – this is different. I *felt* it tighten when you tried to clip it. It was like it knew.'

They looked at each other, and Luke saw his own fear and doubt reflected back in her eyes. He opened his mouth, trying to think of something to say, something that would reassure her, something that would get them out of this unholy mess – when he heard a noise in the yard. He stiffened, his hand on Rosa's, and then as the forge door latch began to rattle, he pushed her roughly down behind the big stone hearth and stood in front of her, his heart banging in his throat, waiting to see who would come through the door.

It was William's voice he heard as the door began to swing open.

'Whoever you are, messin' about in my forge, I'll have your – eh?'

William stood in the doorway, his hair rumpled from his bed, his boots on beneath his night-gown.

'Luke! What are you doing here at sparrow fart, lad? I thought you were abed.'

'I couldn't sleep.' It was almost true after all. He hadn't slept, though in truth he hadn't had the chance.

'But . . .' William took a step forward into the forge, towards where Rosa was hiding. Luke held his breath and prayed. 'Your coat, it's all charred and burnt. What happened? Were you in a fire? You stink of smoke . . . and summat else. Where've you bin?'

'I've been to the Cock Tavern.' That was true too, but it was not the truth. 'There was a fight.' Another truth, another twist. 'I got pushed into a street brazier, boy selling chestnuts.' *Lies.* He felt sick with deception.

'But your skull, lad! You shouldn't be drinking and brawling. You're not two days out of bed!'

'I know.' Luke clenched his fingers inside his coat pockets, begging William in his head to leave, *begging* him to go and stop asking questions. He could hear Rosa's stifled breathing behind him, and from the corner of his eye he could see the shift and swirl of her magic. *Please leave . . .*

William shook his head. He turned on his heel and Luke held his breath. Then, just as William reached the door he turned back.

'Lad, listen.' He came back across the cobbled floor towards Luke. Any second now he was going to come round the corner of the forge hearth and he would see Rosa and it would all be over. Behind him he heard Rosa's panicked gasp and knew she knew this too – he felt her magic flare up like a fire in a draft, knew that she was gathering herself together, readying herself to cast . . .

'No!' He swung round, took a step backwards to put himself between her and William. 'No! Rosa don't – not William.'

There was a sudden, perfect silence, a silence so complete he could hear the wind in the chimney, and then Rosa's skirts rustled and she stood, in full view of William.

Ruth Warburton
Online

Ruth's blog, book news, reviews, FAQs and loads more can all be found on her website.

For all things Witches,
there's nowhere better!

www.ruthwarburton.com